TALES OF THE MALL MASTERS

TALES OF THE

MALL MASTERS

BY

DAVID GULBRAA

RADICAL ROMANTIC PRESS

Tales of the Mall Masters

by David Gulbraa

Published by

Radical Romantic Press
PO Box 66693
Los Angeles CA 90066

A slightly different version of this novel was originally serialized in the magazine RADICAL ROMANTIC, July 1997 through January 1999.

The poem on page 73 ©1997, 1999 by Brian Faulkner.

Printed in the United States of America

ISBN 1891021028

Tales of the Mall Masters

CONTENTS

Acknowledgments

None of the following gentlemen have read this novel in any form, so my acknowledging them here should not be considered any kind of endorsement from them whatsoever. However, what I learned from their work was significant enough to deserve public mention.

First, Dr. Leonard Peikoff, for his talk "Why Ancient Greece is My Favorite Civilization," which was a huge influence on this novel. Thanks especially for introducing me to the Greek concept of arete.

Dr. Gary Hull, for his lecture course "Integration, the Dynamo of Reason." This talk helped me in my attempt to show a passion for integration as one of the key traits of my heroes.

Dr. Harry Binswanger, for his two lecture courses, "Psycho-Epistemology I," and "Psycho-Epistemology II." Some of what I learned from these lectures has found its way into my portrait of how Maurice Sully's mind works.

If I have misunderstood or misapplied any of the ideas set forth in these works, that is entirely my responsibility.

Interested readers can find this material available from Second Renaissance Books. Call 1-800-729-6149. Or go online to www.rationalmind.com.

The Temple of Triumph described in Chapter Five is an actual design done by architect Frederick Gibson of San Francisco, California. Thanks to Mr. Gibson for allowing me to use the temple in my fictional universe. Interested readers can see the drawings on the web at www.gibson-design.com.

Special thanks to Alexandra York for publishing material on the temple in her magazine, ART Ideas. You can visit Alexandra's magazine online at www.art-21.org.

Thanks to my poet friend and loyal correspondent, Brian Faulkner, for cheering me on every month and providing first rate literary criticism while this novel was being written and serialized in my now defunct magazine, RADICAL ROMANTIC. The poem at the base of my fictional Statue of Liberty described in Chapter 3 was composed by Brian, and I thank him for allowing me to use it in this book version.

Finally, thanks to my musical inspirations for supplying the soundtrack to this novel – and to my life while I wrote it: David Arkenstone, Tangerine Dream, and Yanni.

AUTHOR'S NOTE

The culture portrayed in this novel is not intended to be a literal transposition of ancient Greek culture into a modern setting. The culture presented here is fictional; it does not exist, nor has it ever existed. My intention was to portray a culture with an Objectivist substance and a Greek style.

By the unwritten rules governing the writing of alternate histories, an author is required to provide a rational and historically sensible explanation for the source of his alternate culture. This is left mostly to implication in the text of the novel, so let me state it explicitly here.

Philip of Macedon was never assassinated. Alexander the Great assumed the throne a much more mature man in his early thirties. Alexander was Aristotle's best student and when he did become King, instead of running off to conquer Asia, he stayed home and united the Greek city-states, enabling Greece to conquer Rome. Greek culture matured and was largely immune to the ideas of Christianity. Greece ignored western Europe and moved east across the globe, influencing Asia, finally crossing the Pacific Ocean and founding colonies on the west coast of the North American continent. These colonies eventually became the Individual's Republic of California.

PROLOGUE

THE HUNCHBACK OF ALBERTSONS

I am Layvanwick and I am the boxboy. For ten years I have labored with artistic intensity in the fluorescent glory of Albertsons Discount Center, in the West Park Plaza shopping mall. I love this grocery store. It is my temple. I worship here daily. For ten years I have raced over the brightly polished tiles, down the spotless aisles, to and fro under the lights, with blue apron, crisp white shirt, black bow tie, soft-soled shoes my proudly-worn uniform. I have stacked cardboard boxes of merchandise in skyscraper towers to the ceiling, and then danced my boxboy dance beneath and between them, sliding and spinning with chaotic graceful efficiency as I stocked my shelves with colorful cans, bottles, boxes of beautiful groceries. I have arranged soup cans face out with scientific precision. I have slipped on cotton gloves to fondle frozen foods to sleep in misty freezers. I have watered vegetables in the jungle produce section, and mopped the floor to keep old women from slipping. I have stacked flour in the baking section till my face was white with dust. I have hurled huge bags of dog food into massive stacks, like an ancient slave building pyramids in Egypt.

And I have smiled at the shoppers as I bagged their groceries with the quick severe precision of a surgeon saving a life, my hands a blur, the groceries tumbling into bags like icons juggled by a magician. I have loaded those perfectly square paper bags of groceries into gleaming metal shopping carts with smooth rolling wheels and then glided out the doors to the warm spring-summer-fall parking lot, eyeing my customers all the way, sizing them up, then amazing them with my boxboy intuition, telling them which car they drive, smiling at their amazement when I guess right. Smiling, because it is rarely a guess.

And I have chased down the shopping carts abandoned all around this mall; I have strided through the heat of summer over sun-baked black asphalt, felt the heat oozing up, trying to suck me down; I have pushed long trains of carts back into the store, shoving hard against the quicksand asphalt of blistering muggy summer days; I have chased down carts through spring rains and stood in the water-drenched parking lot, smiling at all the shiny wet cars; and I have chased my carts through fall wind storms, guided my long trains through swirling tornadoes of leaves and dust. I have shoved carts through deep wet snow and guided them across sheets of ice even while my hands froze to the metal handles.

And inside my grocery temple I have climbed high ladders to hang colorful signs from the ceilings and windows. I have raced along the aisles with a price gun in my hand, kissing products with tiny numbered stickers to tell our customers how low our prices are. I have responded with heroic swiftness to calls of *"Anton, clean up on aisle ten!"* arriving with a mop to sweep away distasteful blemishes to the beauty of this store.

I have baked bread in the bakery during early morning snow storms; quartered chickens in the meat department on wild Saturday afternoons when the store was full of screaming teenagers; made sandwiches in the deli on funky Friday nights when the echoes of Mall musicians throbbed up from the floors; I have stacked tomatoes in produce on quiet, dark weeknights when the store was deserted and the sound of one lonely register clicking away by itself came drifting over from far on the other side of the store.

In the back room I have welcomed truckloads just arrived from the mountains; I have joshed and frolicked with joke-telling drivers eager to relate the harrowing tales of life on the road and all the adventures their groceries had seen on the way in. I have unloaded those trucks and parked pallet-loads of boxed groceries with geometric precision into back room towers.

I have lurked along the rafters high up in the back room and peered down through strategically placed holes in the walls to spy on shoplifters and catch them as they tried to make their way out. I have watched them ride away in police cars with lost, lonely, forlorn and selfless looks consuming their faces. They came to a place of life and reality and tried to fake an understanding of what it all means. They do not know what it all means, and that is why they leave in tears. I know well what it all means, and that is why I stay and smile all day and go home happy at night.

I am Layvanwick and I am the boxboy. These are the things I have done and will continue to do.

And there is one more thing I have done.

I have kissed the lips of Diane Copernicus.

***

Yes, this Mall is a holy place, a sacred place, a place where life is lived, nurtured, supported, enhanced, enjoyed. The Mall is a temple, and the grocery store is the center of the temple, the anchor that holds it all together, the base upon which it is all built. Groceries come first in the lives of men; the rest is all gravy. The Mall supports many stores selling all variety of products and services, but groceries are always the priority. Once your cupboards are full of fine healthy nutritious food, then you can think about movies and clothes and sporting goods and cameras and toys and shoes and hats and cars and stereos and music and videos and new furniture for your den and a new bed for your spouse and curtains for your windows and a computer and new lights and new carpets and new this and new that...can you think of something you need or want that isn't available in this Mall? I doubt it. We have it all because we are the center of the universe, this is where we all converge to trade, this is where we come to revel in our prosperity and success, this is where we come to flaunt what we've got, and to dreams dreams of what our future will earn us. This is where we come to be human and be in love. This is where I saw Diane Copernicus for the first time, dancing with a mannequin, kissing his cold plastic lips.

***

Midnight in October, on a full moon evening, a harvest moon, a big glowing yellow ball hanging in the sky like a balloon, a lost balloon that a child had failed to value. That is how children first learn to value, they lose their balloons, watch them float away into the sky, lost forever, never to be seen again, to be punctured and burst with a pop and expire instantly — a noble death for a balloon, you hope — or perhaps to drift slowly and expire over time, the air seeping out in microscopic gasps, the poor balloon caught by the wind and taken high to the clouds, and the child's heart punctured just like that balloon, and the child thinking to himself, quietly, desperately, before or after screaming in anguish to his parent, *"I must learn to hold on to the things I love."*

I was on the roof, standing alone in the breeze, facing that moon, taking in the crisp evening air, feeling the ache in my bones from a furious day of consumer frenzy. Our annual Moonlight Madness sale. The store had been rampaged by barbarian hordes of coupon-drenched women shoppers intent on taking advantage of the most suicidal deals of the year. Check your economic texts, you'll see it referred to as a "loss-leader." Usually what worked best for us was eight packs of big sixteen ounce bottles of coke or pepsi for fifteen cents — and all coupons doubled. Or in some years it would be cases of toilet paper that would normally sell for fifty cents knocked down to twenty-five cents. You get the idea. Life is expensive. Make it cheap and people will come racing to you and shower you with all they've got.

It was a hard day. I am strong and I have endurance, but days like these always took the most out of me — in a good kind of way. Like a champion athlete, I had been pressed to the max, driven to the wall, forced to reach down deep to my reserves of strength and focus. I had bagged, loaded, rolled, unloaded a warehouse of groceries. I had chased, gathered, and rolled long train after long train of heavy metal shopping carts back into the store over and over, again and again; I had even had to fight and wrestle rude men for possession of carts promised to little old ladies; I always won, the carts were always delivered to the ladies, I would never let them down like that. And when it was over, and the shelves of the store were mostly empty, and the store had an air of a battlefield where bombs had gone off, where the air inside the store hung heavy and moist and was filled with tiny floating pieces of paper, like the last gasps of a confetti storm or a ticker-tape parade — I had disappeared in the back room, climbed the sturdy wooden ladder up the wall to the roof, gone up and out, onto the roof through our roof access hatch, to walk across the wide flat roof of the Mall, heading east, into the moon, staring at it as I walked along, hearing the distant cars rolling and humming away, back to homes and houses and apartments. I had watched the clouds roll over the face of the moon and I had stopped to stare and wonder at that yellow old face of the man in the moon, staring down at me like some friend from childhood.

And I heard music.

It was dim, faint, almost below the threshold of consciousness. But my senses are sharp, and I noticed the music, and I listened.

Alone on the roof of a shopping mall, staring up at a full moon, hearing music, and listening.

And more.

Laughter. Giggling. The high-pitched melodious tone of a girl. A young woman. The laughter of youth and joy and happiness because all possibilities are poised and waiting, waiting to be chosen for use by a radiant creature of pure ecstatic happiness.

Music, and the laughter of a young girl.

These are siren songs to the ears of a young man.

I listened, stopped, turned, found the source of the sound, and moved towards it.

There was an opening in the roof.

Why it was open, I have no idea. Upon such little details as this, our lives and destinies are built.

Just like the grocery, a store below had roof access. Their air conditioning unit was nearby, chugging along in the night, pumping fresh cool air down to that voice and that music...

I bent down and peered into the hole.

The light was dim, but the sound was bright. I listened. I heard a voice.

"You're so handsome! Won't you please dance with me?"

There was no reply, but there was music. And then more laughter from the giddy-voiced girl.

"Oh my, aren't you a fine dancer! Whirl me around again!"

She is with the man she loves, I thought. But if he was there, he was unusually silent, completely silent. Perhaps he was stunned into silence by her beauty?

Would I be?

If this was a rendezvous of two lovers, I did not want to intrude. But I listened. And the only voice I heard was hers. The beautiful music of a vivacious young girl. I listened, hoping to hear a man's voice, a male voice, a deep baritone. But all I heard was her. She. The musician.

I had to see who she was. After listening for a few minutes, it became clear to me that she was a child at play. She was below me, pretending. A young girl pretending to be in love. She was listening to her music, locked alone in the store after closing, and she was celebrating her love for her job by pretending to be in love with a man...

I climbed down into the hole. I descended the ladder quickly but quietly. I inched my way along through the dim back room and found my way to the sales floor of a clothing store, a lush jungle of colorful women's clothing.

And I saw Diane Copernicus dancing with a mannequin.

I didn't know her name. That would come later.

But I knew her soul instantly.

A slender girl with voluptuous curves, wearing a tight skirt that hugged her hips and accentuated her legs and hips; a red sweater over long, wing-like arms ending with delicate hands. Her hair was black and flowing away forever, slightly rippled, but glowing; her skin was pale white, her eyes bright blue, her lips red and smiling, her teeth white and even.

She held a mannequin close as she danced and spun and waltzed around the clothing store with him. Then the music ended and she walked the mannequin back to his post, stood him up straight, kissed him on the lips, said, "Good-night you handsome man! I certainly have enjoyed our dance, and I hope we can meet again soon!" and then she giggled as she turned him around, facing him towards the front doors of the store. And then she gaily skipped away, dancing along to the stereo, turned it off, then headed right for me.

I disappeared into the shadows and watched her turn out the lights, then she left by the front door, locking me in.

I disappeared back up to the roof and closed the roof access hatch. It locked shut on the inside, secure. No one else would gain access to the clothing store.

The mall is my temple. All stores are sacred. I protect them all, just like the grocery store.

I went home, and that night, I dreamed of dancing mannequins.

***

Indian summer lingered that year, late into October, making the days hot and dry. In the middle of that week I was in the parking lot, pushing a long train of shopping carts toward the front doors of the store. This was a very long train, longer than any I had pushed in a very long time, and it was getting the best of me. I had it aimed straight and was set to surge with the power of a locomotive and get those carts inside with one magnificent rush — but a car passing in front interrupted my rhythm and I had to stop, my train was stalled. I relaxed, cursed briefly under my breath, stopped to adjust my necktie and wipe my brow with a silk handkerchief I kept in my apron pocket. This was a brief kind of break we boxboys permit ourselves when faced with traffic and other interruptions in the parking lot. It is permissible. I was watching my carts with one eye, but standing largely oblivious to all else for a second.

And I heard a voice.

"You look so hot. Would you like a drink?"

The voice was feminine and I recognized it instantly.

I turned to my left and she was there.

Diane Copernicus stood gazing at me, smiling just so slightly, holding out a plastic-cupped soft drink container with a straw sticking up out of it.

Her black hair was thick and swept to one side, even more beautiful now in the full sunshine of midday. She was wearing a white blouse and dark blue slacks.

I looked at the plastic cup and the straw. "That's your drink. I really shouldn't."

"I'm all done," she said. "Here." She tore off the plastic top, with the straw left stuck through the hole, and offered me just the cup. "You can have the rest. It's mostly ice. That should cool you down some."

I took the cup. "Thank you." I took a sip, got mostly ice, but also the last trickle of what tasted like Mountain Dew. My favorite.

"I'm Anton. Don't you work at the clothing store?"

"Yes, Pacific Orchid, that's right."

"I think your mannequins are very well done."

She smiled. "Yes, they are." She looked at my long train of carts. "You are a strong master of your carts!"

"Yes, I am. Are you a master of your mannequins?"

She smiled a huge innocent smile of pure happiness — and her eyes got strangely large. "Yes! They flirt with me occasionally, but I let them know who's boss!"

"Thanks for the ice," I said.

I took one last mouthful of ice from her cup, then tossed it in a nearby garbage can. Then I bent low behind the first cart and pushed hard, using my legs, and surged once, sending the long train of carts across the street and into the front doors of the store. When I had the carts parked properly inside the store, I turned and glanced back.

She was not there. She had not followed me inside.

I went back to work.

***

The next day she showed up again. This time she passed through a checkstand with only an apple. I walked up and smiled at her as she paid for her apple. "Would you like that apple in a bag?" I asked.

She smiled. "No thank you. I'm having it for lunch. It will be gone shortly."

"So you're ruthless with apples."

She looked at me strangely. "Oh yes."

She walked away, out of the store.

Later that day, after my shift had ended, I walked out of the grocery and into the larger mall. Pacific Orchid was only a few spaces east of us. I walked past and slowed my pace, hoping to catch a glimpse of her.

She was there, straightening a rack of clothes, pulling each item off the rack, fluffing it straight, then replacing each size back to it's proper place. I walked in and interrupted her, noticed the name badge pinned to her blouse.

Diane.

"Diane. How do you do?"

"Anton the boxboy! Are you chasing down shopping carts in here?"

"No. I've come for clothing."

"We sell mostly women's clothing."

"Mostly?"

"We have a few men's items."

"Show them to me."

"I'm not sure we have your size."

"Show them to me."

"You're very broad in the shoulders."

"Yes I am."

"You're looking for shirts?"

"Yes. And pants as well."

"Your thighs are so huge. We might not have your size."

"Show them to me."

"Follow me."

She took me to the men's section. It was small. But they did have my size. I tried on an entirely new outfit and stood looking at myself in the mirror for a long time until Diane managed to come back to me from ringing up another customer. She looked me over with severe eyes, and I searched those eyes closely for signs of interest. But she was so professional in demeanor, it was hard to tell.

"How do I look?"

I was wearing a bright gold shirt and black slacks.

"This isn't for work at the store."

"No."

"You look fine. They fit you well."

"Very well. I'll take them."

"Shall I box them up for you, or will you wear them?"

"I'm pressed for time. I'll wear them."

"Very well."

As we stood at the cash counter, I watched her hands. Her beautiful slender fingers were fine and feminine. She was not wearing any rings, no jewelry of any kind. I paid my bill with a one dollar gold coin. When she offered my receipt, I accepted and swore my value oath while staring directly into her beautiful eyes.

"In the name of my sacred ego, and the beautifully selfish life it supports, I pledge to value these clothes with full arete and make them a part of my soul for as long as I wear them."

It was a solemn moment for both of us.

Diane smiled at me. "If my service has been adequate, I will allow you to kiss me."

I am not a fool. I took advantage of her offer and I kissed her.

Our first kiss. I was glad that it sealed a sacred transaction within the mall, she selling me clothes that I would wear to please her.

Our spiritual moment passed.

"Why did you offer me water in the parking lot the other day?" I asked her.

"You boxboys work so hard. I felt sorry for you."

"You shouldn't. I love my work. Do you love yours?"

"Yes, I do."

"Good clothing is a great pleasure, don't you think?"

"Oh yes."

"Have you ever considered working in a grocery store?"

"Do you want to hire me?"

"Yes, I do."

"Shouldn't we do an interview first?"

"Yes, that's a good idea."

"When would you like to interview me?"

"Do you work this Saturday?"

"Yes, but I get off early, in the afternoon."

"Shall I meet you here, then?"

"Yes. That would be acceptable."

"Very well. I'll see you then."

And yes, that is exactly how we agreed to our first date.

***

Our first date was in the mall. I wanted to find out if she loved it as much as I did.

We had dinner in one of the finer restaurants, then relaxed on a bench near the center court and watched all the people passing by. Later, we had dessert at one of the sidewalk cafes. I asked questions designed to draw her out and get her to talk about the things she loved. My own statements were attempts to relax her and make her feel safe, to envelope her in a protective cocoon of benevolence so that she would feel free to confess her values, loves, desires, dreams.

I didn't have to work very hard.

Diane Copernicus told me, "I've thought about becoming a Mall Master some day. But I want to own every store in my mall. That's an original goal, isn't it? Has anybody ever done that before? I don't think so. That's why I want to do it. Because it's never been done. And I want to design clothes. All sorts of clothes, for all sorts of people. I want to come to work one morning and walk into my mall and see everyone wearing clothes I have designed."

"What's your favorite place in the mall?" I asked her. "I don't mean your favorite store. I mean, physically, your favorite spot, the site you most like to stand or sit, your place with your favorite view...will you tell me?"

She looked at me seriously, as if deciding whether she should tell me or not, then she slowly smiled as she made her decision. She stood up, offered me her hand. I stood and took her hand and she led me away to — surprise surprise —

The roof.

I think it was then that I decided to fall in love with Diane Copernicus.

***

We spent the rest of the night up there, in our private domain, sharing our special intimacy, our special privacy, occasionally peering down through the windows over the center court, taking a peek down into the mall at all the people enjoying themselves on this Saturday night. The sun went down, the wind picked up, clouds swirled across the sky like boiling shadows above us. It was just cool enough to be comfortable, just windy enough to move Diane's hair in exotic ways, just mysterious enough for us both to move slowly with each other. When I suggested we dance together under the clouds she was delighted enough to venture back down into her store and bring up her compact stereo system. We went to the center of the mall, near the windows over center court, played classical music, and waltzed together in the dim light seeping up from the mall beneath us.

"How do I dance?" I asked her.

"Very well."

"You've had practice, haven't you?" I told her.

"Yes, I have," she said, smiling strangely at an inner vision she thought was a secret. But I knew.

It got late, the music ran out, we both grew tired and sat down near the windows, talked for a long time, did not notice that beneath us the mall had grown dim and quiet. Eventually, I looked at my watch and saw the time.

"Do you have to be home at a certain time?"

"No."

"Good. Now I have something special to share with you."

We made our way down from the roof, back into Pacific Orchid. Diane replaced the stereo system in her store, then I led her out the front doors of the store, into the mall. It was quiet and dark. It was about one-thirty in the morning. All the stores and restaurants were closed, the mall was quiet and dark. "Follow me," I said.

I made my way to the mall management offices, found my way into the office of the Mall Master, Maurice Sully. His name was on the door. "Have you met Maurice?" I asked Diane.

"No. I haven't been here that long, you know."

"Maurice and I are friends. He understands the way I feel about the mall. We're going to have some fun, okay?"

"Very well."

In Maurice's office I found the music control system, loaded in one of my favorite cd's, then led Diane back out to the center court.

We were alone in the darkness of center court at two in the morning. My music came pouring through the mall speakers. It was just the two of us in the mall we both loved. We danced again, this time within the mall. I felt the mall's walls all around us like a fortress and I felt an exquisite sense of ownership. The mall was mine, all mine, for this brief time. And I could share it with Diane Copernicus, and was happy to do so. And judging from the look on her face, she was happy to be sharing it with me.

When the music ended, and our dance was finished, I held her close in the silence and kissed her — and only the mall saw this kiss. Our eyes were closed for a long time.

***

Monday morning at work Maurice Sully came to the store to see me. "The security officer tells me you visited my office late Saturday."

"Early Sunday, actually."

"And you had a friend."

"Yes."

"A lady friend."

"Yes. Her name is Diane. She works at Pacific Orchid. I'll introduce you."

"Security is nervous. They feel you've abused your privileges."

"Have I?"

"Yes, actually, I think you've gone too far this time, Anton."

"Very well. You're the Mall Master. Are my privileges revoked?"

"Yes, for now."

"And our friendship?"

"That depends."

"On what?"

"On Diane Copernicus."

Maurice left the grocery store. He was not smiling. I saw him walk towards Pacific Orchid. I saw him enter the store.

I had to roll a cart of groceries out to the parking lot, so I didn't see him leave. Nor did I know how long he was inside.

***

Maurice Sully, Mall Master of West Park Plaza, was my best friend. Like all friendships, ours grew out of shared values. In particular, the mall. Maurice had a passion for the place that was equal to mine. Managing such a place was a kind of utopian paradise for Maurice, and he lavished his attention on the mall as if it was a beautiful woman to whom he was married. I teased him about it sometimes, but he never laughed.

Maurice Sully stood just over six feet tall and was lean and gaunt. He wore elegant suits to work, carried a cellular phone with him at all times, and knew every centimeter of the mall. He knew all the stores by heart, knew all the owners, and each employee in all those stores. He knew all the products, all the sales, all the special promotions. He knew more about the stores than the people who worked in them and ran them. He had a computer-like memory that sucked up facts instantly, filed everything properly, accessed those files at the speed of light, and when information became useless, it was erased and replaced with new information with ruthless efficiency.

Maurice had blond hair and blue eyes and a relaxed elegance that disarmed men and alarmed women. Women thought he was gay — and the men wished he was. I had never known Maurice to be in love — except with the mall. I had seen women throw themselves at him — but he was always oblivious because his eyes were always up, looking around at the mall. I always felt that Maurice was like me: if any woman was going to capture his heart, she would have to be given to him by the mall. I think that is what Maurice was waiting for.

The first time I met Maurice was a few years ago at springtime during the greatest hail storm in anyone's memory. One afternoon the sky turned gray and heaven opened up and unleashed an avalanche of golf-ball size hail pellets on the city. Inside the mall, it sounded as if the roof was being pounded on like a drum. The power went down and we were left in darkness. In the grocery store, we evacuated our customers out into the mall so they could wait in safety for the storm to stop. If we could get the power back up, we would invite them back in, but we had no idea how long that would take.

After the evacuation, the assistant manager came up to me. "Anton, take one of the other boxboys, grab one of our big ladders, and meet the Mall Master down at the jewelry store. They've got a problem and they need a big ladder."

I pegged Fred to assist me. We grabbed a big ladder and hauled it out and down the mall to the jewelry store. We were met there by a tall, relaxed young man of about my age who seemed rather blasé about the entire affair. He had a walkie-talkie in one hand and a flashlight in the other. "I'm Sully," he told us. "These folks had their roof access hatch open when the storm hit. Now they've got a back room filling up with hail pellets and we can't get the hatch closed because the hail is still coming down — stuff will knock you out if it hits you."

"Hell, probably kill you if you spend long enough in it," I said.

"But that's not the main problem here. The hail is coming through the open hatch and knocking a bank of electric circuit breakers silly. We've got to close the hatch before it does too much more damage."

"I can do that," I said. "But you've got a more serious problem." I pointed out of the jewelry store and across the main concourse of the mall, to the area beneath the crystal windows over center court.

Instead of covering the center court area with bubbles of unbreakable plastic – which would have been the practical thing to do – Maurice had installed a special delicate crystal designed to prism sunlight in spectacular and entertaining ways. At noon, those at center court could behold a rainbow. At certain other hours of the day, prism-beam ribbons of color seemed to flow down from the skylights.

But right now, people were congregating beneath the windows and looking up like idiots at the hail smashing into the glass. Inside the jewelry store the noise was deafening, so I couldn't hear the sound of the hail pellets smashing into the glass — but I knew what the hail storm had to be doing to that delicate crystal. "You'd better evacuate those people before those windows collapse."

"*Mother nature, you hoary old bitch, leave my mall alone!*" bellowed Maurice Sully. Then he yelled into his walkie-talkie, "Security, evacuate the center court! Those windows could go at any time! Get those people out of there!" And he ran off to do what he could, leaving me in charge of the pellet-bombarded jewelry store.

I turned and looked at the two women employees of the store, Julie and Doris. They looked up at me with huge, imploring eyes. "Anton, what can you do?"

"Come on, Fred."

We hauled the ladder back, got it into position beneath the open hatch and right in front of the bank of circuit breakers. The ladder acted like a kind of shield against the hail pellets. They were coming down only a few at a time now, but when they did it was with a terrific, devastating, bomb-like impact. They started denting our ladder right away. There were melting hail pellets all around our feet. We slipped and slid and stumbled over them briefly until we found firm footing and stood our ground.

"I'm not going up there," said Fred.

"You don't have to. See if you can find a broom, or anything you can use to sweep these hail stones away."

Fred did that while I carefully edged up the ladder toward the open roof access hatch. I got pelted good a couple times by hail stones that came zinging down and ricocheted of the roof hatch and then plunked me in the legs and chest. It stung like hell, but I kept going up until I was close enough to the hatch. "Hey Fred, hand me your broom!" He tossed it and I caught it and with one swift swinging motion I slammed the angled metallic supports that held the hatch in place and the thing came slamming down with a thump, locked closed. A few hail stones knocked loose by the falling hatch fell harmlessly at my feet.

I flew down the ladder. "Help the women clean this mess up."

"Where are you going?"

"To save the mall."

Maurice had evacuated the center court area. The hail storm was subsiding. But I could see out of the corner of my eye as I ran by the center court, accelerating towards the mall offices, that there was a huge pile of hail stones piled up there on the weakest part of the roof windows and there was still a chance it could collapse. Unless somebody got up there and removed the hail stones.

Maurice Sully had the same idea and was right behind me as I scurried up the ladder to the main roof access hatch just west of the center court windows.

"What happened at the jewelry store?" Maurice asked as we climbed.

"We saved the day."

"I hope we can do it again!"

"We will."

I hit the hatch and gave it a shove, but it wouldn't open at first, there were too many hail stones piled up on it and around it. So I had to brace myself good on the ladder and give it a long two-handed, two-armed shove with all my strength, using my legs for leverage and power. The thing opened and I climbed out to a scene of utter devastation. The roof had been punctured with thousands of little holes, as if some giant shotgun in the sky had blasted a load of pellets into the roof. I looked up at the sky and glanced quickly all around. The storm was pretty much over, but there were still a few stray hail stones flying down. I felt and heard one whiz past my head and thump into the roof as I began stepping gingerly across the roof, making my way towards the glass windows above center court.

I yelled back at Maurice before he made it all the way up. "Have them send up some push brooms. They should work okay for the job we've got here."

"Right." Then he barked down to the security officers to hurry up with the brooms.

I came up to the edge of the glass windows, saw the hail stones spread out all over it in a huge icy swath, as if frosting had been spread over the windows. Most of the hail stones had accumulated in the crevices between the curved windows. And there was one flat rectangular area between two banks of curved windows in which most of the hail stones had piled. I couldn't even see the glass beneath the stones, they were piled so thick. I bent down and used a hand to carefully, slowly, brush away some stones, until I could see the glass beneath. I pressed my fingertips to the glass and pressed very gently, as if the glass was skin and my touch a soft loving caress.

It was silent up on the roof now. An eery, unearthly quiet. Even the cars in the streets surrounding the mall had been pounded into submission by the hail. There was no sound. So when I pressed my fingertips to the glass, I could hear clearly the very faint sound of the glass cracking and the supports that connected it to the roof starting to give, starting to whine and wail like tired animals over-taxed in a long race to freedom from carnivorous predators.

The mall was weeping.

"Hurry up with those brooms!" I shouted.

"Here they are," said Maurice Sully, right behind me.

"Careful, this section here is going to collapse."

"Let's get the stones off there first, then." he said.

We swept together. A good boxboy knows how to use a broom efficiently. I thought I was fast and would out-sweep Sully, show him how it was done, humble him with my brilliant boxboy skills. But he was as fast as me, as good as me, as quick as me. We had the thing cleared off in no time. We shoved all those glowing white balls of ice away from the glass, spread them out over the roof and let them start melting.

When we were done, the first little sliver of sunlight started poking through the clouds. I stood at the edge of the glass windows and leaned on my broom, resting, smiling at Maurice Sully in his soiled white suit pants and dirty silk shirt with the bright, gaudy tie. He smiled back at me and dropped his broom. "Time to celebrate!" he shouted. He ran across the roof and hit the rectangular section of glass, slid across in his leather-soled shoes, like a kid ice skating on a lake.

I lurched forward and screamed, "You damn fool, that glass is weak!"

He slid across the glass and stopped just at the edge and stood beaming at me, standing on the glass, fully supported.

"And it could collapse at any time!" said Maurice Sully.

I stood waiting, watching, flabbergasted as the glass supported him.

"But it won't. Do you want to know why?"

"Why?" I asked.

"Because this mall loves me and it won't do anything to hurt me."

I lurched forward and grabbed his arm just as the glass gave way.

I braced myself with my legs and pulled back as Maurice fell down into the mall.

But I had his arm securely and he only went so far. I watched the glass fall below him, all the way to the floor of the center court far beneath him. I heard screams and shouts coming from people below.

"Perhaps you'd better reconsider your relationship with this mall," I said.

"Perhaps you'd better pull me up," he said.

I pulled. He climbed up my arm like a scared monkey running from a tiger. I had him up in a second and we both collapsed on the roof, far back from the glass windows, lying there exhausted, not minding the aggravating pellets of melting hail stones poking us in the back and butt.

Maurice looked at my Albertsons name badge pinned to my apron. "You're a good man in a pinch, Anton. I'll recommend to your manager that he give you a raise."

"Actually, I am the manager. I just pretend to be a boxboy."

A flabbergasted Maurice stared at me. Then he burst out laughing. "I like your style!"

"I like yours."

We didn't shake hands. We had already done that, when I pulled him up from certain death.

That's a pretty good foundation for a friendship, don't you think?

***

I told that story to Diane Copernicus on our first night together.

It was after midnight, she stood naked at the end of my bed, her exquisite female shape outlined in silhouette against the billowing sheer white curtains of my open bedroom windows. The breeze was wafting in and the street lights from outside were beaming twin spotlights at her. She raised her arms over her head, shook her lush hair back, bounced slightly on the balls of her feet, sent delicious jiggling quivers undulating through her breasts — which were the focus of my attention. Then she came back to bed, crawled up over the white sheets and spread herself out over me like a blanket, rested her head on my chest, squirmed briefly into a comfortable position, then relaxed like a big cat, her breath soft and gentle and sweet against my chest.

"Your such a delicious kitten," I said.

"Meow."

"What is your name, sweet kitten?"

"Meow."

"Her name is 'Meow,'" I told my bedroom. "What a sweet name for a kitten."

"Anton?"

"Yes."

"I'm sorry if I've damaged your friendship with Maurice."

"You haven't. Think nothing of it."

"I met him today."

"Oh?"

"He came to the store."

"What did he say?"

"Nothing of consequence."

"Oh?"

Maurice was the type of man who *always* spoke with consequence.

"Did you like him?" I asked. It was important to me that Diane like my best friend.

"I was impressed with him."

"Good."

"Now let's go to sleep. We'll dream together, okay?"

"Yes."

***

We slept.

I dreamed. Diane was there, Maurice was there, but I was nowhere to be seen.

In my dream, I watched the meeting of my best friend and my love.

Diane was alone in the store, dancing with a mannequin. It was the middle of the day and the store was drenched in full sunshine, Pacific Orchid a tropical paradise of cotton colors bursting like neatly folded man-made flowers. There were no customers. Maurice strode in from the bright and deserted mall and tapped a mannequin on the shoulder. "Excuse me, may I have this dance?" The mannequin stepped aside and Maurice moved in, took Diane in his arms, glided around the store briefly, then maneuvered her out into the mall.

"Do you like dancing with mannequins?" he asked her.

"Yes."

"Do you like dancing with a real man?"

"Oh yes!"

"You move exquisitely. Your practice has served you well."

"Thank you."

"I'm Maurice Sully, Mall Master of West Park Plaza."

"I'm pleased to meet you."

"I designed this mall and built it myself. Are you impressed?"

"Very much so!"

"I suppose you'd like a mall of your own someday."

"Yes, that is a dream I've held and a goal I want."

"I can teach you the ways of malls. Would you like to learn?"

"What can you teach me?"

"Everything. How to build. Where to build. How to get shopkeepers and customers to fill your mall with wealth."

"If you teach me, what must I give you in return?"

Maurice smiled.

***

I know Maurice. I know what he wanted.

The next morning at breakfast, I told Diane about my dream. "Is that the way it happened?"

"Yes," she said. "That is exactly how it happened."

Now it was my turn to smile.

"Are you afraid Maurice is going to fall in love with me?" Diane asked.

"Oh, there's no doubt that he will fall in love with you. The question is, are you going to fall in love with him?"

"And if I do?"

"I want you all to myself. But I am a selfish man, so if you choose Maurice, I can deal with it. There is logic in such a choice."

"Very well. I promise you that I will not fall in love with Maurice."

I stopped eating and stared at her seriously. "Now I am afraid."

"Don't be. Tell me about Maurice. I want to hear about this Mall Master. Is he a man of high character? Is he a man you would recommend to a woman? Should I pursue him? Should I be interested? Will he be good to me, and good for me?"

I sat back in my chair. "You want to know about Maurice? Well, let me tell you about him..."

BOOK ONE

THE REASON

OF

MAURICE SULLY

CHAPTER ONE

MASTER OF THE MALL

Maurice Sully lived on top of the mall.

He had designed and built the mall himself at the age of twenty. It was no great detail to integrate a small penthouse structure into the roof of the western end of the shopping center, just above the mall management offices, to provide himself with easy access. His home was a rectangle of two L-shaped walls facing each other. One wall was stone and faced south across the parking lot to Grand Avenue. The north-facing side was all glass, one window looking out to the great sandstone cliffs of the Rimrocks that framed the city of Billings; the short end of the glass L faced east to the city skyline. Maurice liked to stand alone in his penthouse at night and stare across the empty roof of his mall and see the glowing tops of the buildings of downtown Billings twinkling in the night. They didn't have malls downtown.

In the morning, Maurice would rise, shower, dress, have a small breakfast, then descend in a private elevator to the management offices, check his schedule, answer his messages, do some brief paperwork, then, cellular phone in hand, prowl out into the mall and tour the entire structure, first inside, then outside, checking on the tenants, making sure the floors were clean, garbage dumped, signs in place, security present, stores open and trouble-free. He would stop in and chat with merchants, deal with issues outstanding, get feedback on what he could do to make his tenants happy, productive, prosperous. He would listen to complaints and sometimes make notes. He would give advice to the younger, less experienced merchants, or to tenants new to his mall. He didn't miss a store. He couldn't stand the idea of one of his merchants feeling left out. They were like children. He had his favorites, but he wasn't going to let any of them know just who.

Special events and celebrity appearances happened almost every week and took up a lot of time. There were always negotiations and special arrangements to be made. He was always on the phone to someone or reviewing plans or requests sent in the mail. There were always film crews wanting to use his dramatic architecture as a background for their dramas. They always wanted to film his penthouse.

That was strictly forbidden.

His official duties usually ended around four in the afternoon, although depending on circumstances, he could sometimes be found in his office until early evening, or later. He usually liked to end the day with a foraging expedition to the grocery store, buy a few items, then stroll through the mall with a sack of groceries in his arms, anonymous amidst the swirls of happy shoppers. He would vanish into the maze of mall offices and be whisked up to his penthouse for a relaxing evening.

One door in the south-facing wall of his penthouse led to the mall roof. It was his front yard. He had a telescope and liked to look at the stars. But mostly, he liked to sit in a chair when weather permitted, listen to classical symphonies and opera, sip rare liqueurs, and watch the traffic stream by on Grand Avenue.

"I only have one mall," he would say to the traffic. "But that is enough."

Every spring, on June 17th, he would, at some point during the day, go to the roof and raise a toast of rare wine to the flag of his nation, the Individual's Republic of California. June 17th was Freedom Day. He would smile at the flag: a gold dollar sign against a dark blue background. He would drink the wine, savor the flavor in his mouth, savor even more the feeling of security that flag gave him. His government was pledged to protect individual rights for all eternity. If you owned a mall, you took that promise seriously and knew what it meant. Maurice knew.

***

"I'm going to be a Mall Master some day!"

Maurice Sully was nine years old when he made that announcement to his family. His parents smiled. All the kids wanted to own malls at one time or another. It was a stage they all went through. "That's nice, darling," said his mother. His father was a little more hard-headed. "Well, what are you going to do about it?"

Maurice liked to pull down all the books from his parent's library and stack them out along the floor in various geometrical shapes: sometimes a rectangle, sometimes a square; once a daring octagon. When he had the shape, he would park his toy cars and trucks all around the structure, then populate it with his toy soldiers. "Look mommy and daddy, see my mall!"

"That's beautiful, darling!" said his mother.

"Who's your anchor?" asked his father.

"JC Penney!"

"They'll never last. You want a major retailer with real teeth, kid. I'd go with Sears."

"No father, you're wrong."

"Oh yeah? Why?"

"Their management is inefficient and lacks a long-range vision."

"The hell you say."

Young Maurice always had to close down his malls by bedtime. But he kept notebooks in which he drew pictures of all of them. He included indexed lists of tenants, making sure to cover every area of retailing and all the major service industries.

When Maurice graduated from the local lyceum at the age of fourteen, he was ready to apprentice himself to a regional developer.

At that time there was no mall in his home town. Nobody thought it was a good market — except the people who lived there. Maurice promised himself to bring his neighbors a mall. It was to be his mission in life.

He was sent to the west coast, to Seattle, to work in the office of the leading mall developer in the country.

He had thought he would have plenty to learn. Instead, he did much of the teaching. By the time he took up his apprenticeship, he had studied every mall in the country. He knew them all so well he could have written books on each; big, fat, thick, scholarly books detailing every aspect of each mall: location, size, architectural style, demographics, traffic both in numbers of people and dollars; category breakdowns by business and sales for each business. He knew the demographics of each state of California, each major city in each state; every region of the nation: coastal areas, mountains, plains. He had studied in particular the malls in areas bordering the Mississippi River and the United States of America.

He had never been across the river and into that strange sister country. He was not sure he wanted to go. He knew he would go eventually, because everyone made the trip at least once. But it was not something he was looking forward to, and certainly not something he lusted after and felt necessary to fulfill his life. The USA was still a welfare state, actually taxed its citizens and regulated business. Maurice did not want to do business with companies laboring under such a system; it was certain to put his capital at risk. So he didn't think about those issues. But he did very intensely study the malls along the river; they were the busiest malls in the country, mainly because hordes of shoppers from the USA came across to shop and get products not available at home — or available cheaper and at better quality. Those malls had special circumstances and much could be learned from them. In the first year of his apprenticeship, Maurice went to St. Louis and spent a week at the Show Me Mall.

The most serious problem the malls along the river had to deal with was criminals from the USA coming over and entering the malls and asking for sanctuary.

It was just such an incident that provided Maurice's first great test as a Mall Master.

The nation of California had been founded by businessmen explicitly for the purpose of securing free trade, and the entire country was, in effect, one gigantic free trade zone. But even within this context, malls were in a class by themselves and were given special consideration both by the citizens and the legal authorities. As the business culture of California had developed over time, it had become the custom for businessmen who were experiencing legal problems to ask local Mall Masters to mediate their disputes. The Mall Masters were sufficiently admired by the people and respected by the authorities that this situation was accepted as natural by both. Ninety per cent of the people in California were pagan atheists, so the leaders of the few churches that existed were not taken seriously. The handful of universities that existed were populated mostly by scientists who wished to remain aloof from social problems. So in a business culture, it was the businessmen the people turned to for moral leadership. And this was a function all Mall Masters took very seriously, trained for, prepared for.

Soon, however, the logical implications were played out fully when common criminals of all types took advantage of the custom, escaping into malls to seek justice from Mall Masters known to be fair and wise — and sometimes overly benevolent. Usually what happened to some thief running from the law was that he went to a mall, was granted sanctuary, his case was examined, facts were presented, depositions given, arguments made for and against, and, if the guy wasn't actually a murderer or rapist and had not used a weapon to inflict bodily injury on some citizen, he usually ended up signing a contract with the mall management agreeing to live and work exclusively in the mall for a certain period of time. He would be watched carefully. He was kept to strict quarters and strict hours. He was usually worked like a slave. The Mall Master assumed personal responsibility for the guy. He was referred to euphemistically as a "part-timer." If the guy broke the terms of his contract, the Mall Master would "fire" him. This consisted of his being booted off the mall premises — and into the waiting arms of the police, who would haul him off to a slightly less benevolent social milieu. But this rarely happened.

The authorities outside didn't mind this set-up because the guy was essentially in jail as far as they were concerned. Even though he had contact with the community, it was a segment of the community that had not been harmed by his crimes. His actions and movements were strictly delimited. And if he left the mall, the local cops would have him in a real jail in a flash. And in California, even such petty criminals as did exist had a semblance of rationality about them, so they usually took advantage of the situation, and when it was time to leave the mall, they did so with some money in their pocket and the hard-earned good will of their fellow citizens. "Hey, there goes that guy who stole from the Jones'! Been workin' at the mall the last two years. Not a bad guy. Does good work!"

But along the Mississippi river, the situation was a little more serious.

It happened on a weekend. Maurice and his team of apprentice Mall Masters had been at the mall for a week. They had been closely supervised at first, but gradually their leash had shortened, and now, as was custom during these training exercises, the leash was gone and they were on their own for the weekend. The regular mall management had taken the weekend off and had gone across the river into America with the senior mall instructors. They wouldn't be back until Monday.

Maurice was sharing a hotel suite with three fellow apprentices in the Hilton across the street from the mall. They were high up and had windows facing the mall facade across a narrow band of parking lot. A train platform stood in the middle of the wide avenue separating the hotel and the mall grounds. Every few minutes a load of passengers would pour out and head for the mall.

Maurice's bed was next to a window. Every morning he had stood at the window for a time, staring down at the mall, studying it, analyzing the parking lot and surrounding structures, watching the trains try to compete with the cars in a contest to see which could deliver the most people. The cars were big shiny powerful sedans driven by elegantly-dressed Californian's. The trains were filled with grubby Americans. It was hard to say exactly who was winning.

At night, before sleep, Maurice would stand for a time and meditate on the mall by night, all lit up in blazing neon finery, beckoning the night to withstand its ferocious gayety. Maurice would stare and remember times as a child when he had dressed his toy malls up in Christmas lights.

Maurice was the youngest of the apprentices on this training mission, but he had naturally assumed leadership of the group because he was the tallest and he knew the most. The others had come to the ways of malls late in childhood, or early in their teen years; but Maurice had been consumed with mall passion almost from the instant of birth. He radiated such a distinctive intensity for every aspect of mall life that the others looked up to him simply as a kind of logical inevitability. To be with Maurice was to be with a mall.

His roommates were Frederick Wilson from Denver; Halston Stiggs from Seattle; and Evan Philips from Portland.

Across the hall, sharing a suite, were the two female apprentices from California: Gloria White from Atlantis, and Ann Thurston from New Athens.

Maurice rose early and dressed in a dark blue suit. Pinned to his lapel was a name-badge identifying him as an apprentice.

He decided to skip breakfast with his colleagues and went on across to the mall on his own. On the way, waiting for the light in front of the train station, a load of morning-eager Americans were pouring off a train. He glanced over and caught the eyes of a slender, intense young woman who slid past him, glanced at the red lights facing her, saw the street was clear, then made a dash across to the mall parking lot and kept jogging to the moving walkways that swiftly carried shoppers into the mall.

Maurice thought nothing of it. When the light turned green, he strolled across the street and had a relaxing, slow-paced reconnoiter of the parking lot and front entrances.

As he moved along the slideway towards the front entrance, he noticed a cruiser from the St. Louis police department pulling into the lot on his left. He glanced off to his right and saw another cruiser far off at the end of the parking lot, moving slowly. An officer inside the car was directing a searchlight beam into the cars they passed.

Maurice glanced at his watch. "Damn. I should have eaten breakfast."

***

"I'm asking for sanctuary here in the mall."

The woman sitting across the desk from him was the same he had seen rush off the train and hurry across the street. She had beat him to his own office.

"What kind of crime have you committed?" asked Maurice.

"I'd like to discuss this with the Mall Master."

"I am in charge of the mall at this time."

"You're nothing but a boy!"

"I'm fifteen years old. How old are you?"

"You're an apprentice, for God's sake!"

"No, I'm an apprentice for *my* sake. Now, if you want me to help you, please answer my questions. What crime have you committed?"

The woman took a deep breath. She stared hard at Maurice with eyes that had seen much. She was a good judge of people. You had to be when you lived in a criminal infested cesspool like America.

"Tax evasion," she said.

"Okay. What else?"

"I violated some stupid regulatory laws."

"What business are you in?"

"I owned a bookstore."

"They regulate bookstores in America now?"

"They always have."

"What did you do?"

"I carried books that weren't printed on recycled paper."

"And they shut you down for that?"

"On the surface."

"What was happening below the surface?"

"Small press stuff critiquing the government."

"I see. How much do you owe the tax hounds?"

"Fifty thousand dollars."

"That translates roughly into five hundred in IRC money."

"I guess so."

Maurice smiled. "Do you have a weapon?"

"Not anymore."

"Did you have one on the train?"

"Yes."

"What happened to it?"

"I dumped it."

"Where?"

"Here in the mall. In a rest room."

Maurice hit an intercom button. "Maintenance? I need someone in here right away." Maurice looked back at the young woman. "Now I think it is time for a name."

She looked at him. "Sarah Fletcher."

"Sarah, when the maintenance man comes in, I want you to tell him which rest room you were in, okay?"

"What are you going to do?"

"We'll need that weapon. It's better we have it and keep it then leave it to chance that it find its way into the hands of the American authorities."

"How could that happen? I thought they can't set foot on mall property. This is a sacred place, isn't it?"

"Yes, it is, but it's also on the border with America, which makes the rules a little more fluid than for a normal mall off in the wild rustic greediness of California."

"Are you going to sell me out?"

"Not a chance. If you're honest. And if you're rational. And if you mean to do well here."

"I mean it."

"Miss Fletcher, have you been to California before?"

"No, this is my first time. But I've always wanted to come, I've read a lot, and heard stories—"

"You'll find that Californians are more focused on actions and results than on words. Say whatever you will, you're going to be watched carefully, held to high standards, and judged ruthlessly. That is the California way. Make terms with reality — or go to hell."

"You sound like my grandfather."

"He must have been a good man."

"He was a drunken son-of-a-bitch. No, I mean, you sound like an old man."

"I'm an apprentice Mall Master, dear lady. It goes with the territory."

A maintenance man in crisp brown overalls walked into the office. "You wanted me, Maurice?"

"Yes. This is Miss Fletcher. She lost an item in one of our rest rooms. Miss Fletcher, please tell Alfred here which rest room you visited."

Sarah Fletcher explained to Alfred the maintenance man which rest room she had visited after entering the mall. When Alfred left to perform his assigned task, Maurice excused himself and intercepted Alfred outside just before he left the mall management offices. "Alfred, it's very important to be as discreet as possible with this job. My advice is, when you've found the wastebasket in question, don't even look inside, just bring the entire thing to my office. Take a replacement with you so we don't end up with garbage all over a rest room, okay?"

"Yes sir."

Maurice went back to Sarah Fletcher. "How long have you been on the run?"

"Three days."

"Where are you from?"

"Kentucky. Am I going to be granted sanctuary?"

"When I've decided, you'll be the first to know."

"What else do you need to know?"

"I've already told you."

"Aren't there some special procedures we have to go through?"

"Once a Mall Master has decided to grant sanctuary, there are some traditional statements that need to be made, some public announcements and a ceremony. And the authorities have to be notified, of course. It's kind of like getting married. But the actual decision to grant sanctuary is entirely up to the Mall Master."

"You mean, there isn't like a council that votes on it?"

"No. Forgotten the name of this country already?"

"Oh, yes..."

"All values are personal, Miss Fletcher. Only individuals are fit to make value judgments. So no, you'll see no voting on things as important as this."

"Well, when do we start?"

"We already have."

"Then how am I doing?"

"You're flunking."

Sarah Fletcher looked shocked.

The phone rang.

Maurice picked it up. "Management."

A tough, gruff voice on the other end of the line said, "This is Captain Chester Kaiser of the St. Louis police department. I'd like to speak with Mall Master Clemens, please."

"He's out of the country, sir, on a weekend sabbatical."

"Who is this?"

"Maurice Sully. I'm an apprentice, sir."

There was a long pause on the other end of the line. Maurice waited patiently, knowing what was going through the mind of the older gentleman on the other end.

Finally, the law officer said, "How old are you, son?"

"Fifteen."

"First apprentice assignment?"

"Yes sir."

"Where are you from, son?"

"Billings, Montana."

"First trip to a big city?"

"No sir. I've spent time at the Mall Development Training Center in Seattle."

"Well, I guess you're ready for anything then, huh?"

"You haven't told me what your problem is yet, officer Kaiser."

"*Captain* Kaiser, son. I suspect you already know what the situation is."

"I'd like to hear it from you, sir."

"Very well. There's a young woman on the run. American wanted for tax evasion and violation of regulatory procedures. We think she's heading for the mall to ask for sanctuary. We think she might already be in the mall."

"Do you have a description?"

"Female, twenty-five years old, blonde hair, blue eyes, athletic build. And she's armed and considered dangerous."

Maurice had listened to the description while staring directly at Sarah Fletcher. Every detail fit her. "Do you have a name?"

"Son, you have a situation here that's going to be a little more than you can handle. I suggest you get on the phone and contact Mall Master Clemens as soon as possible."

"If I do that, I'll flunk this exam, Captain Kaiser."

"To hell with exams! You've got a real-life situation here that needs to be dealt with seriously, you can't be thinking of school-boy tests!"

"That's what I was talking about, Captain Kaiser. Life gives the real exams; that's the one I want to pass. So let's not talk anymore about Clemens. I'm going to handle this situation because that is what a Mall Master is supposed to do — and I am a Mall Master, Captain Kaiser, even if the title hasn't officially been granted yet. This is not a job, a career, or a 'calling' for me. It's an identity. So tell me what makes this request for sanctuary so much more serious than any other?"

There was a long pause.

Maurice stared at Sarah Fletcher. The young woman couldn't hear half the conversation, but her eyes were large enough to indicate that she understood what was going on.

Finally Kaiser spoke again. "She's the daughter of the Governor of Kentucky. They don't want her in California. They want her home."

"How old did you say she was?"

"Twenty-five."

"She's a grown woman. They have no authority over her."

"Son, I told you that this is more complicated—"

"You haven't told me anything, Captain Kaiser. I suggest you start. I need all the information you have. If you won't give it to me, you're of no assistance and I'll have to end this conversation."

"You pretentious little boy—"

"And I'm also going to request that from now on you address me as Mall Master Sully."

"The hell I will!"

Maurice hung up.

"Kid, you've got balls," said Sarah Fletcher.

"Don't be disrespectful," said Maurice. "Your life is in my hands right now, so I suggest you act accordingly."

Maurice took out his cellular phone and dialed a number. When the other end answered, he said, "Fred? Are you guys still at breakfast? Well, cut it short. We have a situation. Get everybody over here right away. I'll brief you when you get here. Make it quick." When that conversation was over, he dialed another number. "Security? This is Sully. We've had a request for sanctuary. I'm taking it seriously, so this mall is off limits to all police and militia until further notice. Get everybody you've got on this. There were patrol cars from the St. Louis PD in the parking lot when I came in. Politely ask them to vacate the premises. Post guards at all the doors. Make sure everyone understands this is the real thing, not a drill. Call people in if you're short-handed. Do whatever it takes. But be cool, stay calm, stay professional. No reason to get shook up just yet. Excuse me, what's that? No, Clemens has not been notified. He will not. I'm handling it. Yeah? Well, if that's true, then you can be a pallbearer." Maurice hung up.

"So, I'm not flunking anymore?" asked Sarah Fletcher.

"Are you really the daughter of the Governor of Kentucky?"

"Yes."

"I don't follow American politics. How powerful a man is your father?"

"He's a candidate for President."

"What are his chances of winning?"

"He's a worthless son-of-a-bitch, so — pretty good."

"Do you think he'd actually violate a sanctuary request?"

"That custom means nothing to Americans. If they want me bad enough, they'll come and get me."

"Even if it means war with California?"

"I think they want war with California. I think they want to loot all these malls along the Mississippi. And the communities that surround them."

"That's insane. Nobody could be that stupid."

"You don't know my father."

"When did you last see your father?"

"Three days ago. When I shot him."

Maurice sat back in his chair and stared silently at her for a long time. She gazed back, holding his glance severely, as if to say, "Well, you wanted the truth."

"That changes things," said Maurice.

"Does it?"

"Yes. Did you...kill your father?"

"I don't know."

"What part of his body was shot?"

"I think his stomach."

"Was he conscious when you left him?"

"Yes."

"Why did you shoot him?"

"Does it matter?"

"For me personally, yes."

"He knew about my trouble with the law. He knew about my tax problems, and my scuffle with the regulatory agencies. I asked him for help. He refused. He wanted to make an example of me. He wanted to sacrifice me to prove he was worthy of the Presidency."

"That's the most obscene thing I've ever heard in my life."

"He was going to have me put under house arrest. I had no choice. It was my only way out."

"How did you manage to escape? Doesn't your father have bodyguards?"

"Yes. But they never considered protecting him from family."

Just then there was a knock on the door. "Maintenance!"

Maurice got up and opened the door and let Alfred in. He had a garbage can on a hand truck. He unloaded it in front of Maurice's desk, then excused himself.

"Let's take a look," said Maurice.

He took the lid off the garbage can and looked inside. A plastic bag lined the metal can. At the bottom were a few scraps of paper and tissue. Maurice reached down and grabbed one of the moist paper towels and used it as a glove as he searched the bottom of the can. He found what he was looking for. He pulled a gun up out of the bottom of the can, held it up in front of Sarah Fletcher. "Is this your weapon?"

"Yes."

Maurice carefully set the gun down on his desk, stared at it for a second while stroking his chin, thinking.

Sarah Fletcher stared at the gun, her eyes wide with a memory that made her sick. She took a deep breath and straightened her back and waited for Maurice.

"I know nothing of guns," he said. "Never handled one, never touched one. I think this is the first real gun I've ever seen."

"Don't be frightened. It won't spontaneously shoot you."

"Is it loaded?"

"No. I flushed the remaining bullets down the toilet before I trashed it."

"Open it up and show me."

Sarah came forward, picked up the gun, popped the cylinder out, showed it to Maurice. There were no bullets. Sarah flipped the cylinder back into place, left the gun on the desk where Maurice had placed it.

Maurice went to a drawer in his desk — the Mall Master's desk — and got out a manila envelope. He picked up the gun — again using the towel as a glove — and placed the gun back into the refuse-filled plastic garbage bag. Then he wadded up the entire mess and stuffed it into the over-size envelope. He sealed the envelope and then used a marker to write in big, bold letters on the front: "Various receipts." Then he just tossed the envelope off to one side of the desk. And he gave Sarah Fletcher a good long look.

She sat looking back at him, her arms crossed, one eyebrow arched up in inquisitive sarcasm.

Maurice said, "Generally speaking, sanctuary is not granted to individuals who have committed violent crimes. But that rule is intended to apply to California citizens who live in a free country. You are not the citizen of a free country. If your story is true, then your actions were in self-defense. Therefore, I'm going to grant you sanctuary. But there is one condition."

"What's that?"

"You have to marry me."

She burst out laughing. "Get real!"

"I am serious, Miss Fletcher."

"And you lecture me about honoring reality!"

"Being the wife of a Mall Master counts for much in our society."

"I don't doubt it."

"You have time to consider my proposition. And think about all the ramifications. No need to answer immediately. But when you are officially granted sanctuary, you will have to sign a contract. These sorts of contracts are enforced most rigorously by the authorities. They have no choice in the matter. If they didn't enforce them, this whole system of sanctuary would fall apart and be useless. So do take this seriously. And understand that if you don't agree to marry me — there will be no contract. You will not be given sanctuary. You will be turned over to the authorities — who will be obliged to send you back to your father."

"Just my luck to get mixed up with a horny teenager."

"I like the idea of a woman who takes her values and life so seriously that she would shoot her own father and abandon her country to get to freedom."

"I'm not some romantic goddess, young man."

"Stick with me — and you will be."

The door flew open and Fred Wilson strode in, stopped short. "Excuse me, hope I'm not interrupting."

"Perfect timing, Fred. Come on in. Everybody else behind you?"

"We're coming, boss," said Gloria White. Behind her, the other three apprentices, Halston Stiggs, Evan Philips, and Ann Thurston streamed into the small office.

Sarah Fletcher stood and stared grimly at the crowd of mall apprentices. They all smiled back at her.

"Here is the situation," said Maurice. "This young lady is Miss Sarah Fletcher, recently of Kentucky, USA. She has requested sanctuary and I have decided to grant her request. The situation is dangerous because Miss Fletcher is—"

"The daughter of the Governor of Kentucky, the leading American Presidential candidate," said Evan Philips.

Maurice smiled at his friend. "Evan, your fascination with America politics is perverse, but potentially useful in this context, so I'm glad you spoke up. Your job is research. I want you to get online and gather as much information about the governor as possible. Sarah here can help you fill in any missing pieces, possibly provide you with useful dirt. Just dig for now. When I need you and what you've found, I'll let you know."

"I'm on it, boss," said Evan. He was twenty-three years old and had a full beard.

Maurice continued with his orders. "Fred, I'd like you to manage security during this situation. Supervise them closely, make sure they stay on top of things, don't let the situation get loose. Don't try to micro-manage, let them do their jobs, just keep close tabs and make sure everybody understands what's going on and what's at stake. I'm planning on a twelve noon sanctuary ceremony, so plan accordingly."

"It's as good as done," said Fred, and he was out the door.

"Ann, you're from the capital, so you know something of ceremony. I'd like you to start setting up the sanctuary ceremony at center court.

All we need is a bare-bones, essentialized ceremony. You have three hours. Is that enough?"

"It'll be close, but if we don't get too fancy, we'll be fine. Should I notify the media?"

"Yes. But don't give out any names or details. Low key it. Make it seem like just a run-of-the-mill thing. If memory serves me—"

"And it usually does," said Ann, smiling.

"—the last sanctuary granted at this mall was nine months ago. So they'll probably be hungry for some juicy news like this."

"I'm gone," said Ann, turning on her heels and wheeling out the door.

Sarah Fletcher's head was spinning. She looked at Gloria White. "You're all older than Maurice. Why is he the leader, and why do you all jump when he barks?"

"Because we're all impeccably selfish egoists devoted to our best interests and highest values. So naturally, we all get along. Maurice is simply the best. Besides that, he's my hero, and when he grows up, I might marry him."

"You'll have to wait in line," said Sarah.

Gloria raised an eyebrow.

"Enough," said Maurice. "Gloria, I want you to take Miss Fletcher out into the mall and buy her some new clothes. Something appropriate for a sanctuary ceremony. Use the mall management credit card. Make a point to introduce Miss Fletcher to all the merchants you deal with. Be loud and theatrical about it. Make sure they all understand who she is and where she's come from. Stop by security and get two escorts before heading into the mall."

"Yes, sir."

Maurice motioned with an arm. "Miss Fletcher, off you go."

Sarah stood up and followed Gloria White to the door.

"Gloria, when you're done, bring her back here."

"Yes, sir."

When they were gone, Maurice sat down and picked up the phone, dialed the number for the commander of the local militia, General Kent McKnight. When he had the General on the line, he said, "Sir, this is Mall Master Maurice Sully at the Show Me Mall. We've got a sanctuary situation here that I think needs your attention."

"The hell you say. I've just been on the other line with Captain Chet Kaiser of the SLPD."

"I see."

"So you're fixin' to try on a fancy new pair of britches, huh son?"

"I'm wearing them, sir."

"I hope they fit. Captain Kaiser was unable to confirm that a certain young lady was actually in your custody. Are you now going to confirm that she is in fact in the mall?"

"Is this a secure line?"

"Of course it is."

"And are you the only individual I'm speaking to?"

"You're insulting me, son."

"Very well. Miss Sarah Fletcher is in the mall. I have granted her sanctuary. The ceremony is scheduled for twelve noon today."

"So you've already decided?"

"Yes sir."

"Are you aware of the crimes this young lady has committed?"

"Tax evasion and regulatory violations."

"Son, she shot her father. He's in intensive care right now. The whole American political scene has been spun topsy-turvy. They want her back, and they want her back with a vengeance."

"So you've been on the phone with some other folks as well."

"All last night, and all damn morning."

"Who have you talked to?"

"Never mind. Listen son, the fact is, she's a violent criminal. You can't give sanctuary to a violent criminal. You have to let her go."

"She's the victim of a welfare state that *sacrifices* the rights of its citizens!"

"Don't use foul language, son."

"Well, that's what they do, and you know it. Now listen to me, General. You know the history of the malls in this region as well as I. They've granted sanctuary to Americans for years. But never when violence was involved. Never to violent criminals. I am telling you that we have to appreciate the context here and understand that the political situation in America has become so twisted that individuals there have to become violent in order to maintain their sovereignty, secure their property, and exercise their rights. What we take for granted in California, they have to fight bloody battles for. Do you know why Sarah Fletcher shot her father?"

"I know what the Americans have told me."

"He was going to turn her in. He was going to give her up, his own daughter. He knew about her troubles with the law, and instead of trying to work something out and save his own daughter, he was going to sacrifice her, he was going to serve her up on a sacrificial altar to the people, to the government, and say, 'Here fine people, to prove my moral worth to you, I'm giving up my own daughter. I'm sacrificing her to the country. I'm giving her away to you.' General McKnight, can you believe such a thing? Can you conceive of the mentality of a human being who would do such a thing — and call it virtue? Can you conceive of the sickening powerlust that must consume this man? I say it is time the Individual's Republic of California starts granting sanctuary to *any* citizen of America who asks for it. I say this is a test case for us. I intend to make the most of it and to use the moral authority that comes with being a Mall Master for all it is worth. I've spoken with Sarah Fletcher. I think she believes in, understands, takes seriously, and desires all the values we Californians hold dear. I say she is a greedy, selfish egoist — and we have to save her!"

Evan Philips and Halston Stiggs had turned from their tasks to face Maurice and listen silently. When Maurice finished, they both raised clenched fists in the air. "Right on, boss!"

"Get back to work!" snapped Maurice.

"Yes sir," they responded.

There was a short pause on the other end of the phone as General McKnight took a deep breath. "Okay, son. It's your mall. You're the Mall Master. If that's the way you want to play it..."

"General, I'd like to suggest that you attend the sanctuary ceremony. It would send a message to have you here. And it would give you a chance to meet this young woman personally, speak to her, get a sense of who she is and where she's coming from."

"I was going to insist on it, son."

"If your reason tells you she's lying and really is a dangerous criminal, you can hold me responsible."

"I certainly will, son."

"Also, General, although it's not my place to presume knowledge of military matters, I'd like to officially request, as a Mall Master, that the largest show of force possible be displayed here at the Show Me Mall. I'd like to send an unmistakable message to the Americans that we take this sort of thing very seriously."

"I'll consider your request, Mr. Sully."

"Thank you, sir."

"Have you contacted the other Mall Masters yet?"

"That was to be my next task."

"I'll let you get to it, son. I'll see you at high noon."

The General clicked off.

Maurice sat back in his chair and took a deep breath.

His stomach growled.

"I should have eaten breakfast," he said, picking up the phone again.

***

After a conference call with the five nearest Mall Masters close enough to make a twelve o'clock sanctuary ceremony, Maurice took a break. It was nine forty-five. He sat back in his chair, closed his eyes, took a deep breath, meditated for a moment on the structure of events developing around him. He didn't notice when the office door opened and a restaurant delivery person entered with a tray of hot food, sat it down on the desk without saying a word, and vanished soundlessly from whence he had come. Maurice caught the scent of pancakes and eggs and opened his eyes, saw the food, smiled, leaned forward, pulled the tray to him, picked up a fork, said, "Thanks guys," as he took his first bite. "Don't mention it, boss," said Halston Stiggs, smiling at Evan Philips as they continued their intense work.

Maurice ate breakfast, staring occasionally at the manila envelope on his desk marked, "Various Receipts."

After breakfast, he got on the phone again and called the mall's General Counsel, Mike Charles. "Sorry to bother you at home and ruin your weekend, Mike, but we've got a situation here at the mall."

"What's up?"

"I'll brief you when you get here. But I need you to draw me up a contract. A sanctuary contract."

"I see. I knew you kids would have a wild weekend."

"Never mind. Do you have a pen? You need to make some notes. I want some special clauses in this contract."

"Very well. Shoot."

Maurice outlined the contract for him, gave him the exact wording of the special clauses he needed. When he was done, Mike Charles whistled through his teeth.

"That needs to be ready and in my hands by noon for the ceremony. Can you do it?"

"I'll be there. Wouldn't miss it for the world."

"I'll see you then."

After hanging up, Maurice picked up the manila envelope labeled "Various Receipts," carried it out of the office, down a hallway, through a locked door, down a long stairway to another locked door, then deep into the bowels of the mall until he reached a hot, dark area where an incinerator burned and glowed. Maurice opened a small port in the incinerator and tossed in the envelope, slammed the port shut, watched the thing burn through the slits in the port. He saw flame and sparks and soot and ash swirling together in a flaming miasma that resembled water flowing through a prism. He watched it for a long moment, feeling the heat on his face, closing his eyes for a second and catching the weight of the mall on his shoulders, all of it up there above him, all that life and wealth, together, integrated, and he supporting it, like Atlas supporting the world. It was his job. He was a priest of commerce. He was responsible for establishing and securing the link between life and wealth and making sure it was never severed. Making money and spending it was to be a beautiful, sensuous experience, the spiritual center of human life. That was his life's work. This was the first act in his life's drama. It seemed he was having a climax even before he arrived on the stage. How would he ever top this? What could the future possibly hold for him?

It was a question he needed to ask, but did not need to answer. He could not think of the future now. It was not necessary. He had it all in his hands, on his shoulders, above him now, supported by his mind, his knowledge, his devotion to sacred values. He smiled. Those people above him thought he was a child playing an adult game, out of his league and out-matched and about to be crushed into nothingness and sent crying back to his mother.

He yawned. The truth was, this was just another day at the office.

***

Preparations for the sanctuary ceremony moved along swiftly.

A stage had been raised at center court. The area had been roped off with heavy velvet finery brought out of storage. Ann Thurston placed a golden "S" carved out of wood at the front of the stage. This was a symbol that immediately changed the character of the mall. Relaxed shoppers strolling by saw the S and paused, smiled, looked around, then raced off to the nearest pay phones, or else turned to face a pillar or wall in privacy as they brought out their cellular phones and placed urgent calls to people who wanted to know, needed to know — which was every citizen within a ten mile radius of the mall. Anybody who could get there in person, would.

And the merchants who hadn't already been faxed or called by Halston Stiggs stepped out across the thresholds of their shops and into the greater mall and looked this way and that way, checking out mall traffic, spying on neighbors, gauging reactions. Some stood for a long time, watching the mall and thinking. Others retired instantly to back offices, to place calls, to check employment records, to make calculations of hours usage — just in case. Others turned on radios, tv's, or accessed the internet to see if they could find a clue as to who it was that was about to be granted sanctuary.

The mall was normally a busy, active place filled with swift, purposeful people. Now it shifted into high gear, like an engine pushed into overdrive.

Alone together in the mall management offices, Halston Stiggs and Evan Philips paused in their work. They sat silently, listening to a distant hum growing just at the fringe of their consciousness. They placed fingertips gently against a wall and felt the mall vibrating, ever so gently. They smiled at each other — and went back to work.

Maurice Sully returned to the offices after his brief trip to the basement and opened the large walk-in closet at the rear of the offices. He took a brief inventory of the sanctuary uniforms hanging on the rack, then picked out a robe for himself, set it aside. Then he returned to the office. "How are the merchant notifications coming?" he asked Halston Stiggs.

"Ninety per cent done, sir."

"Very well. Evan, keep digging."

"I'm a gold miner, sir," said Evan Philips, smiling.

Maurice sat down and placed a call on his cellular phone. "Fred, any problems with security?"

"We're handling it, sir."

"Any evidence of military presence yet?"

"Not yet, sir."

"Let me know as soon as you see something. But I want you in uniform at the sanctuary ceremony, so give yourself time."

"Yes sir."

Then a call to Ann Thurston. "Are you on schedule, Ann?"

"We'll be ready."

"What's the mood out there?"

"It's buzzing. Everybody is getting very excited, I think."

"Good. Any media yet?"

"They're unloading their trucks right now."

"Very well. Be nice to everyone, make sure each station has a good camera position."

"We'll do."

Then a call to Gloria White. "How are you doing?"

"She's being fitted right now."

"Good."

Maurice hung up, then went back to the private rest room to change into his robe.

***

At 11:45, Maurice was at his desk, talking to Fred Wilson about security when Mike Charles was escorted in. Mike was clean-shaven and wore his best suit, looked ready for business. He opened his brief case and slapped down the contract Maurice had asked him for. "There you are, Mall Master Sully. Just what you asked for."

"Thank you, Mr. Charles," said Maurice. He glanced over the contract briefly, then handed it to Sarah Fletcher, who was sitting in a chair against a wall, demure in her new gown, an elegant purple satin evening gown. "Please read this contract, Miss Fletcher. Basically, it says you are being granted sanctuary conditional on your accepting matrimony with the Mall Master, and that you agree to the terms and conditions of mall sanctuary, namely, that you agree to live within the mall for a specified time, that you are forbidden from leaving the mall at any time, for any reason during that period, and that you will engage in productive work for one or more mall businesses during your stay."

Sarah Fletcher read the contract. It was not a long contract. The language was simple and straightforward. When she was done, she looked up at Maurice, her face blank. "Two years. I have to stay in this mall for two years."

"Technically. Please note that as my wife, you'd be able to travel to other malls with me."

"So you'll take me wherever you go."

"Yes."

"Where are you going next?"

"I don't know. I haven't been told. Probably depends on how I handle this situation."

Sarah Fletcher signed the contract, then sat back in her seat.

Maurice placed the signed contract inside the inner pocket of his sanctuary robe. Then he stood up. He was wearing a dark blue sanctuary robe with beautiful gold dollar signs on front and back. His fellow mall apprentices all wore similar robes.

"Are we ready, Fred?" he asked.

"All set," said Fred.

"Let's go," said Maurice, motioning Sarah Fletcher to rise.

They all marched out of the mall offices, to a waiting electric mall cart driven by a security officer. The officer pulled away from the offices and accelerated down the long hallway and out into the greater mall.

Out in the mall, the cart zoomed down a narrow, winding, velvet rope-lined highway framed with shoppers and curiosity seekers. The people who watched the cart pass by stood quietly at attention and gazed intently at the woman in the purple dress. Some recognized her and gasped. These were Americans. Most of the Californians had no idea who she was.

CHAPTER TWO

SANCTUARY

Maurice Sully and Sarah Fletcher sat together, holding hands, in the middle of the electric cart, flanked on either side by a security officer who rode standing up, holding on to the top of the cart with one hand, facing out at the gathering crowds of shoppers, one hand lightly on his baton, ready for action.

As the cart moved out into the mall, the shoppers turned as one and pressed in slightly against the velvet-rope lined path. Bright flashes popped chaotically on either side as cameras clicked and photographs were taken. They swept past murmuring voices and never caught the questions being asked. The Californians were quiet and respectful, merely whispered to each other as the cart passed by and they caught a glimpse of who it was to be granted sanctuary. The Americans present screamed and shouted in desperate hope it was someone they knew; those who recognized the young woman in the purple evening gown were overcome with emotion and choked on screams and convulsive gasps of hysteria. Some tried to rush forward, screaming her name, but were stopped and dragged back by Californians committed to maintaining order.

The cart zoomed down a long straightaway as it flew along one wing of the mall. When it hit center court, it swooped into a long sweeping curve that carried it around to the back side of the raised stage that faced a wall of shoppers pouring in from the front doors. The cart stopped, security jumped down and escorted Maurice and Sarah out of the cart and up the steps of the stage. On either side were Maurice's assistants: Evan Philips, Halston Stiggs, Fred Wilson, Gloria White — and, at the top step, just one step down from the actual platform itself, stood Ann Thurston. Maurice stopped before her, bowed very slightly, smiled subtly, winked at her as he handed over Sarah Fletcher. "Wait here with Ann a few moments," Maurice told Sarah. "I'll have to say a few words before I introduce you."

Sarah nodded. Ann took her hand and held it tight. Too tight. As if she was afraid she would run away. Sarah looked hard into Ann's face. Ann smiled with severe goodwill. Sarah turned her head and looked back down the steps. Security stood looking up at her, grimly erect and imposing, as if to say, "This is it. Nowhere else to run."

Then Sarah looked up and around at the surrounding mall. The stage was surrounded on three sides by balconies hanging out from the upper levels of the mall. Shoppers stood hanging over railings, staring down intently, some pointing, others aiming video cameras at the stage, some popping flash bulbs as they took pictures. Staring up around the mall was like looking up into a huge crystal bowl shot through with flickering facets of silver light. It made Sarah dizzy to stare too long, so she looked away, her eyes following Maurice as he strode across the stage.

Maurice walked with serene grace, head high, shoulders erect, the sanctuary robe falling over him in elegant folds. His blond hair, blue eyes, and sun-tanned face caught the light flashing down from all sides of the mall and seemed to catch it in a glowing nimbus that radiated like a halo. As he strided across the stage in swift, purposeful steps, he didn't hear the questions shooting through the crowd like electric impulses:

"Who is it?"

"It's Clemens!"

"The hell it is!"

"It's just some kid!"

"He's an apprentice!"

"Ah!"

"What's his name?"

"Maury something..."

"Where's he from?"

"Don't know. Out west somewhere."

"Who's getting sanctuary?"

"Some woman."

"Which one?"

"The one in purple."

"Ah!"

"Who is she?"

"Where's she from?"

"What'd she do?"

"She's an American!"

"No!"

"Yes!"

"Ah!"

Maurice Sully raised his arms and the mall fell silent.

Television cameras on all sides trained lenses on him and came into focus, broadcast his image instantly across the country — and also into America. Maurice didn't know it, and would never be told, but at that precise instant, Mall Master Clemens, on vacation with his wife in America, was sitting before a television in a hotel. "Well, looks like the kids are having a wild weekend," said Clemens to his wife. "Let's see how they do."

"Do you think Maurice can handle this? Look who it is getting sanctuary!"

Mall Master Clemens chuckled as he saw the beautiful young woman in purple standing behind Maurice, just off stage, waiting to be introduced. "Well, if he does, I'll have to promote him and give him a raise."

Back in the mall, Maurice lowered his arms and spoke into the microphone that stood perfectly adjusted in front of him. "Welcome. Thank you for coming to witness this event. Today, sanctuary will be granted to a sovereign individual seeking to live free."

The crowd applauded vigorously, until Maurice raised his arms for silence once more.

"I am Mall Master Maurice Sully, Apprentice to the Show Me Mall, First Assistant to Mall Master Richard Clemens. Are there any equals present to witness this event?"

As the question was asked, down in front of Maurice, at the bottom of the stage, five Mall Masters in flowing robes rose as one and walked up the steps to Maurice, stood off to one side.

"Please state your names and the malls you preside over," said Maurice.

Individually, each man stepped forward and introduced himself.

"George Kilgore, St. Charles Mall."

"Andrew Blackstone, Jefferson City Mall."

"Christopher Dvorak, Columbia Mall."

"Julius Tourney, Washington Mall."

"Clay Johnson, Perryville Mall."

After speaking, each Mall Master stepped back and faced Maurice, who addressed them as a group.

"Have you each individually reviewed this case?"

"We have."

"Do you concur with the grant of sanctuary?"

"We do."

"Thank you, gentlemen."

The five Mall Masters bowed to Maurice, then sat down in chairs placed along the far edge of the stage, where they could see the proceedings, but were far enough away so as not to compete for attention with Maurice.

Maurice inched a touch closer to the microphone and straightened his back even more severely, raised himself another inch in height, and stood before the multitude, his eyes scanning across — up — down — taking the entire mall into his field of vision, as was his custom, as he had trained himself to do. He relaxed his mind and shifted intellectual gears consciously, ignored details, concentrated on essentials, sent a loud order to his subconscious to remember details for him because he would need them later, then he immediately put that order out of his mind, knew his subconscious would save it for him and give him the information he needed later.

He looked out and saw the crowd but thought of only one person. He would not address a mob today. He would speak to the individual mind of one single person. He pictured that person's face in his mind.

Inside the mall, those present could not see the color change in Maurice Sully's eyes. They only saw him stand tall and proud, the idealized portrait of an idealistic young mall apprentice.

But those watching on television saw something different.

The camera had Maurice in full close up. His twin blue eyes filled the screen. The confidence, serenity, and clear focus shown through his eyes. And when he shifted gears mentally, although none watching knew what was happening, they saw his eyes grow brighter, his face seemed sharper, more intense, as if he had been animated with a new spirit, as if something inside him had been activated, turn on, switched up to full power. Those watching didn't understand what they were seeing, they were merely mesmerized by it, could not take their eyes away, listened with a focus that matched what they saw on Maurice Sully's face.

"Today, sanctuary is to be granted to a citizen of the United States of America. Her name is Sarah Fletcher. She is from the state of Kentucky."

Maurice paused a moment to let those facts register. From the mall, there was a brief intake of breath, then random shouts, some positive, some negative. Those who were disturbed by the news controlled themselves and waited for more information.

Maurice continued. "Sarah Fletcher has been accused of tax evasion and the violation of various regulatory laws. As you know, in California, we have no such laws, so here, Sarah Fletcher can live free from such violations of her individual rights."

A slight ripple of applause undulated through the mall, then dissipated quickly.

"But this is not why I have granted her sanctuary," said Maurice. "Sarah Fletcher is the daughter of the Governor of the state of Kentucky, a leading candidate for the American presidency. As many of you might already be aware, this man has been shot and is in the hospital. The person who shot him was his own daughter — Sarah Fletcher."

That split the crowd into ragged, screaming fragments, like a stone shattered by a chisel. The Californians present suddenly jumped up furious and bewildered.

"What the hell!?"

"Has the kid lost his mind?"

"Who trained this brat? What's he think he's doing?"

The Americans present could only shout one word: "Traitor!"

The merchants present who had dealt with Maurice in the last week did not panic, did not leap to conclusions. They shouted, "Context! Context!"

That was the word Maurice was listening for, the only word that mattered now. He smiled very slightly, turned halfway back so he could catch a glimpse of Ann Thurston still holding on to Sarah Fletcher. Ann's face was shocked and suddenly very serious. This she had not known. She twisted her neck and looked closely at the face of the woman she was escorting.

Sarah didn't notice. She was watching Maurice.

Maurice turned back to his audience, facing them squarely. "You want reasons?" he asked.

"Yes!" they shouted.

"Here is my first reason!" Maurice turned and motioned down to Sarah Fletcher. "Sarah Fletcher, please present yourself to the people of the Show Me Mall!"

Ann Thurston let go and stepped back, like a child letting go a balloon. Sarah Fletcher drifted away slowly, moving up the steps of the stage, hesitant and slow at first, but gathering speed, momentum, confidence as she rose up and saw more and more of Maurice Sully. When she was finally fully on the stage and could see Maurice clearly, she smiled broadly at him. "My future husband," she thought. And she strutted across the stage to him, feeling the eyes of the crowd beaming down at her, pressing down on her, and she rising effortlessly against the pressure of those eyes, knowing some wanted to push her away, but most would welcome her, she was sure of it. And she heard the words from somewhere, she wasn't sure if they came from inside her own mind, or if someone in the crowd had yelled it at her, but she heard it nonetheless: "Work it, girl!" Her smile sharpened and her nostrils flared. She gave an equine flick of her head and tossed some curls from her eyes, then ran a hand through her hair, a quick brushing motion. She felt the motion of her legs moving her forward; the smooth texture of her gown flowing against her skin; warm air and lights against the bare skin of her arms; the undulating rhythm of her breasts bouncing slightly in motion with her body; and the matching rhythmic metronomic shimmer of her hips beneath her gown, drawing the eyes of men to her, and she working it, knowing she was selling herself to a group of pagan Californians, knowing this was not irrelevant, not to these men. Reasons would be given, arguments presented, logic used as a hammer to pound her case into a shape that would stand. But at the base was a simple fact: she was a beautiful woman, and Maurice wanted every man present to know it, remember it, appreciate it.

Sarah didn't mind, either.

She stopped in front of Maurice, he took her hand, and, like an ancient courtier from the age of Kings, he presented her to the crowd, displayed her briefly to the full glare of lights and television cameras, then pointed at her with his free hand and spoke forcefully into the microphone. "Citizens, *this* is not an object of sacrifice!"

Every man who had watched Sarah Fletcher walk across the stage answered Maurice:

"No!"

"Save her!"

"Sanctuary! Sanctuary!"

Maurice whispered in Sarah's ear. "Introduce yourself, dear. Very briefly."

Sarah nodded, then approached the microphone. "My name is Sarah Fletcher. I ask for sanctuary. Thank you."

She stepped back and the crowd was silent.

Maurice stepped forward once more and took command. "Citizens, as you know, sanctuary is generally not granted to violent criminals, or to criminals who use a weapon to commit a crime. The penalty for bringing a weapon into a shopping mall is loss of shopping rights and expulsion from that mall forever. With that context in mind, I must inform you that Sarah Fletcher did in fact shoot her father, and she has admitted as much."

This stunned the crowd into paralyzed silence.

"I have determined that her action was in self-defense. I have granted her sanctuary and assumed responsibility for her case. If it is discovered that she did in fact bring a weapon onto this property, I alone will be held responsible. If a weapon is in fact discovered on this property, I alone will be held accountable. I am responsible. It is my mall rights in question. It is I who face expulsion and banishment. It is I who risks losing his freedoms. Sarah Fletcher is not a citizen of this country and has nothing to lose. She has in fact fled a country that routinely violates the freedoms of its own citizens, a country that does in fact regard those citizens as objects of sacrifice.

"I have used that word repeatedly today. I hope it has offended your ears and soured your stomach as much as it has mine. But I have abused your sensibilities on purpose. I will not allow the obscenity of sacrifice to take place on the sacred property of a shopping mall. This is the reason for my radical actions, and this is the purpose of my stand: to defeat sacrifice, to obliterate it from our lives, our minds, our spirits, our souls. Here on the Mississippi, on the border of our sick sister country, we are witnessing a slow seepage of this evil idea into our own country, our own culture. It must be stopped. It has throttled America. It must not touch California.

"I am a Mall Master, a priest of commerce. Since the earliest years of my childhood I have made it my purpose to know the source of life, to nurture that source, to make it grow. I have made it my honor to dedicate my life to the creation of wealth, the refinement of wealth, the enjoyment of wealth. I know the principles of wealth. They are the same as the principles of life.

"The source of wealth — the source of life — is in people like Sarah Fletcher. She is exactly the type of person who founded our country. Our founders did not submit. Sarah Fletcher will not submit. If our country is to continue growing and prospering, we must continue to support and nurture individuals like Sarah Fletcher. We must welcome them into our country. We must grant them sanctuary when necessary.

"The violence committed by Sarah Fletcher was in self-defense. The principle of self-defense takes precedence here. That is your context, citizens.

"Here in California, we have long regarded individuals as ends in themselves. We have held that there is nothing more valuable or sacred than an individual human life. More so when that individual life is rational and productive. We have acknowledged individual rights as absolutes not subject to violation or abridgment at any time, by any one, for any reason. I am asking that you, as a community of sovereign individuals, apply these principles to the case of Sarah Fletcher and acquiesce to my judgment of sanctuary. Welcome her into your community. Let her productivity add to your own wealth. And strike a blow to the American advocates of sacrifice! Let them know that those they choose to immolate on their bloody altruistic altars will find a home here in California, that they will live free and prosper, and that if they continue their policies, America will be reduced to an anemic husk filled with nothing but human zombies stumbling blindly into graveyards. Let us be an example to our brothers across the river — a wealthy, prosperous, living example!"

Concluding, Maurice turned and swung out a pointing arm at the row of Mall Masters sitting off to the side. "Mall Masters, what say you?" he asked.

The five rose up as one and proclaimed their verdict: "Here here!"

Maurice pivoted on the balls of his feet and raised his arms to the multitude. "Merchants, what say you?"

The mall exploded into a ragged filament of sound that swirled down and washed over the stage like a foaming wave crushing a beach.

"Here here!"

"Sanctuary!"

"Down with sacrifice!"

"Hurrah for Sully!"

"Sarah Fletcher, marry me!"

Maurice lowered his arms, bowed his head in acknowledgment. Then he turned and glanced at Sarah Fletcher.

She stood with head raised, eyes shining, gazing around the mall at the people who had accepted her.

It grew quiet again. Maurice spoke into the microphone. "The term of sanctuary is for two years. Sarah Fletcher has agreed and has signed the contract." Maurice brought the sanctuary contract out of his pocket and held it up for all to see. "Before this contract is finalized with the seal of the Individual's Republic of California, there is one last responsibility I must execute. I must ask this, and mean it seriously: is there any individual present who believes that sanctuary should not be granted? Under the law of sanctuary, no group, association, or collective of any sort will be acknowledged or allowed into discourse. Only an individual will be allowed to speak against sanctuary. Is there any one present who wishes to do so?"

The mall fell deadly silent. Each individual held his breath and stood frozen like a statue, waiting.

Down front, almost directly in front of the stage, one lone person stood up. "I wish to speak against sanctuary."

It was a young man.

Maurice looked down at him, his eyes narrowing. "Very well. Please ascend the stage. You will be allowed to speak."

The crowd parted, a path appeared in front of the young man, leading directly to the stage. He walked forward slowly, hesitantly at first, uncertain about the crowd and how it would react to him. But they left him alone. This was, after all, a sanctuary ceremony. The Californians present knew how important it was to conduct themselves with impeccable civility.

The man reached the bottom of the stage and started to walk up. All eyes were on him.

Maurice watched the young man rise up to him. He studied the young man, drawing in details first in a generalized way, then, as the young man got closer, in a more detailed way.

The young man was skinny in a sickly kind of way. He walked with an awkward, gangly gait, as if his knees weren't functioning properly. He wore an ill-fitting gray suit, ragged, threadbare, several years out of fashion now. His hair was mussed and poorly cut. He had several days worth of whisker stubble smeared across his cheeks in a dirty salt and pepper pattern. He wore huge, heavy-rimmed, thick-lensed glasses precariously perched on his nose; as he made his way up the steps, they kept sliding down and he had to keep pushing them back into place so he could see. The thick lenses hid his eyes. They were either blue or gray; maybe brown, it was hard to tell.

When he reached the stage, Maurice motioned him to the microphone. The young man approached timidly. When he reached Maurice's side, Maurice said, "Please introduce yourself — and then state your case."

The young man positioned himself in front of the microphone, tried to adjust it, made a mistake; the microphone stand slid down to a height of two feet, as if awaiting the words of a midget. The young man bent down to fix it and his glasses fell off his face, clattered to the floor. In reaching for his glasses, he smacked his head against the microphone and a loud boom reverberated through the quiet mall.

The Californians could have laughed at him. But this was a sanctuary ceremony. They remained silent, waiting.

The young man found his glasses and put them back on his face. Maurice helped him adjust the microphone to his height. Then he was finally ready to address the mall.

As he first tried to speak, his voice broke, his throat full of phlegm. He turned and coughed, cleared his throat, then tried again.

In the moment it took him to do that, Maurice turned and glanced at Sarah. He knew who this young man was. He wanted to see how she was reacting to him.

She caught his glance, showed him the pain in her eyes. This was causing her to suffer. But it was an impersonal kind of suffering, as if she knew this young man, but he wasn't of much importance to her.

The young man finally spoke clearly, and everyone understood what he said.

"I am Stephen Fletcher, the brother of Sarah Fletcher."

A gasp from the mall acknowledged that statement.

Stephen Fletcher continued. "I have no desire to speak to a mob of pagan money-grubbers. My words are only for my sister's ears." He turned and faced his sister. "Sarah, we need you."

"I need me, too," said Sarah, to no one but herself.

The mall saw her lips move, but no one heard what she had said.

Stephen Fletcher continued. "Your family needs you, Sarah. I need you. Your late mother, God rest her soul, needs you. Our father needs you. He is a good, kind Christian soul. He loves you, and he forgives you. He wishes you to return to our family. Together, we can help our father regain his health, we can help him get elected. In the White House, with the power of the presidency, we can make the sacrifices necessary to make our country strong again. Don't listen to these merchants and shopkeepers. They have brainwashed you. You have been hypnotized by their bright and gaudy lifestyle. But theirs is an empty universe, Sarah. These people have no souls, no spiritual qualities, no appreciation for the mysteries of the universe. They are arrogant in the face of God. You must be humble and return to your family.

"Also, dear sister, you should know that I have been authorized to inform you that the Attorney General of the United States has agreed to drop all charges against you. Both the tax evasion and regulatory violations, as well as the shooting of our father. He has acknowledged that it was an accident, an unfortunate misunderstanding, an issue to be resolved within the family, and not in the public courts. So you see, you don't need to remain in this place. They are not offering you sanctuary. They are making you a slave for seven years. They simply want you to work for them for free. This is not what you want, to be the slave of strangers. Come back to your family. Come back to your country. Come back to the people who love you."

Sarah Fletcher now had a microphone near her face. Ann Thurston had brought her one. So when she spoke, everyone heard her. She said, "I cannot return. I am to be married."

"To whom?" asked her brother.

"To Mall Master Maurice Sully."

The mall liked that. Cheers and applause rippled through the crowd.

Maurice crinkled his face in a brief spasm of discomfort. He had wanted to announce his impending wedding himself, and at a time and place of his own choosing. It was not necessary to do so at the sanctuary ceremony. But now it was done, so he would have to deal with it. He composed himself and watched the befuddled face of Stephen Fletcher as the young man tried to dredge up a response to his sister's confession. All he could manage was:

"So, you're to be a concubine as well as a slave."

The mall booed him roundly.

Maurice Sully raised a hand to silence them.

Stephen Fletcher stared at his sister with desperate eyes. He saw her standing proud and straight in a beautiful evening gown, the shimmering material glowing beautifully in the lights, her background a mass of elegant and prosperous Californians staring up from the floor of the mall, as if worshipping her from below; and others hanging from balconies above and all around, gazing down with yearning eyes, like souls lost in heaven, aching for earth, and seeing all of earth in the person of this young woman. Stephen Fletcher looked at her in the same way. He had been told to bring her back. He knew now that he was going to fail. He could hear the voices berating him on his empty-handed return. He knew what they would say. "Never send a boy to do a man's job." So he was a boy. He would not argue that point. He had always been a boy, and that would not change. He did not know what a man was.

His sister, he knew, was a woman. He could see that. He could feel her energy and confidence radiating at him across the stage. Even here with the Californians, she stood out. Maybe she had been born in the wrong country. But not him. He had been born in the right country. He wanted to return. He needed to feel comfortable again.

Maurice Sully asked him, "Is that all you have to say?"

Stephen Fletcher stared at him, his eyes suddenly empty. "Yes, that is all I have to say."

"Very well. Thank you for your comments." Maurice turned to Sarah. "Miss Fletcher, do you wish to respond to your brother's appeal?"

"I do not."

"Have you been moved by his plea?"

"I have not."

"Do you acknowledge the need of your family?"

"I do not."

"Will you submit to the need of your former country?"

"I will not."

"Do you wish to accept citizenship in the Individual's Republic of California?"

"I do."

"Very well. Upon completion of your term of sanctuary and your release from this mall, you will be acknowledged as a citizen of the Individual's Republic of California."

"Thank you very much."

"You're welcome." Maurice reached into his inner pocket and brought out the sanctuary contract. He held it in the air for all to see and strided across the stage to the five seated elder Mall Masters. They rose as he approached, stopped with perfect timing as Evan Philips appeared out of nowhere with a portable standing desk, set it up between Maurice and the Mall Masters, then swiftly retreated. Maurice placed the contract down on the desk. "Gentlemen, please sign as witnesses."

While the Mall Masters signed, Maurice signaled to Ann Thurston, who understood, came forward, escorted Sarah Fletcher to the desk. Maurice signed the contract, then handed the pen to Sarah Fletcher. She signed her name at the bottom — and it was done.

Maurice raised the contract in one hand, led Sarah to the front center of the stage by the other hand, presented both to the mall and boomed into the microphone, "Shoppers and merchants, please welcome the newest employee of the Show Me Mall — Miss Sarah Fletcher!"

The greatest actress on the grandest stage in the most solemn theater in all of drama never received such applause. They welcomed her with exuberant benevolence of an intensity that brought tears to Sarah's eyes.

Maurice folded the contract and placed it back in his inner pocket, then motioned the mall for silence. When they gave it to him, he said, "I had not intended to intrude my private affairs on this ceremony, but my future bride has trumped me and made it necessary. It is true that I have asked her to marry me and that she has accepted. Would you folks like to stay on for a wedding?"

The mall answered enthusiastically, sending a gush of applause and well-wishes down to the stage.

Maurice motioned to the Mall Masters. They conferred briefly, then Senior Mall Master Clay Johnson from Perryville stepped forward to perform the ceremony. Maurice and Sarah stood side by side and faced Mall Master Johnson. He turned first to Sarah. "Miss Sarah Fletcher, do you take this man, Mall Master Maurice Sully, to be your lawfully wedded husband?"

"I do."

"And do you, Mall Master Maurice Sully, take this woman to be your lawfully wedded wife?"

"I do."

"Then by the authority granted me by the Perryville Mall, I now pronounce you man and wife. Wealth and happiness to you both."

Maurice turned to Sarah, took her in his arms, and kissed her deeply, and for a long time.

Mall Master Johnson had turned away at first, but turned back quickly, saying, "And by the way, you may kiss the — oh, never mind."

The mall applauded again, cheered again, and kept right on doing both until there was nothing and no one left to cheer and applaud.

***

Up on the roof of the mall the military had established an observation post. It consisted of a small mobile tent set up over some tables and chairs. On the tables were lap top computers, maps, communications equipment. In front of the longest table, standing at the edge of the roof, General Kent McKnight stood looking through a pair of binoculars, scanning the parking lot of the mall — the streets and buildings across from mall property — and the far horizon off towards the Mississippi river. An aid stood to his right and just behind his elbow, close enough to hear any comments or orders, but not so close as to crowd the General and make him feel smothered.

"What does intelligence say?" asked General McKnight.

"Looks like some officials from the American State Department are on mall property, making inquiries."

"Who are they asking for? Me, or the kid?"

"You, sir."

"Very well. What does intel say about the probability of sanctuary being broken?"

"They think it is quite high."

"So do I. Any info on infiltration?"

"None yet, but they're watching and listening."

"Very well. We'll try to keep things quiet for the kid. It is his wedding night, after all."

"Yes sir."

"Where did they put them up?"

"Bridal suite at Nordstrom."

The General chuckled. "I remember it well. Very good. Make sure they aren't disturbed."

"Yes sir."

"Try to direct any American inquiries to Captain Kaiser. I'll have to talk to them eventually, but I want them to sweat first."

"Yes sir."

"I want the men relaxed, but alert."

"Yes sir."

"Nothing's going to happen we can't handle, but the men don't know that. Let them know what's going on — but only what they need to know. I don't want any bizarre rumors starting about who Maurice Sully is and what he's up to. So make sure they're clear on that. And Miss Fletcher, of course. The rest, they can pretty much judge for themselves. Our soldiers aren't stupid brutes."

"Very well, sir."

"If you need me — I'll be shopping."

"Yes sir!"

***

Down in the parking lot, Captain Chet Kaiser of the SLPD rested a booted foot on a concrete tire stop at the head of an empty parking space in the VIP section of mall parking. He hooked his thumbs into his belt and watched a big black sedan roll to a stop in the space. The big car was dirty and dusty, as if it had driven quite a distance. Thick exhaust poured out the back briefly, then dissipated quickly, like the last exhaled breath of a dying beast; the engine sputtered and shook as it cranked down; a sound akin to two robots clanking at each other with wrenches issued forth from under the hood as the engine stumbled into silence. Captain Kaiser noticed the front tire on the right side looked slightly bald, and the rear on the same side was low on air.

The passenger door on the side facing Captain Kaiser creaked open. Flakes of rust fell to the pavement. From out of the car, a scuffed brown shoe stepped out and ground the flakes of rust into dust.

Captain Kaiser sized up the man he saw.

He wore an over-size black suit that made him look like an undertaker. His pant legs were too short, showed off some ratty old socks that kept falling down around his ankles. His head was shaven completely bald, like a monk. He wore huge, thick, black-rimmed oval glasses that gave him an owlish demeanor. As he stepped out of the car, he paused, glanced around with quick, ferret-like movements, pressed the fingers of his hands together into a steeple briefly, then came forward to Captain Kaiser.

"Who's in charge here?" he asked.

"Mall Master Maurice Sully."

"You mean, the boy."

Captain Kaiser shifted his weight in a motion of impatience and asked, "What can I do for you, sir?"

"I am Filbert Duckworth, Special Counsel of the American State Department. I'm here about the Sarah Fletcher situation."

"Sarah Fletcher has been granted sanctuary."

"I would like to talk to her."

"Not possible. She's with her husband right now."

"Excuse me?"

"She got married. Right after the sanctuary ceremony."

"Married? To whom?"

"Mall Master Maurice Sully."

"She married *the boy*?"

"That's right," said Captain Kaiser, a slight smirk of satisfaction turning his lips upward.

Filbert Duckworth looked back at his associates who had followed him out of the big black car. "Why wasn't I informed?"

His associates shrugged inside their ill-fitting black suits.

"Just happened," said Captain Kaiser, trying to be helpful. His muscular torso shivered slightly with suppressed laughter.

Filbert Duckworth stepped forward, close enough to read the name on Captain Kaiser's uniform. "Uh, officer Kaiser—"

"*Captain* Kaiser."

"Captain Kaiser. You should know that I will file an official protest with your Foreign Office."

"Okay."

"I see evidence of a military presence around the mall. Who's the commander in charge?"

"They haven't told me."

"Highly unlikely. Captain Kaiser, I have the distinct impression that you are playing games with me."

"Not at all. I'll tell it to you straight, Mr. Diplomat. Sarah Fletcher has been granted sanctuary. It's a done deal. There is nothing you can do about it now. You can not talk to her. You will not be granted access to her of any type. You will not be allowed into the mall."

"What if I want to go shopping?" asked Duckworth, smiling.

"You'll have to choose another mall."

"I'd like to talk to Sully."

"He won't allow that."

"Answer me one thing, Captain Kaiser."

"Sure."

"I really don't understand why it is you adults let a kid call the shots in a situation that could very well lead to a serious breach between our two countries."

"This isn't your first job in California, is it?"

"Actually, I have much experience here."

"Then you should know the answer to that question. Idealism and a sense of responsibility are qualities we value highly in California. We like to encourage these qualities in our young people whenever and however we can. Most especially in future Mall Masters. Those who wish to assume a position of moral leadership in this country are held to very high standards. And we demand extraordinary competence. I'll grant you, Maurice is young. But he's also gifted."

"I wonder what the First Citizen would think of this situation."

"I couldn't tell you."

"Have you ever met him?"

"No."

"I have."

"Is that supposed to impress me?"

"How long has it been since he's been seen in public?"

"I couldn't tell you."

"Ten years, I think."

"That long, huh?"

"Doesn't that make you wonder?"

"About what?"

"About if your leader is doing his job."

"I don't have a leader, sir. No Californian does. The First Citizen doesn't lead, rule, or order anyone — not the way you Americans would want him to."

"Didn't the First Citizen start out as a Mall Master?"

"Yes, I believe he did."

"Do you think Maurice Sully has any ambitions?"

"Yeah. His ambition is to run a shopping mall. It's all he cares about."

"Sounds like a very limited life."

"Not in this country."

"By the way, has anyone found the gun?"

Captain Kaiser stared hard at Duckworth, but said nothing.

Duckworth chatted on. "I don't suppose the First Citizen would think highly about some fifteen year old kid granting sanctuary to a violent criminal who brought a weapon onto mall property, would he?"

"It's none of his business until Maurice Sully makes it his business."

"Oh, I think the First Citizen has the moral authority to make it his business — if he wanted to."

"Listen, friend," said Captain Kaiser, a new tone of impatience in his voice. "You Americans might be impressed by the power and authority of government, but here in California, it works a little different. You're not going to scare me by sicking somebody you regard as a Big Daddy on me. You're not going to scare Maurice Sully, either. If the kid scared easily, he would have never taken this situation this far. So you can yammer on all you want about First Citizen this and First Citizen that, I don't give a rat's ass. I don't believe you ever met him. I don't believe you've ever talked to him. I don't believe he would spend even a split second having anything to do with a little weasel butt like you. And the reason he hasn't appeared in public in ten years is because he hasn't had to, doesn't need to. The First Citizen is not a government official. He's a private citizen, just like the rest of us. He has private affairs to take care of, just like the rest of us. Our First Citizen just happens to be a man the majority of the populace has a great deal of respect and admiration for, looks up to, and would tend to look to for leadership in a time of national crisis — which doesn't happen very often, which is why he hasn't been seen in public in ten years. Because when you have a nation of men and women who regularly produce kids with the quality of a Maurice Sully, you don't need some snoopy-ass would-be dictator sitting on a throne and giving orders and trying to micro-manage every aspect of life, up to and including going to people's homes and reading them bed time stories and tucking them in at night, which, I gather from the papers, is what the majority of your fine citizens over there across the river expect from their 'President.' No thank you, sir. I'll take a fifteen year old Mall Master with some self-respect and a firm concept of individual rights to that bozo set up any day, any year, any lifetime. So why don't you take your monkey crew here, get back in your hearse, and drive back across the river and go about your business of digging more graves. And while you're at it, fall in one."

Filbert Duckworth smiled very slightly at Captain Kaiser, nodded his head in acknowledgement of the older man's passionate statement, then he said, "You must be very proud of your nephew."

Captain Kaiser was stunned into silent immobility for a moment. He stared hard at Duckworth with cold eyes for a few seconds, while the shabby diplomat stood smirking, knowing he had finally reached the Captain.

"Well, you got me," said Captain Kaiser. "So you have done your homework after all. I underestimated you."

"A common mistake."

"But now you've made our conflict personal. That's a big mistake with a Californian, sir." Captain Kaiser reached for his radio, made a brief call. "This is Kaiser. Move in."

Within a matter of seconds, the big black sedan was surrounded by police officers. Two cruisers pulled up nearby and positioned themselves so that one could lead the black car out of the lot, while the other followed.

"This is no longer a debate, or even a discussion," said Captain Kaiser. "You are on private property sir, and the owner has informed me that you are not welcome. It is my professional obligation to protect the property rights of the citizens in this community. So let's go. Back in the car, follow my cruiser out, and don't try coming back."

"I haven't talked with the military commander yet."

"Nor will you. Not here. Now let's go."

"I'll be back."

"If you are, it will only be to buy yourself a new suit."

Filbert Duckworth and his associates piled back into the big black car, then drove off, escorted by the two police cruisers. Captain Chet Kaiser watched them go. As they were moving away toward the exit, he got on the radio and put out a general order to all units: "Any more inquiries from American government officials, refer them to the Foreign Office. I'm not talking to the bastards." Then he got on the radio to General Kent McKnight. "General? Kaiser here. I'm pulling the plug on these bastards."

"Okay. Fine by me."

"Now it's your turn. I hope your boys are up to it, and I hope your intelligence is good, because I'd bet New Athens on these punks trying a snatch."

"We've assumed that from the start."

"The bastard knows Maurice is my nephew."

"I see."

"So I'm going to take this little affair personally from now on. And I'm not fooling around with any of these ghouls they send over. Every chance the law gives me to bust their chops, I'm going to take it."

"Maintain your discipline, Captain. Don't let your boys get out of line. Don't give the Americans any opportunity to accuse us of being the aggressors here."

"Hell, their police force has guns, not ours."

"I'm your gun, Captain. Remember that."

"Hope you're loaded."

"We're always loaded, Captain, you know that. And we shoot

straight. So let me worry about violence. You just look after the law."

"You guard the boy well."

"He's getting the security a Mall Master deserves. Trust me."

***

Inside Nordstrom's bridal suite, Maurice and Sarah sat in the spacious living room. They were together on the couch, sitting beside each other, close, but not actually intimate. They each held a glass of wine and sipped conservatively. They had both pointedly ignored the bedroom so far.

"Is it your intention to consummate this marriage tonight?" asked Sarah.

"Certainly. In a situation like this, we should find out immediately where we stand with each other. If it's going to be a love relationship, I want to know right away and make the most of it. I hope you do as well. Sexual compatibility is an essential part of a good romantic relationship, so we need to find out about each other right from the start. If it is not to be a love relationship, then we can act accordingly and conduct ourselves with dignity and mutual respect, but just have a business relationship."

"There's one question you haven't asked me."

Maurice watched her. She was waiting for him to speak, volunteering nothing, watching him carefully, closely, occasionally taking a tiny sip of wine.

Maurice smiled. "You're not going to tell me what question it is I haven't asked?"

"No."

"You want to see if I know it. If I don't, you're going to completely lose respect for me."

"Yes."

"Very well. The question is: did you leave anyone behind? Did you have a lover in America? If you did, will I help you get him out, bring him to you, reunite him with you? If that is the question, then I am asking it now."

Sarah looked up at him, her eyes wide and dark, her lips parted, her hands holding her wine glass in a trembling grasp that slowly lowered to the table in front of the couch. She set the wine glass down and looked up at him. "That is the question I was hoping for."

"And now you're worried about how the answer will affect us."

"Not worried. Merely curious."

"And more specifically: how your answer will affect me."

"Yes, I am most curious about that."

"So I have asked. Now what is your answer?"

She stood up, picked up her wine glass, walked across the room to the curtained window. She parted the curtains. Together — she close to the window, he far back, admiring her figure within the frame — they looked out to the west, to the far horizon of the Individual's Republic of California. The bridal suite had no windows facing east, toward the river and America. That was what she wanted to look at. But instead, she saw her future. She looked through her future, imagined she could see all the way around the world, her sight circumnavigating the globe at the speed of light, her eyes in an instant in touch with her past, the country, world, life, memories, events of what she had just recently left behind in America. She saw it from above, like a spirit that had left the world and was drifting above it all, detached and uninvolved now, but still able to remember it all, she having lived it, felt it, all the pain and joy, all the values pursued and lost, all the people who had held no interest for her, and just one lone solitary and struggling man who had held her view of life, who had seen his own self in her, who had found his own values in her person, and she in his; she remembered that man, but she did not speak his name, not even in the privacy of her own mind, and certainly not out loud to the hearing of Maurice Sully, this new man who was suddenly her husband, for to do that would have been to lose that man forever, to have him wiped out by Maurice Sully, who was young and a stranger, but still her kind of man, she knew it, had known it from the beginning; even though he was young, he had a spiritual power that radiated into her female bones and made her wish to submit, to bow down, to worship, to take commands. But she wanted to remember that other man as well, she wanted to hope that somehow he was still alive and would find his way, get across the river and come to California to find her and be with her and love her as he had in America...

She turned away from the window, away from California, away from her future. She faced east and all she saw was the figure of Maurice Sully, standing across the room from her, watching her, relaxed, at ease, confident, unworried, a young man already with power and security and responsibility, and set to rise even further, a man who could accompany her to places and values she could not conceive right now. Did she want to go with him? Would she find her own values with him? Were they set to travel the same road together? Or would they join themselves only to be ripped apart at some future juncture where his values conflicted with hers?

And what of her love? Should she gamble that he would make it to her? Or should she count him out and carry on with what was right in front of her now?

The filthy word Maurice had denounced on her behalf drifted half recognized in the back of her mind. She knew it was there, waiting to be acknowledged. It was taunting her. It was telling her to name it, to make it conscious, to say out loud what she was really doing and what it really meant. But she couldn't face that word in relation to her beloved. She could not. And was that *really* what she was doing?

Say it, said a stern voice inside her. *Name it. Say it out loud and see how it feels to say that word while picturing the face of your beloved.*

Maurice watched her, mesmerized. He knew she was fighting an epic battle within herself, the kind of inner fight that could make or break a life, the kind of private spiritual war that would determine the course of an entire lifetime. He stood immobile, like a statue, not even breathing, not even blinking his eyes; he stood staring at her for so long without blinking, concentrating just on her, that his eyes began to tear up, and if she had glanced up, she would have thought he was weeping. But he was not. He was waiting, and watching, and gathering his inner resources for whatever action he would have to take next.

He saw her close her eyes, bow her head, tremble briefly, then her shoulders slumped, she exhaled a long breath of air into the room, as if she were a balloon deflating and fluttering to the ground. Then she opened her eyes and looked at him honestly, her eyes filled with pain, but also with a dignity crying out to him not to spare her, not to pity her, just to see her for what she was.

And inside her mind, in the moment before she spoke to Maurice Sully, her Mall Master husband, she named her deepest, darkest thought to herself: Yes, she was leaving her beloved behind. Yes, she was going to stay. And was it a sacrifice? Was it? Was she sacrificing the man she loved? For a fifteen year old stranger who would give her opportunities not possible any other way, with any other man? Is that what she was doing?

She looked at Maurice and said, "Yes, there is a love I left behind. My first love. My greatest love. My only love. The love after which there can be no other. And I have left him. I have abandoned him. And I have sacrificed myself for him..."

Maurice walked forward, took her face in his hands, looked deeply into her eyes while brushing her tears away with his fingers. He whispered, "It was this man who shot your father, wasn't it? You've done all this to protect him, have you not?"

She couldn't answer him. She could not speak. She simply fell against him, trembling, sobbing, knowing inside the exquisite ecstacy of suddenly loving another man when she had not thought that possible.

CHAPTER THREE

THE LIGHT OF FREEDOM

"Well, did they consummate their marriage that night?" Diane Copernicus asked me.

"I don't know. Maurice never told me."

"Didn't you ask?"

I smiled. "That's not the sort of thing gentlemen discuss, darling."

"So what happened next?"

We were sitting in my back yard, under the shade of a giant oak. I had told most of the story in my living room, but when it got exciting, Diane could not contain herself; she got up and started jumping around my living room, acting out the events I was relating to her. And I joined her. I acted out the part of Maurice, gave his famous sanctuary speech from memory, while Diane stood by, playing the role of Sarah Fletcher. We both became so excited, the house could not contain us, so I moved our little drama outside, to the back yard, to the afternoon sunshine and the presence of the oak. At this point in the story we paused to reflect — and to share tall glasses of cold lemonade I had prepared.

"I was just a child when all this happened," said Diane. "I have a dim memory of it. I remember my parents getting very shook up watching a sanctuary ceremony on television one day. I was too young to take much interest in it. But now that you tell the story, I'm starting to remember some details. I do vaguely remember seeing a very young, tall, blond Mall Master on TV. My goodness! So this was my dim memory of childhood, the very first time I ever saw a sanctuary ceremony on TV. I'm ashamed now that I wasn't conscious enough to take more interest in the event."

"Don't blame yourself. You were only a child."

"Oh, I know. Don't worry, I'm not attacking myself. It's just strange that now I am working in his mall. This raises many questions in my mind."

"I know those questions. I have asked them myself."

"Do you know the answers?"

"Yes, I do."

"Then continue the story! I want to know. There is no Sarah Fletcher here at West Park Plaza. So obviously, Maurice lost her somehow. Did they really fall in love? Did Maurice really love her? Did she love Maurice? And why is Maurice Sully, the greatest Mall Master who ever was, managing a very small and relatively average mall here in Montana, instead of reigning in New Athens as one would hope?"

"Don't let him hear you call his mall average!"

"Oh, never mind! Continue the story!"

"Very well. More lemonade?"

"Yes, thank you!"

I poured.

She listened.

***

The morning after, without even waiting for the urging of the military, Maurice Sully acted quickly. He left his bride slumbering in the bedroom and he paced the living room of the suite, talking on the phone. His first call was to New Athens. He had a brief conversation with Mall Master Shane Pavoc of the Apollo Mall. Then he was on the phone to the management office downstairs, inquiring on the status of Mall Master Clemens. After that, another brief call to Mike Charles. Mike was already up even at such an early hour and had anticipated Maurice's request and had everything ready for him.

After that call, Maurice connected himself to the military watch command and asked a simple question. "Have there been any attempts by the Americans yet?"

"None that we have detected, sir."

"Very well." Maurice clicked off, feeling nervous and thoughtful. The Americans should have acted swiftly if they wanted Sarah as badly as they had indicated. The fact that they had not acted swiftly was inexplicable. He would have to consider exactly what that meant.

When his calls were done, he sat down in a chair facing the windows and looked out at the sunlight spreading out across the morning landscape. He watched it for a few moments, then he settled into his chair, closed his eyes, and meditated on the problems facing him.

He was interrupted an hour or so later by his bride.

"Good morning," Sarah said.

"Good morning."

Maurice called room service and had breakfast sent up. They ate together, and Maurice explained what was to happen today. Sarah listened, understood, was not surprised, showed no excitement at the prospect. It was all much too profound for her to get hysterical.

They showered together to save time. It was a quick, efficient, well-mannered cleansing in which they both observed proper decorum. Then they dressed, left the bridal suite, were escorted down to the mall management offices.

Maurice's staff was present. Mike Charles stood off to one side. Mall Master Clemens sat behind his desk.

"Apprentice Sully, thank you for handling the mall in my absence."

"My pleasure, sir."

"I understand you wish to buy out Miss Fletcher's contract, and then be transferred, with your bride, to do service at the Apollo Mall in New Athens. Is that correct?"

"Yes sir."

"Very well. I will sell the contract for two hundred dollars. Is that sum acceptable?"

"Yes sir."

Sarah's face remained calm.

Mall Master Clemens motioned to Mike Charles. "The contract, sir?"

Mike Charles placed the contract down on the desk. Clemens signed first, then Sully.

Maurice asked, "Will it be acceptable if I have the money wired to you within twenty-four hours of my arrival in New Athens?"

"That would be fine."

"Very well."

Mall Master Clemens stood up and offered his hand to Maurice. "It was a pleasure doing business with you, Sully. I wish you much happiness and wealth in the future." Then he bowed gravely to Sarah Fletcher. "Ma'am."

Sarah bowed in acknowledgement.

Maurice shook hands with Mike Charles. "Thanks for your help, Mike. If you're ever in New Athens, stop in and see me sometime."

"I sure will."

"And give my best to your wife Patty."

"I will."

Maurice turned to his staff. "Are you kids packed and ready?"

"Yes sir!" they all chimed.

"Off we go. Good logic to us all." Maurice took his bride's hand and that was the end of his association with the Show Me Mall.

***

They had a military escort to the airport, where they boarded the private jet of the Show Me Mall. Earlier, it had flown Clemens back from America. It had refueled, been cleaned slightly, and the crew replaced. The plane took off a little after ten AM and headed west. There was no incident on the way to the plane. There was no incident while boarding the plane. There was no indication of a hijacking once they were in the air. Maurice was not relieved by any of this.

Maurice and Sarah were left alone at the rear of the plane. Sarah was quiet for a long time, waiting for Maurice to speak. But he remained silent, merely glanced at her occasionally, held her eyes for brief moments, did not smile, seemed severe and business-like. She finally decided that he was waiting for her to seize the initiative and say what needed to be said. So she did.

"Is this the proper time to speak of it?"

"If you wish to speak, then yes, it is the proper time."

"I am your wife now, so it is acceptable to ask you for help or advice. If you have any to offer me, I will gladly accept."

Maurice only asked, "What was his name?"

"Alan. Alan Benton."

Maurice was silent for a long time. He took her hand and held it, stroked her wrist with his fingers, caressed her hand in a loving and caring fashion. She watched his fingers with an impersonal detachment. He finally stopped caressing and simply held her hand. He said, "Sarah, I'm not going back. You're not going back. He is lost to you. That's a fact. That's the way it is. This is the result of choices both of you have made. Don't evade that. Accept it. He did what he did because he wanted you to get away and to be here, in California, alive, with a chance. You have a chance now. A very good chance. You could have stayed with him and stood beside him and suffered whatever fate the Americans had for him. You made your choice. I believe it was a rational and moral choice. But still a painful choice, so don't think I don't appreciate that. I won't be presumptuous and say I know how you feel. I have no idea what it feels like to make a choice like that. I will simply point out that the pain you feel is the result of being put into a perverted position by the manipulations of evil. These evil bastards have put you in a situation where you cannot make a rational choice of values. Anything you do will cause you loss and misery. Stay in America with Alan, and you die with him, or else watch him die and live as a slave.

Escape to America and live, and feel pain for losing your love and not fighting with him and taking every chance possible, even the chance that means certain death. You are probably feeling guilty because you're alive and he's probably dead, and you wish you could be with him. If you can't have him, you want death. Is that how you feel? Is that what this love meant to you? Is that the type of love you had? Is this the type of love you wish to have, want to live up to? If so, you probably feel guilty for taking the easy way out, for just running away, getting free, not looking back, and carrying on with your life. If that is the way you feel — don't. Don't feel guilty about being alive. Not even in a situation like this. Don't ever feel guilty about pursuing life. If you truly have lost Alan, all you can do is hold his memory within your mind, to think of him as you knew him and loved him — and don't stop loving him. He was a real person who really lived, and that you really knew. Your love existed, if even for a short time. It was real, the two of you were real, your love was real. Your love doesn't have to end. So don't stop loving him. Nobody and nothing can stop that feeling within you. So keep it, hang on to it, relish it, enjoy it, love it, love your memories, and love even the pain you feel on losing him. That is what you have now. I can't take that from you. Nobody can. That is the freedom of the mind, the freedom of your spirit, the freedom to choose values and to hold them — and after you've lost them, to hold simply your capacity to value, to remember the experience of valuing, to remind yourself that without values, human life is empty and meaningless. Your life must not be empty and meaningless, and it will not be. You are not the kind of woman who will let that happen."

"It sounds like you're telling me to become an obsessive."

"No, that's not what I mean. You're too rational to let that happen. You know what I mean. Stay focused on reality. Don't fake it. Don't pretend that Alan is back, is coming back, or might come back some day in the future. Never let yourself forget that he is gone, and will be gone forever, and you will never ever have him back. You know that. That must be an absolute in your mind. But even knowing that cannot stop you from loving him. Your love belongs to you and only to you, and it can be a real love, and a meaningful love."

"Aren't you hoping that I come to love you in that way? And could you stand the competition?"

"There is no competition in love. Each love is a self-contained universe of exactly two people, no more. Your love for Alan is completely yours. I can't touch it. If you come to love me in any way, that love is completely yours and can be touched by no one. No one else can gain entrance. Not even me. All I can do is love you back. And truly, darling, I think I will. And very soon."

Sarah took Maurice's hand in hers. She held his hand as if it was a lifeline. Soon she closed her eyes and sank comfortably into her seat, relaxed into a deep meditative state, reflected on what Maurice had told her.

Eventually, Maurice felt her hand go limp. She had fallen asleep. He let her snooze. After a few hours, she woke up. Snacks were served. Maurice switched seats with her so she had the window and could watch as the plane approached New Athens. He wanted her to see her new home. It was beautiful from the air. As the plane began its descent to New Athens International Airport, Sarah turned smiling to him and said, "So tell me about the Apollo Mall."

***

New Athens from the air was an endless plain of sun-drenched sprawl stretching from the mountains encircling the New Athens Basin to the beaches at the edge of the continent caressed by waves from the Pacific Ocean. The plane approached from the west, descended over the outskirts of New Athens, cruised low over the south central district of the city, enabling Sarah to stare down at the classic center of the city, the place where the first Greek settlers had built the original settlement when they arrived in their steamships. Then the plane swooped out west over the ocean, traced a long graceful circle out across New Athens Bay, then approached the airport from the ocean side, coming even lower, cruising over ships and boats coming and going from the harbor, the plane going lower still, as if someone had ordered this landing choreographed in some special way, for some special purpose. Sarah thought they were going to land in the water when suddenly she realized why the plane had taken this route. The Statue of Liberty materialized in her window, was held there framed like a picture for a short time as the plane circled and lowered, moved on past towards the airport, giving Sarah a long, lingering look at the famous symbol of freedom.

The white stone of Liberty's naked body was brilliant and glowing against the twin blues of sky and ocean. She stood facing out to sea and the ocean breeze could have actually been blowing her flowing hair, streaming behind her in a frozen stone flow, like a waterfall turned to ice. Her upraised arms and hands seemed to reach for the sky even as her long legs held her anchored to the earth; she was reaching for the heavens while remaining firmly in touch with an earthly reality. Her right hand was slightly higher than her left, and in this she held her torch. Her pose was deliberately ambiguous, and much debate had raged over the years, but the sculptor had never spoken to indicate his actual intention: was she offering her flame to the heavens — or bringing it down? How one judged her action always seemed to indicate a wider view of life. Sarah felt certain she knew the truth. She spoke. "Maurice, what is your view on her flame?"

"Her flame is her own. And she should be careful who she offers it to."

Sarah smiled, her hunch confirmed.

As the plane moved past, she caught a glimpse of Liberty's breasts glowing in the afternoon sunlight, her fine flat tummy, the curve of her hips, her long legs spread wide apart, and the flower of her womanhood beckoning, unhidden, between her legs. She was a finely muscled woman, and Sarah knew each muscle and every detail of the model's body had been reproduced in perfect idealized detail. But from the plane she saw only the essential shape, and that was enough. She was shocked at what an impact the sight had on her. As tears flooded her eyes, she closed her eyes and recited the poem inscribed at the base of the statue:

"For love of life I stand;
Who does want me, come.
Take light of freedom from my hand
And count yourself the sum."

Then she felt Maurice's hand on her back, the plane's wheels touched ground, and they were landed on the soil of the freest city that had ever existed in the history of the human race.

***

They were met at the airport by a white and gold limousine from the Apollo Mall. Sarah and Maurice went alone in that vehicle; Maurice's staff and all their luggage followed in a van. They were whisked away out onto wide palm-tree lined boulevards. As the cars moved north toward the Mall, Sarah stared out at passing images of meticulously ordered wealth and beauty such as she had never imaged. She had heard stories, seen pictures, read accounts; but the reality was something she had not really conceived.

The entire city was a pristine garden of beautifully integrated and exquisitely stylized structures designed to make the flow of purposeful human action a never-ending esthetic experience. Here, the daily routine of life was a masterpiece of art, the simplest domestic task took place in a context of breathtaking beauty; each action by each person, no matter what they were doing or where, was stylized by the frame of the city, and each citizen, no matter how humble, acquired the status "heroic" simply by virtue of doing his work within the context of the city. Each individual who lived in New Athens had the attitude that the entire city was an integrated, organic whole, and at any given moment, it all depended on him. He had to be rational, responsible, and productive in all his actions, or the city would be injured and die. Or, at worst, it would simply be made ugly, and thus, anyone seeing that ugliness would suffer a spiritual death of some degree. So the city lived by virtue of the intense devotion its citizens gave to it. Its beauty, energy, grace and livability was the sum result of the selfish individual passions of all the greedy people who lived within its borders. They all wanted a certain kind of city and acted accordingly, and the result flowed as logically as a mathematical equation.

And Sarah Fletcher was the newest citizen who's own personal, selfish loves would add to the total spiritual and physical wealth of this city.

And all Sarah could think of was the road.

Back in America, the roads were publicly owned and constantly filled with potholes because nobody was responsible, and there was never enough public money available to fix them. So you drove across rutted landscapes, had your teeth jarred out of your mouth, and had to fight crazy drivers, irrational beasts behind the wheels of complex machines, insane individuals convinced that they were the only person allowed on the road, everybody else had to get the hell out of the way or pay; there was no manners, no politeness, no consideration — no sanity.

Here in New Athens, the streets were all privately owned and kept in pristine condition. To be the owner of a pot-holed street was considered a breach of integrity. And each street was named for its owner, so you knew on who's street you were driving. Right now they were on "Frederica's Road North." Traffic flowed smoothly along, thick, but functioning perfectly thanks to ingenious lane designs, well-integrated traffic lights, and occasional bridges and tunnels that kept traffic moving through particularly busy sections of the city. The drivers all seemed unusually polite and considerate from Sarah's point of view.

Back in America, the streets had taken her past boring run-down boxes of unimaginative hovels, homes, and office buildings, all publically owned, and therefore, no one's responsibility. Any lengthy trip through a city in America was a boring, depressing journey filled with sights of poverty and despair.

Here in New Athens, the big quiet limo sped past examples of the wildest, most individualistic architecture she had ever seen. Distinctive, flowing shapes shot up and out, away from the edges of streets, out off into the community. In the business districts, the buildings were tall and most connected to others with skybridges, escalators, moving-slidewalks.

The economic vitality of this city — and the nation that grew outward surrounding it — was evidenced by the number of banks she saw.

Back in America, there was only one bank, the government-owned Bank of America. All of their offices were drab and ugly, the service was poor, and the currency issued by the government was constantly being inflated into worthlessness. When you went to the bank, you had to wait in a long line for the chance to be treated like dirt from a person who didn't care to do his job properly, who couldn't be fired because he was in a government union, and was more than likely to steal from your account if he decided he didn't like you.

Here in New Athens, it seemed there was a different bank on every corner. The buildings were beautiful, the windows wide and clean and shining, the doors busy with prosperous people coming and going. The banks had names like, "Wealth Source of New Athens," and "Capital Bank of California," and "Greed Incorporated," as well as more traditional names like, "First National Bank of New Athens," and "Bank of California." Sarah's favorite was "Money R Us."

And these banks all had something that didn't exist in America: automated teller machines, usually a whole line of them out on the street in front of the bank. But as intrigued as she was by those machines, Sarah wished she could go inside one of those banks and see what service was like, see how the people treated her, and see if the interiors were as gorgeous and well-designed as the exteriors.

She probably wouldn't have the chance until her period of sanctuary ended at the mall.

As the limo continued north, she saw grocery stores, theaters, restaurants. And although there was a lot of business activity, certainly compared to America, there wasn't as much as she had expected. The streets were really not that crowded, not that busy. She knew the reason why. Most business was done in the malls.

So she watched and waited for her first glimpse of a mall.

Her first sight of the Apollo Mall was as dramatic as the designer had intended.

Frederica's Road North had curved and swooped through some residential districts, then shot out of a long curve right at the base of the Pericles Hills. The mall loomed in front, a glowing white crown set onto the brow of the hills. At first, it seemed a small white jewel set in a field of green. But as the limo got closer, the mall grew larger, and instead of the mall decorating the hills, it was obvious that the surrounding green of nature was intended to decorate the man-made glory that ruled wild nature. The hills were subservient to the mall.

The limo disappeared into a tunnel underneath the mall. Luggage was unloaded and handled by mall staff. Sarah didn't even have to think of it. She merely was escorted along with Maurice into an elevator that would take them to the mall management offices and their first meeting with Mall Master Shane Pavoc.

Sarah saw no sloppily dressed people. Here in New Athens, more than anywhere else, shopping was seen as a sacred, exalted experience, and when people came to spend money, they dressed accordingly, and gave the experience the full emotional attention it deserved. In her brief time in the mall, on her way to the management offices, Sarah saw some of the most passionate and emotional people she had ever witnessed.

There was in particular one woman in a bright yellow dress who had just completed a transaction for housewares for her kitchen. The sale was final when she kissed the manager of the store full on the mouth.

And there was a young man in an exquisite silver suit who was at a jewelry store buying a ring. He had a look of such intense ecstacy on his face that Sarah felt next he would either faint, or start speaking in tongues. He did neither. His sale was finalized with a kiss as well. It was the custom in New Athens.

"I will have to practice my kissing," Sarah remarked to Maurice.

"Just as long as you do it on me."

***

Shane Pavoc was a short, dark-haired, intense man who sported the latest fashion rage in New Athens: golden eyes. He had been fitted with contact lenses to make his eyes appear gold. It was a good choice for him. With his dark hair and tan skin coloring, gold eyes looked just fine. Sarah thought it strange at first, but she got used to it quickly. She had seen other golden-eyed individuals in her brief trip through the slice of mall she had seen on her way to the management offices. At first she was put off by the alien feel of people with strange colored eyes. But when she saw Mall Master Pavoc interact with Maurice, and when she talked with him herself, the alien sensation left her. He was an earthly Californian, nothing else.

The discussion with Pavoc was brief and focused mainly on living arrangements. When those issues were dealt with, Pavoc turned to Sarah and asked her, "Have you thought about what trade you wish to pursue here in the Apollo Mall?"

"I had assumed I would be assigned a position."

"That's possible. But we like to give sanctuary cases a choice in what work they do. What did you do in America?"

"I ran a bookstore."

"Then I would suggest trying that first. You should discuss it with Maurice. I'm sure he has some ideas on the subject. Don't you, Maurice?"

"A few."

"Very well. I'll let you two get settled in your apartment. But please understand, Miss Fletcher, that your sanctuary transfer went into effect the second you entered the Apollo Mall. You are bound by the contract. You are forbidden from leaving this mall for a period of two years. Or until the authorities have examined your case in full and have determined that you are actually innocent of the charges brought against you by the Americans."

"Or until they nullify the charges," said Maurice.

"Quite right. So my advice to you is: make yourself at home, but don't be in a big hurry to do everything and see everything. You will probably be here for a long time, and the mall has much to offer, so pace yourself. Take small bites. Stick to the golden mean, as our ancient teacher Aristotle taught us. We'll work you hard, you can count on that. We do good business here. And there's bound to be much curiosity about you, so you should expect a lot of shoppers coming in your direction, no matter what you do. Now then, have you been properly greeted as a new employee of the Apollo Mall?"

"No, she hasn't," said Maurice.

Mall Master Pavoc smiled, stepped forward, took Sarah's face in his hands, said, "Welcome to Apollo," and then kissed her full on the lips.

"You won't need much practice at that," said Pavoc.

***

And so began her life at the Apollo Mall.

After a brief discussion with Maurice, they agreed that she should try to get a job in a mall bookstore. She toured each store, interviewed with the different managers, decided to pursue a position in the Parnassus shop on level three. Since she had management experience, the store manager was eager to see what she could do, so he let her loose. She plunged into the work intensely, lost herself in the job, let her focus on the new store push all thoughts and memories out of her mind.

The number one bestseller in the store her first week was a new book called, *Objective Principles of Inductive Logic*, by a woman named Alice Rose, who, Sarah gathered from the biographical information on the book jacket, was a private detective of some note who was highly sought after by law enforcement, Mall Masters, and private citizens who found themselves faced with apparently intractable mysteries. She had been so successful in her field that now, like many Californians, she had entered the field of philosophy in order to explain her techniques. Sarah wouldn't have noticed the book or had any interest in it herself, but everyone was talking about it. When she went to lunch, she over-heard conversations at the tables next to her, highly animated arguments between people who had read the work and wanted to hotly debate various aspects of it. The interest in the book seemed to cut across all age categories and professions. The book was a sensation. Everyone was reading it, discussing it, arguing about it. Sarah was impressed. She had heard Californians took ideas seriously and had a very active and volatile intellectual life. But seeing it firsthand was something of a shock to her. She had witnessed nothing equivalent to it in America. There, all the debates were religious in nature, and centered on arcane gibberish from the Bible. None of that had ever moved her emotionally or intellectually. So she found the spectacle of the Californian's philosophic fervor very refreshing.

And Maurice bought a copy, of course, and sat up in bed late at night reading it, occasionally quoting excerpts to her. Even though she found it all very abstract, she still tried to discuss it with Maurice. She got the impression that he was disappointed with her inability to discuss it on the level he could. She just didn't have the philosophic training that he had. Californians received rigorous training in the laws of logic and in the wider science of philosophy at very young ages. So even grade school kids knew more about some of this than she did. There was certainly nothing like any of this in America, on any level of education.

But she did the best she could, while feeling lost and disoriented much of the time. Her natural rationality asserted itself and guided her through the more difficult moments. And the people she worked with and met were very helpful and benevolent, appreciative of her context, and eager to answer her questions. So she learned quickly.

It was a different universe of literature here in California. The most popular subjects were philosophy, science, and business, in that order. But the Californians also had a great passion for poetry, drama, and huge sprawling epic novels. The most popular fiction writer in the country was a guy named Richard Julbran, who wrote a series called *Tales of the Mall Masters* that was very popular with kids and adults alike. Sarah gathered that he had to stretch things quite a bit to come up with stories that topped what real-life Mall Masters had done over the years. This series interested her quite a bit, so she asked Maurice about it and had her suspicions confirmed when he told her that he had read the entire series as a young boy. He recommended certain episodes to her and she plunged in, read it eagerly. It was the first authentic Californian literature she had ever had access to. She found the tales wonderfully benevolent, briskly written, cleverly plotted, and the characters invariably idealized portraits of how Californians saw themselves at their best. And unlike America, where the Christian ideal of self-sacrifice was impossible to practice, and so wasn't; here in California, the ideal was considered not only possible, but actually necessary to daily life. If you weren't an idealist, you were considered a fool.

Sarah had difficulty at first gauging how her fellow citizens felt about her. At least several times a day she was approached in the bookstore by people who knew who she was, knew her story, understood her context, and wanted to talk to her about what had happened, how she liked New Athens, what life in America had really been like, was it as bad and as crazy as everyone said? But even the bold and extroverted people who dared to speak to her seemed to hold back a little, as if there were certain things they could not, or would not say. It was clear that her status as the wife of an Apprentice Mall Master intimidated some people. And she was actually surprised that more people didn't acknowledge who she was. She did, after all, have a name badge identifying her as a sanctuary case. So she assumed that everyone she came in contact with, every single customer she helped in the store, and every merchant in the mall, and every customer she saw while she explored the mall, knew who and what she was. And had an opinion of it.

But only a few bold individuals bothered to express those opinions. And most of them were positive, so she felt welcomed and valued. If there were any citizens who thought she had been granted sanctuary in error, and who disagreed with the way in which Maurice had handled the situation, she never heard from them.

She asked Maurice if he had. She was curious. What was his situation here at Apollo? Was he welcomed? Was he respected? Was he operating here with the kind of regal authority he had used at the Show Me Mall? Or was he being thwarted by sophisticated Athenians who resented a young hick from the mountain regions coming to town and showing them up?

Maurice smiled at that assessment. "No, dear. Envy is peculiar to America. Californians are hero worshippers. We don't feel diminished by those of high achievement; we feel enriched. But don't get me wrong: we are still competitive as hell, especially here in New Athens. I have been welcomed here by other apprentices who admire what I did on the Mississippi. But they have informed me in no uncertain terms that they intend to learn from my example and surpass me in thought and action the first chance they get. And I have wished them well."

Sarah could only smile at that.

But wasn't that exactly what she had experienced in the bookstore, so far? And wasn't this kind of social atmosphere exactly what she had been starved for in America?

Going to work every day felt like the most refreshing and invigorating adventure. There was no tension about it, no pathological dread. The bookstore was a temple of reason, an oasis of calm even within the Apollo Mall. The people she worked with were competent and helpful. The customers were passionate and emotional like all shoppers in New Athens, but maybe just a little bit more understated than in other shopping venues. Book buyers tended to be a fraction calmer and more elegant in their emotional demonstrations than other shoppers. But that wasn't saying much. The religious quality that these people brought to the simple act of shopping never ceased to mesmerize Sarah. Several times a day she had the experience of finding a book for a customer who had trouble locating it himself. When she had found it, she always received a rather passionate kiss in reward. She had expected to be aggravated by that custom. Instead, after the first week or so, it all seemed perfectly natural and she didn't mind at all, she actually came to enjoy it. What did surprise her was the first time she was invited to an orgy. She declined, explaining that she was unable to leave the mall. Later, she asked Maurice how common that sort of thing was in New Athens. "Not very. Mostly its something young people do, teenagers who haven't discovered the spiritual nature of sex."

"Have you ever...?"

"Been to one? No. I've always valued the spiritual aspect of sex."

"Will I be expected...?"

"No. All things sexual are strictly optional and open to personal choice. Most Californians over the age of twenty-one eventually settle down into sexually exclusive relationships with mates. The orgy custom is simply a way for teenagers to explore sex completely, satisfy their curiosity, then move on into the realm of serious romantic relationships."

"You must have an incredibly high rate of teenage pregnancy."

"Hardly any at all. As you know, Californians value personal responsibility more than practically any other personal virtue — behind rationality — and responsibility in sex is one of our most encouraged virtues.

"I'll tell you a story. Before my initiation last year, my father gave me copies of two books. One was a lavishly illustrated edition of the *Kama Sutra*. Beautiful book. Everything you could possibly want to know about sex is in that book."

"I've never seen a copy. They've banned it in America."

"They should have it at the bookstore. Take a look. My other book was a copy of the novel *Frankenstein*, by Mary Shelley. My father told me to read both books, then tell him what the connection was. I read them. I didn't have to think about it long. I told my father, 'Frankenstein was a man who engaged in the irresponsible creation of life. He created a monster that eventually killed him. The connection to the *Kama Sutra* is: sex is how we procreate. If I am to have sex, I must not be irresponsible and bring an unwanted life into existence; if I do, it will become a monster and destroy me.'

"'So what am I telling you in practical terms?' my father asked.

"'Use protection. Make sure my partner uses protection. Make sure she understands that I have no intention of getting her pregnant.'

"'If she's a good girl, she'll tell you.'

"So you see, kids in California know everything about sex from a very young age. We drown them in sex, club them over the head with it. It is not a forbidden subject in any way. It's just treated as a natural, common-place fact of life. But adults who attend orgies are regarded as immature and undeveloped. Unsophisticated and uncouth."

"This is all very disorienting for me."

"Have you noticed any difference in the way men treat you and respond to you here in California? Compared to men in America?"

It was the first time she had thought about it. There was a difference. Back in America, most men were what the Californians would have called "selfless" in regard to women; that is, they acted unconsciously, mindlessly, without any consideration of the woman's thoughts, feelings, or context. There, when a man wanted a certain woman, he took her, usually by force, and it was irrelevant to him if she cared for him, liked him, loved him, or was even interested in him at all. Men didn't seem to pursue women out of any personal desire or need; it was more as if they were in a competition to impress other men with what great studs they were, so they had to go after whichever women were considered by general consensus to be the most "desirable."

Sarah had managed to avoid relationships with men like that, but she had seen them in action, known them, known the women they were involved with. Most of the women never even questioned the actions or motives of the men in their lives. It was simply "the way men are." But why were they like that? Was it actually part of their masculine make up, given to them by nature, a sort of sexual programming that couldn't be denied? Or was there some other factor at work?

Here in California, she suspected very quickly that there was another factor, that the Californians knew it, understood it, used it to achieve their personal goals. What was that factor?

Sarah had observed that the men here in California had a much greater reverence for and respect for women, treated them with impeccable manners, and acted consciously and purposefully in regard to women. If they were interested in sex, they never hid that, were quite blunt about it. But sexual overtures were never made until a context was established, a personal rapport, a spiritual link. Adult Californians were much more interested in and focused on the spiritual dimensions of sexual relationships. It was widely accepted that sex was 1% physical and 99% spiritual. What she saw around her seemed to prove that.

The men didn't seem to be competing with each other. They displayed strongly held personal standards and desires; they sought women who could satisfy those standards. And they always seemed conscious of the fact that sexually, women held all the cards in this society. There was a slogan that she heard repeatedly, mostly from teenagers: "Men choose, but women decide." Men chased women, just as nature intended. But whether a woman was caught or not was completely her choice.

She became curious about sexual perversion and rape in California society. She did some checking in reference volumes in the bookstore. What she discovered astounded her. Incidents of rape were almost non-existent. It happened, but statistically, the numbers were so small as to be insignificant. And the literature on sexual perversion was tough to find, there was so little of it. Child molesters, flashers, and the like, were extraordinarily rare in this society.

So was California a sexual utopia? And wider still: a social utopia?

The first time Sarah raised the issue to Maurice, he had some interesting comments to make:

"Utopia is not a social concept. All utopias are private in nature. Individuals make their own utopias. That is the only way it can be. Lives have to be lived individually, by individuals. If paradise is to be made, it has to be made by an individual choosing rational values and then achieving them. I don't even think the idea of a 'perfect society' is a valid idea. There is no such thing. There are only people who are rational and competent — or people who aren't. What a free society is, is simply a system in which people have to be rational and competent to live – and if they aren't – they don't."

She liked the idea of utopia as a private universe created by individuals pursuing passionately held values. She liked the romantic love angle: "Utopia is a happy marriage." That was another slogan she had heard. It was even the title of a popular book on relationships. It seemed to be what most Californians wanted and worked for.

And what about she and Maurice? Is that what he was building with her?

Every afternoon she returned to her apartment from her day at the bookstore. Most of the time, Maurice was not home yet. He worked long hours. An apprenticeship at the Apollo Mall was a demanding thing. He didn't talk much about what he did, what kinds of projects they had him doing, and what kind of training he did. Occasionally he would mention little details. She quizzed him a little, because she was very curious. But he didn't seem to want to talk about it. She watched him carefully, trying to discern if he was happy or sad in his work. He was neither. He was simply Maurice, the consummate professional, coolly going about his business. What kind of pressures were being put on him? She could not tell. Sometimes he was tired. Most of the time he was invigorated, and he brought that energy home with him and radiated some of it at her, let her soak it up, when she needed it.

When they spent time together, it was normally just the two of them. They would sit and talk for a whole evening, she telling him about life in America, or what her day had been like at the bookstore. If Maurice was late, sometimes she would take off and roam around the mall, explore what it had to offer, have dinner at one of the many restaurants, try a movie at one of the theater complexes. Or go window shopping, picking out items she someday thought she would buy, but couldn't afford right now. A sanctuary case had to save.

When she came home late, sometimes she would find Maurice asleep on the couch. She would leave him there and go to bed. Later, she would be awakened by him climbing in beside her. Then they would fall back asleep together.

Sometimes he would be in bed, and it would be she who climbed in beside him. If she woke him, he would acknowledge her with a touch, nothing more. Then it would be her choice about how close to get.

For a pagan Californian, she was surprised at how gentle Maurice was with her. He was not pushy about sex at all. Compared to the American men she had known, he seemed almost to have no interest in it. At first, she was worried about whether he even found her attractive. But she knew he did because of the way he kissed her. His kisses left no doubt that he found her arousing.

Their problem was that there was a ghost between them.

She hated herself for it, but she couldn't help it. She thought about Alan Benton all the time. When Maurice touched her, it was Alan's hand she felt. When Maurice held her close, it was Alan's arms around her. When Maurice kissed her, it was Alan's lips she tasted. She wanted to experience Maurice completely. She wanted that special intimacy which comes from two people loving each other in a way that obliterates the rest of the universe, creates a universe of two. She wanted what Maurice had known she had had with Alan. But her wanting alone could not make it happen. The ghost was there. Nothing either of them tried to do or say would make it go away. Finally, she stopped trying, stopped worrying about it. She took Maurice's advice. She held on to her memory of Alan. And she looked to Maurice to force Alan out of her mind. He was the man. It was his responsibility. If he really loved her, he would do it.

When she experienced frustration with the way Maurice was handling their situation, she reminded herself that he was only a fifteen year old boy, after all. So how much could she reasonably expect from him?

But he was no ordinary fifteen year old boy. He was a Mall Master. Even at his tender age, he was more experienced and better educated than even the most accomplished adults back in America. And he had been raised in a rational culture, programmed with a rational philosophy that had saturated his subconscious — and every cell of his body. He knew much and was capable of much, so she felt certain that he would not disappoint her, he would come through in the end. But so far, she could not understand what he was doing.

When they made love, he liked to turn the lights down low, lie with her naked on the bed, stroke her and kiss her, hold her face in his hands, study her eyes, make love to her with words. She loved the sound of his voice. She listened to him and watched him, followed wherever he led, found herself swept away for brief moments. When it was over, Maurice was beside her – and the ghost was still between them.

What amazed her was how acutely he could sense her feelings. He always knew. And sometimes he would speak of it to her.

"Was it I who made you come – or was it him?"

She could not lie to her husband. "It was his absence."

"Could any man make you feel what you just felt?"

"No. Only Alan."

"Well, it's my own fault. I advised you to keep his memory."

"It will take time."

"Yes. Time."

"Perhaps we shouldn't speak of it."

"What the mind does not acknowledge, the heart lets run wild."

"Shall I forget him?"

"No. I want you to remember him. I told you to remember him, and never let go, not for anybody, not even me. No, this is my problem, not yours. If Alan is coming between us, it's because I am allowing him to. I have not been logical enough. I must try to find a way to achieve greater intimacy with you."

She wondered what he would try.

She only had to wait a few days to find out.

She came home late one evening after working a late shift at the bookstore. It had been a long day and she was tired, but when she saw Maurice waiting for her, she read his face instantly and knew something would happen tonight. She remembered that look. She had seen it so often at the Show Me Mall, when Maurice had saved her life. It was burned into her memory. That was something she would always be able to call to mind.

She changed her clothes, combed her hair, then they left the apartment. Maurice took her to a private elevator and they rose up to the roof of the mall. She knew there was an observation deck up there on top, but she had not bothered to visit it yet. Perhaps she had been waiting for an invitation like this?

The roof was empty. It was late, the middle of the week, so the weekend crowds were gone. They had the roof mostly to themselves. Maurice took her to the middle edge, hung over the railing, stared out at the glittering lights of New Athens as it stretched towards the dark ocean. Low clouds hung like a curtain over the city, so they saw no stars. But it was clear to the ocean and they could see the blurred edge of the horizon where the bay met the city. A glittering star of light sparkled like a distant star, just on the horizon, a sharp pinpoint of focus on the blurred horizon of their sight.

Sarah followed Maurice's eyes as he scanned the view, then looked at her. She smiled at him, then turned to face the city.

Silver stars sparkled in shimmering little fountains of white foam, as if the ocean had come to shore and caught fire. The silver flowed out and swirled into a spinning chandelier of light that seemed to float upon the land. It was a city of marble and crystal, gold and glass, steel and plastic; all this lit up with neon rainbows so that skyscrapers looked like giant Christmas trees and homes in the darker residential areas glowed like mysterious jewels. From a distance, it was an eye-popping mosaic of color that seemed alive, that moved and breathed as if life had somehow taken hold.

"Listen," said Maurice.

She closed her eyes and held her breath. A slight breeze moved hair across her face, but made no sound.

"Do you hear it?" asked Maurice.

She could hear the city. It was quiet at night; it tended to whisper. You knew it was there, resting easy, waiting to be brash and loud once more in the morning. It was giving you a rest, and you knew it, so you took the chance to rest yourself so that you could match the city once more in the morning.

"I hear the city," said Sarah.

"Do you hear the mall?"

"No."

"The mall is talking to the city. And the city is talking to the mall. What do you think they are talking about?"

"I don't know."

"Let me show you."

Maurice turned to the telescope and put in a coin so it would operate. He focused the lens on what he wanted, then he tightened a clamp to secure the device squarely on what he needed Sarah to see. Then he moved away and motioned for her to look and know what he wanted her to know, to gaze upon that which the mall and the city were talking about.

She looked.

Lady Liberty, naked in the night, her flame glowing, stood within the frame of her vision.

She had been beautiful in the day, bathed in clean sunlight, and framed with the pure blues of ocean and sky. But the night suited her as well, perhaps more. And darkness was not a cloak she wore close; it was a robe she tossed aside, still holding her nakedness proudly for all the world to see, and holding her light of freedom high so that those lost in the night would find her, come to these shores, find this city, join this rousing carousel of light and color.

Lady Liberty was gazing out to sea, to the far shores of worlds and countries that had not yet found her. Sarah wanted her to turn and look for her, see her here, a prisoner in the mall. "Set me free, Lady Liberty. I am earning my freedom here. When the day comes, I will leave this mall and work for you."

Maurice watched her face as she stared, then pulled back, blinked, then let her sight flow across the city once more, taking in the night scene, holding it a moment, then glancing back through the telescope at Lady Liberty, and holding her for a longer moment. Then there was a loud click as the telescope stopped, and Sarah pulled back, turned her head away, her eyes closed. She turned her back to the city and the statue in the bay, she walked away a few steps, to a dark shadow close to a wall of the mall, and she listened now to the mall. Was it speaking to the city? Was it talking of Lady Liberty?

She knew enough about Californians by now to know that their spiritual link to their city was a real one, a palpable entity that could be known if one understood the way in which these people held their ideals in their minds. What they valued was real and they always wanted to see it, touch it, feel it, hold it, show it off.

Liberty was real, and they saw its reality in the form of the statue in their bay.

Love was real, and they saw all the myriad aspects of that value in the physical presence of their city; this was a woman with whom they were in love, and every step they took through her streets and within her buildings was a kiss of love from them to her.

Man was real, and all his works were great, and they displayed his wares in a secular museum they called a shopping mall, where men were free to come and choose, take what they want and pay for it, then go out into the sun-drenched city to show off their love before the judgment of Lady Liberty, saying to her, "I am as good as you knew I could be. And you are better than I ever dreamed."

Maurice watched Sarah. She finally turned around, came out of the shadow, back into the tender evening caress of the city, and she smiled at him.

"Have you seen what I wanted you to see?"

She told him what she had seen – and what she had thought.

Maurice smiled at her. "You've understood it in the way I have needed you to understand it." He took her in his arms, hugged her, kissed her, then they turned together and faced the city. They just gazed for a long time, standing together, holding hands. The city was happy. They could hear laughter drifting up from far below.

Maurice finally turned to her and said, "I am not a man yet. I am still mostly boy. I have always felt that to become the man I want to be, I must master the mall enough so that the mall gives me the woman I need. The woman I need is a woman who sees the mall as I see it, values it and loves it the way I do, and understands how it all fits into a city. A mall is a city within a city, and has the same type of life a city has. I hope you understand. I went to the Show Me Mall and was virtuous enough to be rewarded with you. But I haven't won you completely yet. I have to do that here, at the Apollo Mall. But I can only win what exists to be won. If you do not master the mall as I have, at least in spirit, then there will be nothing for me with you, and no possibility of true love between us."

"What you want is a mall in female form."

"Yes."

"Then I want to be that mall. And I want you to be my master. Be the master of my mall."

He kissed her then, for a very long time, and the city bathed them in a soft gentle rain of orange and purple light, until they pulled apart and vanished down into the mall, secure and at home, protected within their city.

When they made love that evening, she finally understood who Maurice Sully was, and what he wanted, and what he would become when he was finally a man. If this was what the boy could make her feel, then the man would surely scorch her soul, melt her and mold her, burn her straight into another kind of existence. It was what she wanted and needed, to enter the pulsing core of a great-souled man, to stand within the fire, to feel the heat and know it was a life-giving fire, not a killing one. Those alien to this soul would be burned into non-existence by it; but not she. She would be forged by it. She would be made into an Athenian sword that would cut through reality and find the joy inside, the true life, the total existence.

She found it with Maurice that night, and for the first time, she was happy, and there was no ghost with them that night, and she did not think of her lost love, she only thought of Maurice, and the Sarah she had become, the Athenian Sarah Fletcher, and she understood why the people who shopped in this place were so exultantly happy. They had known what she was now knowing.

She held Maurice all night. She would not let him sleep. She took everything he had, and more.

The next morning, without even having slept a wink, she stood happy and beaming behind a cash register in the bookstore, and the first customer she faced that day was Alan Benton.

CHAPTER FOUR

THE SWEET CHAOTIC MADNESS OF IT ALL

Sarah Fletcher smiled at the young man who stood facing her, thinking at first that he was some freak of nature, a look-a-like, a twin she had never heard about, a secret from Alan's past that he had kept hidden from her.

But in an instant the radiant serene power of his face impacted her mind, the light from his blue eyes connected with a link to her soul, and the glow from his face radiated waves of subtle communication to her heart and mind — and she knew it was really *her* Alan Benton, before he even spoke.

But then he did speak. He said, "Sarah. It's me, Alan."

And that was too much. A wave of nausea overtook her. She heard a roaring in her ears; a strange kind of sound she had never heard before.

It was the sound of her soul crying out and her inner world crashing from an overload of experience.

She fainted.

She hit the ground softly, because Alan had caught her.

That is what kind of man he was.

***

"Damn you!" cried Diane Copernicus. "How dare you throw a twist like that into this story!"

"I'm just the messenger, dear," I said. "This is all true. It happened exactly as I tell it."

"But you said he was dead!"

"They just thought he was dead. They had no idea at the time what had really happened to Alan Benton."

"So now I know what happened to Sarah Fletcher, and why she is no longer with Maurice — even though they were in love."

"You know nothing, dearest. I haven't finished the story. Now you must learn how Alan Benton came to be standing before Sarah Fletcher in the Apollo Mall on that particular morning."

"You're going to digress again."

"Just briefly. But you must know the context of Alan Benton. Else none of what follows will make sense to you. Just as it did not make sense to Sarah Fletcher."

"Very well. Proceed." She settled back in her chair and closed her eyes. But her face was alert, her ears waiting, her mind receptive.

I continued.

***

Alan Benton fell in love with Sarah Fletcher the first time he ever saw her. He had come to her bookstore looking for a rare book; instead, he found a rare woman. He forgot about the book he had wanted and talked to the woman. The next day, he remembered the book and he went back. It was a good excuse to see her again. In the end, he got the book — and the woman. After two weeks, they were dating. After one month, they knew they were soul mates destined for each other. After two months, when he knew who her father was, Alan Benton knew this girl he loved would be the greatest challenge of his life.

He almost chickened out. But that was only a passing attitude; in the end, there was only one choice for him. After three months, he had decided he would ask her to marry him.

But by then, they were both doomed, because Sarah's father had found out about Alan.

Alan was a journalist. He wrote the truth. It was all he saw, all he knew, all he cared about, all that mattered. He brought to the profession of reporter a passion for truth that made one of his editors refer to him as "a religious zealot." That editor had fired him. The next called him, "a saint of journalism who bore the stigmata of objectivity across his shoulders like a cross." That editor had fired him as well. The latest had called him "a perverted scientist in journalist's clothing, on a mad quest for a truth that did not exist." That editor had fired him as a favor, as a means of saving a young man from a future he could not conceive and would not survive. "You're in the wrong profession, kid," that editor had told him. "There is no room for the truth in journalism. You should get a job with the sanitation department. The only truth today is garbage. That's all that exists for certain."

Stunned with disillusionment, Alan Benton tried to get a job in the government's Ministry of Information. He did it just to play a joke on reality, just to thumb his nose at the world in which he lived and the people who ran it. But it was too late. They knew all about him and were not going to let him slip through. What he would have done in that job he had not considered. And he didn't have to. He never saw the report in which he was referred to as a "pimp to the whore of truth." And he never knew that his file was sent to the CIA and the FBI with a recommendation that he be watched.

After those disappointments, Alan Benton simply went underground.

There was a flourishing underground press in America. You couldn't earn a living writing for it. But you could write. And you could search for the truth, find it, and have the satisfaction and pride that came from that — never mind that most of your fellow men wanted to skin you alive for offering it to them.

So Alan Benton went underground and wrote for newspapers and magazines that were circulated secretly, in small editions, at great personal expense and risk, by people who had to do it because they simply knew of no other way to live or think.

Alan's special interest was politics. When the governor of Kentucky announced that he was a candidate for the presidency, Alan did some digging, examined the man, his personal history, and his campaign. Then he wrote an editorial analyzing all this. It was published, and Gerald Fletcher got a hold of it, didn't like it, sent his boys out to take care of Alan Benton — and the magazine he had written it for.

But by then Sarah Fletcher was so intimately involved with Alan that she constituted a major road block for her father's hired muscle. When they learned that their boss's daughter was sleeping with the man they were supposed to rough up, they backed off and told the boss and let him decide how to proceed.

Gerald Fletcher had feelings for his daughter that he would have described as "love." He told everyone who would listen that he loved his daughter, that he valued her and needed her. This was true. He did. But in his own peculiar way. He valued her the way a drunk values a bottle of booze; the way a drug addict values a needle full of heroin; the way a midget values a warped mirror in a carnival fun house. That is actually what Sarah was for her father: a narcotic that soothed his wicked soul and kept his mind fogged from the true reality of his own character, which he did not want to face. When he looked into his daughter's eyes and saw the reflection of his own soul combined with hers and beamed back at him, he saw a reflection he liked; he saw a soul pure and true, clean and good. He wouldn't let himself know that he was using his own daughter as a funhouse mirror, and that the reflection he saw was distorted, that he was seeing mostly his daughter's virtue. She was good and she loved him, so *he* had to be good. Nothing could challenge that axiom in his mind. To destroy that certainty, would be to destroy Gerald Fletcher.

Alan Benton was the man who destroyed it.

When Gerald Fletcher learned that his daughter had a boyfriend, and when he was informed who that boyfriend was and what he had written about him, he sat absolutely still, was quiet for a long time. Then he finally smiled. "Let's take a drive," he said.

He went to visit his daughter. Paid an unexpected visit to her bookstore.

When the Governor of Kentucky came strolling in, with his sleek-suited, sun-glass clad boys in tow, the patrons of Boulevard Books paused in their browsing, took notice, watched the procession pass by with a kind of frozen panic, mesmerized like deer staring into on-rushing headlights; hypnotized like small, furry, cute, helpless animals watching a massive predator pad by, and wondering if those glowing eyes and that fanged mouth was going to take notice and perhaps stop to sample some of the local flavor.

That is the way the fine upstanding citizens of the state of Kentucky saw their Governor. Gerald Fletcher was a good man who loved his daughter.

Sarah's store was a long narrow rectangle cut into the side of an old building on an undistinguished street in the older part of town. It didn't get much sunlight. But the lights were bright. When her father entered, Sarah was at the back of the store, alphabetizing the history section. Not far from her, sitting in a chair in the corner, paging through a big pictorial history of ancient Rome, was Alan Benton. He looked up from his book quite often, smiling, watching the movements of the poetry in motion he called his girlfriend. Because he looked up so often, and because Sarah's back was turned to the aisle down which her father came, Alan was the first to see Gerald Fletcher stroll up behind his daughter. Alan was silent. He said nothing, did not warn Sarah. But he forgot his book immediately, let it fall open on his lap, a garish picture of two gladiators staring up at him. He watched the men. He watched Sarah. She would have warned him, had she known. She would have thought it necessary. Alan didn't. He watched the sleek-suited, sun-glass clad muscle spread themselves out through the bookstore, none of them very far from the Governor. Alan did not watch them the way the other patrons did. He was not mesmerized, hypnotized, afraid. He was simply watching.

The Governor took no notice of him. His eyes were on Sarah. "Hello baby doll," he said, smiling behind his daughter.

Sarah turned, saw her father, smiled. "Daddy!"

"You got a hug for your old papa?"

"Of course." Sarah stepped into his arms and was hugged briefly, then set free. "You didn't call! What's going on?"

"Just in the neighborhood. Thought I'd stop in and say hi to my little girl. Heard you've got a new boyfriend."

"Oh?"

"That's wonderful," smiled the Governor.

Sarah cast a quick glance sideways to Alan. Her father followed the glance and turned his eyes on Alan for the first time. Still smiling, he said, "Is this the young man?"

For a split second, Sarah and Alan looked at each other. Neither believed in telepathy, but for that split second, they both had the closest thing possible in this universe. Each was flooded with emotion. The emotions consisted of a universe of thoughts. The thoughts concerned values. Those values were threatened. What was the best course of action? Yes or no? What each knew was communicated via nothing more than eyes and face; eyes glowed suddenly bright with an intensity of consciousness; face muscles sculpted flesh into frozen masks of thematically transparent art stylized to communicate intent and conviction. Yes or no?

Alan slammed the book shut and stood up sharply. "Yes sir, how do you do, Mr. Governor." He held out a hand.

Gerald Fletcher took the hand and tried to crush it. He could not; Alan Benton had a firm handshake and strong hands. He used a manual typewriter.

"How do you do, son," said the Governor, smiling. He looked at his daughter. "How about an introduction?"

Sarah was pale, felt she had turned into a ghost and would drift back into her bookshelves and vanish in a swirl of dust. But she focused on Alan's strong face and was able to speak. "Daddy, this is Alan."

"Alan...?" said her father.

"Alan Benton," said Alan.

"Ah. I've heard that name before. Seen your name in print. You're a reporter, aren't you son?"

"Yes I am."

"I've read your stuff, you're pretty damn good." The Governor refocused his attention exclusively on his daughter, seemed to lose all interest in Alan Benton, as if he was of no significance. "Listen baby doll, I'm having a little dinner party at the mansion in a few days. Love to see you there. It's been so long since you visited me in Frankfort.

Promise you'll come? Bring your new boyfriend along, I don't mind. Promise?"

Sarah nodded. "Of course, father."

"That's my girl. I've got business to attend. So I'll see you in a few days. Alan, nice meeting you."

The Governor turned and left the bookstore. The muscle swirled after him like ashes from a fire.

When the coast was clear, the browsing patrons left the store one by one, quietly and precisely. None of them bought anything. Alan and Sarah were left alone in the store, at the rear. Alan sat down in his chair, his arms on the rests. He looked at Sarah. She said nothing. She went into the back and washed her face with cold water.

***

They went to dinner at the governor's mansion.

Alan wore a tuxedo. The last time he had worn it was when he had attended an awards dinner for investigative journalists. He had not won an award.

Sarah wore a black party dress, as if she were attending a funeral and was happy about it.

The dinner party was small and private. It was them — and the Governor.

They had dinner in the dining room of the Governor's private residence. When Alan and Sarah arrived and were escorted in, they were surprised to see the room empty of people. "We must be the first to arrive," said Sarah.

They were fifteen minutes late.

Alan was a little more realistic. "No, dear. We are the party. Just you and I."

"You think?"

"Oh yes."

"Sometimes I tend to give my father the benefit of the doubt."

"I can't afford to do that, darling."

"Don't worry. I'll protect you from my father. He won't hurt the man I love."

Alan was silent.

The Governor finally arrived and they sat down to eat dinner at a large wood rectangular table. The Governor sat alone on one side in the middle of the table and faced Alan and Sarah, who sat side by side facing the Governor across a narrow band of food. The Governor ate heartily and tossed off inane comments. Sarah picked at her food. Alan ate slowly, precisely, consciously — like a prisoner enjoying his last meal.

Halfway through dinner, the Governor brought out a magazine and tossed it on the table beside him, with no comment. Just let it sit there. Did not draw their attention to it at all. Just it tossed it like it was garbage worthy of no comment. And then he abruptly changed the subject of conversation.

Alan and Sarah both recognized the magazine as a copy of *Freedom Forum*, the magazine for which Alan had written his piece on the Governor.

Alan gave a quick glance at the magazine, noted what it was, but said nothing. He continued eating, glancing up occasionally at the Governor, waiting for him to make his intentions clear.

Sarah noted the magazine, smiled at her father, but said nothing upon seeing the flat dull iciness of his eyes.

"So, you interested in politics?" the Governor finally asked Alan.

"I take an interest."

"Know what a politician's job is?"

"I know what a politician's job *should* be."

"What's that?"

"To protect people from force."

"Is that what you think I do?"

"When you're at your best, that's what you do."

"I'm always at my best, son."

Sarah said, "Daddy, I didn't know you read *Freedom Forum*."

"I don't, baby doll."

Alan said, "Did you invite me here tonight to question me about my essay, sir?"

"I didn't invite *you*, son. I invited my daughter. You're just along as a courtesy."

"Very well."

"Daddy, I understand how you'd be angry—"

"Let's read a little, shall we?" said the Governor, picking up the magazine. "Here's a nice juicy tidbit: 'Close study of the career of Gerald Fletcher reveals a man who pursues power for the sake of power and is willing to walk over corpses to grab whatever authority he can get his hands on.' Now isn't that charming. Seems to me you're insinuating that I've committed murder, young man."

Alan put down his fork and knife. "I see now that it was improper for me to accept this invitation, sir. It's not right for me to sit at your table and eat your food when I've written this about you."

"You show quite a moral sense there, son. Glad to know you're that discriminating. Time for another tidbit. I quote: 'Evidence exists which clearly indicates that Gerald Fletcher attained the governorship of the state of Kentucky by instigating a concerted campaign of bribery, blackmail, coercion, election fraud, and even murder.' Now, what would you know about all that, son?"

"I gained access to files held in the offices of the Attorney General for the State of Kentucky."

"Is that a fact? And why hasn't the Attorney General acted on that so-called evidence?"

"That's a good question, sir."

"Maybe I've got him in my back pocket, do you think? Here, let's check." The Governor twisted around and reached into his back pants pocket, saying, "Hey, Attorney General, you in there?" He finally yanked something out of his pocket and held it up while smiling. "Well, it's just my little hanky." He blew his nose into the white cotton handkerchief, then wadded it up into his jacket pocket. "As it happens, son, the Attorney General is actually a friend of mine. He let me know about some information he possessed that was of a — how should I put it? — scandalous nature. I asked him to send the files over so I could take a look. But when he went back for them, they were gone. I don't suppose you would know anything about that, would you, son?"

"I'm a journalist, sir, not a thief."

"Stealing files from a government office is a serious offense."

"Yes it is."

"So if you know anything about it, you'd best come forward."

"Don't be so stupid, Governor. You'd never make such a thing public. That would reveal the files and you'd be sunk. So you won't scare me with that one."

Sarah sat with her mouth open, watching Alan and her father stare at each other, realizing the little game they had quietly been playing had changed drastically, that the issue had been named and thrown out into the open, and now they would have to face each other honestly. She also realized that she was about to see a side of her father that had remained hidden from her. What kind of truth was she going to discover? Somehow, the possibilities did not frighten her, shock her, intimidate her. The prospects caused her no distress, no anxious trembling. Whatever it was, she had known it in some form, on some sub-verbal level for a long time. She had know it in an abstract, detached, emotionless kind of knowing. The sentence in her mind was: my father is a beast, but it has nothing to do with me. And even now, when suddenly it was going to have something to do with her, she was not frightened. Whatever he was, that is what he was. Whatever she felt about it, that would be what she felt. And however it affected her life — that is how it would affect her life. She would deal with it, live with it, learn with it, grow with it.

She never even wondered if she would survive it.

Governor Fletcher said to Alan, "I just want to hear you admit that you are the guy who stole those files."

"Okay," said Alan, lightly. "I admit it."

"Is that true?" asked the Governor.

"What do you think?"

"Did you steal the files?"

"I stole the files."

The Governor looked at Sarah. "Baby doll, do you love this boy?"

"Yes."

The Governor looked back at Alan. "Are you gonna lie to me in front of the woman who loves you?"

"Governor, to defeat you, I'll lie like hell."

"You didn't do it."

"Does it matter who did it?"

"Some other bastards at this little rag did it."

"Does it matter?"

"It does now. They're all in jail."

Alan said nothing to that, simply looked at Sarah, who held his eyes for a moment, then looked down at the napkin in her lap.

The Governor looked at his daughter. "Sarah, do you know what your father's job is?"

"You're the Governor."

"So I am. Do you know what that means? Know what it is that I spend my days doing, what I think about all night when I can't sleep, what kind of decisions I have to make to fulfill the responsibilities of my job?"

Sarah looked up at him. "I never wanted to consider it."

"I know that. Innocent children like you and your friend never want to consider these issues. That's left to men like me. I make the decisions. You want to know what it is I do? I'll tell you. This is your political education. This is all you need to know. Everything else is details. What I do is facilitate the morality of the human race. Do you know what it is that life requires of us? Sacrifice. That is how we pay reality for the lives we live. Life requires sacrifice. But because men are low, men are fallen, men are evil and wicked by nature, they can't see individually, inside their own egotistical skins, what it is that life requires from them. They can't see that when they live in a society, a collective of evil, selfish, wicked men, that sacrifices have to made for the good of the whole. So we elect governments to take care of the sacrifice for us, to do it morally, and fairly. To decide who gets sacrificed, when, to whom, and how much. And that is why governments and the men who run them are universally reviled. Because we do the dirty work. We do the job nobody wants, the job nobody will admit needs to be done, the job nobody else has the courage to face. That is what I do, daughter. I sacrifice. I make the choices, I do the deed. I pluck the little lambs from the flock and I slaughter them. And I sit here at dinner with you and my bloody hands and ask your forgiveness and understanding. Did I get this job by force? Yes I did. That's the nature of the venue in which I work. If government's job is to use its legal monopoly on the use of force to make the sacrifices that need to be made, then it doesn't make sense to give that job to an elected official. The man who gets the job is the man who's willing to do what it takes. A man like me. I was willing to use force to enter into a position of power in which I could use that force for good. So it's nonsense to talk of not deserving the position and not being worthy of it. It's mine. I took it by force, I'll keep it by force, and I'll use the force I have for good. I'll make the sacrifices that need to be made. And anybody who gets in my way gets stomped on."

The Governor stopped and took a long, slow, languid drink of wine, held it in his mouth for a long time, sloshing it around behind his greasy red lips while he watched the two innocent young people sit and stare at him with wide eyes. Then he finally swallowed, belched, then smiled at Alan. "How's that for political philosophy, young man?"

"At least you're honest."

"I'll continue to be honest." He looked at his daughter. "I have before me a situation in which a sacrifice has to be made. I'm not going to chicken out in front of my daughter and not face the situation honestly. One of you has to be sacrificed. I'd prefer it be the journalist. But if it isn't, it can very well be you, my dear."

Sarah stared at her father. "What do you mean?"

"I've protected you for a long time, because you're my daughter. You know I have. I know all about your bookstore, how you run it, the unauthorized books you carry, the underground publications you support. If my protection vanishes, you'll be wide open to authorities who would love to take you down as a way of getting back at me. It would happen very quickly."

"You wouldn't do a thing like that," said Sarah.

"I would. That is what I'm telling you. I want you to know that your father is a man of integrity, honesty, justice. I would sacrifice my own daughter for the good of the community, the state, the country. I may have to anyway just to prove I'm worthy of the presidency. Once the campaign heats up, the opposing camp will make your indiscretions public and I will be forced to either deny them — or act on them decisively. Or I can deal with it now and make it a moot point. What I am telling you is, father to daughter, that I would prefer to deal with your boyfriend here, to make him a public sacrifice, and spare you."

"To harm Alan is to harm me, father. We are not separate. We are one."

"You've never really had a taste of power, daughter. If I give you a little morsel to sample, you'll feel the rush and change your mind. Exercise power in the manner I have known, you will know your own human nature for the first time. Then you'll stand beside me as a princess at the altar of power."

"Make I be excused to go to the bathroom?" asked Alan, starting to stand up.

"No, you just sit there and pee your pants," said the Governor. "You're not going anywhere until I say."

Alan sat back down, slowly.

The Governor hit a button near his hand and some muscle entered the room. Two men in dark suits stood behind Sarah and Alan and waited attentively, watching.

Alan felt the heat from the two men on the back of his neck.

Sarah sat prim and proper and dabbed at her mouth with a napkin. "Very well, father. What are you suggesting?"

"I suggest nothing, daughter. I order. I command. Here's the deal. You remain untouched and protected. Alan here joins his friends in prison and their stupid rag gets shut down."

"If we refuse?" asked Sarah.

"Then I'll make a public sacrifice of you, my daughter. And of Alan — a non-public sacrifice."

"I see," said Sarah.

"I still have to go to the bathroom," said Alan.

"Tough," said the Governor. "Sit and suffer."

Sarah stared at her father, found she couldn't see him, as if light rays went straight through him, rendering him invisible. She looked past where he had been sitting — or was sitting, invisibly — and out the French doors behind him, to the garden just outside. The garden of the Governor's mansion. It was night, so the place was a tangled mass of twisted shadows. In daylight she would have seen beautiful flowers glowing in sunlight, a bright and gaudy place filled with mirth and sweet scents. She had walked through that garden in younger days, innocent days when her father first occupied this office, this mansion, this altar of power. In those days she had the garden to herself because she was the only one who enjoyed it. Not even her mother loved the garden as she did. Her father never entered it except at night. Her brother was allergic to it, so never went near for fear of a sneezing fit. So it was her garden. For a time. Then she left and tended a garden of books, a jungle of ideas. She tried to plants seeds and make them grow. But this world she lived in was difficult, the soil wasn't good, she could not make the ideas grow. What she planted came up weak and small, like *Freedom Forum*, a plant unable to defend itself when her father came to stomp it out of existence, then pull up the roots and make sure nothing like it ever grew again.

She wondered about her mother's death. Her mother was buried out in the garden. Who had put her there? And why? What had necessitated that sacrifice? Were the roses she saw red with blood from her mother's body? Had the gnarled plants that grew dark and twisted in that dim jungle been nourished with remains from the woman who had given her life? If she asked, her father might tell her. He was drunk on truth today. He was a man who could be made drunk by the truth because he had tasted so little of it, it was a shock to his system.

It was not a shock to her system. What she knew now about her father did not collapse her inner world, it expanded her. She was growing spiritually. Spiritual growth was not like physical growth, which was limited by the physical nature of existence and could only progress at a slow, methodical rate. Spiritual growth took place at the speed of thought and so was unlimited. Her soul was traveling at the speed of light away from her father and toward her new sun, her new galaxy, the new center of her universe: Alan.

Her love for Alan, and the bright, sun-lit universe they had created together, was not to be sacrificed. It was not to be given up, turned in, turned over, offered up as a plea for life to others who could not live. It was to be kept, held, protected, nourished, and lived daily, every succulent second of joy was to be drained from it, then replaced each day as their love recreated itself, and their universe multiplied, expanded, flew out and up and away into the universe, a galaxy on its own, spinning up and away from the reach of those with sacrificial hands. This was her world, her universe. She finally turned to look at it.

Alan was smiling at her in a strange way. Had he been thinking these same thoughts?

Sarah spoke. "Darling, we seem to be stranded in this wilderness, surrounded by wild animals. Have you heard these growls?"

"Yes."

"Don't they sound ferocious?"

"Yes."

"I think they want to eat us."

"I think you are right."

"What weapons do we have?"

"None, my darling," he said, a forlorn tinge to his voice.

"Well, there is still one weapon left. The most powerful weapon of all. I think I shall use it now."

"Very well darling," said Alan. He sat back in his chair and relaxed.

The Governor smiled at his daughter. "Don't think you're gonna try some hanky panky on me, baby doll. You play that game, I'll win every time."

Sarah smiled at her father. "Of course, papa. You're right. So no hanky panky. No lies. No scam. Just the naked, brutal truth."

She thought about how ironic it was — that word was too weak, she couldn't think of a word that described the curious nature of this situation — but it was still ironic, to be telling her father that she was going to lie to him, and he refusing her lie, but then she standing up and launching into the lie, knowing full well that she would win, her father would take the lie, because it was unreality, it was fake, and it was what he wanted. She did not know when she had learned that the way to defeat evil was to give it what it wanted, that it would die instantly, because what it wanted was unreal, couldn't be made real, and the attempt to live the unreal would always end up killing. Perhaps she had learned it just this moment, while listening to her father. Perhaps she had known it years ago and just had never had a chance to put the theory into practice. But now the chance was here. It was going to be an interesting experiment.

She stood up and faced Alan. "You lying son-of-a-bitch!" She slapped his face. "How dare you call my daddy a murderer!" She slapped him again, only this time her fist was closed and it was more of a punch. Alan's head flew back and he suddenly had a bloody lip. "You can go to hell, you bastard!" Sarah screamed. "You'll not use me as a whore any longer, do you hear me? You can go to hell, and take your cheap silly ideas about freedom with you! I'll stand by my daddy." She moved around to the other side of the table and stood behind her father's chair. She waved at the two suits standing behind Alan. "You boys get rid of this lying bum! Take him away, get him out of my sight!"

The two suits looked at each other, then stood loosely, arms dangling, ready for action, but not moving because they had not heard their master's voice command them. They were like two well-trained attack dogs confused by strange voices.

The Governor twisted around in his chair and glanced back at Sarah. "You don't expect me to fall for this. You're so transparent."

"Am I?"

Sarah rushed back around the table to Alan, grabbed him, dragged him out of his chair, hauled him across the room and dumped him at the feet of the muscle. "You boys haul this garbage out before I puke all over it and give you a real mess to clean up. Didn't you hear me? I'm the princess of power, I stand with my father, the Governor of Kentucky, soon to be the President of the United States. So you'd best step lively!"

"Sarah, you come over here and sit down," said the Governor.

Alan got into the act. "So, you're selling me out? This is what love means to you?"

Sarah sneered. "I never loved you. Go ahead, boys, rough him up."

"Stand easy boys," said the Governor. He stood up behind the table, came around after his daughter. "Girl, I'm not falling for this crap, so stop it, right now. Boys, take the punk away, get him out of my sight, I need to deal with my daughter."

The muscle moved in and grabbed Alan. They held him facing Sarah and the Governor for a split second. Alan looked into Sarah's eyes and saw that she loved him, that she was acting to free him, both of them, in the only way possible. He did not think it would work, and did not like to see Sarah gamble with their lives in such a daring, brazen way. But his own plan could not be put into action. Because he had not had the chance to go to the bathroom. But maybe there was still a chance...

"Guys, I need to get to the bathroom—"

"You don't let him get anywhere near a bathroom!" said the Governor. "You just let him poop his pants and then sit in it. I know what he's got up his sleeve and he's not getting a chance. So get him out of here now!"

While the Governor was talking, Sarah had moved quickly behind him to the dinner table, picked up a steak knife, then moved in behind her father, using his body as a screen so the two thugs couldn't see her, and as her father finished his last sentence, she plunged the steak knife into the side of his neck. The Governor screamed and spun around, reaching for her and the knife at the same time, but Sarah hung on tight and twisted the knife in her father's neck, ripping a deeper, wider wound, then hitting bone and bending the blade freakishly as her father howled and sagged to the floor while the closest muscle lunged forward, diving for Sarah. She caught him in the face with her high-heel and he flipped over and landed on his back.

Behind this, Alan had uppercut his palm into the nose of the second thug, hoping to deliver a blow that would send the guy's nose bones jutting into his brain. The blow was off-angle and not hard enough; he merely managed to smack the guy in the side of the face and send him sprawling to the floor as he reached for his gun. He was drawing it when Alan pounced on him and jack-hammered his elbow directly into the bridge of the thug's nose; this did some serious damage, breaking the guy's nose and sending blood spurting out down his shirt front. The thug managed to pull the trigger of his gun without aiming and sent a bullet flying off into the wall. Alan stood up and stomped a foot down onto the guy's hand and squashed the gun out of his fingers, then picked it up, pulled the trigger without aiming or thinking, shot the guy through the heart, turned quickly to face Sarah, not knowing he had just killed a man.

Sarah was on top of the man she had kicked in the face. He had reached for his gun as well, but Sarah beat him to it, had it in her hands, pressed the barrel briefly against his forehead to silence him, then stomped on his groin as she moved away and whirled on her father, who was gurgling, "No guns! No guns!" even as he pulled up a pants leg, reaching for a gun he had strapped to his ankle.

Sarah didn't see this.

But Alan did. He took aim on the Governor and fired as the door to his left exploded open and a pile of people came spilling in like beans from a tin can.

Alan's bullet hit the Governor in the stomach. The old man froze in shock, then slumped back, his leg stretched out in front of him at an odd angle, the small gun strapped to his ankle clearly in view.

Leading the crowd invading the room was Sarah's brother Stephen. He rushed in and saw Sarah waving a gun in his direction and hit the floor. Behind him, more muscle came tumbling over him, sprawling out over the floor in a comical skid of turmoil typical of any event Stephen was involved in. "The Governor's been shot!" someone screamed.

"Daddy, what have they done to you!" howled Stephen Fletcher from beneath a pile of muscle.

The pause in pursuit was long enough for Sarah and Alan to act in tandem, both of them picking up chairs and crashing them through the windows behind the dead thug. They followed, dancing over the dead body and hearing only cries and sobs and hysteria behind them — then nothing as they flew through the air and landed in the bushes below. Both of them were cut to hell in the one-story fall, but they bounced onto sturdy ground quickly and dashed away from the mansion while lights popped on all around, sirens went off, alarms rang, and the windows of the house screamed like a living beast wounded in a fight.

Sarah went one way, Alan another. They would escape and meet up later.

Alan ran into darkness and lost himself in shadows, moving on foot away from the mansion, hoping for a link to the surrounding neighborhoods, hoping for an avenue of escape, hoping for a sewer to fall into, or a trail to get lost on, or a cave to hide in, or a tall tree to climb. Behind him, he could hear the barking of dogs.

Sarah jumped in an open Jeep and drove through the front gates of the mansion, in full view of the guards, and with spotlights beaming on her as she smiled and waved to the guards like a happy teenager on a lark. They let her pass just seconds before the message came through to stop her. Moments later, they gave chase, but when they found the Jeep, it was empty.

Sarah escaped.

Alan did not.

None of this was what Sarah had in mind. But it was done, and now it had to be dealt with.

***

Sarah ran, and they were chasing her the whole time, but they couldn't guess her route, and they couldn't read her mind. It never occurred to them that she would go shopping, so she slipped through and ended up at the Show Me Mall and was rescued by Maurice Sully.

Alan was not so lucky.

They had him and they held him. Stupid and paranoid as they were, they asked him all the wrong questions, and he had no answers for them, so it got ugly. They beat him, tortured him, drugged him, threatened him. They found his family and took in the family and tried to use them against him, but the family folded easily and turned against him, they all hated him anyway, had for years, and the chance to watch the government stick it to him while they cashed in was the dream of a lifetime for these people, so they watched Alan suffer while they maneuvered to profit, made deals, took pledges, informed on friends, ratted out still others, and trumped up charges against people they had never met, never heard of, would never know. They lied like hell up one side and down the other, and danced like puppets gleeful to be held on strings and directed to live the life of power and lies and schemes and subterfuge. They reveled in the sweet chaotic madness of it all, and when it was over, they were taken away and shot in the back of their heads and died believing utterly that they were practical and knowledgeable and on the cutting edge and hip and so secure to be at the center of power and seeing it all happen and knowing what it was all about. They were buried in unmarked graves and nobody ever knew they were gone, and nobody missed them, most of all Alan, who had his hands full trying to stay sane.

All he could do was think of Sarah and wonder how it had all gone so wrong. But he knew. They shouldn't have split up. They should have stayed together. But better one to get free. Could he hold out until she came for him? And would she ever come? How would she manage that? It wasn't possible. No, it wasn't going to happen. He was dead. They were going to put him down. They were going to take him out. Very well. Let it be done, he thought. My Sarah is free, and that is all I really wanted, so let them do anything to me, anything at all.

They lied to him, of course, told him Sarah was dead, that she had been shot trying to escape, but he acted like he didn't care, and eventually, they stopped that story. They gave him drugs and found out that he did care. But that was all they found out. They wanted to hear lies, the kind of lies they told each other, but Alan only had truth inside him. And the kind of love he had for Sarah was something none of them could relate to, it was so confusing to them, they didn't know what to do about it.

And meanwhile, Sarah eluded their grasp.

And then turned up on TV from the Show Me Mall in America.

And all was well once again.

Filbert Duckworth was put on the case, and he knew what to do.

When Sarah flew off to New Athens with Maurice Sully, Filbert Duckworth knew the Americans were expecting a snatch.

Duckworth intended to give them a snatch.

***

The Americans excelled at one thing: stealing. They regularly managed to steal all sorts of technology from California and then adapt it to their peculiar American purposes.

This was the case with Alan.

Filbert Duckworth kept up on all the technology his country stole from California. He kept up with developments on how that technology was used for purposes of state security. So when the case of Sarah and Alan was thrust on him, he had a good idea about what he would do to bring the girl back.

What they did to Alan Benton was this: they performed an operation in which an interesting piece of nano-technology was implanted into his brain. This tiny microscopic device was a bomb keyed to a radio signal. The first signal initialized the bomb and set its atomic timer on a ten day countdown. When the countdown ended, the bomb would explode, blowing Alan's head off, killing him and probably anyone else within twenty feet. The bomb could only be turned off by pressing a deactivation button attached to a broadcasting unit in Filbert Duckworth's State Department office. And this button was designed to respond only to a preprogrammed fingerprint that it would detect via an infrared scan. That fingerprint would belong to Sarah Fletcher.

"Bring Sarah back, or your head will explode," Filbert Duckworth explained.

Alan Benton laughed in his face.

They didn't dare rough him up at this point. Smack him in the head and the bomb was likely to go off. Or so the superstitious brutes who worked for Duckworth thought.

So they left Alan untouched. Gave him a chance to recover from his other beatings.

And they set him free.

With ten days to get to New Athens and bring Sarah back.

Before they let him go, though, they gave him some demonstrations, in case he thought he was being scammed. They showed him film of the operation they had performed, to prove to him that they had indeed inserted the bomb.

And they showed him what would happen to him by doing the same thing to a chimp and then letting the bomb explode.

It was not a pretty sight. Those watching with Alan had done so grimly, seriously.

Alan was the only one who laughed.

He felt sorry for the chimp, and was sad to see what the sadists had done to it, but he still had to laugh, because in the instant when he watched the chimp's head explode, he knew that Sarah had been right after all, and that she had won, just like she had told him, they were both going to be free, he would walk out of here just like a man going on vacation.

Which is exactly what he did, later that day.

His trip to New Athens was very pleasant.

***

When Maurice Sully saw Alan Benton, he realized immediately who he was and why he had been sent. "You're the one, aren't you?"

"I'm Alan Benton. Maybe Sarah told you about me."

"She has. But she doesn't know why you have come. I do."

"Do you?"

"Yes."

"Why have I come?"

"To take her away."

"Oh really?"

"They must be holding some incredible blackmail over your head."

Alan smiled. "You have no idea."

"Why do you smile like that?"

"Never mind. Listen, do you love Sarah?"

"Yes I do."

"You're a Mall Master, so I believe you. Then she is yours. She must remain with you. You must love her and help her to be happy. I am just passing through, I can't stay, and I can't let Sarah come with me. I have to leave her with you. So promise me that you'll take care of her."

"I promise you. But tell me what they have done to you. I can help."

"I don't think so. Don't concern yourself with me. Sarah is your only concern, okay?"

"She's waking up. We should go to her."

"Yes."

***

Alan had made up his mind to see Sarah one last time, then go off alone to let the bomb explode and kill him. He would take her picture, record her voice, then die staring at her face and hearing her voice.

Maurice and Sarah knew none of this, could not know, would not know. Not if Alan had his way.

***

When Sarah woke up and saw the two men she loved looking down at her, she smiled, thought that fainting again wasn't a very good idea. She liked this. She liked seeing them together. But she was worried. "Do

I have to make a choice?" she asked.

"No, darling," said Alan. "The choice has been made."

"Who made it?"

"You did, darling."

"Whom did I choose?"

"Maurice."

Sarah looked up at Alan. She reached out and touched his face. "You look so happy. If I have chosen Maurice, then why are you so happy?"

"Because you're alive, darling. And I'm here to see you."

Sarah remembered then. What she and Alan had gone through in that other universe. The things they had done, the choices they had been forced into making. She sat up and looked more closely at Alan, touched his face, checked his body to make sure he wasn't missing any limbs. "What did they do to you?"

"That's not important now."

"They must have done something to you."

"I survived and I'm here, that's all you have to know."

"I want to hear about it."

"Later."

Sarah looked up at Maurice. "Maurice, my husband...is there room for three in our bed?"

"Yes, darling, of course."

"Then Alan can stay with us?"

"Yes."

"For how long?"

Maurice looked at Alan.

Alan said, "I have to leave on Saturday. I have an appointment at noon on Saturday. I can't miss it."

"Alan can stay with us until then," said Maurice.

"I've got a headache," said Sarah. "Can we go home?"

"Yes darling," said Maurice.

"Alan, why are you crying?" asked Sarah.

"I'm just so happy to see you, darling. So happy to see you..."

CHAPTER FIVE

THE TEMPLE OF TRIUMPH

To celebrate his sixteenth birthday, Maurice Sully rose before dawn and traveled alone up the coast to the Temple of Triumph, and there, he watched the sunrise and thought about love.

The Temple of Triumph was a simple structure of steel, glass, and concrete built into the side of a cliff facing the Pacific Ocean. From most angles, it resembled the prow of a ship jutting out over the sea. Personally, Maurice had always thought of it as "the cutting edge of Western Civilization," because the leading edge of the temple sliced out away from the cliff like a blade, out toward the horizon. Here on this cliff at the far western edge of the North American continent, it was a symbol of both the beginning and the future of the universe the Greeks had brought to this land. It was a temple of explicit Man Worship of a type that only Californians felt comfortable with.

The temple was small and intimate. Only individuals were allowed inside, never groups. It was traditional for a visitor to disrobe and enter the temple naked. Once inside, Maurice walked down a series of spiral stairways leading to the main floor of the temple. This was transparent glass. So were the walls and ceiling. He walked out over the ocean, suspended in space over the sea, blue sky all around him and blue ocean below. Behind him, halfway between the front edge of the temple and the back wall, the statue of a naked man hung suspended in the air. The statue had arms raised, greeting the dawn, and seemed to be flying.

As did Maurice. He did not close his eyes and bow his head. He opened his eyes and raised his head, stood up straight and proud, looked around at the beauty of the sky and ocean. He smiled at the sunrise, then broke the silence with his own laughter. Here was a temple to his own happiness, and he had come this morning to reclaim it. The temple demanded that he laugh, and he obliged.

Glory in your pain, the temple told him. You are alive and hold your values seriously. Your pain is proof of your love.

Naked, Maurice felt the warm sunshine float through the transparent walls of the temple and caress his skin. He was naked before nature. Naked before the sea, which reached up for him, but couldn't touch him;

naked beneath the sky, which wanted to rain on him, but missed, because it was blind; naked to the earth behind him, which yearned for him to return to it as dust. But Maurice wasn't ready for that just yet. Not at the age of sixteen. Not on his birthday. So nature couldn't touch him, because he was protected by a temple of triumph.

And also he was naked before himself, his soul bared and reflected back at him from the glass walls of the temple. This was a place young men came to claim their manhood, and old men came to remember. Maurice was here on the morning of his sixteenth birthday to ask himself a question and demand an answer.

"The mall gives, and the mall takes away," he said to the ocean.

He turned and looked back at the statue of the hero. The stone man had nothing to say.

Think, Maurice commanded himself. You are a man, you survive by thought. Now your thoughts must match this temple in beauty and rigor. To achieve your values, your thoughts must each be a temple of consciousness, each thought a beautiful little conceptual sculpture equaling this temple in design and functionality. Your thoughts must work. They must help you to understand the complexity with which you deal.

So he thought. And what he thought was: Now I must follow my own advice, the advice I gave Sarah on the plane when we both thought she had lost Alan forever. Now I have lost Sarah back to Alan. I have lost Sarah, a fresh new love, my first love, the love I wanted, the love given to me by a mall, the love I earned by virtue of being a Mall Master, the love I created by mastering events thrust upon me at the Show Me Mall. The world had said, "Show me what you can do," and I obliged. Sarah came to me and said, "Show me who you are and what you value," and I obliged. Mall Master Clemens had put me in charge and said, "Show me how responsible you can be." I showed him. I showed them all. Now they know who Maurice Sully is and how he operates. Now I have proved my love for the universe of the Mall. My competence in these matters flows from my love for these values. To be competent, one must love. To be competent in love, one must love as logically as one works.

Staring down through the glass, he watched the ocean swirl silently, waves foaming up to the rocks below.

Was there a chance that he would *not* lose Sarah to Alan? He didn't want to think of the possibility. He did not want to consider the idea, because it was not realistic. He knew Sarah's love for Alan. It had been a palpable thing between them. Alan was here, and he was whole, so that was that.

But there was more to consider. He was still convinced that the Americans would try to kidnap Sarah. Was Alan somehow that attempt? And if so, how could it work? He seemed healthy and free, so what could they hold over his head? What value could they use to blackmail him? And if they were trying that, why wouldn't Alan simply say so and seek the help of the military?

He needed to spend more time with Alan to properly gauge this situation. He needed to spend time with Alan and expose his subconscious to all the facts implicit in Alan's voice, body language, comments, plans, interactions with Sarah. It would be a tough job for his mind to solve a problem that big and that subtle in only one week, but he had trained his mind well over the years. It was that very training which had identified Sarah Fletcher as an honest person with an affinity for his values. It was his very ability to grasp big problems quickly via a powerful subconscious that had convinced Mall Master Pavoc to bring him to the Apollo Mall. He was here precisely to develop that ability further. This was exactly the kind of challenge he needed. And since his happiness was at stake — his future with a woman he loved — there would be no dreary academic scholastic rationalism involved. Life demanded he solve the problem, or suffer. So let the processing begin.

He walked to the edge of the temple, stood with fingers pressed lightly against the glass. He struck a dramatic pose. The temple held him, as if a creature of stone and glass were offering him to the sea, showing the spectacle of a man.

That is why the temple had been created. To showcase Man. But not for nature's benefit, and not for alien creatures who might not know who and what Man was. The temple was for men. So that they might be reminded. As Maurice had to be reminded on his sixteenth birthday.

Now he had been reminded. In the spiral structure of his life and values, once more he had swung back on himself, to see what he was, what he knew, what he loved, and where he was going, and how he intended to get there, and why he wanted to be there in the first place. So now, to spiral back up, this time knowing more, this time with his certainty more solid and profound; with his knowledge an ever-expanding fractal mosaic of intricate, beautiful, fascinating details; with his purpose reviewed and confirmed and connected to the center of time and existence.

What did the temple teach him?

That he was perfect — and getting better every day.

***

Cocooned within the mall, soothed by early morning dimness, Sarah drifted slowly up out of a deep and refreshing sleep, opened her eyes to see Alan staring at her, his eyes bright, his face glowing with a restless energy indicating that sleep had not visited him. "Have you been watching me?" she asked.

"Yes."

"How long have you been awake?"

"Forever."

"Aren't you tired?"

"No. I'll never be tired again."

"You need your rest."

"I don't wish to visit the realm of the unconscious."

"You'll make yourself sick."

"I'll rest when I'm dead."

Sarah sat up, reached out, touched Alan's face. "My husband has left us alone together. He has made a gift of you to me."

"You should thank him when he returns."

"I will, I assure you."

"I have never made love to another man's wife."

"You are my husband, Alan. Maurice knows that. It is he who has been making love to another man's wife."

"I'm not here to ask you to make a decision—"

"There is no decision to make, dearest."

Those were the last words they spoke that morning. Alan silenced her with a kiss, and after that, she spoke only with her body. And Alan listened.

***

"You must ask for sanctuary," she told him.

"No, that isn't necessary."

"Darling, I can't leave the mall. I am forbidden."

"I will visit you every day."

"I don't want to be visited. I want you to live with me."

"I can do nothing but live with you, darling."

"We'll talk to the Mall Master, we'll get you a job here, Maurice will help us."

"I need to talk to the authorities about what happened to us in America."

A shadow crossed Sarah's face. "Maurice feels certain that the Americans will still try to kidnap me. Even here in New Athens. I don't believe it. It can't be possible, not here. What do you think, darling?"

"You're safe. There will be no kidnapping."

"I hope you are right. But Maurice is usually right about everything, you know. He is spooky that way."

"Everybody makes mistakes, dear. Maurice is wrong. Trust me. The Americans have given up."

"Have they?"

"Yes."

"Alan, did you see...or hear...from my father? Afterwards?"

"No, not directly. He lived, that's all I know."

"It's strange. I don't know whether I'm sad or happy about that. I mean, my father still alive."

"You need time to work it all out."

"I would have shot him, if you hadn't."

"I know."

"It wasn't my intention to get violent, but the dumb bastard wouldn't swallow my lie the way he was supposed to!"

"There was no time. He would have, eventually, if we could have played the scene out a little longer, or even dragged it out over weeks. He would have gone for it."

"What did you plan for the bathroom?"

"Just a chance to escape. Surprise my shadow, get out a window, lose them. Nothing fancy. Just get the hell out of there. I knew you were safe with your father. But I wasn't, not for a second."

"Well, it's all over now. We're together again. They can't touch us here."

"No, they'll never touch us again."

***

Sarah had to work, so they went together to the bookstore and it was just like old times. Sarah rolled a cart full of books to a section and began shelving. Alan followed her, sat nearby in a comfortable chair, held a book in his hands just to keep her happy — and to make it look like he was a customer. But mostly he just stared at her, watched her work, watched her move in her beautiful new Athenian-style clothes. She chattered away at him about this and that, how wonderful it all was, the mall, the city — what she knew of it from her perch on the mall roof — the books that were being written and read here, the movies she had seen, the music she had discovered, the people she had met, the life she was leading. She did not feel she was in prison, she did not feel she was leading a restricted life, she felt more free and more alive than she had even in her best days back in America. And now she had him back. Her life just seemed to keep improving.

Despite himself, Alan fell asleep in the chair, finally.

Sarah let him be.

***

In the afternoon, Maurice returned from his sojourn to the temple, tracked Alan to the bookstore, showed up and spoke with Alan. "Can we take a walk? I need to talk to you. Sarah will still be here when you get back."

"I know."

"Can you stand to be apart from her for a little while?"

"I think so. But you should ask *her* that question, too."

"Let's get out before she objects."

"Shoo!" said Sarah, chasing them away, ignoring the sting of trepidation inside her.

Maurice and Alan walked the mall. "Tell me about your appointment on Saturday," said Maurice.

"It's personal."

"Does Sarah know about it?"

"No. She doesn't need to know about it."

"Doesn't she?"

"Trust me."

"Do I need to know about it?"

"If I decide you do, I'll let you know."

"You understand Sarah has a sanctuary obligation to the mall. It will be impossible for you to take her away until that obligation is complete."

"I understand that. I'm counting on it. I don't want to take Sarah away. I want her to remain. It will be good for her. She'll need the mall. And she'll need you."

"The sanctuary term is still two years. What kind of relationship do you intend to have with her?"

"You are her husband, Maurice. That will not change."

"Athenian law allows for plural marriages. Do you wish to become a co-husband?"

"No, that will not be necessary."

"You don't think so? I expect Sarah will ask you to join our family.

And then join her here in the mall, undertake an apprenticeship. Does that interest you?"

"No. I'm a journalist. If I pursue a career here in New Athens, it will be in that field."

"You sound as if you have some doubts."

"Does it?"

"Is your meeting on Saturday about a job?"

"Let's talk about Sarah. Is she really going to pursue an apprenticeship?"

"Yes, I think she is quite serious about it."

"That's wonderful. I think she will do well."

"I'm sure. Alan, would it mean anything to you if *I* were to invite you to become a co-husband?"

"I would be flattered. But I would have to refuse. At this time."

"Perhaps in the future?"

"It won't be necessary."

They had stopped in the middle of a sky bridge linking two of the upper levels across a lower courtyard. Alan leaned over the rail and looked out across the mall, took in the whole scene. He smiled, his eyes bright.

Maurice watched him closely. Alan's smile was a touch too large, his eyes a touch too bright, as if his face was riding the edge of an emotional wave that was large and moving very fast and Alan was barely hanging on. Maurice noticed his hands grasping the edge of the rail. His knuckles were white. The tendons on his arms stood out, and his muscles trembled and shivered. He was grasping the rail tightly and seemed to be almost trying to rip it to pieces. But he could not. He relaxed somewhat and stood back. The fire went out of his eyes and for a moment he looked impenetrably sad, as if this scene before him was all a great tragedy. Then he smirked and cocked his head in a gesture of resignation. "Isn't this beautiful," he said.

"You seem saddened by it."

"Do I? I guess us Americans really don't know how to appreciate the finer aspects of civilization."

"Some might not. But you do. Why so sad?"

"Sarah gets to spend two years here. In the end, she won't want to leave. The world outside will seem colorless, tame, irrelevant."

"Not at all. That is not how I feel about it."

"The entire world is a mall to you, isn't it?"

Maurice smiled. "Yes, I think it is."

"The world is wide open, all spread out before you. And all you have to do is take what you want — and pay for it."

"Yes. That is the basic structure of business. And of life."

"The complicated part is the paying for it. Am I right?"

"Everything has its price."

"What's the most expensive thing you've ever purchased?"

"Sarah."

"What did she cost you?"

"I don't know yet. The price is still being tallied."

"Well, I hope you can afford it."

"I can. What about you, Alan? Can you afford it? Or have you paid too much?"

Alan looked at Maurice. "You can read me like a book, can't you?"

"If I can, you are a book written in a foreign language which I still have to translate."

"Well, so it is a slow process. But you'll understand the story eventually."

"That is why you're sad, isn't it? You fear you've paid too much, more than you have?"

"Perhaps," said Alan, quietly. He watched Maurice for a moment, sized him up seriously, looked him over as if appraising him. What he saw was a slender youth standing straight, tall, proud, his manner and movements a stylized expression of pride, self-esteem, self-love, egoistic self-reverence of a kind only an American could be conscious of. Because this sort of healthy human vitality was so rare over there on the other side of that damnable muddy swamp they called a river. Alan liked what he saw, was comfortable with it, did not feel threatened. Would he have been if his situation had been different? He didn't bother with the question, it was irrelevant. His situation was real, and serious enough that he had to consider only it, nothing else. So he admired Maurice, felt relaxed and comfortable — and thankful that this was the man he would leave Sarah with. This was a man who would teach Sarah to stand as he stood, to exist as he existed, to live as he lived, to think as he thought.

He would never see Sarah as a Mall Master. So he had to imagine it now. He looked at Maurice and saw what his Sarah would become.

And then he felt compelled to say something to Maurice. "You have a great wealth of spirit, don't you? That is how you can afford to be what you are. All of life's values have to be purchased first with an act of consciousness. Perception — thought — value. You are rich in thoughts. And your thoughts are like individual gold coins stored in the vault of your mind. So when the world confronts you with choices, you have the means to pay. You know what you want, and you know why you are worthy. Before a man can be wealthy in fact, he must first be wealthy in soul."

"If you understand what you have said, you are not far from being a Mall Master yourself."

"But that is not my road."

"What is your road?"

"To leave this mall."

"And?"

"Pay for it."

"For what?" asked Maurice.

No answer came.

***

That evening, Maurice was home alone when Sarah returned from her shift at the bookstore. Alan was gone. Maurice had assumed that he was with Sarah. But she returned alone, looked around, asked, "Alan's not here?"

"No."

"He must be out exploring the mall."

"Yes."

"Did you talk to him today?"

"Yes."

"What did he say?"

"It's best that he tell you that, darling. What's important now is for us to talk."

"Very well."

Sarah sat down on the couch and faced Maurice. He sat down beside her and they both twisted to face each other close, grasping hands, her hair wafting onto his arms, the fine dark strands outlined against his white shirt, some of it brushing against the skin of his hand. Her breath was sweet and warm against his face. Her eyes were large, wide, bright, eager, unafraid. She was ready for the future, whatever it would bring.

"I'm still in love with you, of course. That's an absolute," he told her.

"Yes."

"I invited Alan to join our family as a co-husband, but he refused. He seemed to think that it would not be necessary."

"Was he offended by the idea?"

"He didn't seem to be."

"Then Alan wants me all to himself."

"I don't think so. He seems to believe that you and I are to remain together."

"Then what—"

"As I said, darling, you should discuss that with him yourself. He did not give me any specifics. I got the impression that he was holding back from me so he could say these things to you himself. So we'll both be patient and let him speak."

"I can't imagine why Alan doesn't think he can be a part of our family."

"I don't want to speculate on that. I don't think you should, either. Just relax and talk to Alan when the time comes."

"Yes, of course."

"Now, about us. As long as your sanctuary term is still in effect, you'll live here in the mall. But if you are to have a relationship with Alan, that is going to affect us. So I'd like to tell you how I wish to handle this situation."

"Very well."

"I would accept Alan as a co-husband — especially if it will make you happy."

"It would."

"But if he refuses that offer, and you still wish a relationship, then I will withdraw so that you and Alan can be a couple."

"What if I choose you?"

"Then I will remain your husband, happily. Have you made a choice?"

"I should wait till I've spoken with Alan."

"Yes."

She looked at him closely, studying his face. In her short time with him, she had learned to read the contours of his face, the shape of his mouth, the light in his eyes. What she saw now was a calm certitude in his mouth, a resigned understanding in his eyes, an acceptance of facts he could not change across all his face.

"You think you know my choice, don't you?" she said.

"Men choose, but women decide," he said, smiling slightly.

"In this case, it seems I get to do both."

"So you do."

"I have no wish to hurt you, Maurice."

Maurice smiled. "You're not in America, darling. Don't act ashamed, and don't apologize. Make your choice, then relish every once of pleasure from it you can, and don't look back, don't regret. You're not hurting me, silly woman. I love you. I told a crowd of shoppers at the

Show Me Mall — not to mention a nationally televised audience — that you are not an object of sacrifice. You are not. You were not then in that place. Nor are you here in this place. I allow no sacrifices, and I ask for none. This is the California way. I love you. It would be unbearable to see you give yourself to me, knowing full well that you love another. So don't be afraid of hurting me, of breaking my heart. My pain is not your concern. Your love for Alan is. If he is your choice, then not to choose him would be an obscenity against life, reality, reason, logic — everything that makes love possible. I wanted to learn about love from you. I wanted it to be real so I would learn a real lesson. My love has been real, still is, always will be. You have taught me about love. Taught me what it feels like, how it makes one more conscious. The greatest way to explore the spirituality of reason is through love. True love is the greatest expression of reason there is, the greatest integration one can make in life. All of existence tied up in the person of a love, all of reality implicit in the fact of her existence, her body, her mind, her soul — everything. You have shown me all of that, and now, you can teach me the ultimate lesson — what it feels like to have it, then lose it, have it taken away. So go ahead. Break my heart. It was made to be broken. I'll mend it and put it back in place. It will be stronger because of what I have learned with you. And I have a spiritual wealth that runs deep. I can afford to lose you. What a preposterous thing for me to say, yes, I know it is, but there — I said it. I'm arrogant enough to say it. I'll say it again. I can afford to lose you. I don't want to, but if you go — my love remains. I have a future. It will be more of a future for having loved you. So if Alan is your choice, I'll simply kiss your hand — and say thank you."

Sarah sat looking at him for a long moment. Then her hands rose up, covered her face. She bowed her head to her lap, shook and shivered momentarily, convulsively, either crying, or laughing, neither of them knew, least of all she. What could she say to a statement like that?

She sat up straight, lowered her hands. She felt his presence on the couch beside her. He did not touch her. She looked at him. "You know me so well, don't you?"

"Do I?"

"How can I choose you after what you've just said?"

"Then it is done."

"Yes. It must be done. There. Yes. I can feel it now." She looked away, to the other side of the room, to the wall, then beyond the wall, outside into the mall, then on into the city, to wherever her Alan was. He was waiting. She must go to him.

She came back to the room, brought her attention back to Maurice. "Alan is my true love. He is my husband in spirit, as you are before the law. I must make Alan my husband in fact, in public. If he'll have me. If he'll ask me."

"Ask him yourself, if he does not. Put the question to him. Let him make a choice."

"I must go to him. Soon."

"Tonight."

"What am I waiting for?"

"I don't know."

"Then I'll go. I don't have to worry about hurting you. So I won't." She stood up, walked to the door, opened it, then stopped, came back leaving the door opened, stood in front of Maurice. "Maurice, someday you'll find your true soul mate. The mall will give you the woman you deserve. Maybe not this mall. Perhaps the mall you build yourself."

"Yes. I think you are right."

"I hope I can visit that mall and meet that woman."

"I'll look forward to it."

"Excuse me now. I must go find Alan."

"Yes. He is waiting for you—"

***

Earlier in the day, Alan had found the tourist information center inside the mall and done some small research, found some particular information that was useful to him.

"Down in the bay, is there a place where I can rent a boat?"

"Yes."

"Just for the afternoon, a small craft, one person is fine. If I can pick it up at eleven AM on Saturday, that would be ideal."

"It can be done. Just call this number."

Alan called the number and made a reservation. A one-person pleasure craft was reserved in his name. He would pick it up at eleven AM on Saturday, take it for a cruise in the bay, see the statue, enjoy the sea, look back at the cityscape of New Athens gleaming along the coast. He was glad for the bay and the lady. She would be good to see. He would be looking at her, she would be—

Noon on Saturday. That is who his appointment was with. The lady and her lamp. The Statue of Liberty. She would give him his final freedom. Wouldn't that be something?

Late that night, he found himself up on the roof, in a strange spot, alone, no crowds, where was everybody? He was looking through a telescope, sighting far out to the coast, to the statue, with the lights gleaming off her in the night, she all lit up and glowing as if a flame burned within her, as if the stone of her form held a radiance within, as if she had been sculpted from chunks of sun come too close to earth, and Man, that imperious bastard, had snatched her away from the sun, brought her down to earth, stood her in this bay to light the way, to show the road, to point to home.

He did not know it, but he held the same telescope Sarah had used when seeing this same sight. He could not sense her residue on the scope. But he felt what she had felt when he saw what she had seen.

When his viewing time was done and the telescope had shut itself off, he stood at the edge of the roof and looked down at the city, listened to what the city had to say. It was quiet for a long time, and when she walked up behind him, he heard her footsteps first, the sound of her shoes on the stone. He knew the rhythm of her movement, was sure it was her before he turned to see her. When he did, he smiled.

She was not smiling. "I've spoken to Maurice tonight. I've made my choice, and he has given it his blessing. I have chosen you, Alan. You are my love. I wish to be your wife, if you'll have me. I'm sorry. I didn't mean to ask like that, but — there is nothing else to say. That is what I want. But I do have questions. Do you have something you wish to tell me, darling?"

Alan smiled gently. "I was afraid you would do this to me."

"What have I done?"

"Darling, I cannot join you. I must go away."

"Why? For what?"

"I cannot tell you."

"Why not?"

"You will know by the end of this week."

"Why can't you just tell me?"

"There is nothing to tell."

"So you're going away. Will you be back?"

"No."

"Why not?"

"It will not be possible."

"My father's people are blackmailing you, aren't they?"

"How can they blackmail me? With what? You are what I love the most. And you stand right before me, untouched by their corrupt hands. So what can they do to me?"

"They can kill you."

"Can they?"

"Is that it? They've threatened you with death?"

"They did that back there, on the other side."

"And what happened?"

"I died. And came here to heaven."

"Alan, we must be serious. Don't talk that religious slop."

"I am serious."

"Where are you going?"

"Nowhere."

"What are you going to do?"

"Nothing."

"I want to be with you."

"Impossible."

"Let me come with you and face them."

"There is no one to face."

"I don't understand."

"Darling, understand this: you are torturing me with your questions. Please don't ask. Please accept that I am here now, and when I am gone...Maurice will take care of you."

"They have done something to your mind."

"Sarah, there is nothing to figure out. Don't think about these things, you will only make yourself crazy."

"Is that what happened to you? They made you crazy?"

"No. I am completely sane. More sane than I have ever been. I can't help but be sane. Even if I wanted to be a lunatic, I couldn't do it. I'm locked in to sanity now, no choice in the matter. So don't be afraid."

"You don't sound like yourself."

"I've never been to New Athens before! My God, what a beautiful city!"

Sarah smiled gently at him. "The correct phrase is, 'By Man.' If you speak of gods here, you will offend."

"Refreshing, isn't it?" he said. "You've become sober in your time here. But I am still drunk! I was just looking through a telescope at Lady Liberty. Oh my, what a sight!"

"I have used that same scope."

"I'm going to visit her." He made the statement, then stopped, looked hard at Sarah, searched her face for pain, found none. He wanted to tell her more, to speak in detail of his plans for the bay and his desire to see the lady up close. But he could not hurt Sarah. "I'm sorry," he said, gently.

"Don't be. If you're planning an excursion I can't take, I want to hear all about it. And when you've returned, I want to hear all the details. So you're going to see the lady. Do you promise to give me a report?"

He nodded subtly. "Very well. I promise."

"Thank you. I look forward to it." She walked past him and went to the edge of the roof, stood leaning against the edge, staring out at the city. "You know, I think on the day my sanctuary term is complete, my first venture out of the mall will be to visit lady liberty myself. Seems like the right thing to do."

"By Man, you're right!"

She smiled at him. "You always were a quick study."

***

They walked the mall all night, talked as if they were suspended in time and hadn't a care in the world. For Sarah, morning would never come. For Alan, Saturday would never come.

When they got tired, they went back to Sarah's apartment, let themselves in. Sarah said nothing, simply followed Alan into his room, left the door open. He had noticed that the door to Maurice's room was open slightly and a dim sliver of light shown out. But there was no sound. Sarah ignored that, but Alan made a note and remembered.

They spent the night together. Sarah had adopted a favorite custom of Athenian wives: she turned on the love lamp in the corner so they could see each other during their lovemaking. It bathed the room in a dim yellow glow, a gentle light just right for nocturnal sex.

Alan counted her kisses, and tried to be quiet when they made love, but Sarah would have none of that. "It will make him happy to hear us," she said. So she didn't hold back. When he took her, she howled, and when her ecstacy came, she screamed with delight, and he joined her, his voice harmonizing with hers in a twin chorus of joy. Hers was innocent and unbridled. His was desperate and fierce, as if he was an animal soul transported into a man's body and knowing self-consciousness for the first time. He knew the meaning of life, knew that it would end, saw that end coming, saw it closer than it had ever been before. At the moment when he held her in his tightest embrace, felt his manhood rush into her, felt his ecstacy spark into a white nova — he saw the moment of his own death, and he cried out her name. The force of his passion shook the room, thundered against the walls, silenced the woman beneath him, her body suddenly attuned somehow to what he was feeling, seeing, knowing. She went limp beneath him, opened her eyes to see him above her, saw what was on his face and in his eyes, did not understand what it was, only knew that it was something dark and powerful and fearful, and she could not touch it.

It was gone as they collapsed and melted into each other, lay for a long time stroking and caressing, seeing each other through dim love-drunk eyes in the soft glow of the love lamp. Eventually, like a good Athenian wife, Sarah rose when Alan's eyes were shut and he was at the edge of sleep, and she turned off the lamp, returned to Alan in darkness, and sank into sleep beside him.

***

Maurice lay in bed listening. This was a music he had always enjoyed. He had listened to sex all his life and knew all the subtle nuances of sound. The human voice was an expressive instrument and could be made to communicate emotional depths as lucidly as music. What Maurice heard from Alan frightened him. He knew immediately that this was important and that he must remember. He commanded the memory into place within his mind, then proceeded to contemplate it intently, hammering it down to the attention of his subconscious over and over, knowing this was a clue, a key perhaps, and if he could learn the meaning of this, he would know the truth about Alan. So he heard the sounds, went to sleep with his mind analyzing the content of those sounds.

Lost in all this was what music Sarah had shared with him.

***

In the morning they all three had breakfast together.

Alan spoke first. "Did you sleep well, Maurice?"

"Yes. Did you?"

"Too well."

"Oh?"

"Ever notice when you sleep more than normal, you wake up feeling tired?"

"Yes. I've experienced that."

"So have I," said Sarah. She was at the stove, preparing food.

"Did you dream?" asked Maurice.

Alan frowned. "No, I didn't."

"Is that normal for you?"

"No. Usually, I have vivid dreams, I remember them clearly, and I can analyze them, know what they mean, relate the symbols to the events of my life."

"But nothing last night?"

"Nothing I can remember."

"Well, maybe tomorrow," said Maurice. He smiled. But inside, he was worried. Not to remember your dreams meant your subconscious had no advice to offer on your current situation. Or else you didn't want to listen. So if Alan was getting nothing from his subconscious, it meant he was in trouble. It meant he had a problem his subconscious couldn't crack. It meant he was getting no advice from the deepest reservoirs of his mind. Which meant he was going to have to be mentally muscular enough to analyze things consciously. And then honest enough to face reality and take his own advice. Would he be able to do that?

"You two sounded wonderful last night," said Maurice.

Alan blushed, glanced at Sarah, who responded with a smile. "I told Alan you would enjoy us."

"Alan, do you feel uncomfortable with this situation?" asked Maurice.

"You have no idea."

"Don't. This is a good experience for you. You're plunging right in to California culture in the best way possible. You already know that sacrifice is a dirty word here. You've probably thought about the political implications of that. But there is a more important realm: the arena of love. In this realm, sacrifice is an even dirtier word. So relax."

"In America, the men kill their rivals in love."

"And they don't achieve happiness, do they?"

"I would say not."

"Don't worry, I'm not going to kill you. I'll tell you what I told Sarah: don't feel guilty. Get every ounce of joy out of Sarah you can. She belongs to you now."

Sarah sat down and smiled at Alan. "See. Told you. Now let's all enjoy our breakfast, shall we?"

***

Saturday came way too soon.

Alan tried to slow time down by staying awake as long as he could, and by focusing so intently on the details of daily life and of all his new experiences, that every moment stretched into a slow motion film, as if reality had a projector he could slow down. But the slow motion film wasn't enough to satisfy him. He wanted a photograph, a painting of one perfect moment, a moment that could be lived for all eternity, he wanted to freeze that moment and then step inside, become a conscious part of the moment forever. And Saturday would never come. He would never have to face Lady Liberty with the clock in his head ticking.

But Saturday came, methodically, relentlessly. The great cosmic clock counted off the seconds, minutes, hours, days...and then he was there. It was Saturday morning.

How do I say good-bye without letting her know I am saying good-bye? He didn't know. But he had to do it anyway.

He didn't sleep, and on Saturday morning, he was first to stir in the apartment. He left Sarah alone in bed and went to shower, shave, change into fresh, new clothes she had bought just for him. A classic Athenian shirt and slacks. The shirt was of fine white linen and had been tailored just for him; the slacks were a soft white cotton also tailored perfectly. They were the finest clothes he had ever worn.

He went to Sarah and woke her. "Join me for breakfast?" he asked.

"Sure," she murmured, her eyes brightening as she drifted up out of sleep.

They sat together at the dining room table in the silent apartment and ate toast, fresh fruit, juice.

"When will your meeting be over?" Sarah asked.

"Quickly. I don't expect it to last long."

"I have the afternoon off. We should do something together."

"We'll see."

The phone rang.

"Let it ring," said Sarah. "Maurice needs to be awakened."

The phone rang five times before Maurice picked it up in his bedroom.

"I doubt if it's for me," said Sarah, smiling.

"Definitely not for me," said Alan.

"Why do you stare at me like that?" asked Sarah.

"Am I staring?"

"Yes. More than usual."

"If it makes you uncomfortable, I'll stop."

"If it makes you happy — don't stop."

"It does make me happy. Very happy."

"You haven't touched your breakfast! Did you invite me just to watch me eat?"

"Yes, I think so."

"Where has your appetite gone?"

"I don't need a lot of food right now."

"Then let me have your toast. I'm starving!"

"It's yours."

Sarah continued to eat, happily making a pig of herself. Alan watched, smiling at her, his eyes bright with a touch of hysteria that he couldn't feel, and she couldn't see, both of them unaware of the effort he was making to ignore emotions that kept fighting to the surface, looking for expression. He held them in with an iron force of will. They would be let out soon enough. When they were, she would not be there to see it or hear it. That would be only for him, and the statue in the bay. Lady Liberty would be his symbol, a stand-in for his real love, this woman who sat eating her breakfast in front of him.

He thought of Sarah. Wasn't he being cruel to hide his death from her? Shouldn't he share it with her? Wasn't that the Athenian way? Isn't that the way a true love would act?

But he could not. It was cruel any way he looked at it. And she must not know. If she knew, she would try to save him, and there was no way to save him, he knew that. And he did not want her close. That was the main thing. She must not be near him when it happened, she must not see it or hear it. He had to be alone. So he kept it to himself. My life is hers, he thought. But my death will be mine. Only mine.

Sarah was almost finished when Maurice walked into the room dressed for business in fine slacks, white shirt, and an apprentice vest.

"Who was that on the phone?" Sarah asked.

"Mall Master Pavoc. We've been called to a meeting. It concerns your sanctuary. So let's get ready and go. He wants us in his office right away."

"Now?"

"Right now. Alan, you should come too, you'll want to hear this, it concerns you as well."

"But I have an appointment."

"Now you have two."

***

On the way to the meeting, as they approached the mall management offices, Alan said, "I need to use the rest room. I'll meet you two there, okay?"

He swerved off down a short corridor and headed for the rest rooms. Maurice and Sarah merely nodded in his direction, noted where he was going, then remained focused as they continued on to the management office.

Mall Master Shane Pavoc wore his sanctuary robe and had removed his golden eyes. He stood behind his desk, stern and serious, his natural brown eyes giving him a hard aura of realism. Off to one side was General Kent McKnight. On the other side was Mike Charles. Maurice took all this in and knew immediately that much of consequence was about to happen. Sarah merely waited, wide eyed.

"Where is Alan Benton?" asked Pavoc.

"Using the rest room, sir," said Maurice.

"He should be present to hear this. I don't want to have to repeat myself."

"What has happened?" asked Sarah.

Pavoc held up a piece of paper. "I have received an official communication from the American State Department, directly from Mr. Filbert Duckworth. The Americans have officially relinquished their claim on you, Sarah Fletcher. They no longer want you back. At the same time, new evidence has come to light in the matter of the criminal actions that led to you entering the Show Me Mall. McKnight?"

The General stepped forward slightly, addressed Sarah. "California intelligence sources in America have confirmed that the person who actually shot Governor Fletcher of Kentucky was Alan Benton. We've informed the Americans of this fact and have presented our evidence — an extraordinary thing for us to do, let me assure you — but the Americans don't care. They had Alan for a time and are satisfied with how they handled him. They don't want him back, either."

"Does this mean I'm free?" asked Sarah.

Nobody answered. Maurice turned and looked at Mike Charles. His presence here was inexplicable. "There's more to this. Let's hear from Mr. Charles."

"Where on earth is Benton?" asked Pavoc. He motioned to one of his assistants. "Go find Benton, get him in here."

The assistant started to leave. "Let me go with him," said Sarah.

"You stay!" said Pavoc, his voice loud and commanding, holding a tone no one had heard from the Mall Master in many years. There was a tinge of anger in his voice.

"Very well," said Sarah.

"Go ahead, Charles, tell him," said Pavoc.

Mike Charles stood up straight. "Maurice, I represent the Show Me Mall. Our investigation and analysis of your handling of Miss Fletcher's sanctuary case has determined that she did in fact bring a weapon on to mall property. We've discovered evidence of a melted down gun in one of the furnaces in the basement. It was warped out of shape slightly, but still obviously a gun. Of American design, and fitting the exact description of weapons in use by bodyguards at the Governor's mansion in Kentucky."

Mall Master Pavoc looked at Sarah severely. "Is this true, young lady? Did you in fact bring a weapon onto the property of the Show Me Mall?"

"Yes sir, I did."

Pavoc looked at Maurice. "Sully, overall, I admire the way you handled that situation. I followed it closely and admire the way you took responsibility. But we are not on the Mississippi here. We are in New Athens and we have a higher standard. Because of what she did in America, I cannot allow Miss Fletcher sanctuary in my mall. And I cannot allow you as the man who brought her here to continue your apprenticeship. Therefore, I have ordered the following: that Sarah Fletcher, by virtue of bringing a weapon onto a shopping mall in the Individual's Republic of California, is hereby banished from the Apollo Mall. Your sanctuary is at an end. You are free to leave and pursue your self-interest elsewhere. Maurice, your apprenticeship is terminated and your sanctuary fee is forfeit. You are banished from this mall forever. You are requested to leave at once."

Mike Charles said, "Maurice, if you wish to contest this decision, I can recommend a good lawyer."

"No," said Maurice.

Sarah looked at him, shocked to her core. "Maurice! This is unbelievably unjust, and, if I may be so presumptuous to say so," she said, turning to Mall Master Pavoc, "Stupidly irrational!"

"Not for a Mall Master," said Maurice, quietly.

"We have the highest standards here, Miss Fletcher," said Pavoc.

"I am here to enforce the Mall Master's orders," said General McKnight.

Maurice bowed to Mall Master Pavoc and then removed his apprentice vest, handed it to an assistant who came forward to receive it.

"Thank you for the knowledge you've shared with me in my time here," said Maurice. "I intend someday to surpass you in thought and action."

Pavoc bowed. "Good logic to you, sir."

Maurice turned to General McKnight. "Sir, may I have a word with you in private?"

"Certainly," said McKnight.

"Is that all?" asked Sarah, incredulous. "That's the end of it? Just like that, and we're gone?"

"Yes," said Maurice. "It was a voluntary association which has now ended. Come along, dear."

Sarah turned back to the Mall Master. "Pavoc, you're a cold-blooded son-of-a-bitch!"

Pavoc smiled and bowed very slightly. "And you, madam, are obviously an American."

Maurice took her by the hand and escorted her out of the office, with a little help from General McKnight, who held her right hand while Maurice held her left. She walked between them stiffly, but didn't really struggle. She wanted to get out of Pavoc's sight.

As the three were leaving the management offices, Pavoc's assistant was returning alone from his errand to fetch Alan Benton. Maurice was first to notice the stricken look on the assistant's face and he asked, "Did you find Benton?"

"No sir, I did not," said the assistant, as he walked on past, obviously not relishing the reception his boss would give him.

Maurice turned to General McKnight. "Sir, this is what I was afraid of. It is Benton who has been sent by the Americans to snatch Sarah back. They've lied to you. It was Benton all along. But the twist is, Alan isn't playing along. He's not going to make a snatch."

McKnight crossed his arms and regarded Maurice seriously. Coming from anyone else, the General would have laughed these comments away. But he had watched this kid function at the Show Me Mall, so he was willing to listen to Maurice.

"You're saying Alan is a kidnapper who won't do the deed?"

"No, he won't."

"Then what do we have to worry about?"

"Alan's been acting like a man with a disease who doesn't want anyone else to know about it. I think his life is in danger."

Sarah turned in the direction of the rest rooms, suddenly remembering Alan's strategy against her father. "Oh my God!" she said, unconsciously reverting to her American upbringing. She wrenched free of Maurice's hold and went running down the corridor toward the rest room Alan had entered.

"One moment, please," said Maurice. He followed her.

When he entered the rest room, he saw Sarah standing in the middle of the immaculately clean room, mirrors shining on her left, a row of stalls to her right. Her back was to him, but he saw her stricken face reflected from the mirrors.

The rest room was completely empty. There was no one in any of the stalls, no one at any of the urinals. Just the two of them.

Maurice walked up behind Sarah, took her by the arm, guided her out gently without saying a word.

General McKnight was waiting at the door, looking like he was about to enter. "Well?" he asked.

"We'll need your help, sir," said Maurice. "Put out a call immediately. Have your men bring Alan Benton into custody."

CHAPTER SIX

THE UNSACRIFICED

Alan Benton left the mall at eleven o'clock, was in a cab and on his way to the harbor at about the same time General McKnight sent out a radio call to have his men apprehend him. By eleven thirty, Alan had checked in at the boat dock and had his private pleasure craft moving slowly, methodically out to sea, away from the shore, out towards the Statue of Liberty. But not too close. He didn't want what was going to happen to take place too close to her.

He wanted to go faster. An insane impatience boiled up within him, urging him to open up the boat full throttle and get out to sea quickly, before anyone caught him from behind. But he held his inner discipline. He could not attract attention to himself. There could be no one near him when the moment came. He must be alone and his end must not harm anyone else. The boat would probably be damaged, and whatever was left of him would probably sink to the bottom with it, but that couldn't be helped. The boat would just have to be sacrificed.

Sacrifice. What an ugly thing, he thought. What a truly miserable, vile thing that is. And that is what I am now. I am a sacrifice.

He tried to feel what that meant. He tried to experience the reality. But he was frozen now. His emotional mechanism was gone, shorted out, blown away, useless now. He could feel nothing. All he could do was stare out to the horizon and wish it would come, wish it would end.

If the earth was flat, I could fall off the edge and vanish. That would be convenient. But impossible. As all was impossible now.

He looked at his wristwatch. Time was sliding by just as it always had, always would. All week long he had tried to slow time down, had not succeeded. Now he wanted to speed it up and end this thing swiftly. But time would not move fast for him, just as it had not slowed down. It just stayed the same, tick tick ticking away, monotonous, steady, reliable, absolute.

He looked back to the coast to see if any boats were moving in his direction. There was nothing. Sail boats slid across the sea moving left and right, the sails flapping at him, their bright cheerful colors mocking his impending doom, the boats themselves seeming like tiny toys cast to sea by children. Their innocence mocked him.

I am not innocent, he thought. Not of anything. Most of all the meaning of life, the shortness of life. I wish they would have killed me quickly back in America. Put a bullet in my brain and sent me to darkness in one swift plunge. Not like this. Not this long, drawn-out horror. This was cruel and unusual punishment. The most cruel, and the most unusual ever conceived.

And it occurred to him, Why should I wait? If I know it is coming, if I know what my fate is, if I know the exact time and date, why wait, why let them do this to me, why let them torture me like this? I have it in my power to end it myself. I have volition, I have free will. I can do the deed myself. I could jump out of this boat and drown myself here in the bay. I can do it quickly, end it now, and when the moment comes, when twelve o'clock strikes, there will be nothing left to murder, the clock in my head will hit twelve, the alarm will go off, but I won't be there to hear the call, to feel the twinge, to experience the last flash of sensation —

He glanced at his watch. Fifteen minutes till noon. And the boat was still moving so slowly. He glanced up to the horizon, in the direction of the statue. She was there, small, white, beautiful. She seemed so far away. She too was like a toy. Like some plastic doll sticking up out of the ocean. He did not want to remember her like this. Just let me get a little closer, I want to see her close up, I want her to be huge, I want her to be larger than life. And then, when I am satisfied with my last view, then I will go. Then I will end it myself. And she will be my witness.

He turned his back on the coast. He faced out to sea and concentrated on reaching his lady.

He did not know that Sarah had figured out where he was going. She was only a few minutes behind him.

At five minutes of noon, she caught him.

***

Sarah had stood by and watched, waited, while Maurice went into his Mall Master act and ordered General McKnight to put out a radio call to his men to bring Alan Benton into custody. The General had not heard Maurice's request as a command, but that is what it had been. Sarah had heard the tone of voice. And she saw the light in Maurice's eyes. He was in his element now. Even after having been dismissed from the mall and asked to leave, he still had the moral authority to boss around one of the highest ranking Generals in the California military. McKnight did as requested, then went back to Pavoc's office, leaving Maurice and Sarah alone together in the hallway.

Maurice came to Sarah. She searched his face, wondering if he understood what she did, if he knew what she did. She was so angry at him right now, she said nothing, just listened.

"Darling, return to our apartment and start packing. I'll find Alan and we'll take him with us, okay?"

"Very well," she said.

She walked in one direction. Maurice walked in another.

She did not return to the apartment.

She walked out of the mall.

She was stopped once by security. They placed a call to Pavoc and the situation was resolved quickly. She was a free woman. She walked right out of the mall, found herself a cab, ordered the driver to the coast, told him to step on it.

She didn't even have time to feel anything about being free.

All she could think about was why Alan had to visit the Statue of Liberty. Who was he going to meet there? Why had he been so secretive about it? Why did he think he couldn't tell her or Maurice about it? And why was he willing to run out on a meeting with Mall Master Pavoc and vanish from the mall to get to this meeting?

There was never any doubt in her mind where to look for him. He had said he was going to this place, so she simply followed.

She called from the cellular phone in the cab and reserved a boat, made sure they had it ready for her, that it was running and ready to go. She had the cab driver charge her ride to the Apollo Mall — care of the office of the Mall Master — and when the cab skidded to a stop at the dock, she bolted out the open door and ran across the heavy wooden boards of the dock and jumped into her reserved two-person pleasure craft and gunned the motor, sending the boat spewing foam as it jolted out into the harbor.

She ignored the speed limit. Actually, she didn't even know there was one. It was the first time she had ever been alone in a boat on the ocean. She sped past other boats, steered her craft into wild swerves to avoid sailboats crossing her path. The harbor patrol was alerted and gave chase behind her, but she had a big lead and if they caught her, they could simply help her bring Alan back.

She brought out a pair of binoculars and found Alan cruising through the water ahead of her. When she first spotted him, he was traveling fast, his boat skidding over the water, kicking up foam behind, shooting across the bay towards the Statue of Liberty as if in a race and he was running out of time. But then as she watched, his boat inexplicably slowed down, then stopped, and just seemed to drift in the water. She was within a hundred yards of him by this time. Through her binoculars, she could see him clearly, as if he was standing right in front of her. She caught a flash of his face as he turned in her direction and he seemed hysterical and desperate. He seemed to be talking to someone, actually screaming almost, his face red, his hair flying in all directions, buffeted by converging winds and the movement of his boat. He didn't seem to realize there was another boat close. She put down her binoculars and tried to accelerate her boat even more. It was already going as fast as it could. She was slammed and jolted as the boat skipped across the bay, bouncing hard from wave to wave, her eyes focused on Alan standing in his boat. She heard the first vague cries of sirens behind her as the Harbor Patrol converged on her position, but she didn't relate that sound to what she was doing, how she was driving her boat across the busy bay. She thought it was Alan crying out to her. She thought she could actually hear his voice. He was screaming. He was calling out to her, or someone, to come and save him.

From what?

Didn't matter.

She was so intent on reaching him as quickly as she could, so focused on his position, so hypnotized by the sight of him, that she didn't slow down as she approached. By the time she cut her engine, there was no avoiding smashing her boat into his. When she realized it was going to happen, she screamed as loud as she could, screamed his name, told him to hold on, brace himself —

***

What does it feel like to stand in an elevator plunging down a shaft to certain death?

How does it feel to be at the controls of an airplane taking a nose-dive into the side of mountain?

How does it feel to stare at a gun pointed at you, then to hear that gun fired and see the flash and to wait for the impact of a bullet into your flesh?

Alan Benton knew.

He had glanced at his watch one last time. It was five minutes till noon. If he was going to own his own life, now was the time. If he was going to take his death out of the hands of his murderers and do the deed himself, now was the time.

But then he glanced back and saw the boat coming towards him. And he saw, standing up in that boat, hair flying behind her, her voice screaming and being carried away by the wind so he couldn't hear what was being screamed, the face of his beloved. Sarah. Sarah Fletcher come riding to his rescue.

And *he* screamed.

He screamed in defiance of those who had put them both in this situation; he screamed in misery at not being able to tell her why this was happening; he screamed at time for running out on him; he screamed at the Statue of Liberty for the appointment he was missing; and he screamed at himself for having been the man who fell in love with this woman, the one woman who would lead him to this day when he had to die like this instead of live with her. He screamed at himself for having a nature that made it impossible for him to do anything other than love her, no matter the circumstance, no matter the difficulties, no matter the danger. Yes, even this. This is the price I have to pay. What an expensive love I have purchased today. My mother would not approve. Very impractical, this. Why love someone who would destroy your life?

He screamed at the stupid bastards who would never understand.

And then he plunged off the side of his boat, dove into the sea, swam for the bottom.

There was no bottom.

It just got darker and darker, colder and colder.

But he kept swimming.

***

He dove at the instant her boat smashed into his. She jumped from her craft into his, held on for a moment, until she could get her footing, then she hung over the edge and peered into the sea. She saw a dim shadow moving far beneath the surface.

She stripped off her clothes, kicked off her shoes, then, clad only in panties and bra, she dove in after him.

Thirty seconds later, the Harbor Patrol arrived. They had

watched two people go overboard. No one had come up. "Get a diver over immediately!" said the Captain.

In the distance, the Statue of Liberty gazed out to sea, oblivious to them all.

***

Back at the mall, Maurice Sully returned to his apartment to help Sarah start packing. When he discovered that she was not there, he got on the phone to security and asked them to locate her. He was informed that she had left the mall. "Do you know where she went?" he asked.

"She got into a cab and drove off."

Maurice hung up the phone and sat quietly, his eyes closed. What did Sarah know that he didn't? Where Alan was going. She was chasing him. To where?

He didn't know. Or did he?

One of Maurice's favorite mental techniques to use in situations like this was to tell himself, "Well, if I did know, what would the answer be?" This is where having a powerful subconscious was a great gift. He was still working on the problem, he didn't have all the facts, but this was a situation that demanded immediate action. So he had to think and decide quickly: where is Alan going? Because that is where Sarah would be. And that is where he had to be right now.

If his theory about Alan was correct, his life was in danger. But not by any conventional means. He was being blackmailed: kidnap Sarah and bring her back to America, or you die. Maurice knew what he would do in a situation like that. He felt confident that Alan would do the same: leave Sarah in freedom and die to protect her.

So if Alan was leaving, it was either to meet his blackmailers — or to keep Sarah out of danger.

If any Americans had followed Alan to California to kill him, the military would know about it and would have dealt with them. So there could be no meeting with blackmailers.

Which meant that Alan's "meeting" was simply an excuse to get himself away from Sarah to protect her.

Sarah was in great danger right now.

But from what?

He picked up the phone and had himself connected to General McKnight. "General, if I wanted to kill someone remotely, at a specific time, what is the most effective, efficient, and untraceable way to do it?"

"That's classified, son. And not the sort of thing I'd like to discuss with a Mall Master."

"Very well. This 'classified' method: do the Americans have access to it, or have they recently gained access to it?"

McKnight paused.

The pause was long enough to confirm Maurice's suspicion. "General, whatever that 'classified' method is, I believe that is what the American's have used against Alan Benton. Whatever it is, it is going to happen today at noon." Maurice looked at his watch. On the other end of the line, he heard McKnight say, "Son-of-a-bitch."

"General, Sarah Fletcher has left the mall. She knows where Alan is heading. If you can't save Alan, at least save her."

"You don't know where he's going?"

"I haven't figured it out yet."

"When you do, give me a call." McKnight clicked off.

Maurice got back on the phone with security, found out which exit Sarah had used when she left the mall.

The mall had four different entrances and exits. One facing north, to the hills. One facing east, to the center of the city. One facing west, to the most luxurious residential neighborhoods. And one facing south, to the ocean and the bay.

Sarah had left using the south entrance.

Maurice didn't even have to use his subconscious. That was enough information to make the necessary leap. Just fill in the blank.

He got on the phone to McKnight, told what he suspected, then hung up.

McKnight had men in motion in machines in the air. They could be there in seconds. The Harbor Patrol was already there and could be alerted to the situation immediately.

Maurice looked at his watch. It was too late for him. He wasn't going to make it. It was out of his hands. Whatever was going to happen to Alan, was going to happen in just a few minutes.

And wherever Sarah was — Maurice couldn't stop her, couldn't bring her back, couldn't tell her what he knew.

I should have warned her, he thought.

But it would have been useless. She would have acted the same, even knowing what he knew.

So he relaxed a moment, took a deep breath, stared at his watch, looked at the seconds ticking by.

Just let it happen. Then I'll act, he thought.

As soon as his watch said twelve noon, he was in motion.

***

She swam down into the chill darkness, her eyes open, but just as well closed, it was getting so dim. She saw shadows. She felt nothing. She had followed his line. He had been moving straight down, and so was she, following a shadow darker than all the rest. Her eyes stung from the sea water. She couldn't go any further, and she needed to suck in a breath. But the air she had in her lungs was all she was going to get. It would have to do. If that was her last breath, than this is what it would be spent on. And even though she couldn't swim down any deeper, her arms kept moving, her legs kept kicking, and her head still pointed down, towards the ocean floor.

Then she collided with something. Instead of pulling back, she grabbed out. It could have been a shark or an octopus or some other disgusting squishy sea creature that would kill her and eat her. Didn't matter. She had to hold it. Her hands closed around body parts. Felt familiar. She held on, pulled it close, saw through the murk that it was Alan. He was limp, his eyes were open, he was staring at her with utter despair and terror. She had never seen such a look on a man's face before. As she watched, he exhaled his last breath and a cascade of air bubbles went flowing away to the surface. Horrified, she held him tight and reversed direction, pulled him up with her, heading for the surface. He made no protest, didn't move. Was he conscious? Possibly not, though she thought she saw some recognition in his eyes. If he was conscious, why didn't he try to swim with her? Think about that later. Now, just move, swim, get back to air, get back to breathing and land, and bring Alan with, get him out of this wet world.

The trip down had been hard. But the trip up was just like floating, only a guided float, an acceleration up. On the way up, she saw a series of criss-crossing light beams scintillate through the water. And with the beams came divers in full scuba gear. Two came from one side and grabbed her, pulled her away from Alan. Two more had Alan and pulled in the opposite direction. She tried to scream in protest under the water, sent off a shout of bubbles flowing angrily to the surface. She watched Alan drift away as she reached the surface. Then she didn't care about anything except getting air into her lungs.

***

Maurice met General McKnight on the roof of the mall as a military helicopter landed to pick up the General. There wasn't room for Maurice, but the General squeezed him in anyway.

They headed in a straight line for the Statue of Liberty.

***

After they pumped the water out of his lungs and stomach and got him breathing again, the first words out of Alan's mouth were, "What time is it?"

"Five after."

"Five after what?"

"Noon."

"You're clock is wrong," said Alan.

"Oh yeah?"

"Hell yeah."

The medic picked up Alan's limp wrist and looked at his watch. "Yours is still working. It says the same thing."

"Aw hell," said Alan. He held his head in his hands. "Aw hell."

Alan was at one end of the rescue boat, Sarah at the other. Sarah recovered from her dangerous swim quickly and was up on her feet while they were still working on Alan. She walked to the rear of the boat, looked down at Alan, saw that he was breathing and that his eyes were open. She fell down beside him and put her head on his chest. But very lightly. Just enough to feel his chest rising and falling with each breath he took. He didn't seem to realize who she was or what she was doing at first. But he finally noticed her. "Nurse, what are you doing?" he asked.

"I'm not your nurse," she said.

He finally focused his eyes on her. "Oh my God," he said.

"What were you doing down there?" she asked him.

"Trying to save your life, darling."

"You have saved it."

"Well, as long as you're here, give me a hug."

She hugged him.

He held her so tight, she thought she was going to stop breathing again.

"I'm not letting go," he said.

"No, darling, don't let go."

"By the way, what time does your watch say?"

She snuck a peek at her wristwatch. "Ten after noon."

"Ah, well, what the hell," he said.

The seconds and minutes just kept on ticking by, ignoring the two young lovers lying wet together on the deck of the rescue boat.

***

At midnight, Maurice stood alone at the north entrance to the Apollo Mall, waiting for a car that would take him north, out of the city, into the valley beyond the hills, and then out into the desert, and then on, away and away, to the mountains, and his hometown in Montana. Driving seemed the right thing to do. He was going to have to think a lot, feel a lot, process a lot.

Outside, the city was a cold dark green sprinkled with flashes of diamond light sparkling in the air. It was quiet and there were no people on this side of the mall. There wasn't even a security guard to be seen. Just Maurice standing with his back to the mall. It was a mall he would never see again, so he wasn't even going to look back. Just get in the car when it came and then head for home. There was a mall waiting to be built when he got home. The folks back there didn't know it, but it was going to happen. Maurice Sully was a Mall Master, and he was going to build them a mall. His mall. His kind of mall. What exactly would that be? Wait and find out. He had the plan in his mind. That is what he had to think about now. That is how he would heal his broken heart.

He thought back to the words he had spoken to Sarah when he had urged her to choose who she really wanted, and not to spare his feelings. Brave words from an innocent young man. And now he had to live with them, live the reality of them, every day for the rest of his life. Because he didn't have Sarah, he would never have Sarah.

He heard footsteps behind him. He didn't turn, even though he was curious to see who had come. Some lost shopper finally finding his way out of the mall at this late hour?

No.

It was Ann Thurston.

"Hi boss," she said.

"Hello Ann," said Maurice.

"Congratulations on your graduation."

"Thank you."

"What did Pavoc have to say?"

"'Get out.'"

"Well, he is a bit old fashioned."

"Yes."

"What happened with Alan?"

"They did a brain scan. He's got a bomb in his head, but it didn't go off. Incompetent Americans screwed it up, as usual. But they're afraid to take the thing out, don't want to tamper with it, might set it off. So they're just going to leave it. Alan has to wander around the rest of his life wondering if the next instant might be his last."

"He'll be okay."

"You think so?"

"Yeah. Sarah will be good for him."

"True."

"Maurice, do you know why the bomb didn't go off?"

"Why?"

"You stopped it."

"How did I do that?"

"You refused to sacrifice Alan. You let him be happy with Sarah, and you took away all his guilt. That is what saved Alan. Simple brain chemistry. You know that certain emotional states produce chemical reactions in the brain. Alan's emotions produced a chemical reaction that shut down the bomb. And with Sarah by his side, that bomb will stay dead. So don't worry about Alan. He'll be fine."

"You're serious, aren't you?"

"Of course I am. And I'll tell you even more. If the Americans captured you and stuck one of those bombs in your brain, it wouldn't explode either. Your body would turn it off. Your subconscious would know what it was, know how to do it, and the thing would be killed. You could do it because you're a completely integrated man, reason and emotion working in perfect harmony, conscious and sub-conscious in perfect sync."

"How do you know all this?"

"Because I'm a woman."

"Remind me to marry you someday."

Ann smiled with girlish delight. "When I graduate. When they kick me out."

"Hell of a system. Are they always so cold-blooded and brutal about it?"

"Of course they are. You know as much about it as I do."

"Yes, I do, don't I. And to think I'll have to do the same someday, when I have trained young apprentices into Mall Masters."

"You'll be good at it. You'll be the best, Maurice."

His car arrived. The attendant parked it, then got out, left the driver's door open for Maurice, came forward and loaded Maurice's suitcase into the trunk. Then he collected a tip, bowed, and disappeared.

Maurice turned to Ann, took her in his arms, gently kissed her on the lips. "Good logic to you, Ann."

"Good logic to you, Mall Master Sully. Have you decided on a name for your new mall?"

"West Park Plaza."

"I like the sound of that."

"What about your mall?"

"Oh, I've got a ways to go before old Pavoc kicks me out."

"I know you will become beautifully rich."

"Yes. We will all be gorgeously rich, that is a certainty!"

"And Ann, about Alan and Sarah—"

"Yes?"

"I don't need to hear about them. So — no news, please."

"As you wish."

"Give the others my best."

"I will."

He got in the car and drove away from the Apollo Mall. He drove up through the hills, then out into the desert, across the desert and into the mountains, then all the way home. In the end, there was snow on the ground and he thought it was beautiful.

INTERLUDE

LAYVANWICK SPEAKS:

It was late at night by the time I finished my tale. Deep into the evening, cold and dark, with a wind kicking up outside, brushing the tree branches against the walls and windows of the house. Diane sat in a big easy chair in the corner, her legs pulled up tight to her chest, her eyes closed, her face a relaxed mask of meditative reflection.

I tossed a pillow to one end of my couch, sprawled out, relaxed, eyes to the ceiling, ready for sleep if it came to take me; or ready for Diane, if she sought my arms.

But she stayed in her chair.

"So now you know," I said.

"Yes."

"Now you know who Maurice Sully is."

"Do I?"

"You know more than most ever will."

"Can Maurice tell similar tales about you?"

"Yes. But you'd rather hear them from me, I'm sure."

"Another day."

"Are you spending the night, darling?"

She smiled. "I want to go home, be alone, reflect on what you've told me."

"Very well."

She rose, got her jacket, then came and kissed me on the forehead. "Good night, darling. Until next time."

"Yes."

And she left me sitting alone on my couch, and went out into the cold windy night, and found her way home to be alone with her private thoughts of my best friend, Maurice Sully, Mall Master, whom I had just given to her.

Because I knew it was what she wanted.

And probably what Maurice wanted, as well.

***

The next day I had lunch with Maurice. I left word with his secretary early in the morning that I wished to lunch with him and asked for a confirming response; I got one mid-morning, and when lunch time arrived, I made my way to our designated favorite, a sidewalk cafe at the eastern end of the mall, to Maurice's reserved table on the upstairs balcony over-looking the eastern entrance. People flowed past beneath us as we sat eating and talking.

"Maurice, I've been wondering."

"Oh?"

"You've never taken apprentices at this mall. Why is that?"

He looked at me in his wide-eyed manner of complete attentiveness. "Do you wish to become an apprentice?"

"No."

"Do you know someone who does?"

"I might."

He raised an eyebrow. "I see."

"You've been here ten years. No urge to teach?"

"Have I taught you anything?"

"Of course."

"I only teach those I love."

"I'm flattered."

"You should be. Anyone who wishes to apprentice under me must be willing to become my lover."

"Does that include me?"

"I love you in the manner proper to men. Is there someone else you had in mind?"

"Yes."

"Let me guess: Diane Copernicus?"

"Correct."

"Has she expressed an interest in apprenticing?"

"No. But I know her well, and I think she will express an interest very soon. Either to me — or perhaps directly to you. She is a bold girl."

"How much have you told her about me?"

"Everything essential."

"I see. Tell me Anton, do you think we two are capable of sharing a woman?"

"Under certain circumstances."

"Let's not discuss hypotheticals. The real case is this: if Diane Copernicus wishes to apprentice with me, she must agree to become my lover. If you wish to apprentice with her, the best course of action will be for us all to be married so that you and I can be co-husbands. Those are my terms. If you are in love with Diane and wish sexual exclusivity, this could be a painful situation for you. So you must know your mind before making a decision. And make sure Diane understands as well."

"I love you enough Maurice that I think I could share a woman with you. But I have never been in this situation before, so perhaps I really don't know my own feelings."

"You must learn your feelings before we act, otherwise it will be too late. So here is what I suggest: if Diane wishes to seek an apprenticeship, she will come to me alone and spend the night and I will initiate her in the customary fashion. Then I will send her back to you to report on her progress — in graphic detail. She will invite you to spend an evening with us in what we will call a 'pre-initiation ceremony.' When we are all three together, I will outline the structures of your apprenticeships, — and then you will know for certain if this is the right thing for you. Not to mention, Miss Copernicus will have the chance to choose between us if we are not to be co-husbands."

"I know how she will choose. Her desire to be a Mall Master is great."

"So be it. Very well, does this sound logical to you?"

"Impeccably."

"Now answer me a question: you've been managing the grocery store for ten years. Why do you still refer to yourself as a boxboy?"

"My customers feel comfortable relating to me in that way. And I think the idea of a boxboy as artist appeals to their sense of esthetics."

"And does it appeal to yours?"

"You know it does!"

"If you become an apprentice, will it be to run a mall, or to benefit your grocery?"

"I love the grocery business. I'm in a position to have my own store soon. I only need one last investor. Then I can build my new store. I have ideas. I will operate the most exciting and original grocery business in history."

"I would like to hear your ideas. But tell me — why haven't I heard about your plans for a grocery?"

"You're my last investor. If you sign on, the deal is done. But I have to explain some things to you first."

"So as usual, you will be teaching me even as I teach you."

"Exactly."

"We trade well together, don't you think?"

"That is why we love each other." I offered a toast. Our glasses chimed and we drank together, to the past, to the present — but most of all, to the future!

BOOK TWO

THE

PURPOSE OF

DIANE

COPERNICUS

CHAPTER SEVEN

DIANE COPERNICUS
BARES HER NAKED PAGAN SOUL

I never believed in miracles until I saw the fat man fly.

When I was a little girl I decided that someday I would marry a Mall Master.

In my early teens, I amended that decision: why not just become a Mall Master myself?

I was a slow child. I didn't reach the conceptual level of consciousness until the age of eleven. Yes, I know: that is a perfectly normal age to become conceptual. But my family had high standards, and higher expectations. Most of my siblings showed signs of conceptual level functioning at the ages of nine or ten. But it didn't happen for me until eleven. I remember the day, the hour — and the event that triggered my mind and pulled me up to the adult level of thinking. I remember my first wide-scale integration, and the sensations of power and control it gave to me.

I will tell you the story.

You want to know the meaning of my strange first sentence? My story will tell you the meaning.

***

I grew up in the city of Denver. When I was eleven years old, my parents took me and the rest of my siblings to the Mile High Mall to witness and participate in the Festival of Youth. On the first day I joined a crowd of children around the center court of the mall. We were to be welcomed by the resident Mall Master, a man named Klaus Santemeyer.

Klaus was the happiest man I'd ever seen. He was short and fat and wore loose-fitting robes of bright red trimmed in white. The white trim matched his beard and hair, which was a fuzzy bright white. He looked like a furry red ball rolling down the floor of the mall the first time I saw him. He came bouncing through a crowd of children, laughing and smiling at us all, greeting us with bombastic laughter, like a clown without paint — except that he was no buffoon — he was a Mall Master. At that age, we knew this commanded respect, but nothing more. We had no idea what kind of issues the man dealt with, or what special competencies he possessed. We only knew that he was laughing and happy and seemed glad to see us.

He climbed up on an octagonal stage and beckoned us to crowd around. Then he proceeded to do something that I have never heard of another Mall Master ever doing: he put on a magic show.

He performed all variety of magic tricks. He made bright balls appear out of nowhere, juggled them for us, then made them vanish one by one, until he had only one left. This he turned into a bright yellow handkerchief. From beneath this, he produced a bird, which flew out across the heads of us children, then swooped in a low circle around the stage, finally returned to the Mall Master's hand, chirped briefly in a sweet bird farewell, then was transformed into an egg. The Mall Master passed the egg down into the audience and told a child to break it open. This the child did. Inside the egg was a yellow handkerchief. "Keep it, it's yours," said the Mall Master. The child, a young boy, promptly tied the handkerchief around his neck.

I watched, both amazed and confused. I had been taught that magic was false, a lie, that it did not exist, and that those who claimed supernatural powers were to be treated as lunatics and ignored. A Mall Master was the human embodiment of the highest standards of reason and logic; his commitment to reality must remain unblemished, otherwise he would be forced to resign.

But here was a Mall Master doing magic tricks for the children.

On the way to the mall that day, I had asked my father, "What am I to see today?" He had told me, "An exercise in logic. A test of your skills of induction, deduction, and the holding of context."

"I have no skills in these disciplines, father," I told him. "My class has just begun the study of these subjects."

"The most important tests come from reality, daughter. You watch, and think hard. We'll discuss it later."

"Very well."

As the Mall Master continued his show, I watched, serious and stone-faced. Around me, all the other children laughed and cheered, gasped as more miracles flowed from the hands of the jiggling little man in red.

I was near the front row, close to the stage. Perhaps he saw me because my white face stood out against my black hair. My mother had made me up that morning; my first serious application of make-up. I was an elegant little lady with huge dark eyes and scarlet lips. Perhaps he saw me because I was the only one not laughing and smiling.

But the Mall Master did see me. He came to the edge of the stage, bent down on one knee, pointed at me, motioned me forward. For the first time, I noticed how loud the other children around me were. I heard them as they parted at the command of the Mall Master and he motioned me forward. I did not want to go. But then he smiled and laughed and I saw the bright light of a majestic gayety in his eyes, and I stepped forward, not fearing him, but still serious, giving no hint of a smile.

He took my hand at the edge of the stage. "Why do you not smile and laugh, young lady?"

"Magic does not exist, and those who claim supernatural powers are bad!"

"But I have not, and do not, claim to have supernatural powers. I have merely performed tricks for the amusement of these children. Now why do you suppose I have done that?"

"I do not know."

"Why, to welcome them to my Mall! The Mall is a place of miracles! This is where your dreams can come true!"

"I do not dream of miracles. I dream of what is real."

"Then my lesson to you, young lady, is this: what is real is not only that which exists; but also that which can exist through your mind, your power, your creativity. What do you want to be when you grow up?"

"A Mall Master."

"Bravo!"

And with that, he stood up and moved back to the center of his stage, raised his hands above his head, and shouted, *Welcome to the Mile High Mall!"*

And then he rose up into the air, levitated right in front of my eyes, flew around above us, laughing and bouncing in the air like a big red balloon floating above us.

My jaw dropped.

The children around me cheered and screamed. They thought it was marvelous and could not contain themselves.

I did not laugh. I did not smile. My face remained cold calm stone.

I was not angry, nor upset. Merely curious and puzzled.

The other children ignored me. They pressed forward to the stage, and I was shoved back, jostled away from the stage. My eyes were raised, I did not take them off the Mall Master as he flew high above us, floating up and up, into the high reaches of the mall. He was parallel to the fourth level and adults gathered at the railings and balconies were laughing and cheering and tossing confetti at him. It rained down on the stage. And I suddenly had a thought.

I would test this Mall Master. I would challenge his magic and see if it was real. I would learn the truth. I would learn this lesson.

I shoved my way forward back to the stage, made it, then climbed up and stood in the center, looking up at the flying Mall Master, pointing my right arm to him, and raising my eleven year old voice as loud as I could. *"I want to fly!"* I screamed, as the confetti floated down around me, lacing my hair with strands of bright color. *"Let me fly with you!"*

I heard him laugh and watched him slowly circle down to me. He did not even touch the stage when he finally lifted me into the air. He just swooped in and scooped me up and away, flew up into the high rafters of the mall.

I did not know then how he did it. I do not know to this day how he did it. I only know that it was the most thrilling sensation of my life, to fly with him, to rise up into the mall, to feel the wind in my face, to feel weightless and unafraid.

For the first time that day, I smiled. I smiled and I laughed and I screamed with glee.

He took me up to the fifth level and deposited me onto a balcony, into the eager arms of laughing adults, who stood me again on firm ground and sent me on my way. I left the balcony, ran along the railings, following the Mall Master as he rose higher and higher, all the way to the top of the mall, eight levels up. I watched him as he disappeared into a hatch in the ceiling.

I watched for a while, wondering if he would reappear, but he never did. The show was over. The lesson was over.

I made my way to an elevator and rejoined my family on the ground floor. We made a day of it in the mall. We did some shopping, saw some shows, had dinner and dessert, played games in the arcades. I was in a daze the whole time. My consciousness had been altered. I could not tell if for good or ill. Was I stupid now, or had my mind been expanded? I was too numb to tell. It would take time.

On the ride home I was silent. My father tried to talk to me, asking me questions about the meaning of what I had seen. But I did not wish to answer him at that time. I had nothing to say. I told him that.

"If you *did* have something to say, what would it be?" he asked me.

Without realizing what an odd question that was, I immediately answered back. "Magic is fun, and a fine puzzle for the mind."

"Which part do you like best — the fun, or the puzzle?"

"The flying!" I answered.

"Have you thought about why watching magic can be an exercise in logic?"

I thought about my introductory courses in logic. "Logic is the method of proving the existence of that which is not directly seen. The Mall Master's magic gave the appearance of violating causality. But logic tells me this is only an appearance."

"How do you think he does it?"

"Obviously, he has at his disposal technology and methods that I am unfamiliar with."

"So you don't think he can really violate laws of nature?"

"No, certainly not!"

"How do you know that?"

"Well, I'd say it's simply a matter of princ—"

I stopped and stared out the window at the city of Denver flowing past. But nothing I saw registered. I was back at the mall, flying with the Mall Master, understanding in a brief violent flash what it meant to be a Mall Master, why the mall was the center of existence, and why my future would be there.

And what a principle was.

I had named my conviction with precise words. My idea was based on observation of reality. And as I introspected further, followed the structure of my own thoughts, observed in retrospect the order in which information and conclusions had entered my mind, I glimpsed my first understanding of what a principle was, and how a principle can be used. And most importantly, I now had my first experience and first honest, self-known understanding of a word I had heard my parents and teachers use, but which had — until now — held little firm meaning or reality for me. That word was: integration. Now I understood. I had reached a new method of thought, a new level of consciousness. I felt warm, secure, and powerful. When I finally let the sights register on my mind, I saw the city pass by with a new, special kind of focus. Everything meant something, and everything was connected to everything else. It was a fun challenge to figure out how!

My dad didn't press me, the darling. My mom was silent as well. They let me meditate and introspect on what had happened — both inside the mall — and inside me.

***

Have you ever noticed that children develop avid interests — and sometimes abilities — in the various arts at exactly the same time their conceptual capacity is blooming? It was this way with me. In the year leading up to my conceptual flowering, and in the years after, I delved intensely into all the major arts: drawing, painting, music, sculpture, writing. I explored them all, became adept at several. I've always thought this phenomenon of childhood to be a clue to the nature of art. If the philosophers are right, and art is the means of bringing our most abstract concepts down to earth in physical form, then is a child's youthful obsession with art his own quest to explore and control his newly discovered conceptual ability?

And more: turning abstractions into concretes, and vice versa, is merely the epistemological angle on this question. There is a metaphysical question as well. The artistic impulse is primarily metaphysical: the urge to grab reality by the throat and mold it consciously into a form that reflects your values, your image, your life. It has been said that the artists create their own universes. So they do. Novelists, painters, sculptors, composers — they all re-create reality in their own image. And for the child just reaching the conceptual level, art is a first taste of metaphysical power. At a time when he is still dependent on his parents, a child can explore a crucial kind of power to move through reality, to understand it, create it, control it. For most, this is a child's first taste of significant independence, and the beginning of his birth as a distinct individual.

Mall Masters are the ultimate artists.

The mall is a stylized universe created by Man. A world into which men enter a new kind of existence, something different from that beyond the doors of the Mall. It is a place of wealth, beauty, splendor, manners, ritual, exaltation, worship, and sacred production and trade. It is a place where logic reigns, where logic rides a wild horse called passion, where logic rules in a beautiful integration of thought and emotion, of science in the service of human life, of philosophy in the service of human joy, of business in the service of human ecstacy. The mall is a place where people come to find themselves, create themselves, meet themselves. The mall is an abstract concept in concrete form. Do you know what concept I mean? You are a child. You should think about it. I'll ask you again later.

But I will answer one question for you now: did I know all this before I served as apprentice to Mall Master Sully? Yes I did. This is just the basics, just the essentials.

What I learned from Maurice Sully was more, so very much more.

You think it is easy to be a Mall Master, and that anyone can do it?

No. Not even in our exalted culture is this true. The Mall Masters are the rarest of the rare.

And if you dare to love one, good logic is the least of the weapons you'll need to survive.

***

Although I am a pagan slut as my mother taught me, I did have my share of sexual problems growing up.

I understand that over in America, to call a woman a slut is a grave insult. It means she does not value herself and will give her sex away to any low man who asks.

Here in California, the term is used a little differently.

Here, the meaning is closer to "worthy of sexual attention." Here, the term has a connotation of self-worth. To be a slut is to be a woman who knows her value and displays it not because she wishes to invite every man to her bed; but because she wishes to be known to those few heroes who have the soul and character to earn the right of passage into her arms.

I learned to be a woman from my mother. From my father and brothers, I learned about men. And by myself, I learned of my own sexual power and value. Like everyone, I was taught that romantic love is the highest expression of reason and logic — and that sex is the means of integrating the spiritual and the physical. And like many young people, I went to orgies to see if I could test the theory and find out if it is true. And also to avoid the social death of being known as a filthy virgin.

But I suspect that the orgy custom they encourage for youth has an ulterior motive. And we don't know of it until we are much older — most of us — and we really fall in love for the first time. I don't mean fake love, puppy love, and what one of my teachers called "falling in love with the *idea* of being in love." I mean real, true love of the most serious and adult type. Life and death love.

The ulterior motive is this: the orgies are just to occupy teenagers with sex until they are really ready for love. And to make sure that they know the difference between sex and love. And, I think, to get them burned out on sex, so that when they are ready for love, that is actually what they find, not sex.

What a tragedy it is that some people never learn the difference. Because you have to do that before you can unite the two, integrate them into the spiritual glory of romantic love.

All of the important lessons in life are learned the hard way.

The orgy custom is simply a way of making a hard way easy.

But of course, you cannot attend orgies until you have taken the Oath of Womanhood and been initiated.

I was initiated at the age of fourteen. My ceremony was a quandary for me because I couldn't decide if I wanted to actually submit to a real sex act, and dispense with my virginity immediately — or do so merely symbolically and just go through the motions of ritual sex. This is what the gutter-mouthed young boys refer to as "screwing the ghost." It is not an act which garners one high marks for character. My mother, and all my sisters, had all been initiated in the proper physical fashion. None of them had said a word to me. But I knew what was expected.

My problem was: if I was to be initiated, I wanted it to be by a Mall Master — or an apprentice. But I was not personally acquainted with either. And I was not about to let a stranger initiate me. So my best option was to ask a Mall Master to perform a ritual initiation. But this would have been an insult to my father. Normally, if a girl wishes to relinquish her virginity merely on the spiritual level, it is her father who performs the ritual. If I was to deny my father this honor, no telling how I would hurt him. Not to mention the rest of my family.

Teenagers are initiated between the ages of twelve and sixteen, normally in conjunction with a birthday, and almost always at the request of the child. Parents are silent on the subject until the child comes to them and requests an initiation ceremony on a certain date. Then they comply happily, glad to push their child forward into adulthood. The only exception to this is if the child reaches the age of sixteen without having asked for initiation. If this occurs, parents will, in effect, push their children out of the nest, as the birds do. "It's time to fly, little one!" Shove. And then it's now or never.

That is a situation I wanted to avoid. When it comes to sex, it is always best to be in control, know what you want, and make your own choices.

So after announcing three months prior to my fourteenth birthday that I wished to be initiated, I became a fixture at the nearest mall, hoping to befriend an apprentice and establish a relationship that could develop into an initiation ceremony.

Meeting a Mall Master is difficult. Unless you are a merchant within the mall, an apprentice, or someone taking part in a ritual or ceremony within the mall, the Mall Master is not going to see you. And the apprentices are so busy and so immersed in the intense training they receive, the odds there are not much better. You would think healthy young men with boiling testicles would jump at the chance to initiate all the young women who yearned for them. But it is not so. Those studying for their calling to the Mall approach sex with artistic idealism. Everything, especially love, must be integrated into the universe of the Mall. This is actually a principle the Mall Masters follow. I did not understand this completely until I became intimate with Mall Master Sully.

That year in the mall, as I prepared for my initiation ceremony, I learned two difficult lessons.

First: that I was not original. I was not the only one. After one week in the mall, I noticed all the other lonely, wide-eyed, slightly frightened young girls ghosting around trying to bump into apprentices and Mall Masters. And I noticed what contempt the merchants had for these girls. It was bad enough that they were virgins. But to be virgins who begged was disgusting to those within the mall. And that is what these girls were like: beggars. Not the ragged, filthy type we had heard about in America. No, these were clean, well-groomed, beautiful young girls innocent of the fact that they were spiritually dirty, that they were showing a massive lack of self-esteem and self-confidence.

On the day I realized there were other young women prowling the mall with me, I went into a rest room and stood in front of a mirror and looked at myself. I did not like what I saw. My hair was fine, my face was flawless, my clothes were the latest style. But my eyes were screaming with ignorant, youthful desperation.

I left the mall and did not go back. It was a spiritual defeat for me. And what made it worse was the second lesson that I learned: how far above us the Mall Masters really were. I had not comprehended this completely until that moment. I think very few really do know this, even those who admire the Mall Masters intensely. But now I knew. Until you approach that universe and try to gain entrance, you have no idea what is involved, and what quality of mind and soul it requires to excel in that world.

So I was humbled. And when the time came for my initiation ceremony, I screwed the ghost.

It was almost not a ceremony for me. When I took the Oath of Womanhood from my mother, I could see the dark disappointment in her eyes. I was the first of her daughters not to consummate my womanhood with a loving male friend. My father took it better than my mother, but not by much. Afterwards, the celebration at home was muted and restrained. My brothers didn't speak to me. But my sisters were kind and supportive.

However, in the weeks and months following my initiation

ceremony, it was like my family abandoned me. I was suddenly the black sheep of our clan.

Again I was unoriginal. Most young women in my situation take off on their own, leave town, start over somewhere else. And that is exactly what I did.

I could have gone to the coast, to one of the great cities, New Athens, or Atlantis. But I was intimidated by those places, especially after my experience at the local mall. Those cities were for those at the top who never made mistakes and were certain of success. I didn't feel that confident.

So I headed in the opposite direction.

I looked at a map one day and saw the state of Montana, up near the Canadian border. I noted the towns and cities named on that map. None of them were very big. Montana was the least populous state in the country. There was no city of more than 100,000. That is what I wanted. That is what was right for me. A small town. A provincial arena. Coming from Denver, I would probably seem sophisticated to all those hillbilly barbarians.

I put my finger on the city of Billings. Yes. Right there. That is where I'd go. What a perfectly drab name for a town. What a boring, dull place that would be. Probably didn't even have a mall. Even if it did, whoever ran it would be of no significance. An amateur Mall Master. A pretender, an incompetent, a buffoon.

Why had I decided on Billings? Even then, my subconscious seemed to tingle slightly, as if it was trying to send me a message, but I was too weak to hear it — and my subconscious was too undeveloped to make the message unmistakable. But I do believe now that somewhere deep inside, I knew. I knew what was waiting for me there, and who was waiting for me. I held knowledge of which I was unaware. And this was a good thing. Because I really think if I would have known what was waiting for me — I would not have gone.

***

It was this mall that healed me, brought back my self-esteem, my confidence, my love of life, my expectations for myself.

West Park Plaza was by far the most beautiful mall I had ever seen.

This shocked me, really angered me at first. How could such a place exist in this tiny backwater burg? How could they let such a place be built anywhere other than New Athens? And why had we never heard of it?

Because in Denver, we didn't listen.

But now I was here, and this mall spoke to me.

The first time I saw it, I was not impressed.

It was only two storys high. From the street, it was just a pedestrian sprawl of unimaginatively linked rectangles surrounded by two huge parking lots. From the main entrance off Grand Avenue, facing north, you saw the low-lying mall framed by trees rising up to the Rimrocks; then the sandstone cliffs of the Rimrocks rising up to the blue sky, which arched over the mall like a blue canopy. It was as if the mall itself was a prairie at the base of mountains. Although it did seem to have a simple elegance, I just thought it too tame in presentation, not flashy and sophisticated enough. The great malls in the great cities are all visual marvels that make a statement immediately. You can't take your eyes off them. But this mall seemed to have no pretensions, and no personality.

This pleased me. It was exactly what I had hoped for. And so, I was unprepared for the actual, living, working mall — the interior.

The designer of this mall had applied all his creativity to the interior.

Inside was a marvel of beauty and design.

From the outside, the mall seemed small. But once inside, space seemed to expand, and the interior gave the impression of having somehow been doubled. There was space everywhere, all of it scaled to the human form, framing human bodies in motion, and leading the eye and the feet in directions intersecting merchant space.

The ceilings were unusually low for a mall. This helped to generate an atmosphere of close intimacy as one moved through a wing to the center court. There, the walls flared up like open flower petals into a bloom of light and space that brought sunshine down from the sky. The light that entered through the ceiling skylights over center court was a muted, soft, intimate light that gave a sense of being outdoors on a mild cloudy day. It was the kind of light that made the neon signs seem to glow with a sweet intensity that could evoke strange feelings of child-like wonder and expectation. And being held within this light at center court, and seeing the various wings of the mall branch off away, one glanced down those wide corridors with a growing urge to exploration and discovery. Even if one worked in the mall, as I eventually did, and knew each shop by heart, had browsed and shopped and hunted for treasures many times, one still had the certainty that there was much unknown still waiting for your eyes.

Most of the mall was on the first level. However, the northern and eastern wings featured sunken subterranean levels, as well as raised upper levels, giving these sections three levels for shops and attractions. Here again, the designer had used clever techniques to induce a child's sense of adventure and play to the discovery of his mall. To reach the north wing, one passed through the center court area, then approached what appeared to be a cliff. The cliff was actually a stairway leading to the lower level. On either side of the stairway, one saw the ground floor and second levels shooting away in a frame of violent color and activity. The ground floor level was set well back on both sides, with the lower and upper levels jutting out, so that the lower level's ceiling was a walkway for the ground level, and the ground level's ceiling was a walkway for the upper level.

If one stood at the top step of the stairway leading into the north wing and looked straight across to the far end, one had a sense of staring down a spacious, elongated tube of liquid light flowing like a stream away from you, and pulling, tugging, urging you along with it. At the far end, from the ceiling, a long slender stream of silver water poured out of the ceiling and fed a tiny stream that ran swiftly down the center of the floor, disappeared beneath the steps of the stairway. Even though the water was flowing towards you, the vision of that long thread of sparkling waterfall at the far end beckoned with a natural resonance that urged people to get close.

The lower level was just a short few steps down. If one wanted the ground level, one simply detoured past two sets of escalators. But if one wanted to reach the upper level, one rode those escalators up.

This north wing held the arcades, movie theaters, virtual reality chambers, and entertainment of all varieties. As such, it was a loud place, frothing over at the edges with energy and motion and color. It had the sense of some wild street in a foreign country, something intimidating and hard to understand, something moving away from you as you approached, something you would never touch or get close to. And even when you entered and experienced what was offered, you still had the feeling there was something important you missed.

The eastern wing was much different.

This was a quiet wing of shops dealing in clothing and personal necessities of all variety. There were stores catering to every physical need imaginable. Instead of a stairway cliff to the lower level, this one had a long gentle slope that you simply walked down. The upper levels were reached by a pair of stately white marble stairways that curved up from the ground level in a seashell swirl. Taking these steps usually induced the urge to dance or skip, regardless of what direction you were heading. Many people skipped up in defiance of gravity, as if the mall had made them weightless. On the way down, sometimes it was easier just to let gravity slide you down. If you wore the right kind of shoes, it was like skiing a gentle slope.

Facing east from the center court, one saw, at the far eastern end, framed by a dark royal purple background, a huge glowing white marble statue of Athena. Down this wing, one entered a perpetual dusk. There were no skylights in this wing. The ceiling was vaulted and low. The lighting was soft and intimate, comfortable and relaxing. All lines of sight led to Athena. She beckoned to follow the path through the mall. A stroll through this wing was like a quiet walk through an elegant museum — except this was a living museum, and all the art wanted you to buy it and take it home. There were actually several galleries in this wing specializing in sculpture and painting. The mall itself had been decorated with sculptures placed in the intervals between shops, and in other strategic spots where space was available and the eye was sure to wander. The colors here were all warm and soft, nothing dazzling or eye-popping. There was no neon; all of the shop signs here were various forms of sculpture. Some of it was back-lit, so it had a kind of gentle radiance.

In the north wing, shoppers were assaulted. In the east wing, they were seduced.

And there was more to the mall: the individual shops. Each shop was like a star held in the gravity of a great galaxy. The mall was a galaxy, spinning in a stately waltz through space. The shops spun alone, distinct and separate worlds held within the power of the mall. You could enter a shop and be swept away, completely forget where you were, lose track of time, then wander out finally back into the mall and be disoriented at discovering where you had come from. It happened to me, and still does. And I know well the look on people's faces after they have spent the day inside, touring shop after shop, spending passionately and being pampered by the merchants; then they come out back into the mall and have an odd, lost look on their faces, as if they are aliens and don't speak the language, don't recognize any landmarks.

And this is where the mall is truly a work of genius.

It brings them back. It always brings them back, helps them regain their focus, reestablish their context. How does it do this? I haven't figured it out, yet. That is for the Mall Master to teach me.

But I have experienced this effect in the most profound way possible. This mall literally brought me back to myself. When I came here, I was a spiritually injured young woman who wanted to find a mall I could hate so I could degrade myself in it. Instead, I found a mall I loved, and it brought me up, helped me to a new level of happiness.

Here in California, production and trade are sacred activities, and shopping is a form of worship. The relationships that develop between merchants and their customers becomes so intense that in many cases they become lovers. And when a shopper comes to make a special purchase, and is guided through the process by a loving merchant, the resulting experience can be so profoundly intense and emotional, that people are ushered in to another level of consciousness — a state of ecstacy in which reason and emotion are so integrated and intertwined that they are indistinguishable and inseparable from each other. In this state of mind, a powerful emotion gives rise instantly to a logical chain of syllogisms showing the source of that emotion; and every logical thought and identification results immediately in a powerful emotion, as thought and value are integrated into one and reinforced. Here, clear thoughts lead to deep emotions; deep emotions lead back to clear thoughts. Here, in this state of hyper-focus, one sees clearly the rational source of all one's most deeply felt emotions. And one experiences a bright flash of emotional electricity from every true thought one holds in one's head. To know this form of shopping is to know the ultimate power of integration in human life.

I never knew this kind of intense shopping at any other mall. Perhaps it was just because I was young and hadn't matured, hadn't grown spiritually enough to experience these kinds of emotions. I think that is part of the answer. But the other part is this mall, and the people who work here, and the people who shop here. There is something very special here. I know now what it is and how it works. But at first, I was clueless. And nobody told me. No one spoke of the Mall Master. None of the merchants spoke of how they had been trained. None of the customers spoke of the guiding spirit of this place. I think they were all beautifully selfish: they wanted to hold their joy within, totally private, shared with no one. Certainly not the snooty young girl from Denver with her haughty manners, her nose in the air, her shoulder burdened with a chip that rivaled the Rimrocks.

Well, I wasn't really that bad. But I was still learning too slowly to satisfy my own standards.

I am still amazed at how long it took me to think of the Mall Master.

For some reason, I just assumed that the person who ran this place was an old man, of no interest to me, of no personal significance, holding no special value. He was not someone I could ever become personally involved with, so what was the point? Why wonder about him, why worry about him, why go through all those painful little-girl games I had finished with in Denver? I was through with that. I didn't come here to worm my way into a Mall Master's arms. That was the silly dream of a silly little girl. I was here to grow up, to learn business, to establish myself in a trade I had a passion for, and maybe open my own shop, maybe even within the walls of this fine mall, but if not, somewhere else, downtown maybe, there was much to be said for the cosmopolitan aroma of a center city location; it wasn't the magical world of a mall, but it was still business. And maybe I would find a soul mate here. Perhaps I would meet a fine young man.

The mall didn't even have a picture of the presiding Mall Master hanging up anywhere. There was no notice saying who ran the place and where to find him. And I never asked. Didn't want to deal with it. Nobody talked about him. It was as if the place was run by a ghost. Or somebody who kept an unusually low profile.

And then I met Anton.

The western wing of the mall is just one short level connecting to the grocery store. My shop, the Pacific Orchid clothing store, was on this wing, about halfway down, close to the grocery. On slow days, I could step out into the mall briefly, glance to my left and see the great glass windows of the grocery blasting my eyes with precise arrangements of geometrically ordered color. I liked to watch the grocery. That place was a constant swirl of motion and color. The place vibrated with an energy other shops lacked.

It was my habit to shop in the grocery every day, usually after I got off work. I liked to buy groceries before going home because the grocery cheered me up. It was such a bright, clean, happy place. Everyone who worked there seemed to be very much in love. I was so impressed with the place, one day I asked one of the girls in produce who managed the store.

"Layvanwick."

"Who?"

"Anton Layvanwick, he's the manager."

"Have I seen him?"

"Look over there."

I looked across the store to the checkstands. A shopper had just rolled her cart of groceries into a scan stall. A flurry of red beams flowed into a holographic circle around the groceries, scanned every item in the cart, then the stall beeped loudly and released the cart through to the other side of the counter, where a finely muscled, dark-haired, sun-tanned young man began bagging the groceries. The woman customer examined her price print-out and then thump-printed her credit code into the checkstand. In the time it took the woman to get her receipt and walk through to the other side, this quick-handed boxboy had all her groceries bagged and carted and ready to roll. The woman kissed him briefly, then they held hands and walked together to the doors, the boxboy expertly steering the shopping cart with one hand while giving all his attention to the woman customer at his side. They disappeared out the doors.

I glanced back at the produce girl. She was working on her vegetables with a strange smile on her face. "That was the manager?" I asked.

"Yes. Layvanwick is the manager."

"I always thought he was just a boxboy."

"He is a boxboy. That is the way his customers love him."

"Is he a good boss to work for?"

"What kind of a dumb question is that?"

"Quite right. I was illogical. Never mind."

I continued shopping. I bought much more than I needed. And I timed my approach to the checkstand just to be sure it was Layvanwick who bagged my groceries and helped me out to my car.

I was so busy watching his beautiful hands fondle my groceries into bags that I didn't notice the checkstand beeping madly at me to take my receipt. Anton noticed the beeping before I did and he looked up. Our eyes met. We considered each other for a split second before he said, "Your receipt, dear lady."

"Oh yes. Thank you."

I took my receipt. Anton had my groceries ready and was waiting attentively. It is the customer's prerogative to kiss a clerk if she wishes her shopping experience to be that intimate. Usually, if she is satisfied with the service and quality of the merchandise, it is the proper thing to do. That evening, I waited too long. I did not kiss Anton. I merely nodded, and led him out to the parking lot. If he was unhappy, he didn't show it.

Outside, as we approached my car, I said, "I understand that you're the manager of this grocery."

"Yes ma'am, that's right."

"Why do you pretend to be a boxboy?"

"It is the best way for me to be intimate with my customers."

"Your store is very clean."

"Thank you."

"The produce department especially was very impressive."

"Thank you, I'm glad you're happy."

"You're very beautiful. You must get much female attention."

"I do."

"You'll excuse me if I don't kiss you tonight. Please don't take it as dissatisfaction with your service."

"Was this your first time in my store?"

"Oh no! I've shopped with you many times. I enjoy your store very much."

"I'm glad it has made you happy."

"Thank you for helping me out with my groceries."

"My pleasure."

"Good-bye!"

After that, I returned regularly. I kept my eye on Anton. I observed his habits, noted his schedule, asked discreet questions of store personnel, learned as much as I could about him. Which wasn't much. One thing I did learn was that he loved to spend time up on the roof after work, to relax and meditate on the sky, watch the city from his high perch.

So one night when I was closing Pacific Orchid, I left our roof access hatch open on purpose, hoping Anton would see it and come to investigate.

He did. He spied on me as I danced with a mannequin. That was how I learned that he was my kind of man.

After that, our relationship progressed very quickly.

***

Looking back, it seems highly unlikely that I would have missed meeting Maurice Sully as long as I did. But that is how it happened. Our schedules were out of sync. He always stopped in Pacific Orchid on my days off. My manager never mentioned the Mall Master to me, and I never asked. So it went. Until I met Anton. Maurice was Anton's best friend, so after becoming involved with Anton, learning about Maurice and then meeting him followed very shortly.

Our first meetings were professional, well-mannered, dignified. Nothing of consequence was said or done. We were merely introduced.

But then Anton told me the history of Maurice Sully, his start, his apprenticeship, his career. Coming from Anton's lips, it was like I was knowing Maurice directly, personally, in the flesh.

And on our first meeting after hearing the tale, Anton told me more.

"I have spoken with Mall Master Sully. I have hinted that it is your wish to apprentice with him."

"What did he say?"

"Are you serious about pursuing an apprenticeship?"

"Yes, you know I am."

"Maurice believes in full integration. He will only apprentice one who is willing to become his lover."

"I see."

"Do you?"

"Does this mean I have to choose between you and Maurice?"

"Not necessarily. Maurice has indicated that he believes the best course of action for us all is to become a family, with he and I co-husbands, and you our wife."

"But that is only possible if you wish to apprentice."

"Yes."

"And if you are willing to relinquish sexual exclusivity in regard to me."

"Yes."

"Are you willing?"

"I haven't decided."

"I see."

"Diane, I love you. But I also love Maurice. And I do wish to pursue an apprenticeship. So I must examine the logic of this situation, and establish a clear hierarchy of values. Right now, my values are: you; Maurice; apprenticeship. That is the wrong order for this to work."

"So you are telling me that if I pursue an apprenticeship with Maurice, it means possibly losing you."

"Yes, that is a possibility. However, there is a part of me that believes it would be good to share a woman with Maurice Sully. And the potential spiritual development possible through an apprenticeship makes the situation even more reasonable. So you see, it is all a question of what I want, and what I am willing to pay."

"Anton, I don't want you to have any illusions or misunderstandings about me. I want an apprenticeship. I want it more than anything, and I am willing to pay any price. If that means losing you — I can pay. I've had you, known you for a very short time. If that is all I get of you, then that will have to be enough."

"You've fallen in love with Maurice already, even after just hearing my stories."

"Yes, you are right. But I've been in love with a Mall Master since I was a little girl. I've just never met the one who could bring my love into reality."

"You think Maurice is the one."

"I want him to be the one. Whether he is or not, remains to be seen."

"Very well. If you are willing, Maurice is ready to initiate you at any time. But before you speak to him of it, I have a suggestion."

"Yes?"

"There is a way to present yourself to him that will impress him a great deal. Have you ever participated in an Arete ceremony?"

"Oh yes!"

"Then you know what I have in mind. If you want to do it, I will nominate you as the lead dancer in this years ceremony. That will give you the chance for your first dance with Mall Master Sully to be a sacred occasion."

"Can you do such a thing? What are my chances?"

"I have seen you dance, dear. Your chances are most excellent."

***

And that is how it happened that I came to dance in the Festival of Arete. Anton and Maurice conspired on my behalf, and I got the job.

The Festival of Arete celebrates the symbolic marriage of Apollo and Dionysus — a metaphor for the integration of reason and emotion in human life. It takes place every December 25th and is our most sacred holiday.

On the evening of my dance, it was snowing outside, and so cold and dark, that the mall was like an oasis of light and warmth glowing up from a ghostly frozen landscape. I was glad to be inside. For a festival of human greatness, it gave the evening even more meaning to take place on a night when the human conquest of nature and the elements was so starkly obvious that even an American could understand it. Within our glowing warm mall, the wealthy merchants would present the most beautiful women in the city to dance for the Mall Master. One dancer would stand out to be presented alone to the Mall Master. She would symbolize Dionysus. The Mall Master symbolized Apollo. The two would enter into a symbolic marriage before the eyes of the statue of Athena that stared out across the eastern wing of the mall.

The ceremony began at sundown on a stage at center court. The mall was packed with celebrants, witnesses, citizens, shoppers, children, and visitors from cities that didn't have malls. There were even some Canadians come down to witness the ceremony.

The men present wore cloaks of dark silk decorated with a single ornament: a circle of crystal enclosing a red flame. This was the "crystal flame," the symbol of arete. The crystal symbolized the clear vision of logic; the flame symbolized the heat and passion of emotion. Together, they symbolized passion tamed by reason, emotion ruled by logic.

The women present were stylishly naked. That is, they wore just enough clothing to be considered dressed, but the clothing was worn in a fashion designed to highlight and advertise the female form. These women wouldn't be dancing in the ceremony, but they were dressed in fashions worn in past years by dancers, and they were eager to see what new designs had been created for this new festival.

At precisely six o'clock in the evening, power to the mall was cut and all the lights went off, plunging everything and everyone into utter darkness. The crowd was silent, holding its breath in the blackness. Not even the children cried out.

Directly above the center of the stage, a spotlight flamed to life and shot down a beam to an opening that had appeared. Out of this crevice rose a figure. It was Maurice Sully, Mall Master, dressed in resplendent shimmering white silk robes that flowed about his body like liquid. In one hand he carried a torch with a blazing flame. In the other, a crystal sphere with a wide hole in the bottom. When he had risen out from beneath the stage, he walked forward, holding his hands high, displaying his flame and his clear crystal sphere for all to see. And then his voice boomed out at the gathered witnesses from huge speakers lining the walls, hanging from the ceilings, placed along the floors all throughout the mall. "I — am — Apollo!" The very walls of the mall seemed to speak. "Here you see my reason!" he said, showing his crystal sphere to the crowd. He placed it down on a stand to his right. "Here you see my emotion!" he said, holding the torch high in his left hand. Then he placed the flame in a holder to his left. He stood between them, raised his hands to the sky. Above him were the snow-covered skylights of center court.

"Apollo is lonely, his spirit cut in two. Behold my reason, cold and empty, with no values to fill it with purpose. And behold my emotions, wild and hot, untamed danger threatening to scorch my soul to ash. Great and glorious Mall created by the hand of Man, protector of the wealth and treasures Man has stored up within your secure walls, send your representatives to speak to Apollo. I will listen to those who bring value to Apollo. For I seek a wife, a bride in spirit who will make my soul whole. If there are any here who know of a cure for Apollo's illness, let them approach me now."

I was far away, at the other end of the mall, waiting at the end of a long line, but I heard Maurice Sully speak these words as if he was standing right beside me. His voice came booming out of speakers close by. He was calling to me, speaking directly to me. And soon now, I would march forth and present myself to him.

I was to be the cure for Maurice Sully's soul.

CHAPTER EIGHT

DIANE COPERNICUS
DANCES HER HEART OUT

Since I was the dancer representing Dionysus and was to be presented to Apollo as his bride, I began the ceremony at Athena's feet, ensconced like royalty on an ivory throne, my body covered with swirling silks, saving my nakedness for Apollo's eyes only, waiting for when the time came to announce myself and offer myself to him as a wife.

Ahead of me, at the center court, the ceremony progressed with a procession of seven merchants, each one representing one of the seven classic virtues. First in line was tall Brad Burnett, manager of Sears, representing Rationality. He stepped forward to the bottom of the stage and looked up at Maurice.

"Great Apollo, we have built this mall as a temple to the perfect man. You can build your arete here at the mall. Let us merchants help you achieve your perfection. I am Reason. Without me, you are blind to the world. Accept my eye and see the world clearly."

He then presented Maurice with an elliptical crystal painted to resemble a blue eye. He carried it forward to a stand and sat it down facing forward, the crystal catching the spotlight from above and prisming the light into a flair of colors that beamed out into the darkness, illuminating sections of the crowd nearby. Reason then went to the back of the stage and stood at attention, serenely observing the proceedings.

Next was burly and muscular Dave Wyatt, owner of the mall sporting goods store.

"Great Apollo, I am Independence. With my strong legs you may stand on your own and face the world a man, secure upon supports that will not fail you. My symbol is the pillar. Upon this you may perfect your arete and know it will stand forever."

He grasped a narrow white marble pillar with both hands and swung it up to the stage, sat it down beside the blue eye of reason, then retired to the back of the stage, stood with legs planted wide apart beside the other merchant.

Next was golden-haired John Shultis, head of mall security.

"Great Apollo, I am Integrity. Use my shield to protect your arete and know that any action you take is right action that will not contradict the integration of your soul. With my shield, your identity remains true and unswayed by the urgings of others."

He marched up the stage holding a golden shield, placed it on a stand facing the audience. Maurice bowed to him as he took his place with the other virtues at the rear of the stage.

Next in line was graceful Gary Kaiser, President of the Mall Bank.

"Glorious Apollo, I am Honesty. With me you will know that what you see is true, and what you are is real. Render all fakes and illusions impotent with me by your side. My symbol is my glasses. If your vision fails you, use these to see."

He rose up the stage and placed a pair of glasses on a stand, then retired to the rear of the stage and rotated in a slow circle as he faced each side of the mall and let the gathered crowd get a good long look at him. Then he stood still.

Next in line was Justice. This was silver-haired Guy Rogers of the Mall Legal Offices. He stepped forward with a sword in his hand and held it high for all to see.

"Great Apollo, I am Justice and this is my symbol, a sword with which to slay your enemies and protect your virtues, a symbol held high to let those who would do you ill know that swift retribution follows any stain upon Apollo's arete. Stand with justice at your side and only reason lives in your world."

Guy Rogers stepped before Maurice, bowed deeply while holding out the sword as an offering at Apollo's feet. Maurice made a motion, bidding Justice to rise. The sword was then placed directly into Maurice's hands and he held it for all to see. Cheers rose from the crowd as Justice retired to the back of the stage, took up a severe pose beside the other virtues.

Maurice held his sword as the next virtue approached. This was the magnificent giant Tim Weisner, the 6 foot 10 inch construction mogul. He brought a sledge hammer of solid bronze. He spoke with a deep voice that pounded the walls of the mall.

"Glorious Apollo, I am Productivity. Use my hammer to build your world. Pound the earth into a shape of your liking, mold all creation into a home for your arete. With my hammer you can rule nature and create all you need. Hold my hammer high as a compliment to your sword of justice."

And Weisner approached, bowed to one knee, held the hammer for Maurice to take with his free hand. Maurice raised the hammer as he lowered the sword, and another cheer came from the crowd.

The final virtue was Pride, in the guise of the elegant Mark Thomas, real estate tycoon. He stepped forward with his symbol — a crown of sparkling jewels, glowing gold, radiant silver.

"Apollo, I am Pride, the Crown of the Virtues. With me you are complete. Wear my brilliance upon your head to let all those who gaze upon you know that here resides a man with perfect arete. You are complete and integrated, a total Man. Wear my crown and be looked upon with awe."

Mark Thomas walked forward and placed the crown upon Maurice Sully's head. Then Pride strolled with obvious self-assurance to the rear of the stage and joined the other virtues, completed a semi-circle around the back side of the stage.

Down front and center, Apollo stood tall, holding his sword high in one hand, his hammer high in the other. The crowd cheered and applauded briefly, then was silent as Apollo stood at the edge of the stage and spoke.

"Apollo is complete, his arete built truly and held secure within the mall. I have Reason to see what is true; Independence to support myself within what is real; Integrity to be true to myself; Honesty to check my reason and measure my integrity; Justice to defend against those who would take my arete for their own; Productiveness to build my world and create my values; and Pride with which to live as a man, happy with who and what I am.

"Yes, Apollo is complete! So let him take a bride! Let all women worthy of Apollo come to him now and be judged. Let the feminine arete match my soul in perfection. All women who desire to be Apollo's bride — approach him now!"

Up until this point, the mall had been dim, the participants in the ceremony lit only by narrow spotlights. But now, at Apollo's command, the mall exploded into a violent swirl of color. Lights came on all at once, timed to match the music of the Dance of Arete, which surged through speakers at the exact same moment. The crowd howled with delight, but this sound only merged into the music and was lost in the throbbing chords of a deep and resonant rhythm.

At the other end of the mall, six big men, bare-chested, muscles oiled to a gleam, picked up my throne and began the stately procession to the stage.

Ahead of us, the dancers danced.

They approached the stage in pairs, some of them matched in style and dress, some not. They danced as far as the bottom step, but no closer. Only one dancer would ascend the steps to the Mall Master. That would be she who would be his bride. Before that, these first dancers would tease the audience and the Mall Master by dancing to the edge of the bottom step of the stage, then fanning out around the stage in a circle.

All dancers approached the stage wrapped in thick black cloaks. They marched in stately military cadence, all moving forward in time, first with right leg, then with left, their motion guided by the music and the lights.

The first pair of dancers were twin blondes. They approached the stage slowly, heads bowed, the lights playing on them gently, a chromatic motion urging them on as if through liquid. At twenty feet from the stage, the lights strobed violently and the music surged as they tossed away their cloaks to reveal slender bodies encased in sheer nylon costumes on which delicate designs traced exotic patterns across all the curves of their bodies. Each dancer mirrored the other with perfect precision as they danced to the edge of the stage, strutted and preened briefly, then moved off to either side, towards the rear of the stage.

As the first two dancers moved away, the next two stepped up, tossed away cloaks, and danced forward. One was a finely muscled blonde wearing a broad-brimmed black hat, her body encased in a sheer nylon body suit whose only ornament was a series of black circles up the side of each leg. Her breasts were free and naked, framed on either side by flaring nylon wings.

Her twin was bare-chested above, but clothed below in sheer pink nylon covering her legs with flower patterns, and flaring out at her hips into a frame of shimmering pink bows, so that she resembled a flower as she strutted and danced.

Next was a lusciously curved black-haired beauty dressed in black plastic and made up to resemble a cat. She prowled and strutted with feline grace, while beside her, a long-legged blonde wearing only hip-length pink silk pants spun and pranced for the crowd on the opposite side.

Next was a regal giant of a woman, an amazon with long legs and hair tinted a silvery-blue. Her entire body was encased in translucent blue plastic that caught the light and made her glow as if she were a creature made of water. She shimmered and flowed, the colors twisting across her body as if light itself was making love to her. She danced with impeccable erotic grace to the edge of the stage and raised one leg as if to touch the first step; the crowd saw her and roared in anticipation, liking her so much they wanted her to do it; but she was only the ultimate tease, and she twisted away, flicking her silver hair at Apollo, who stood implacable and unimpressed.

Behind her was a slender dancer made up to be a bird-woman. Her skin was covered with bright white striations from feet to forehead. She wore red boots, red gloves, and red fur panty. Her breasts were bare and her torso was framed by black feathers that sprouted out from the small of her back. She approached the stage and stopped, shivered and vibrated as if possessed, flapped and waved her arms as if they were wings that would carry her into the air. The lights played across her in a manner intended to create an illusion of flight. When she glided away to take up her position off-stage, she was showered with confetti from the observers above.

Next came two flaming redheads done up as exotic clowns. Both wore masks and were decorated like presents, complete with ribbons and bows that flowed and swirled around their bodies as they danced at the base of the stage, causing Apollo to smile down at them with good-natured amusement.

I was close now. There were only a few more dancers ahead of me. I could see the stage in front of me, I could see Maurice Sully standing at the edge, looking down at the dancers. My platform was still in darkness, but soon, the lights would hit me and the crowd would respond.

But first, the strongest and strangest of the dancers had to see if they could win Apollo before me.

Next to last was an ethereal blue-pink bird-woman, completely naked except for thousands of feathers sprouting from her back and lining the edges of her arms and shoulders. Her body had been painted in a fashion that caused the light hitting her to diffuse and glow in a ghostly way. She seemed to drift up to the stage like a blueish mist, tiny movements from her arms and hips sending her feathers into motion. She flowed them to the left, then to the right; she raised her arms and reached up to Apollo and her feathers rushed up, then snapped back, then whipped quickly to each side as she twisted and spun. On a giant video screen facing me I could see her face in close-up: brilliantly cold green icy emerald eyes framed by black feathers flaring up across each temple. Her lips were a piercing red, a shocking touch of color in her sea of pinkish-blue. I saw her mouth the word, "Apollo," as she reached up for Maurice, urging him to come to her and be taken in her arms. She cupped her hands together and gathered them in to her belly, her feathers folding in slowly and gently, covering her chest, hiding her hoped-for treasure. Apollo made no motion toward her, gave no urging for her to rise up the steps to him. She bowed very slightly and ghosted off to her position at the side of the stage.

The last of my escorts were two powerful blondes who approached the stage as the penultimate representatives of Dionysus: their costumes were miasmic explosions of color that jumped off their bodies as they strutted to the stage. They danced in tandem, one girl ghosting the other as they moved in synchronous steps across the front of the stage, their feet skipping in time as the musical tempo increased, their dance steps complex and hinting at the furious motion to follow when Dionysus approached the stage. These two dancers made no effort to win Apollo's attention. Their task was simply to introduce Dionysus and help push up the energy of the ceremony to the next level of intensity. This they did with the speed of their feet as they moved for the first time into the introductory rhythms of the Dance of Arete. The dance was an integration of tap, waltz, and ballet, with this first hint stressing the tap element via two beautiful women skipping along in front of the stage, then spinning and leaping into the air with timing so perfect they both landed and spun at the same instant directly in the middle of the stage, facing Apollo, the crowd now chanting for Dionysus with a rhythm matched by the feet of the dancers as they tapped out a waltz back towards the area where my platform was just edging out of the darkness, to be seen for the first time by those closest to the stage, to be seen for the first time by the great glowing noble one on the stage, Apollo, looking down now with a certain keen interest glowing in his eyes; and his body, encased in flowing white robes, chaste and pure, now vibrating beneath those robes with a subsonic rhythm visible only via the escalating quivers of threads that trembled slightly under the lights, making it seem as if the cloth of his robe was catching fire, sparkling, liquid with a scintillance resembling a waterfall of electricity flowing down from Apollo's golden brow, to the floor of the stage, to be radiated as excess energy to the chanting observers gathered around, taking in this spectacle and this energy as a proper form of spiritual nourishment on the most sacred day of the year, a day set aside to worship what an ego could be, what a beautiful spiritual sculpture the character of a human was who had carved his own soul into a perfection of integrated virtue.

And now Dionysus would come to test that virtue.

The last two dancers moved away to the side of the stage and the lights edged up on my platform. My male escorts lowered the throne to the floor and then escorted me away. I was encased in a round billow of silk that was like a cloth balloon. After several steps away from my throne, my escorts pulled on both sides and tore away my covers. crescendo of sound greeted my naked form. The music rose up into the sacred sounds of the Dance of Arete. The crowd screamed for me to approach Apollo.

I didn't waste any time.

I was clothed only in thigh-high black silk boots with a seashell swirl at the top, and matching gloves that covered my forearms to the elbow. My black hair had been styled into a seashell swirl that matched my boots and gloves, flowing in an arch from my left temple over onto my right shoulder.

Free of my restraints, and now the center of attention, I raised my gloved hands in a stylized presentation of self, and launched into a high-stepping prance to the stage, my knees rising almost to my chest, my boots accentuating my long legs as I jazzed up each step with a little twist of my supporting leg, turning slightly this way, then that way as I approached the stage. My cadence increased in time with the music until I reached the bottom step of the stage. There I stopped, ignoring Apollo, gazing up at the surrounding crowd, displaying myself arrogantly, tapping out a rhythm to the music with my feet as I stood like an energetic horse at the starting gate of a race. The music slowed and I raised a foot high, brought it down slowly, teasing the crowd, flirting with the first step. They howled for me to take it, rise to that first step, bring myself that much closer to Apollo.

Instead, I pulled back that foot, stamped both angrily, then raised the other, teased the crowd again, brought it down slowly, this time coming even closer to the first step. Again, I pulled back.

For the first time, I took a good long look up the steps to Apollo, who stood waiting patiently, gazing down at me with benevolent curiosity. The time had come to ascend.

The music was my guide; the tempo surged and I ran up the steps. I flew up to Apollo and stopped one inch from his face, stared hard into his eyes, saw what was there, spoke into the directional microphone that hung just above our heads: *"Dionysus bows before no man!"*

Then I danced in a circle around his stationary form while the crowd chanted in time with the music, the lights played across our bodies, and Apollo raised his arms above his head, quieting the crowd as the music paused, the only sound a quiet throbbing rhythm of deep bass echoing through the mall, as if the heartbeat of the mall itself was being heard while it too waited for Dionysus to dance with Apollo.

I was standing behind Maurice and he could not see me. His arms were raised, the crowd was quiet, I saw the lights gleaming off his blond hair. I saw his arms stretched high and trembling, his body like an arrow waiting to be shot up into the soul of the mall, his hair on fire with the swirling colored lights, the crowd beyond him a haze of murmuring sound.

Integrate this, you bastard, I thought, as I reached up and snatched his robe away.

The crowd howled and the music seemed to shatter into pieces to be caught by the lights and beamed down to the stage to swirl with me as I spun away from Apollo, danced and twirled to the center of the stage, spinning and whipping the robe with me, then sending it flying to the floor of the stage as Maurice turned to me, his body caught in a golden beam of light, his finely-muscled and elegantly lined male body clad now only in a pair of thong shorts designed to present and highlight the hidden form of his manhood. He was a statue come to life, a god raised to existence in the form of a man. He approached me slowly, methodically, his steps stylized and cadenced to the rhythm of the music. He ignored his robe and reveled proudly in his own fine form. He smiled at me as if he knew he had beaten me already, then stopped a short distance from me, struck a pose of beckoning impudence while I danced madly in a circle around him, my feet flying in a skittering tap, a spinning waltz of rapid-fire thunderclaps as my feet pounded the stage in a circle around naked Apollo, as if my dancing could hold him still, freeze him where I wanted him, leave him helpless as I assaulted him with my fire and fury and boiling out-of-control emotional depths.

Apollo was serene as I stopped, once again behind him, as if afraid to face him, afraid to stare into the power of his eyes, those gleaming eyes flowing with the power of arete, beckoning with the force of a firmly formed character that could not be denied, taunting me with the power of his grasp on reality, a grasp I presumed to match.

Behind him, unseen, I raised my hands to his body, I stroked my glove-clad fingers along the edges of his body, not touching him, but feeling even through my gloves the heat that radiated from his skin. I was close enough to catch the scent of his skin, the aroma of his hair. I brought my lips to the base of his neck, a would-be kiss separated by the width of a beam of light. He was motionless, the immovable mover, while I was a fury swarming around him, dazzling him with my fancy footwork, trying to fool him into thinking that I was in control, not he, but knowing even then, before he had taken me in his arms and begun the dance, that he was my control, he was the force that moved me to display myself as I had, he was the reflection I sought for my beauty, and his was the will I wished to challenge, the strength I wished to face, the virtue I wished to be judged before.

Maurice spun to face me.

His eyes held the music of his soul, was matched by the sound coming from the speakers, but I heard it more clearly from his eyes. I felt his hands take hold of my body and knew that he would lead this dance and I would follow. As we began, I tried to take over, swerve him out of control, but he had done this many times before and I was just an innocent girl from the big city, so I was helpless in his arms.

This first part of the dance was the quickest and most intricate. Our bodies waltzed while our feet tap-danced along in a wide circle along the outer edge of the stage. We danced a zig-zag pattern between the seven virtues, then Maurice spun me into a ballet leap. I flew through the air and landed in the middle of the stage, faced Maurice as he twirled, spun, and leaped to me, had me back in his arms before I had a chance to dance again on my own. We waltzed and tapped in a series of steps that took us back and forth before the seven virtues, our distance from them fluctuating, but our steps growing more complex, our rhythm more intense. The seven virtues remained motionless. Our dance touched each one, then moved back to a small circular area in the center of the stage. Here, the tempo slowed, the music mellowed, and our dance became intimate as Maurice took me in his arms, held me close, and waltzed me in slow languid movements in a gentle circle that showed our integrated movements to every side of the mall, and every eye of each witness.

And we started to rise.

An invisible plastic support was raising us up slowly.

To those watching, we appeared to levitate. Our dance had become a flight.

I heard Maurice whisper in my ear, "Close your eyes."

"No, I want to see."

"You'll make yourself dizzy. Close your eyes."

I couldn't. I had to see.

Maurice held me tight and danced slowly, as slowly as he could without falling behind the music.

I saw the faces fall away, the floor of the mall recede. I saw the seven virtues staring up, their tall taut bodies rigid, their glowing faces twisting to see us rise, their eyes glowing as they followed us.

I saw the other dancers gazing up with rapt wonder. The bird-woman rose her arms and flapped her wings, ushering us higher.

I saw the symbols of virtue illuminated by slender spotlights on the stage below. The eye of reason was hit by multiple beams and tossed out magical rainbow prisms of light that trembled like ghost candy in the color-laced air of the mall. The children laughed and screamed and grabbed for it but got nothing. Their hands were empty, but they were still happy. Their parents ignored the lights and watched our dance. I saw the faces raised, I saw the eyes glowing with man worship, with love of arete. But then we got so high, all I could see was the walls of the mall, the ceiling, the lights facing downward, sending beams to the floor of the mall. From below we must have looked like two swirling froths of color spurting up out of a champagne bottle.

Now we were so high I could reach up and touch the ceiling. The music echoed off the rafters, bounced off the skylights. I was so close, I could feel the chill from the snow that covered the plastic bubbles over center court.

Maurice reached up and grasped a harness I had missed, slipped it around my body before I noticed what he was doing. "Are you ready to fly?" he asked me.

"Yes. I have done this before."

It was all I had time to say. Maurice slipped into his harness just as the plastic riser began to sink back down to earth. It fell away from us in a precipitous descent that I noticed only for a second — because now I was flying, the wind in my face, my feet free, nothing supporting me but the invisible harness, the trick of magic that would give those viewing this part of the ceremony the illusion that Dionysus was flying.

I had flown with a Mall Master before, so I knew what to do.

I went first. I had nothing to do but strike a pose of flight and enjoy the sensations as the harness guided me down. It was computerized technology pre-programmed to take me on a specific glide path back down to the stage. I flew down in a series of ever-widening circles that took me back down into the flurry of lights and sound. I heard the crowd cheer as I glided over their heads. I heard them scream for Apollo, chasing behind me. This part of the ceremony symbolized Dionysus' flight from Apollo. But there was nowhere to go except the stage. He would catch me there.

I spread my arms like wings and enjoyed the sensations of flight. I felt the wind press against my naked breasts, watched the colored lights flow in multi-hued patterns across my bare arms. My long dark hair flowed behind me. The harness fit me so well and the glide down was so precisely measured that I felt weightless most of the time. The speed was great, grew considerably during the middle portion of the flight, as I was lowered down into the mall and the arc of my flight grew longer and longer. As I approached the stage, the flight slowed as my landing grew near. When I finally touched down, it was a gentle landing. I immediately turned to see Apollo float down out of the sky. He touched down and strolled over to me, took me in his arms in what was ostensibly a passionate embrace — after all, he had been chasing me. But this embrace also served the purpose of disconnecting me from my harness. It whispered away back up to the ceiling and our dance continued.

Apollo took my hand and guided me to the symbols of virtue.

"Dionysus, do you recognize these virtues?" Apollo asked.

"I see them."

"Do you value them?"

"I value their personification in your person, great Apollo."

"Then take these virtues, and make them your own. Integrate them into your own arete, and thus be worthy to be my bride."

Each virtue had spent our flight positioning himself behind the symbols that stood on stage. I now went to each and took each into my own person.

I went to the eye of Reason, picked it up, raised it high and touched it to my forehead. "My reason tells me that Apollo is good and worthy of my love. May logic bless our marriage."

Next I approached the pillar of Independence, picked it up, shook it at the surrounding crowds, announced with a powerful voice, "Independence tells me that I am Apollo's equal, able to stand on my own with him at my side." I then handed the pillar to Dave Wyatt, who bowed to me as he accepted it.

I next approached the shield of Integrity. It was held up for me and slipped onto my back by a stern-faced John Shultis. I faced the crowd and told them off in Dionysian fashion. "Know it now that with the shield of Integrity, Dionysus remains as you see her: true to her arete, true to Apollo, true to the mall that is our temple!"

The crowd roared in appreciation for my love of their mall.

Honesty was a pair of glasses. I picked them up, placed them on my face, turned to look clearly at Apollo. "Honesty I accept to see truly who and what Apollo is. There can be no lies and no faking between us." I left the glasses on my face and walked to the next symbol of virtue — the sword of Justice.

I picked up the sword and raised its gleaming blade high for all to see. "Apollo deserves my love — and I deserve his love — so it is just that we marry. I will defend his arete as he defends mine, justice our joint weapon. Let all those who would defile our virtue, take note!" I shook the sword and the crowd howled in approval.

I kept the sword and walked next to the hammer of Productivity. I grasped the handle close to the head and raised the hammer high. "See here the hammer I will use to build a world of virtue within the mall! As logic is the hammer I have used to shape my soul, so my work will be a hammer to shape my world!"

Next I converged with Apollo in front of Pride, a smiling Mark Thomas who bowed to Apollo and receded, let Apollo take up the Crown of the Virtues and place it on my head. Then he took the hammer from my left hand and faced the seven merchants.

"Virtuous merchants, this is my bride, Dionysus. Bless our wedding as you have blessed this mall, wish us happiness and good logic. Shall we be wed in your mall?"

Brad Burnett stepped forward, carrying the eye of Reason in his hands. He bowed to Apollo and Dionysus, gently touched our foreheads with the glowing crystal. "Your union is blessed and you are wed in the mall. Carry your virtues with pride and happiness will be yours."

Apollo took me in his arms and consummated the ceremony with a kiss. This was a real kiss, a true and honest kiss, a kiss completely consistent with the style and principles and values upon which this entire festival was based. Our mouths met, our tongues met, we tasted each other for a good long moment while I held my sword, my hammer, my Mall Master. The glasses did not get in the way. I felt Apollo's hands slide beneath the shield to caress my back. He held me close, the tips of my bare nipples pressed lightly against his bare chest.

When it was over, Apollo took my hand and led me to the center of the stage. We raised our arms and waved to the crowd. I heard Apollo's voice boom out into the mall: "Citizens, rejoice! Apollo has found his bride! Reason and emotion now walk side by side, integrated by perfect arete for the purpose of achieving human happiness on earth, here within this temple to human values, our sacred shopping mall. Now, good logic to you all — *and let the Festival of Arete begin!*"

The mall exploded into a rush of sound and motion as the crowd finally got its chance to participate. Confetti flowed from above as people streamed out into the mall, began dancing with each other, and with those who had been the escorts of Dionysus.

Maurice and I disappeared down into the stage. We ended up in a dark little room facing a bare-chested, well-oiled and most beautiful masked man who had been one of my throne-bearers. He took me in his arms and kissed me, saying, "You were magnificent, Diane!"

"Thank you, Anton."

***

Later that evening, the three of us were alone in Maurice Sully's apartment on top of the mall. Anton had been there before and was at home. It was my first time and I was dazzled.

I stood at one glass wall staring out at the snow-covered roof of the mall, stretching away towards the eastern horizon and the glittering lights of downtown Billings. I could feel the chill coming from the glass. I closed my eyes and pressed my warm cheek against the glass, let some of the cold sink in while I relished my memory of the evening. What a ceremony it had been! One of the best ever, so they all told me. I wasn't sure, I didn't know how to judge. I knew it was the greatest I had ever experienced, but what it had looked like to those watching, I hadn't a clue. Except what they told me, and what I saw in their eyes when they spoke of how they had loved me. Maurice seemed impressed and satisfied. And Anton was beaming more than usual. So, yes, I had to admit, it had been a success. But it had to be, by its very essence: it was a celebration of excellence above all, so it had to be good!

I opened my eyes and stared out into the dark chill. There was enough darkness outside that I caught a good reflection of Anton and Maurice sitting behind me. They faced each other in chairs framed by light from a lamp hanging on the wall above them, shining down soft beams onto a coffee table. They were smiling at me, watching me, waiting for me to come back and sit down. I finally did.

Maurice had poured small glasses of rare liqueur so we three could share a toast. He handed me a glass and then raised his first to me, then to Anton. "Here's to the best Dionysus I've ever married. Well done, Diane. You embodied true arete tonight."

"Thank you, Mall Master Sully."

"We've been intimate. You can call me Maurice."

"Yes, Maurice."

"Diane Copernicus. Was it your relative who discovered that the earth revolves around the sun?"

"Yes, it was."

"I hope someday you will surpass him in thought and action."

"That would please me greatly."

"Anton has hinted that you are interested in pursuing an apprenticeship with me at this mall."

"Yes, that is true."

"Well, after your performance this evening, I would be a fool to turn you down."

"Yes, I think you would," I said, smiling at him.

He smiled back, pleased with my bold self-assurance. "However, there are still some issues to resolve. First: you understand that I believe in full integration. That is what an apprenticeship is all about — at least, in my mall, it is. That means that one of the goals of the apprenticeship is for you and I to be lovers, not in any symbolic way, but in the actual way, a real and honest and true way. And to have it mean the highest possible to both of us. Is this something you feel you would be open to?"

"That is one of the reasons I wish to apprentice, Mall Master Sully."

"Very well." Maurice turned to Anton.

Anton was dressed now in his usual attire: white shirt, black slacks. He seemed relaxed and stress-free. Perhaps it was the festival that accounted for that. Or perhaps he was feeling light simply because of the gravity of the decision he had to make tonight. I had made mine, announced it openly, unafraid of facing consequences. Now it was his turn.

Anton smiled at me. He had known already my choice. But how long had he known his own? He glanced at Maurice briefly, but looked at me when he spoke.

"To be original in love is a worthy goal. To achieve a love beyond the norms requires extraordinary arete. We three are equals and may match each other in spiritual splendor. I'm not afraid to face the challenge of an apprenticeship romance, of seeking a love integrated into all aspects of the mall universe. But I must be honest with myself, and I must be honest with you two — whom I love. I would be committing spiritual treason to my values, to myself, to my happiness, if I did not maintain my claim to sexual exclusiveness with Diane."

He rose from his chair, came to me, took my hands in his. "Diane, you are a true soul mate for me. I have traced the logic of my feelings and the reality of our spiritual affinity is undeniable to me."

"Also to me, Anton."

"I cannot share you even with the man I love above all others — my mall-brother, Maurice."

"I understand."

"I have made my choice. Now you must makes yours. Weigh your choice carefully. With me you have an actual love. With Maurice, you have merely something potential. Neither of you can be sure how your feelings will develop, or how your apprenticeship will go. The mall may reject you. However, I know, as you do, that if you succeed, if your spiritual quest is fulfilled, the rewards will be more than worth the chance you are taking."

I took Anton's strong face in my hands and stroked his cheeks, looked deeply into his dark eyes, saw his yearning, his pain, his nobility. "Sweet Anton, I have searched my logic for errors, I have traced my feelings forward and backward, I have reasoned from opposing viewpoints to prove my convictions wrong — but the answer I see at the end of all my thinking reveals only one truth to me: I was born for the mall. I must pursue my love within the mall. This is the only source of ecstacy I crave. If I fail in the mall, and do not find love here; if I prove unworthy of Mall Master Sully, then I hope you will still see value in my person. But like you, I feel I would be committing spiritual treason not to pursue an apprenticeship. So yes, I must do this thing. Even if it means losing you for a time. But I believe you can never be lost to me forever. When I have finished my apprenticeship, when I have graduated, when reality has tested me and I have proven myself a Mall Master — then you will come back, and I will welcome you."

I kissed Anton. It was a gentle kiss, the kiss of an old love remembering finer times, sweeter days.

"You are right, darling," Anton said, stroking my cheek lightly with a finger as he stepped away. He turned back to Maurice, who was waiting for him.

"Maurice, my friend, for ten years we've worked together in the mall, grown to be friends, taught each other much. For most of those ten years, I've worshiped you as a man of spiritual qualities I've seldom seen equaled. And for several years now, I've hoped for the chance to apprentice with you. And when that chance finally comes, I find that my competition — is the woman I love. I know you've always yearned for a woman that would enter your soul via the mall. Now is your chance. It seems possible that Diane is the woman you have waited for, yearned for, needed to complete your happiness within the mall. She has a grace of arete that runs deep, as you witnessed in the dance tonight. I believe her dance revealed the essence and style of her soul. And the ease with which she mastered that difficult situation indicates the integration of her soul. She is logic and emotion united, truly she is. She has much to learn from you, and may cause you some serious frustrations. But in the end, I think she will win you, win the mall, and win her happiness here with you.

"But I cannot stay to see any of this. So what I propose is this: I will take my apprenticeship outside, into the world. I will apprentice with reality. That is where the ultimate test resides anyway, so why not just plunge right in? My friend Maurice, I have loved this mall all these years, but now I am going out into the world to build my own mall. That will be my apprenticeship: to become your rival. For ten years, this city has had one mall. Now it will have two. I will become the master of my own mall, and when I have built it, I will invite you both to come and dance with me inside it."

"Bravo, Anton!" I cried out, delighted with his plan.

Maurice could not contain his happiness for his friend. He smiled widely, his eyes beaming out a light of friendship and love that lit up the room like a second lamp.

"Anton, the first time we met, you saved my life. So I have owed you, all these years. I have yet to repay that moment. So we have yet to trade equally. Know this, friend: if necessary, you can ask my life. If you find yourself in a situation or circumstance that requires my intervention, know that you can count on me."

"I don't expect you to invest in a competitor!"

"Consider my investment spiritual. And if you put me out of business, I hope you will hire me."

"You know I would."

The two men shook hands, smiling at each other. Then the smiles faded. They kissed each other, then Anton stepped back, looked longingly first at me, then back to Maurice, then finally at me again. "So, let this be our parting, shall we? Diane..."

"Yes, Anton?"

"Good logic to you."

"Good logic to you, Anton."

"And Maurice..."

They simply stared at each other. Neither man could find the words.

I watched their faces. From where I stood, I could see both. They faced each other with implacable serenity. Then Anton bowed slightly. Maurice returned the bow, his eyes closing slowly and gently as Anton moved past him, found the door to the elevator. Maurice did not watch as Anton stepped inside, the doors slid shut, and he disappeared down into the mall.

Maurice was now looking at me.

I looked at Maurice. Perhaps this would stand as an initiation via reality. Should I ask? Or merely wait for Maurice to make a judgment. But any judgment would have to wait for my actions. Should I help Maurice? Or wait for him to help me? And did we need to help each other at all? What had just happened needed to be processed. I decided to conduct myself like an apprentice and seek guidance from the Mall Master.

"Master Sully, what does the science of ethics teach us about an event like this?"

He smiled, pleased with my question. "Sit down, Diane. Let's talk about it."

***

I wore a flowing white gown that evening in Maurice Sully's apartment. I was covered in soft white drifts just like the mall. It got late and I sat back on the couch, listened to Maurice, let him listen to me. Then we were silent for long stretches, both staring out the windows, watching the snow and the dark sky and the blinking lights. The mall seemed surrounded by lights. They shimmered and trembled like jewels in the frozen night sky. They blinked in mysterious rhythms, as if communicating with the mall — or with me. The lights all seemed to be calling to me from the horizon, saying, "Come to me, Diane, I beckon, please come this way, come see my light, see what it is I have to show you." I was overcome with the urge to exploration, but of a curious type: I would explore while sitting still, because I knew those lights symbolized my future. What was there when I finally reached them would be determined by me now as I sat and pondered my future, created it one thought at a time. So I was thrilled by the blinking, it chased away my tiredness as the evening turned into early morning. I was inexhaustible, like those lights. I would shine and blink until the sun came to render me mute.

When I finally noticed Maurice again, he was looking at me oddly.

"Diane, you should be crying."

"Should I?"

"Yes. And so should I."

"Why?"

"Because you've lost your lover — and I've lost my best friend. And the reason we have both lost this one person who is so special to us, is because we have decided that our greatest happiness lies in the future, with each other, in a spiritual quest that can't include that other."

"You're right, I should be crying. Must I mourn before I can be happy?"

"I think so."

"What of you?"

"Me most of all."

"Then I will cry. When the moment comes, I will let it happen."

"That is best."

"Am I to be initiated tonight, or in the morning?"

"In the morning."

"And tonight?"

"Is for talking. You will spend the night, but there will be no sex between us. That must not happen for a time. We cannot force it. I could say the words you long to hear from a Mall Master; and you could say them to me; and we could make love. But that would all be fake, and make us both fakes, and stain our arete in a most disagreeable way. So that must wait. It will be a graduation of a sort. So put it out of your mind. Your job now is to mourn Anton, then focus on what needs to be learned here in the mall. Our personal relationship you must be patient with. Let it develop slowly. Think of yourself as a gardener tending plants. We have the seed of a love within us. It has just been planted and needs gentle care right now. When it is strong enough to stand in full sunshine and weather the storms of angry weather — then we will know it is time. But until then — I am a teacher, you are a student."

"Very well."

"Are you going to cry tonight?"

I looked out at the lights. They trembled, silver dots of brilliant fire piercing the night sky. They seemed like lost planets orbiting far out in the reaches of space. The lights had seemed gay and delightful earlier. Now they seemed sad. Anton was out there with those lights, far away, lost to me now, a traveler to another world, another mall, another universe. And that was sad. I was sad for Anton, sad for me, sad for Maurice.

But I was also happy. Because I had taken my chance, and Anton had been selfish enough to encourage me to take it. I was finally with a Mall Master. I was alone with him in his home. I had danced with him in the Festival of Arete. And tomorrow, I would become a part of the mall.

I suddenly stood up and walked across the room to Maurice. He watched me, curious, but said nothing. I kneeled before him, looked him straight in the eye.

"Today I am a woman. My childhood is over. I am prepared to accept full responsibility for my power as a creator of life. I am responsible for my body, for any seed that enters my body, and for any child that grows from that seed. I swear by my life, and all that is logical, rational, and moral, that any child I bear shall be planned for, cared for, nurtured completely, and taught according to the highest standards of arete. I take this oath before you, myself, and the ultimate arbiter of all that is true: reality. If I have not spoken truly, may reality punish me with pain and misfortune."

Maurice looked at me, a confused smile on his face. "Diane, why recite the Oath of Womanhood before me? Have you never taken it?"

"Of course I have, long ago. But it means more to me now, to say it before you on the eve of my apprenticeship."

"I see."

"I am prepared to accept responsibility for … everything."

He smiled at me, touched my face with his right hand. "You're tired, Diane. You need sleep. We both do. Let's go to bed."

"Yes."

He picked me up from the floor and carried me into his bedroom. He undressed me and tucked me in. Before he turned out the light, he kissed me and said, "My precious Dionysus." Then I closed my eyes and fell into sleep quickly, happy to be snuggled near the center of the soul of the mall.

***

In the morning, Maurice woke me with a kiss, then picked me up out of the warm bed and carried me across the gray bedroom to the glowing warmth of his bathroom. He had prepared a bath for me. While I indulged myself in the luxurious cleansing, Maurice prepared breakfast. After my bath, we shared a small meal together, then we took the elevator down to his office.

Waiting for me, hanging on a wooden stand, was my apprentice robe. It was a gorgeous white satin, trimmed with royal purple, and embroidered with a purple "A" in the upper left breast. It was so beautiful, I was glad I would get to wear it all day long.

Maurice slipped it on over my head, then stood back, liked what he saw. We went out into the anteroom of his office and got his secretary's opinion. Nancy smiled infectiously. "Congratulations, Diane! After last nights performance, I thought you deserved something like this." She turned to Maurice. "And so do you, boss!" She hugged him, whispered in his ear, "Good choice!"

"We're going to take a walk, Nancy. Don't expect me back soon. I'm leaving my phone here. No interruptions during an initiation."

"I understand." She smiled at me. "Good logic, Diane!"

"Thanks, Nancy!"

Maurice took my hand and we walked out into the mall.

It was morning still, about ten-thirty. The place wasn't busy yet. Last night had been a wild festival. This afternoon it would continue, with the mall getting revved up with all sorts of activities, performances, exhibitions. But right now, everything was mild, quiet, pedestrian. Just right for the Mall Master to take a stroll through his domain and see how his world was doing.

With me at his side.

As we walked, Maurice said, "Talk to me, Diane. Tell me why you love the mall, and why you want to apprentice."

"Very well. Anton told me about you. You are famous for pursuing full integration. That is what I seek. The three most important values in life are production, love, and art. Here in the mall, I have the chance to seamlessly integrate all three. I can do work I love, and pursue it on a level that can achieve aesthetic heights. I can learn from a master in a context in which love is free to develop. If I can manage to achieve full integration of these values, my reward will be the most ecstatic state of consciousness possible on earth. And you know that happiness is too weak a word for what I mean. I want to worship ecstacy in the place it belongs: my soul."

"Have you known this kind of happiness before?" asked Maurice.

"I know what is possible. The ego is infinite, it can hold the universe. That is what I want. I want my ego full."

Maurice made no comments, merely noted my words with a nod, his face serene, as if he was a judge filing facts away to be considered and integrated later.

Our first stop on our tour was my clothing store, Pacific Orchid. My boss, Cleone Douglas, was getting the store ready for business when Maurice and I showed up. Cleone was genuinely shocked when she saw me in my robe. "Diane, is this your way of serving notice?"

"That won't be necessary," said Maurice. "She can still work in your store."

"I wouldn't have it any other way!" said Cleone.

"But it will have to be on a part-time basis," said Maurice.

"A part-time apprentice should be as valuable as a couple full-time associates."

"I wanted you to be the first merchant to know, Cleone," said Maurice.

"I'm thrilled to see you've finally found a worthy apprentice."

"Thank you, Cleone. Diane will see you later. Right now, we've a tour to complete."

"Of course. Until later, Diane."

"Thank you, Cleone!" I said.

We left the clothing store. Maurice turned left and headed for the grocery store.

"I need to pick up a few things," said Maurice.

"Oh?"

"And so do you."

"Yes?"

"Your first test, Apprentice. Why am I taking you here?"

It was obvious.

"I will answer myself," I said.

Maurice squeezed my hand, pleased with my understanding.

We entered and walked along in front of the checkstands. A few customers came through, noticed us, paused respectfully to let us pass, some nodding, smiling, waving, pointing at me, reminding companions of what they had seen the night before.

Store personnel watched us move across the store to the produce section. There, Maurice spoke to the wide-eyed young woman tending her vegetables. "Can you call up to the office and let the manager on duty know that Mall Master Sully would like to introduce his new apprentice."

"Yes, very well sir, one moment."

She went back and picked up a phone. Maurice stood examining melons while I watched the swinging doors to the back room.

After a few moments, Anton came out and he saw me for the first time in my apprentice robe.

It made me very proud to see the reaction in his eyes.

He smiled. "I haven't yet been to bed, so this can't be a dream, can it?"

"I am real," I said.

"Of course you are." Anton looked at Maurice. "Your timing is perfect. I was just serving notice."

"I won't let this store suffer, Anton. My apprentice will give it full attention, I promise."

"I will," I said.

Anton bowed to me. "I'm honored, but sorry that I won't be here to see it."

"The mall will miss you," said Maurice.

"I will miss the mall. Now, if you'll both excuse me, I must be going. Thank you for stopping by."

Anton bowed to us, then disappeared back through the swinging doors.

Maurice took my hand and led me out of the grocery. He was walking very quickly and I almost had to run to keep up with him.

When we were out into the mall, he said, "Congratulations, Miss

Copernicus. You have now been initiated. The mall welcomes you."

"And I welcome the mall."

"Let's go to work. Next, I'm going to introduce you to—"

CHAPTER NINE

DIANE COPERNICUS EXPLORES
THE SPIRITUALITY OF SHOPPING

Because of my biorhythms, four o'clock in the morning is the best time for me to rise. No matter how early or how late I go to bed, if I wake up at four, I feel completely refreshed and wide awake, and can usually bounce out of bed clear-headed, limber-limbed, ready for action, able to pounce on any problem, answer any question.

So it was on a Monday morning in May during the spring of my first year as an apprentice. I had taken an apartment in a building just north of the mall, in a property owned by Maurice; he made the arrangements for me and I moved in soon after beginning my apprenticeship. I loved the apartment because it had a south facing balcony. My fifth floor vantage gave me a good aerial view of the mall three blocks south.

On most mornings my alarm would click on with elegant classical music and bring me up out of sleep with soothing ease. I would slip into a silk robe, fix a cup of coffee, then go out onto the balcony and stand in the cold darkness of early morning and look down at the mall, watch the signs glowing with neon brilliance. I liked to meditate on the lights, remembering my first night in Maurice Sully's apartment, the night Anton had left us, had gone away to pursue a solitary apprenticeship, to compete with his best friend, and to wait for me.

When I tired of watching the mall, my eyes would turn east, to the skyline of downtown Billings. Some days it was hard to see in the haze of fog, snow, or rain. But most days the outlines were clear and clean, like drawings etched against the dark sky. I studied the buildings, memorized the forms, grew intimate with the shapes, chiseled their details into the depths of my memory so that later I could close my eyes and visualize the same shapes merely by remembering. It was a skyline I wished to see change. I was waiting for change, watching for change, hoping for change. This was my only form of contact with Anton. He was there, in the center of the city, building his mall. It was to be a skyscraper mall. It would shoot straight up into the sky from the heart of the city. That was all I knew about it, having followed the story in the papers. Anton never called, never visited our mall. I never went to his home, and he never came to mine. That is how it had to be. We would see each other again someday, when the time came. Then we would speak. Until then, my focus was on Maurice, and the mall I shared with him.

So after looking at the city, I always looked back to the mall, to the elegant arrangement of glass rectangles on the roof in the middle of the mall: Maurice Sully's apartment. Didn't matter whether it was dark, or glowing with light, I always smiled, pleased to be waiting to return to that place, pleased to focus on the ongoing process by which I would gain entry to Maurice's most intimate chambers.

After a small breakfast, a good hot shower, and my meticulous dressing ritual, I left home and walked the few blocks down to the mall. It was still dark when I got there, the streets empty, the lights of the homes dim, Grand Avenue sparse with traffic. I walked alone along the north side of the mall, my shoes clicking out a purposeful tap along the sidewalk, the sound echoing back at me from the stone walls of the mall. Sometimes I would spot a security guard on his rounds and he would recognize me. I would wave and he would tip his hat. I kept moving. I toured the mall. It was not only my passion, it was my job, an actual assignment given to me by the Mall Master. He gave it to me because he knew my thirst for the physical form of the mall. And because he knew I liked to prowl the city in the dark early morning hours. So I was out here, scanning the parking lots for illegally parked cars, noting the entranceways to make sure they were clear and clean, checking on the receiving areas and the garbage bins to make sure trash hadn't blown around. I walked by the window displays, noted the artistry of the designs, took special pleasure in some I had done myself, basked in the warm glow of the colorful lights flowing out from inside the mall. I walked the entire outer circumference of the mall. On some mornings, while I was outside, Maurice was inside doing the same for the interior. A few times we had converged on the office at the exact moment, and without even blinking at each other, had launched into our daily reports on mall status.

Today, everything was fine. I finally let myself in where my tour had started: the north doors. Once inside, I made my way directly to the mall offices. On the way, I spotted a security guard and smiled at him. "Happy Monday," I said. "Happy Monday *morning!*" he said back, smiling.

Monday is the most sacred day of the work week, so I was at my best, as Maurice demanded. I was always early on Mondays, always got the week off to an intense and focused start, especially in the early months of my apprenticeship.

In the office, the first task was always my computer and a long string of email messages from mall merchants. They reported sales figures to the mall office daily and one of my jobs was to record and track these numbers. We had sophisticated accounting software that did most of the number crunching for us — but first we had to get the numbers in right. That was what I spent my first few hours doing, sitting erect and alert at my computer, focusing hard on the numbers, seeing through the numbers and into the reality of what the figures stood for: human happiness.

Maurice had structured my tasks with a definite purpose, each part of the day a precise challenge for me. He had told me early in my apprenticeship, "You will learn the mall inductively, get your lessons directly from reality. I am merely a guide. When you feel you have learned a lesson, tell me what it is you think you know and we will discuss it. Remember, integration is the key. Find the connections. Look beyond the range of the immediate moment, the immediate task, and see the broader picture. Expand your context, widen your integrations. Learn how the mall touches all things."

So early in the morning I sat with my computer and crunched the numbers in a deserted office. Maurice was challenging me, testing my focus and my commitment, seeing if I would grow bored and fall asleep. But I didn't because I knew what the numbers were and I loved them.

When I saw a figure reported by a merchant, it was not just a dry mathematical notation with no meaning, no wider context, no connection to anything else. That figure represented money spent by people in the expectation of gaining some happiness from the value it purchased. The sales figures I saw represented countless goods and services provided to make someone's life easier, more enjoyable, colorful, fun, exciting, adventurous. And the happiness those shoppers gained was traded equally for a happiness given the merchants. The numbers I saw represented values gained by merchants pleased with the happiness they supplied their customers. The figures represented happiness they could purchase in the future by expanding or improving their business — or by trading for other values with other merchants both inside the mall and out.

And I saw further behind the numbers. The sums I added were a total of competence displayed by people committed to the virtues I had celebrated during the Festival of Arete. The wealth being created and traded within this mall came from beautifully selfish people in love with their own productive capacities, who valued other people enough to give their best effort always — as I did for Maurice — and who traded honestly with customers, reported honestly to the mall, who put their own integrity on display each day in the form of whatever excellent product they sold, who were independent enough to assume responsibility for how their business was experienced by the individuals they traded with — and all of these virtues flowing from and reducible back to a rationality that found its final eloquent expression in the numbers I saw blinking before me on my computer screen, numbers that stood for definite facts that existed in a real world where real people lived and achieved happiness because they knew what those numbers meant, and what those numbers could do.

"Business accounting is nothing more than the mathematics of morality," I told Maurice later that day, when he asked me what I had learned.

"How so?" he asked.

I told him.

He neither agreed nor disagreed with what I told him. He merely noted my statements with blinks and nods, his eyes watching me ruthlessly, his face showing no emotion, his manner neither congratulating me, nor attacking me. His attitude implied that his opinion of the facts was irrelevant; my primary concern should not be his reaction, but my own relationship to reality.

Of course, I wanted him to tell me how good I was, how brilliant I was, how much I was learning, and how quickly. I wanted him to tell me that I was the most brilliant apprentice he had ever seen, and that I would go far. I wanted him to tell me that he found my competence arousing, inspiring, and that he wished to celebrate my competence in the form of a final integration. After all, that is what this was all about, wasn't it? But I had no right to expect that anytime soon. Maurice was a patient man. When I had earned what I wanted, then it would be mine. Until then, there was work to do.

I enjoyed what I did in the office. I loved accounting, and paperwork, and mail, and talking to the merchants over the phone, and negotiating with business concerns that wished to enter the mall, and studying sales figures, and doing cost estimates, and designing advertising campaigns and marketing strategies. It was exciting to spend whole weeks when I never once set foot out of the office, never once saw the inside of the mall, never once got captured by the energetic pull and lure of the mall, but simply prowled the offices like a military commander in a bunker, not actually seeing and feeling the front lines of business, but planning and directing it nonetheless, knowing exactly how things were going out there simply by the figures and reports I read. I enjoyed all that, and it was a test of my capacity to remain in touch with the perceptual reality of the mall while operating from a conceptual perspective and missing the physical details I loved so much.

But when I went back to those physical details, when I went back out into the mall and plunged in like a trooper on the front lines, actually worked in the stores, had contact with customers and merchants, I remembered the conceptual context and it helped secure the meaning and value of the work I did, made it even more real, because I could relate all the tiny details to the larger principles of business I was learning with Maurice. In the office, my conceptual perspective was strong because of a firm grasp of the perceptual details of the mall; and in the mall, away from the office, drowned in the overwhelming sense data the mall pounded me with, I was able to grasp it all easily because it could all be contained within the principles I learned in the office.

This is all elementary philosophy, of course, keeping ideas real by reducing them back to reality, and making waves of details understandable by relating them to principles. But Maurice never tired of repetition, of pounding it into my head, of reminding me constantly to swing my mental focus back and forth from one side to the other, and thus establish and understand a clear link between the ideas and values I held, and the actual reality of what went on in the mall. Maurice didn't have to nag me too much; this was naturally something I loved doing, mainly because of the way it intensified my conscious experience of the mall.

My favorite context for integrating the conceptual with the perceptual was in customer service. As part of my apprenticeship, I was required to work at least one month in every store in the mall. I was gradually working my way around the mall, working part-time, usually a few hours a day, but sometimes more, in every store. My first experience was in the mall toy store. Here I got to interact with the most elemental valuers alive: children.

When kids reach a certain stage of development and begin to have conscious values, toys are generally their first self-conscious experience with the act of valuing, and with all of the problems and questions that human beings have to consider in the process of choosing, achieving, and keeping values.

I loved the selfish little brats so dearly!

A little man named Sam was escorted into the store by his mother and introduced to me. Sam must have been about six years old; he'd been to the toy store before with his mother, and she had picked out toys for him. But this trip was special: it was his first chance to shop on his own, to choose his own toys, and to spend his own money.

Little Sam was dressed for toy shopping: a pair of blue bib overalls over a white t-shirt, red tennis shoes, and a baseball cap topping off blond curls. He had blue eyes and a slow smile. He was a bit afraid at first, not certain of what to expect, or who I really was. I'm sure his mother had explained to him the special meaning of this trip to the toy store and what was expected of him. It was a little like the first day of school. Mom was going to drop him off, then go do some shopping on her own while her son was supervised by me. Mom had made an appointment for this special shopping experience. It was something the toy store specialized in. Mom was only too thrilled to learn that her son would be handled by an apprentice Mall Master.

When mom was gone, I took Sam by the hand and led him into the store. We sat down on some foam cushions not far from the entrance and I asked him if he knew what a Mall Master was.

"Yes," he said. "He's the man who makes all the toys!"

I smiled. "We'll, in a way, you're right. My name is Diane. I work with the Mall Master here. And he's told me that you're a very special customer and that I should take good care of you, okay?"

"Okay."

"So tell me, how much money do you have?"

"Sixty cents!"

"Wow! You're a rich little guy! What did you do to earn that much money?"

"I cleaned my room every day for a month and then mommy gave me a dime for every birthday!"

"That sounds like a good deal! So now you want to buy a toy, huh?"

"Yes."

"Do you know what toy you want?"

"Yes. I like Captain Logic!"

"So you've made up your mind already?"

"Yes."

"Captain Logic is the toy for you?"

"Yes!"

"Okay." I took Sam by the hand. "Follow me. Let's go this way and see if we can find any Captain Logic action figures."

I led Sam around the corner and into the main aisle of the toy store. The aisle was wide, and in shelves on either side, stacks of colorful, exotic toys rose up to the ceiling and stretched out down the gleaming shelves all the way to the back of the store. As we walked down the aisle, Sam looked this way and that, watched all the toys pass by, his eyes getting larger and larger. I watched his face. He held my hand loosely, was guided by my motion, but was becoming increasingly oblivious to my presence as he was mesmerized by all the different and new toys he saw. Finally, halfway down the aisle, he let go of my hand and went running to a shelf, pointed at a toy spaceship that sat just out of his reach. "Oh, let me see, let me see!"

"That's not Captain Logic," I said.

"I like the spaceship, can I see, can I see?"

"Well, if you really want to." I took the spaceship off the shelf and handed it to Sam. He looked it over, took it apart, put it back together, opened up the cockpit, took out the tiny figure of the pilot, put him back, sat down on the floor of the store with the spaceship, then made sounds meant to mimic a spaceship taking off as he moved the ship through the air in a flying motion.

"I like this!" said Sam.

"Captain Logic can't fit in that spaceship," I mentioned.

Sam ignored me. "Can I have this?" he asked.

I looked at the boxed version of the toy sitting on the shelf. It was priced forty cents. A Captain Logic doll was fifty cents. Little Sam didn't have enough money to buy both. I explained this to him.

"I want the spaceship," he said.

"Very well. Is that your final choice? You've made up your mind?"

"Yes."

"Very well." I took the display model from him and replaced it on the shelf, while taking a boxed version off the shelf and handing it to Sam so he could carry it up to the cash register. "Here you go. Shall we go up to the cash register and ring it up for you?" I started walking, letting Sam linger behind me, struggling along with the huge spaceship box in his little arms. "Do you need some help?" I asked him.

"No, I've got it," he said.

I watched his eyes start to wander again as his feet slowed to a shuffle. He was seeing toys he had missed the first pass down the aisle. Now he was captured by the lure of a bright plastic sports car. He sat his boxed spaceship down and went to the shelf, took the sports car down, examined it briefly, then gave it a push and watched it roll down the aisle, away from us. When the sports car came to a stop at the far end of the aisle, Sam jumped up, ran down after it, then gave it a push back in my direction. Sam came skipping down the aisle after it. "How much is the car, how much is the car?" he asked.

"You want the car, too?"

"Yes, I want both, can I have both?"

I checked the price of the sports car. It was also forty cents, same as the spaceship. I told Sam. "You don't have enough money for both. You'll have to make a choice. Which do you want? Which one do you like the most?"

He looked at the sports car, then at the spaceship. "I want both!"

"Sorry, too expensive, you don't have enough money. It's one or the other."

He was already forgetting the spaceship. He left the box sitting in the middle of the aisle and went to the shelf, pulled a boxed sports car down. "The car, I like the car, I'll buy the car."

"Are you sure?" I asked.

"Yes, I want the car."

"Very well, Sam." I picked up the spaceship and put it back on the shelf.

This gave Sam time to spot yet another toy. This time it was a fancy toy ray gun that used flashing lights in a colored tube to mimic a laser. "Ooooh, I saw this one on TV!" said Sam, reaching with his free right hand to grab a display model off the shelf. He dropped his boxed sports car and fingered the ray gun, then gave it a try. The toy made a loud humming sound and the red barrel flashed bright red as Sam pointed the toy at a row of monster masks on the top shelf of the other aisle and let them have it with a blast of make-believe laser energy.

"Take that, you ugly monsters!" cried Sam. After firing at them furiously for a few seconds, he stopped and looked up at me, smiling. "I shooted them ugly monsters pretty good, huh?"

"You *shot* those ugly monsters very well. But now it's time to pay for your sports car."

Sam stood fingering the ray gun, ignored his boxed sports car.

I heard voices down at the end of the aisle, around the corner, out of sight. A woman and a young child.

"You haven't changed your mind again, have you, Sam?" I asked.

"This gun is integrated."

"It is?" It was a slight shock hearing the child use that word. "Do you know what integrated means?" I asked.

"It's what my daddy says all the time."

"I see. What about the sports car, is it integrated?"

He shrugged.

I heard the voices again, the woman and the young child, this time getting louder, with a few sharp words highlighted by crisp yelling, most notably, the word *"No!"*

"Remember the spaceship?" I asked Sam. "How about that, did you think that spaceship was integrated?"

He looked back down the aisle, to where the spaceships were stacked. They sat gleaming in their packages, unable to blast off or go anywhere.

At that moment a piercing shriek ripped through the store. Down at the end of the aisle, suddenly coming into sight, a woman came striding down the aisle, holding her howling son under one arm. Then, halfway down, as the child continued to scream, she threw him over her shoulder like a sack and swept past us, giving me a quick tense smile of apology for her child's unreason, while I watched the child reach out desperately to the direction they had come and scream, *"I want it, Mommy, I want it!"*

"You can't have it today," said the mother. "You'll have to wait till next time."

Then they were gone out of the toy store and the child's screams echoed into the mall and faded quickly as the mother raced off to take her child out of sight of all those toys, all those choices, all those enticing values which some children just couldn't deal with.

When it was quiet, I looked back down at Sam. He still held his ray gun and was frowning seriously in the direction the screaming child had gone. He finally looked back up at me and said, "That was a baby, huh?"

"Why do you think he was a baby?" I asked.

"He was crying."

"Why do you think he was crying?"

"His mommy wouldn't buy him the toy he wanted."

"I think you are right, Sam. You're a pretty smart little boy."

"How much is this gun?" he asked.

"Space ray guns are sixty cents, Sam," I said.

He fingered the ray gun, then glanced at the sports car, then turned quickly and looked back down the aisle at the stacks of spaceships. Then he frowned again.

I bent down so I could be face-to-face with him. "Sam, are you having trouble making up your mind? You can't decide which toy you want to get?"

"I want all three," he said, his tone indicating his desire was a wish and he wanted me to grant it.

"Well, you know you've only got sixty cents, so you can only afford one. So you'll have to make up your mind which one you want. Do you know how to do that, Sam?"

He shook his head no.

"Well, I have an idea. Do you watch Captain Logic on TV?"

"Yes."

"Well, what do you think Captain Logic would do in a situation like this? How would Captain Logic choose which toy to buy?"

"I don't know."

"Does Captain Logic need a spaceship?"

"No, he already has one."

"Does Captain Logic need a sports car?"

"No, he has a fly cycle."

"Does Captain Logic need a ray gun?"

"No, he has lots of those."

"Of those three items, which one do you think Captain Logic needs the most?"

"His spaceship."

"Good choice! Let me ask you, Sam: how would you like to talk to Captain Logic yourself and ask him some questions?"

"Could I?"

"Sure you can. Here, let me put this ray gun back on the shelf for a few moments. If you decide you want it, we can come back and get it. But right now, you have an appointment with Captain Logic."

I took his hand and led him down the aisle, took a right turn and headed for a private customer service cubicle I had reserved for this appointment. I walked swiftly, but little Sam was so excited, he had no trouble keeping up with me.

Inside the cubicle, a Captain Logic talking action figure stood at attention on a low table in the center of the cubicle. Sleek, long-limbed, dark-haired, laser-eyed, clad in a dark blue skin-tight suit with a white L emblazoned on his chest, and complete with a flowing cape streaming from his shoulders, the foot high action figure filled the small cubicle with a commanding presence that humbled even the eager little Sam. He obviously wanted to rush forward and grab the toy and start playing with it, but I think he wasn't sure if this toy was for real. Maybe this was a different Captain Logic, some kind of new toy that worked in a different way. How was he supposed to know, he was just a kid!

He looked up at me and smiled.

"Go ahead, Sam, let's find out what Captain Logic has to say."

Sam went forward and picked up the toy, pushed the belt buckle button that activated the digital memory chip inside the doll. Captain Logic spoke, his voice confident with certainty and moral authority.

"Captain Logic to the rescue!"

Sam smiled, pushed the belt buckle again.

"With the power of logic, I can solve any mystery!"

"Ask him a question, Sam," I said.

"Hi Captain Logic," said Sam. "Can you help me decide which toy to buy?" He pushed the button.

"Just give me the facts."

Sam looked up at me, smiling.

"Go ahead, tell him the facts, Sam. Tell him about the toys."

"Well…there is a spaceship, and a sports car, and a ray gun. I only have money for one. I can't decide which toy I want. What should I do?" Sam pushed the button.

"Don't be afraid. Any problem is easy when you have logic on your side."

"Push the button again," I whispered.

Sam did. Captain Logic said, *"To be logical means to think and act according to what is true."*

And again.

"Logic is the method of identifying what is true."

"But I know my toys are real," said Sam. "I know my toys exist. I want to know which one is the best."

He pushed the button one more time.

"Logic applies to your thoughts and feelings, as well as to the outside world."

Sam looked up at me and frowned.

"Well, I think Captain Logic has given you plenty to think about Sam, so let's take a break and think about what he said. Captain Logic gave you a good clue about how to solve your problem. Do you know what it is?"

"No."

"Well, you sit tight and think about it a minute. I'm going to step out for a moment. You can keep playing with Captain Logic if you want. I'll be right back."

I stepped out and left Sam alone in the cubicle with Captain Logic. I went back down the aisle we had come up and picked out the three toys Sam had briefly flirted with: the spaceship, the sports car, and the ray gun. I took them with me back to the cubicle. Before going back in with Sam, I sat two of the toys down on the floor just to the left of the door; the ray gun and the sports car. I took the spaceship with me inside the cubicle. As I opened the door, Sam was jumping up and down on the chair and flying Captain Logic through the air. The doll's deep voice was saying, *"You evil bad guys are irrational, and your syllogisms are weak!"*

"Yeah, you stupid illogical bad guys, take that!" said Sam, plunging Captain Logic into the back of the chair and pretending to fight some bad guys.

"Okay Sam," I said. "I think I know how we can solve your problem. Have a seat here and relax for a moment. Keep Captain Logic with you. If you need his help, he'll be right there with you, okay?"

"Okay."

"I brought the spaceship back." I sat it down on the table in front of Sam. "Remember the spaceship?"

"Yes."

"Remember playing with the spaceship?"

"Yes."

"Go ahead, reach out and touch the spaceship, Sam. And while you touch it, think about how you felt while you were playing with it."

Sam reached out and touched the spaceship. He looked up at me.

"Do you know how to remember, Sam?"

"Yes."

"Close your eyes and remember."

"Okay."

"Now think about taking this spaceship home with you. Think about paying your money and then taking it home. Are you thinking about that?"

"Yes."

"Now think about your bedroom. Think about having the spaceship in your bedroom. Where will you put it? Where will you play with it? Will you be able to see it at night, from your bed? Will it be the last thing you see before you fall asleep at night? Will it be the first thing you see when you wake up in the morning? Or will it just be stored away in a closet, out of sight, in a box with a bunch of other toys, and maybe you see it only on the weekends? Are you thinking about it, Sam?"

"Yes." His eyes were still shut. He seemed very calm for a six year old boy trying to decide which toy to buy.

"You don't have to tell me what you're thinking. It's just important for you to know yourself what you think and what you feel, okay?"

"Yes. And Captain Logic, too." he said.

"Okay," I said, smiling.

I took the spaceship away, came back with the sports car. I guided Sam through the same routine with that toy, having him touch it, remember playing with it, and think about taking it home and living with it. Then I did the same with the ray gun. At the end, Sam sat in the chair with Captain Logic tucked in beside him, and three other fabulous toys staring him in the face.

"So you see," I told him. "Your puzzle isn't with the toys. It is with what you think of the toys, how you feel about them, what you want them for, what you want to do with them, how you want to play with them. You can use the power of logic to decide which toy to get simply by identifying your own feelings about which toy you like the best, which toy makes you feel the most excited, which toy makes you experience the most intense fun. Do you understand?"

He raised his big blue eyes to me. "Yes, I do understand. This has all been very logical, huh?" He picked up Captain Logic and pushed the belt buckle button one last time. "What do you say, Captain Logic?"

"Let's go out and kick some mystic butt!"

"Yeah!" cried Sam, jumping up and running for the door. "Captain Logic rules! I'm buying this toy right now!" He threw open the door of the cubicle and ran down the aisle yelling, holding Captain Logic up in the air above his head, flying his new toy all the way to the cash register.

"You've made a logical choice, Sam," I said, closing the door of the cubicle and following him up front.

***

When I discussed that shopping experience with Maurice that night during dinner, I said, "You know, you and I are really not all that far away from little Sam. We have to make the same kind of decisions, the same kind of choices, don't we? The specifics differ, but the principle is the same. I had to choose between Anton and my apprenticeship. You had to choose between me and Anton. Anton had to choose between you and me."

Maurice listened with his eyes shut, a glass of wine held to his mouth, the liquid pressed against his lips briefly, wetting them as he pulled the glass away. Then he licked his lips for a small taste of the wine and opened his eyes as the wine glass was sat down on the table, an accent to my last words. He smiled at me, leaned forward, crossed his arms on the table, stared at me hard. "Next week, you'll be at the opposite end of the spectrum. I'm putting you in the men's store. You'll be selling suits to grown men. Powerful, rational men who know what they want and why they want it. I'll be interested to see how you do there."

"Stop in — and I'll sell you a suit," I said.

So the very next week, as promised, I found myself in the elegant world of Jason's, the finest men's clothing store in the mall. After a few days of becoming familiar with the store's systems and procedures, I was given the task of being prime customer service representative. Individuals wishing for a complete shopping experience called and made appointments, and when they arrived, I was their guide into the spiritual realm of the specific values they wished to explore.

My most significant customer — most memorable and pleasurable — was a man buying a suit for an anniversary celebration with his wife. He had been married for twenty years and wanted everything associated with the celebration to be experienced in a state of focused ecstatic awareness. So he came to the mall to buy a suit and be guided through a spiritual shopping experience.

His name was Ray Curran. He was a surgeon at the hospital downtown. He was a tall, elegant, gray-haired gentleman with blue eyes and beautiful hands. I met him at the entrance of the store and escorted him to a private chamber. Two design associates followed us in and quickly took his measurements, then left immediately with his design specifications in hand. He knew exactly what kind of suit he wanted, what all the elements would be. My job now would be to prime him mentally, emotionally, for the experience of trying on his new suit once it was ready. This would be the suit he would wear for his wife on their anniversary. Most likely, this was the suit she would remove from his body at some point in order to make love to him. He knew that. That is why it had to be special. I knew that. How could I help him?

He was watching me closely while I prepared a drink for him. He was obviously taking pleasure in the fact that I was a young woman. "So you're the new apprentice I've heard so much about."

"Yes, Mr. Curran."

"Please call me Ray."

"As you wish, Ray."

"I operated on Maurice once, you know."

I handed him his drink. An exotic blend of tart fruit juices, spiced with nutrients designed to stimulate his neural peptides. "Oh? What happened?"

"Broke his leg. Fell off a wall while he was building this place. But I fixed him up. Doesn't even walk with a limp."

"I'll have to ask him about that. By the way, what is your wife's name?"

"Helen."

"I've always loved that name. I think if I ever have a daughter, she'll be a Helen."

"I certainly treasure mine."

I went to a nearby closet and removed a changing gown, brought it over to Ray, unfolded it out over the arm of the couch for him. "Please remove your clothes and change into your gown, Ray. Will you be wishing these clothes you wear to be returned?"

"No, not necessary. I chose to wear these clothes one last time because I got them ten years ago while on vacation with Helen. Very special trip, spent time in New Athens and Atlantis. Good memories in these threads. But they're old and deserve to be retired, so now is a good time."

"I'll be right back."

I stepped out while Ray changed into his gown. I checked on the progress of his suit. The design associates were doing good quick work and the suit would be ready soon. I returned to Ray, found him relaxing on the couch, sipping his drink, his old clothes neatly folded beside him. I picked up the clothes, bowed to Ray, said, "The mall thanks you for your trade." Then I took the old clothes to a trash chute and disposed of them. No one else would ever wear those special clothes. The memories held within those threads would remain the exclusive property of Ray Curran.

I went back to Ray and sat down in front of him. "How do you feel? Are you sad to part with clothing you've loved?"

"Yes. But not that much. I'm more interested in the pleasure my new suit will bring me."

"Do you remember your first suit?"

"Oh yes. I was just a boy. My father took me out to buy it. I was fourteen. It was for my manhood ceremony. I took the oath in that suit. Didn't give it up until I bought the suit I married in. I still have that one, I'll never give that up."

"What did that first suit mean to you?"

"It meant I was a man."

"How did you feel about it the first time you wore it?"

"I loved it, the fit was perfect, and I looked great in it. Made me look older, more substantial."

"Do you remember the material?"

"Oh yes. This was a fine linen suit, heavy material, nice sheen to it. Felt great in my hands, and smooth against my skin. Breathed very well. Comfortable suit in any kind of weather. Cool in the summer, warm in the winter. Technically, it was a spring suit."

"Did Helen ever see you in that suit?"

"Oh yes. I was wearing it when we met. At that time she played lead

violin in the Billings Symphony Orchestra. I went to see a concert and I
noticed her, became fixated on her. She wore a flowing white gown,
classic Grecian design, lovely on her. She had long black hair then, kind
of like yours. Presented a striking image sitting under the lights,
performing on her violin. She had a solo, so when that happened, she
stood up, played like an athlete, put her entire body into it. Her dress
highlighted her body so magnificently, I couldn't take my eyes off her. I
was sitting close to the stage, I could see her face and eyes clearly as she
played. I saw that she loved the music and that she took great pride in
her own musical ability. She made eye contact with me. I didn't take my
eyes off her, I held her with mine, and she kept on playing, not missing a
note while she looked right at me. The music was wonderful, it was the
Christopher Shattuck violin concerto, so you understand. I was certain
she was playing it just for me. I heard the music as if it was coming from
her body; her skin and hair trembling with sound, her eyes vibrating into
mine, the sight of her translated into sound so I could hear what she was,
who she was. Every note from the violin was a soft curve of her skin,
every phrase was a quivering section of her body. And her beautiful
dress amplified her sound, highlighted each note as if it came from a
definite part of her body. This melody was her legs, this one her arms,
this next the curve of her back, and this flowing rhapsodic phrase her
hair and eyes and face.

"I was young and that was the most integrated artistic experience of
my life. Made me wonder if perhaps Shattuck had written his concerto
for a woman he had loved.

"Well, I got to meet Helen after the concert, talk to her, find out her
name. I suppose you'd like to know what we said to each other?"

"If you wish to tell me."

"I asked her if she knew the history of Shattuck's piece and what he
was thinking of when he wrote it. She knew the entire history. It had
indeed been written for the love of his life. That music is what she had
made him feel. And that music is so universal, it is actually what *all*
women make men feel. And possibly, what all men make women feel.
Later, Helen confessed to me that her experience of our first meeting
was that she had not played the music at all. Her violin had been a
transmitter, had picked up the spiritual transmissions from my body, and
had simply broadcast them out to the audience. You see, she had the
same experience as I. For her, the music seemed to be coming from me,
the music *was* me.

"And part of it was my suit. My suit was that music expressed in a
clothing design. And Helen knew it. She was more artistically involved

than I, so she knew more than I did about something as abstract as translating a suit into music. I was impressed with her ability to do that, so I asked her to teach me. So she did. And that was how we began.

"Perhaps we would have made a connection even without that suit, but I don't know. There is such a thing as an ugly suit, and if I would have worn one, would she have seen that music in me? I don't think so. And if she would have been less of a woman, wearing clothes that did not match her own character, would I have heard that music the way I did? I doubt it. It was all very logical. We were who we were, and we wore what we wore because of that, and we heard what was in the music because we could recognize it, and see that it was an expression of the values that had formed our minds, and the values that had chosen our clothes — the same values we would now use to choose each other. Existence is identity, and consciousness is identification. See, I remember my schooling. We were both conscious of our identities. We recognized each other. We knew our own natures so completely, and had such an integrated grasp of our values, that we could see those values expressed even in complex integrations like music and clothing.

"So now, is it any mystery why I wished to have a spiritual shopping experience when buying my new suit? Twenty years I have lived with this woman, and loved her every day. That has been twenty years of mornings dressing in her presence, clothing myself in shirts and slacks and suits in which my wife could see my soul and mind; twenty years of evenings undressing in her presence, peeling back the layers of my character to reveal to her my essence. Twenty years of days spent with her, dressed as she would have me dress, as I knew I had to dress to please her and myself. What was the old saying? Clothes make the man? Not hardly. Clothes *are* the man. Show me the way a man dresses, and I'll explain his entire philosophy of life, plus tell you exactly what his character is, what level of self-esteem he has, and what his other major values are. Show me a young man dressed ideally at the age of twenty, and I'll plot out the entire course of his life for you, tell you exactly who he will be and what he will be at the age of fifty. Do you doubt me, young lady?"

"Not at all," I said, smiling.

"I've exaggerated slightly. It was not my wife who taught me most of this."

"No?"

"Not likely. I've been shopping at this mall for ten years, ever since the first day Maurice opened the doors. I've been buying suits and clothes and everything else from Maurice. Especially suits. He taught me how to see my life and values in the clothes I wear. He taught me how to love and value and be conscious of the experience of choosing, purchasing, and treasuring the beautiful things I love that come from the mall. Of course, I had been to other malls and been guided through spiritual shopping. But never by anyone like Maurice. He is more connected to and more integrated with reality than any Mall Master I've ever encountered. You are lucky to have such a good teacher."

"Perhaps I should be buying a suit from you!"

Ray laughed. "Have I sold you?"

"You've made my job easy. But let's see if we can integrate further, deeper, wider. You understand much. Let's discover if there is more to learn. Your new suit is just about ready. Let's find out just exactly what it means to you, and where it fits into your hierarchy of values. Are you ready?"

"I've been ready, dear lady," he said.

"Please stand, and prepare to face yourself."

He stood up. Through the sheer material of his changing gown I could see the faint hint of his body. He was in fine shape for a man his age. But his changing gown made him look old and slightly feminine. I longed to see him in his new suit, a powerful and elegant man. His body had the kind of long classic lines that go well with suits. Here was a man who could not look bad in any suit. And when the right suit fit him perfectly, it was worn as an extension of his soul, a physical manifestation of his own spiritual integration. In the right suit, this was a man who could command an imposing presence and force respect and admiration into the mind of any who faced him.

Now the time was near. I stood behind Ray and placed my hands lightly on his shoulders, whispered in his ear, "Close your eyes, Ray. Close your eyes and think of your new suit. You ordered it. You chose the design. This suit reflects who you are, what you value, how you love. And I know more about this suit than you suspect, Ray. I know that in this suit is your highest value — your wife. It is your wife that you wish to see in this suit, is it not?"

"Yes," said Ray, gently.

"But how can that be?" I asked. "How can you see your wife in clothes designed to present your own self so completely?"

"I know the answer."

"And so do I. Let me speak it, Ray. Let yourself hear this from my voice, from the lips of a woman, from a woman who understands how much pleasure your wife takes in seeing you well-dressed. She will love seeing you in this suit. I know she will. And the reason is this: the suit that presents your deepest self to the world, is also the suit that presents your wife's deepest self, in masculine form, because she is your soul mate, your own self in female form, and if she were a man, this is the suit she would wear, is it not?"

"Yes. It is. You understand that..."

"Open your eyes, Ray, and look at your new suit."

The design associates had brought the suit in while I was speaking to Ray. While they were leaving the chamber, I moved quickly to my control console and told the computer to play Christopher Shattuck's violin concerto.

When Ray's eyes popped open, all he saw was his suit standing before him, hung on a wire stand in an action pose, as if the suit were alive and in motion, and if Ray wished, he could have a conversation with his suit and take it for a walk down the street, buy it a beer at the bar.

I looked at the suit with Ray.

The material was the color of an autumn sky at dusk, the last faint touches of purple fading into black. The lines were sharp, straight, elegant. The cloth itself was enough of an attraction, so the suit carried no ornament, no stripes, no checks, no alien blemishes of discordant color. The suit was a single consistent whole, designed to complete its integration via the body of a man.

Ray stood and smiled at his suit for a moment, then closed his eyes and held out his arms. I removed his changing gown and draped it over the couch behind us.

Naked, Ray walked forward to his suit, stopped, stood waiting for me.

I went to the suit, picked up the first article of clothing he would wear: a pair of custom designed dark green boxer shorts. Ray stepped into them as Shattuck's music rose in a stately spiral toward the violin's entrance. Ray moved to the music, as if he was dancing with the suit. He slipped into the pants and was suddenly made taller, thinner, his waist slimmer, legs longer. On his feet went a pair of triangle decorated Argyle socks, then he accepted my assistance in stepping into his new shoes: shiny black leather loafers that raised him just so off the ground, gave him an aura of subtle weightlessness as he moved slightly this way, now that way as I held out his smooth white linen shirt. He slipped in, buttoned up, tucked in the tail. I held out his belt and he looped it through his pants and fastened it tight. He raised his collar and I handed him his burgundy tie, watched him tie a perfect knot just as the violin entered the concerto, proceeded to skip and dance through musical fields. I helped Ray into his suit coat and stood him in front of a mirror.

"Do you know what recording this is?" he asked.

"Billings Symphony Orchestra; Helen Curran, soloist."

"I recognized her playing," he said, eyeing his suit agreeably. "Just wanted to be sure."

"The suit is exactly what you thought it would be," I said.

"But it's more than that. Tell me how much more it is, Diane. I'm ready to hear it."

I was ready to tell him. "Look at your suit, Ray. And more: look at *you* wearing your suit. What a beautiful integration I see. Your good taste and values are contained in the material. The classic design and the perfect fit reflect your self-esteem. There is rationality in every thread. Do you know what the essence of morality is, Ray? The desire for the best. To have the best, to have it right now, in every context, for your own self, your own use, your own life, your own enjoyment. Even such a simple thing as choosing a suit is an exercise in morality. Have you been moral in choosing this suit? Is buying a suit a moral action? I think so. Just look at you! The way you feel right now, is that a moral feeling? Think about what your wife will feel when she sees you in this. Think of the light in her eyes and the pleasure that sight will give you. Will *that* be moral? What about your desire to experience those kind of emotions with your wife? Isn't that the essence of morality, to experience that kind of joy, and to share it with the woman you love?

"But it is 'just a suit' say the morally deaf. When you desire the best in all of life, there is no such thing as 'only' anything. Every second of your life is precious, every second of your life is important, and every value that fills that life is important, so make it the best you can! Don't buy just any suit, but the best suit you possibly can! And wear it proudly, walk tall with your head held high, don't be shy, strut when you walk down the street in a suit like this. Let other's know that you are a man who loves his life, values intensely, passionately, seriously, and that you are gloriously full of yourself. Advertise who you are and what manner of existence you have. You are a moral man. Choosing, purchasing, and enjoying a beautiful article of clothing like this is no small matter — because for you, *there are no small matters*. Everything is epic for a man with an ego like yours. You want your ego full, you want your ego infinite, you want it to match the universe and contain all the universe.

"And what is your ego? Your consciousness — and every sacred moment that you experience, remember, love; every heartbeat of life lived in the light of reason and loved in the bright glare of self-conscious passion. Buying this suit is something to remember. Trying it on for the first time is something to savor. And letting your wife peel it away to reveal your naked essence will be a moral moment summing up all the rest.

"This suit contains the style of your soul. You are a man of sensuous passions; your suit's soft dark material reflects that sensuality. You are precise and meticulous; so are the lines of your suit. Look at the way they stylize your body, as if an artist designed you. You are a man of wealth; the suit makes that obvious with the bluntness of direct perception.

"And what will your wife see in this suit? She will see what a woman needs most from a man: mastery over reality, metaphysical competence, the capacity to live, the strength to force your will out into the world and change it into a reflection of your self. As you have done with this suit. As you do in the operating room with a life under your knife. A suit worn well is the life force made manifest in an article of clothing. All of the human capacity for knowledge and understanding is implicit in a suit. And yours in this particular suit. So see it all, and relish your understanding, and revel in your man worship. You wanted a sacred shopping experience? Is this what you have had?"

Ray Curran stood tall, back arched slightly, arms hanging loose, hands relaxed. The music of Shattuck's violin concerto still swirled around us; Ray's wife Helen continued her playing. Ray's face was radiant, his eyes bright, intense, his eyes looking up, far away, seeing something outside the chamber. He had seen himself and his new suit in the full length mirror before him; he knew all the details, knew them in the fullest sense, and now he was filled with the meaning of his purchase, an article of clothing that reflected all that he was, all he still yearned to be, and everything he loved, his wife most of all.

"Thank you," said Ray, not taking his eyes from the image in his mind. "Yes, you've given me just what I needed, told me just what I wanted to hear. And I think that is enough."

"Meeting your wife?"

"She's having the same experience — I hope! — across the mall and one level up. I should go meet her now. We've got an epic evening in front of us."

"The mall thanks you for your rational values," I said, bowing.

"Thank you, Miss Copernicus," Ray said, finally looking at me. "You have given me a deep spiritual nourishment today. I think that you are now a part of my memory of this suit."

"That is as it should be."

My final act of customer service was to offer myself for a kiss. Ray was satisfied enough with my spiritual guidance that he took me in his arms with no hesitation and gave me a good long kiss of true thankfulness. Then he paid for his suit, left me a generous tip, and went off to meet his wife.

***

When my work day was done, I went off to be consumed by desire for Maurice. I made an appointment for a shopping experience of my own. I had to buy a new dress. I wanted it to be the dress Maurice would remove from my body the first time he made love to me. When the appointment was made, I had to make it through the day somehow, wondering what I would say to Maurice that evening when we had dinner.

"So, I understand you sold a suit to Ray Curran," said Maurice, as he sliced into a piece of chicken.

"Yes, I did."

"He fixed a broken leg for me once, years ago."

"He told me about that."

"So how did it go?"

"He was satisfied enough to give me a kiss and a large tip."

"Have you met his wife, Helen?"

"No, but I don't feel I have to now. Ray spoke of her extensively. Her connection to his suit was made explicit. I feel I know the woman now."

"You could be her daughter."

"Do you think so?"

"Oh yes. I've guided Helen through many a spiritual shopping experience. She is one of my favorites."

"How favorite?"

He smiled.

I did not smile. "You've made me jealous."

"Have I?"

"Yes. If she has had you, and I have not, I am jealous."

"She has not had me, except in the spiritual sense. So you are equal, so don't be jealous. Never be jealous of anyone. You are an apprentice and they are not, so remember that."

"It is always on my mind."

"Are you getting impatient?"

"Yes."

"Then let me tell you this. Before you can make love to me, you must make love to the mall. If you do not understand what that means, you must learn. That is your next assignment. Show me that you can make love to the mall, and I am yours. You can have the Mall Master. But first, you must prove you are worthy. Do you accept?"

"How much time do I have?"

"As much as you need."

"Very well, I accept." I raised a wine glass in a toast. "Here's to the mall."

"Here's to your spiritual mastery of the mall," said Maurice. "I wish you good logic in your quest."

We drank, then sat smiling at each other. Our smiles gradually faded into seriousness as we gazed at each other. Finally, I could stand it no longer. I skipped dessert, offered it to Maurice.

"Take one bite, then leave the rest for me," he said.

I did as he instructed, taking a forkful of chocolate cake, then pushing the plate across the table to him. He took a bite and sat back, watching me as he relished the sweet cake, his eyes roving up and down my body in explicit admiration and quite frank study.

I watched his face impassively. "If you'll excuse me now, I don't think I can stand to be around you anymore."

"I can't stand it, either," said Maurice, his face austere.

"Then good evening."

"Good night."

I went home and took a long, cold shower.

It didn't help.

So I stayed up all night, thinking about what it meant to make love to the mall.

When dawn came, the essentials of my seduction were set.

CHAPTER TEN

DIANE COPERNICUS CONFRONTS
THE NAKED FACE OF LOVE

Here is how it happened:

Maurice went away to a four day weekend at the Emerald City Mall in Seattle, where he gave the keynote speech at a symposium on integrating the theatrical arts into mall management. He left on a Friday morning, would return on Tuesday afternoon the following week. That is exactly how long I had to make love to the mall, and the second his car left for the airport, I swung into action.

There was never any question of understanding what he meant by "make love to the mall." I knew exactly what he meant, had been planning for my chance since the moment my apprenticeship began.

There had been some preparation. My first task, completed months ago, had been to study mall legal agreements with tenants, especially the standard real estate contract for tenancy. After that, a quick look at my apprenticeship contract made clear exactly how much I could get away with. Because I was an apprentice, the mall was virtually my own. And in the absence of the Mall Master, my authority rivaled his.

Having that information in hand, I prepared a business plan and presented it to a bank outside the mall, asking for a sizable loan. The loan officer of that bank approved my loan. When the loan was finalized, I had the funds transferred into my private account at a third bank.

During all this time, I was closely monitoring available space in the mall, as well as keeping in close contact with tenants whose leases were due to expire. Most would renew. But there was one merchant due to close his business and retire from the mall when his lease was done. He was a seventy-five year old man with no heirs who wished to close his business instead of sell it. He was a jeweler who wished to retire from business and spend his remaining years traveling and doing geological research. Several months before his lease expiration date, I met with him and discussed his business, the mall space, what his definite plans were, how sure he was that he was leaving, what date he had targeted to be out of the mall. We nailed down the details so I knew exactly when the space would be free and I would be able to move in. He would be gone several days before Maurice was scheduled to leave for Seattle. Knowing that, I could plan ahead to move quickly when the time came.

Before all this, Maurice generally paid close attention to lease expirations and empty space within his mall. It was something he was maniacal about. He never left a space empty for long, and if he had trouble filling a space, he could become downright impossible, even nasty. This was one thing that truly frustrated him. In certain rare instances over the years, he had found it necessary to invent completely new businesses right off the top of his head, in a matter of weeks or even days, just to fill an empty space in the mall. Some of these succeeded more than others — but they all did succeed. That always astounded me. I looked up the records and found that Maurice had a record unrivaled in this respect. He always knew what the mall needed, what the community needed, what the market wanted, where the market was headed. He had to know these things: not to would have been a fundamental failure for one calling himself a Mall Master. So for me as an apprentice, this was something I had to look forward to. At some point, I would be called upon to fill an empty space. I doubt if Maurice expected it would happen this soon. I was hoping for it, of course. So when it happened, I moved quickly without consulting Maurice, without asking for advice, without even mentioning it to him. He knew, of course, as he had to. But he did not speak of it to me, offered no advice, even pretended not to be aware of my behind-the-scenes manipulations and preparations. I am sure he knew something was going on. But he had told me to make love to the mall. And I knew he was interested to see me test myself in the highest way possible. So I was free to pursue this issue with total autonomy, and I did.

The architecture I did myself, using computer templates. When my designs were finalized, I took them to Bolt Construction, the same company putting up Anton's skyscraper mall downtown. Roderick Bolt had built West Park Plaza. I knew his capabilities, his reputation, the kinds of materials and techniques he was famous for. But I feared even my special little job would test the limits of his skills. If he couldn't do it, I had to know immediately, so I showed him what I had in mind and asked, "Can you do this?"

"Yes, this is no problem."

"There is one problem. I have an extremely brutal time factor involved. I need this job done to perfection in a certain time frame."

"What time frame?"

I told him.

He blinked, paused, stroked his beard, thought seriously for a long stretch of silence. I watched him. Finally, he said, "Yes, I can do it that quickly."

"Are you sure?"

He smiled at me. "I'll be expecting a sizable bonus."

"I'm willing to pay. But only if the job is done on time."

"You'll have it done on time. You have my word."

So we signed a contract, and I left the plans with Bolt. Much preparation awaited us both.

Before leaving, I asked him, "How is the skyscraper mall going?"

"You can see for yourself by looking at the skyline."

"Yes. Do you have contact with Anton?"

"I speak to him."

"How is he?"

"Busy and happy."

I left it at that.

The day came when the jewelry store closed. I handled all the details. Maurice did not speak of it to me, he asked me no questions. I prepared a report for him and left it on his desk so he could review it upon his return from Seattle. By then, if my plans were successful, that report would be of no interest to him.

The space was empty exactly two days. On Friday morning, when Maurice left for the airport, I called Roderick Bolt and told him to get started. As Maurice's car disappeared down one street, up another came a caravan of trucks and vans. Work began immediately, and proceeded with a swiftness that astounded even me.

Four days later, slightly before midnight on Monday evening, the job was done. The last man I saw was Roderick Bolt. I handed him his bonus check for getting the job done on time, then he left me alone in my brand new store.

I retired, went upstairs, fell asleep between fresh silk sheets on a brand new bed in my brand new penthouse apartment built on top of the mall. Before I collapsed into bed, I glanced out my bedroom window and took a look east, just across the mall roof, at the dim exterior of Maurice's apartment. Whenever he looked out his living room windows, he would see my apartment.

***

I slept deep within the bosom of the mall that night, and there were no dreams, because now, the reality was enough.

For four days I had ravished the mall, consumed by a state of consciousness not unlike sex. For four days I had slept little, instead been swept up in a swirl of creative building enhanced by my understanding of what I was doing and why, of who this was for and who this served. The mall was an extension of Maurice's body, and so my actions upon the mall was action on the body of Maurice Sully. Creating a new store, a new business, and integrating my personal life into it via an apartment, was more than just remodeling the mall. It was an act of love upon the person of Mall Master Maurice Sully. It was an act in which I presumed myself an equal, presumed myself as a desire he held, presumed my own value to match his, presumed my own commitment to the mall to match his own. In this, I made the mall my own. I took from it and gave back in equal trade, integrating myself into the mall, and the mall into me, in a way permissible only to those who presumed to master the mall physically and spiritually. With this act, I was telling Maurice, "I am a master of the mall. Now I wish to be addressed as Mall Master Diane Copernicus. And for this, if your judgment is that I have acted truly and with consistent logic, I wish to be rewarded in a manner befitting my achievement."

And now, like a lady, I simply waited for my man to arrive and make his judgment.

So I waited. But not with idle hands. After all, there was still a mall to manage — and a brand new business to launch.

***

On Tuesday morning, a full-page ad appeared in the *Billings Gazette* announcing the opening of LoveTech, the newest business in West Park Plaza:

LOVETECH
Applying the science of ethics to romance

Do you have questions about love?

Are you having problems in a relationship?

Are you having trouble finding a soul mate?

Do you know what you want — and why you want it?

Do you know how to measure your self-esteem — and how to improve it?

LOVETECH is your one-stop source for answers to all your pressing questions and problems. Our staff of spiritual therapists is supervised by Apprentice Mall Master Diane Copernicus, to ensure the highest level of commitment and attention to your needs.

LOVETECH is short for Love Technology — and we've got it! For the first time anywhere, we offer the benefit of custom-designed Conscious Dreaming technology, to enable you to explore your own romantic values first-hand, in the privacy of your own mind, by yourself — or with your partner hooked in with you.

To experience this unique new service, call now for an appointment, and be guided by logic into the rational realm of romantic love!

Call 1-800-LOVTECH

We started taking calls at eight in the morning, opened our doors for business at ten. A steady trickle of customers showed up, kept my staff of five therapists busy.

As I had expected, the feature most people were interested in was the Conscious Dreaming technology. Using this method, a person can be placed into a dream-state by electronically activating the part of the brain that triggers dreaming. The brain is, in effect, fooled into thinking it is asleep — and you start to dream while still conscious. The link between the two brain hemispheres is tapped into and the content of the dream is produced directly from the individual's subconscious. It is a strange state of altered consciousness in which you are in a focused trance, with conscious access to your subconscious, as if you were accessing a computer database at will, instead of just getting random bits of data burped up by accident. And the theme of the dream is love: you ask your mind to tell you everything it knows about who you love — and why you love who you love. You can consciously follow a long train of complex integrations made over a lifetime and see how your desire for a certain face or body type goes back to values and ideas and premises formed long ago, in your youth — or, sometimes, just last week. You can explore the genesis of your own values. And you can translate your abstract values into concrete form — or concrete forms into abstract values. This happens by feeding your subconscious a long list of spiritual and esthetic values, then asking your subconscious to translate those values into physical form, in effect, drawing you a picture of what your values look like in the form of another human being. Then you know what to look for in another person when you are searching for a lover. And you know if any prospective lovers add up to your own values — or if there are other reasons why you have feelings for them.

Many people have vague ideas of what they want in another person. Searching for a love is a case of not knowing what you are looking for until you find it. When this happens, a person experiences what has been called "the shock of recognition," or "love at first sight." They see somebody and know instantly, because of a jolt from their subconscious, that that person is a soul mate — or at least, a physical manifestation of some deep value or integration of values.

What Conscious Dreaming does is give a person control over this subconscious process and a powerful way of analyzing a wealth of data — the knowledge and thinking acquired over a lifetime.

Have I used it? Of course I have. I wouldn't feature it in a business in the mall unless I knew firsthand that it worked and had value. I used the technology to explore my own thoughts and feelings about love. It did confirm what I already knew. It also took me down into deeper implications of my values.

But I won't go into that now.

You want to know how Maurice reacted when he returned from the symposium and saw what I had done to his mall.

***

I knew what time he was scheduled to return. I had asked security to alert me when he entered the mall. They obliged.

He was on time, as usual. At 2:15 he was back in his office.

I was up in my new penthouse, having lunch, studying Maurice's apartment from my bedroom window. His structure was all clean straight masculine lines of silver metal and glass. Mine was an octagon of alternating stone walls and glass windows. The roof was entirely glass, with retractable blinds open now, flooding the interior with sunlight. An elevator and a spiral stairway led down to my new business. I relaxed, enjoyed my lunch, relished my new surroundings. Then at 2:30, I called Maurice in his office, on his private line. This was a calculated breach of etiquette on my part. "Hi boss! How was the symposium?"

"I was a hit. Even learned a few things."

"Are you ready to learn some more?"

"You've been a busy girl over the weekend, haven't you?"

"Just following orders, boss."

"I saw the ad in the paper this morning. You should know you've aced out every mall in the region on this."

"When can you stop in and take a look?"

"How about right away?"

"I'll be waiting."

Maurice showed up at three o'clock.

He had a woman with him.

Her baring, elegance, erect posture, and imperious face identified her immediately as a Mall Master. When she got closer, I saw the emblem on her classic green gown.

Maurice presented me to her first. "Raphaela, may I present my apprentice, Diane Copernicus?"

"You didn't tell me you had an apprentice!" she said.

"Diane, this Raphaela Capuletti, Mall Master of the Emerald City Mall of Seattle."

I bowed. She came forward and raised my head with a soft finger underneath my chin. I looked up into her huge green eyes. She smiled at me. "That's not a proper greeting, Miss Copernicus." She took me in her arms and kissed me on the lips. Then she stepped back and looked severely at Maurice. "Master Sully, you'll have to explain to me your reticence on this issue."

"I know how you like a surprise, Raphaela."

"Well, you waited a long time to choose an apprentice — but you obviously chose well. Miss Copernicus, you did all this in a weekend?"

She raised her arms in a sweeping motion that encompassed my business.

"Essentially, yes."

"Who was your architect?"

"I was."

"Well, your design seems clean and efficient."

"Let our tour begin here," I said. "I'll explain my thinking to you."

We were standing in the wide entrance lobby just off the mall. On the left was a huge sculpted sign saying LOVETECH. In front of this was a reception counter where a therapist greeted customers. "This is Marlene," I said, introducing her. "She's my most important and valued associate. She has a very subtle job — to make sure prospective customers are not frightened away." To our right was a grouping of four comfortable chairs and a large couch all focused on a table covered with literature and brochures. "When a customer enters the facility, he is greeted by Marlene or another associate. If no associate is available, customers come over here to look at brochures and get some basic information on what Lovetech is all about, what we offer, how it all works. Especially the Conscious Dreaming technology, which is the main attraction, of course." A TV monitor built into one corner caught their eyes, just as it was supposed to. "We've got a demo tape that plays on command," I said. "Shows how the CD technology works, how a person is hooked up to it, and how it affects the brain and body, and so on. Explains what a person should expect to experience. We try to stress as strongly as possible why it is advisable to have at least one therapy session before trying to use the CD technology. This is because it is good to clarify for yourself exactly what your questions are, what it is you want to learn from your CD experience. We all know that the subconscious works best when it is asked questions and given commands. That is what the therapy sessions are for. We try to take customers through a series of three sessions before their first CD experience. It has been found that this makes for a much richer experience."

I guided Maurice and Raphaela through a doorway and into the therapy section of the facility. Along each wall were five private therapy booths. Three were in use right now. I took Maurice and Raphaela to an empty booth and we all sat down inside, closed the door. Inside, simple efficiency ruled. A chair and desk waited at one end for the therapist. The client had a choice of comfortable plush chair or couch.

"Our therapy sessions are pretty basic," I said. "We ask the client questions, find out what he wants, what he needs, what his questions are.

We take them through the standard tests, have them measure their self-esteem, so they have a self-known, objective idea of what level they are on. Then we go into a lot of details. For instance, for most people, they want to have their values translated into a face, a physical form. To do that, we have to find out what their values really are. So we ask questions. I usually like to start with a direct and simple approach. Mistress Capuletti, may I use you as an example?"

"Oh, please do!"

"If you were a client, I would start by asking if you are in a relationship. Are you?"

"Yes."

"Are you married, or do you just have a boyfriend?"

"I have a boyfriend."

"Are you happy in the relationship?"

"Yes. But I want to be happier. And I do have some questions..." She looked at Maurice and smiled.

I had moved around behind the desk and sat down in the therapist chair, so I had access to the remote controls that operated the therapy chamber. I didn't know yet if it would be necessary to use the full array of techniques the chamber made possible, but I wanted to be prepared and in position to activate them. I did push one button that activated the recording and analyzing computer. That was essential to anything else that followed.

"You want to know how deep your value affinity with your boyfriend runs?" I asked.

"Yes," said Raphaela. "That would be a good question to have answered."

"Very well. Let's try the simplest approach first. You are a Mall Master, so we can assume you know your own values better and deeper than the average person. Can you define and state for me in essential, fundamental terms, what is the quality of character you look for most in a man?"

"Yes. I would term it 'ruthless idealism.'"

"Very well. How do you identify that quality in a man? What are some of the characteristics you look for, clues and demonstrations that a man actually has this quality? What do you consider proof of this quality?"

I had picked up a pen and was making notations on a piece of paper in front of me. I glanced quickly once at Maurice to see where his eyes were focused. He was watching Raphaela. She was staring at the blank white wall of the chamber. I noticed again her beautiful green gown, noticed her green earrings and green sandals for the first time. Something clicked in my subconscious and I hit a control button that gradually, slowly, imperceptibly began to change the color of the walls to a shade of green that matched her dress. This was obviously her favorite color, so I would use it to assist the therapy. I also made a note to record how long it would take her to notice the color shift — or if she would notice at all.

After only a moments pause, she answered my question. "The first thing I look for is a man's relationship to his work. An idealist doesn't compromise in his selection of a career and actually chooses work for which he is perfectly fit intellectually, physically, emotionally. If you see a man doing work and he seems out of place, there is a possibility he is not an idealist. If he seems to fit and you can't imagine him doing anything else, then he is the right man in the right place.

"Next, a ruthless idealist integrates all the way, so that every aspect of his life is a reflection of the values he finds in his work. Socially, a ruthless idealist does not have 'halfway' friends. The people in his life are people who share deep values with him. And more: these friends are so important to him that he is willing to trade severely to keep them in his life.

"Artistically, a ruthless idealist surrounds himself with art that appeals directly to his deepest honesty, the part of his mind to which nothing fake or unreal has ever been presented. In the art he loves he sees unraveled strands of the integration of his own thought, own values, own life. This painting here shows him the quality of his sight on the first morning of his childhood when he stood in full sunshine and analyzed his first syllogism. This symphony here opens a flow of emotion stored in memory, the experience of how he felt as a youth the first time he understood what love was, and fell in love with the idea of being in love. And this sculpture here, the one he touches each morning before dressing himself, this brings back the memory of how he first grasped the concept 'entity,' when, as an infant, he lay in his crib playing with plastic shapes, using his hands to grasp, hold, explore, to attempt change, to reorganize and rearrange into new patterns. Now, as an adult, he does all that with his mind. As an adult, he knows what the painting means and why he responds to it as he does — and this frees him to see completely, to relate it to his entire life, to integrate that specific way of seeing into every other moment of his life. So he sees his home and his business and his love with that same beautifully colored, stylized luminosity — and he hears the strings of the symphony in his beloved's voice when she speaks to him — and he sees her sculpted form when she presents herself to him naked and allows his hands to caress her body. This is the idealist consuming art: always making it personal and selfish, pulling out the abstract essence and then draping it over himself like a cloak, seeing it fit his own particular concretes, the details of his life stylized by the metaphysical essence of what is most basic to his soul."

She was looking at Maurice, her face serene, serious, her lips parted, wet, her breath frozen now in her chest, the muscles of her neck tense for just a moment, then relaxed, the only indication of tumult within her a subtle ripple across the skin of her lower neck where blood pumped in time with her heart. She was in love with Maurice. But was this confession intended for him? For me? Or for us both?

I ignored Maurice, sat back in my chair, was able not to look at him through a massive effort of will. Raphaela shifted her eyes to me. Her nostrils dilated, flexed as she breathed deeply, her chest rising and falling gracefully in a relaxed and controlled motion. Her eyes held me coldly. Wasn't I presumptuous in attempting to offer therapy of this sort to a Mall Master? She needed this stuff like the ocean needs water, like the sky needs blue. So sure, I was presumptuous.

But she was not here because *I* had brought her. This had been orchestrated by someone else, for a reason I had yet to consider.

"Let's back up a moment," I said, leaning forward. "I'm interested in hearing more about your concept of idealism. Can you tell me in your own words what an idealist is?"

"An idealist is a person who cannot tolerate a contradiction between his inner world and outer. What is true and good in reality must be believed and understood in the mind; and what is held as ideal within, must have some physical manifestation in the world. If I know that logic is good, then I expect to find logic in nature, and in the men I deal with. If honesty is good, then I expect to find honesty in the world. If love is good, then I expect to love and to be loved in return. An idealist is a person who sees that man and nature must be integrated, that man can only live by fitting himself seamlessly into what reality really is, and be true to his highest nature, and thus raise nature up to the level of man. The earth is dirt; Man's presence makes it gold. *That* is an idealist. If he sees a man walking in the dirt, he gets furious, wants to understand where the gold is."

"I see. Now then, you characterized your ideal man as a *ruthless* idealist. What other kinds are there? And why the distinction and the stress on the term ruthless?"

"A ruthless idealist does not surrender his intellectual sovereignty even for a split second. He does not toy with any alien viewpoint, or any alien values. He maintains his personal connection to reality always, at all costs. He has no consideration, no pity for anyone made uncomfortable by his idealism. He uses the concept in a selfish, practical way, like a dirty man cleaning himself with soap. Idealism is spiritual soap. It cleans the spirit, keeps it fresh and inoffensive. Show me a man with an unclean soul, I'll show you a man who's never been washed by the cleansing power of idealism. Have an uneasy feeling about a man you meet, feel there is something 'off' about him, something not quite right, something your subconscious is nagging you about, but you can't put your finger on just what it is? Look to this principle first. You are probably catching a nasty whiff of a filthy spirit with no trace of idealism.

"And more. This is the quality I look for in the face, above all else. How do you recognize idealism in a human face? Would you like me to reduce the issue and analyze the elements involved, so your fancy computer can draw me a picture of my ideal face, show me what it is I've been looking for all my life?"

I smiled. "Please continue."

She turned to Maurice, raised an arm and pointed an elegant finger at him. "Take a look at *this* man. Have you ever really studied his face?"

"I have."

"Let me tell you what I like about it. As an integrated whole, grasped by its essence and felt immediately as a sum — it is a perfect sense of life expression of what I am talking about, of ruthless idealism. The first time I ever saw him, he gave me such a feeling of comfort and satisfaction, as if all was well in the world. I asked myself why that was, how just a face had the capacity to color my entire metaphysical viewpoint. It was not just that it was a human face. We all see hundreds of human faces every day. We react in *this* way only to a special few. Over the course of a lifetime, perhaps a handful or less. And the first time I saw Maurice, this is what I felt. And as I talked to him and learned the quality of his mind and character, his face grew even more beautiful. Instead of being disappointed by what was behind the face, the face grew more beautiful knowing what animated it.

"Now then. Why did it hit me so hard? Look at his eyes first. Yes, they are blue and beautiful, and they light up his face in an aesthetically pleasing manner. But look beyond that. See the way his eyes react to seeing you — and seeing everything else in his field of vision? Do you see anything registering in his eyes? Yes. You can see his basic intelligence in the focus he brings to his sight. You can see the mind and values behind those eyes in how they respond to what — or who — they are seeing.

"The first time Maurice looked upon my person, I saw that he knew exactly who and what I was — and that this changed him not in the slightest. He would not adapt himself for my benefit. He would not edit or abridge his soul for my sake. He would not change his manner of existence just because another consciousness happened to be present. He simply saw me for what I was. If he felt anything special for me, that was his concern, not mine.

"So I saw a ruthless individualist, first of all. Most people are attracted to faces that make them comfortable. Most people want a face that is friendly, accessible, outgoing, giving, a face that does not challenge or inspire or frighten. Not me. Seeing this face was a command to rise. And I am not afraid of rising. Looking upon Maurice's proud features is like being told, 'If you want me, come up and get me.' That is the exciting core of romantic love. The challenge of pursuing a difficult value, a challenging value: another consciousness that will not accommodate you — but will respond if you have equal value. It has been said that finding a soul mate is like looking into a mirror. But have you ever considered how cold and hard and unmalleable a mirror is? A mirror is not like a pillow upon which you rest your head. And it is not soft putty that you mold into a shape of your choosing. It is hard crystal and if you attempt to bend it, it shatters into shards and you loose the reflection. That is what Maurice's face was to me. It made me uncomfortable — but in a good way. If he was a mystic, or lacked self-esteem, being confronted with another self-confident consciousness would have been a frightening experience for him, and that fear would have colored his face in a different manner, an unattractive manner, and that would have turned me away, not held my interest. But because he is rational and is a creature of high arete, another mind is not a threat to him. Reality is what he knows it to be, and no other opinion holds sway over his mind. And his own soul is what he knows it to be, and no set of eyes looking at him without recognition can change the self-known facts of his own inner self.

"And then there is his mouth. Next to the eyes, the mouth is the most expressive part of the human face. What is present in the eyes is also in the mouth, although much more subtly. Analyzing the mouth is usually only necessary when the eyes are still a mystery and you are not certain what it is you have seen there. It helps to talk. A mouth in repose is a contextless oasis, and one can only infer character by using what one has learned from the eyes. But if you talk, see the mouth in motion, see a smile or a frown, watch what the lips do when he is listening to you speak, observe how the mouth stretches the rest of the face into specific patterns, watch how the facial muscles stretch and pull across the skull, and how the brow creases, how the temple flexes, the tilt of the head — all of this follows from and has been integrated by the basic ruling element of the soul. Independent or dependent? Self-known or fake? Self-esteem coming from within, or is he looking for his worth to come from you? Is he focused on what you are — or what you think of him? Is he self-sufficient — or does he need something from you to complete his self-esteem?

"And the body flows from the face. Body language and style should be consistent with what you see in the face. If it is, you are looking at an integrated man."

"So in sense of life terms, what you are looking for is a face like a fortress. Something unyielding."

"Yes. It is not right for a man to surrender himself to every other mind he meets, to be a spiritual shape-shifter and change to accommodate other values. You see, if a person believes that other people exist to serve his needs, or that he exists to serve the needs of others, then he does not look at other people as ends in themselves, and he does not experience himself as an independent soul. So when he meets and interacts with another person, he does so either as a spiritual beggar — or as a spiritual vampire. The proper attitude should be: I am what I am, I'm not going to change, take it or leave it. And that attitude finds expression in a certain kind of face, what you have called 'unyielding,' which is a good term. But it is better to see the physical reality of that kind of face. And for that, we have Maurice."

We both looked at Maurice. He sat relaxed but attentive, his face neither agreeing nor disagreeing, his manner indicating no special pleasure or displeasure in being the object of such a serious, detailed discussion by two beautiful women who both wanted to sleep with him. He said, "Have you noticed that the walls have turned green?"

Raphaela looked around, smiling. "Yes, I had noticed that. Thank you, Diane. I appreciate you being so attentive to my needs. That is a beautiful hue of green."

I sat forward and glanced at my notes. "So here is what we have so far. Your essential character value is 'ruthless idealism.' You see this best expressed in a face you term 'unyielding.' You've made it clear that Maurice is the best expression of this kind of face you've ever seen. Would you like to proceed further and see if our computer draws a different picture for you?"

"If I have expressed my value preference consciously, what does it matter what a computer thinks?"

I smiled. "Forgive me Mistress Capuletti, but you have misunderstood. The image is generated by your own subconscious, during the Conscious Dreaming experience. The images come directly from your own deepest mind. They are the images to which you have always been attracted."

"But I already know what these images are. I know my mind. I see no point in having dreams to explain myself to myself."

"You are right. It is perhaps irrelevant for a person of your spiritual development to learn anything new from the CD experience. But of course, this is is not a real therapy session. You may experience the Conscious Dreaming just so you know what clients here are actually going through."

Maurice spoke up. "I would like to take the next step. This business is in my mall, it has been created by my apprentice. I am obligated to test this technique, see how it works, what it means, what it actually does, and what its potential is. So I will experience the Conscious Dreaming. It would please me, Raphaela, if you would join us. Correct me if I am wrong, Diane, but in our context, would not a linked CD session be the most interesting and intense?"

"It would."

"That is what we should do. We have an actual situation here. Raphaela is in love with me, has been for years. This trip is perhaps her last chance to consummate that love. Or so she believes. And then she learns that I have an apprentice, and that we are seeking full integration in this relationship. She is afraid of you, Diane. She is afraid you will take away her last chance to have a love with me.

"And Diane. Your situation is even more challenging. Now you believe you are in competition with a full-fledged Mall Master, a woman years ahead of you in spiritual development. How can you hope to match her quality and win my soul? You are just an apprentice. So you must be feeling great turmoil right now.

"And then there is me. What are my real intentions here? Who do I really love, who do I really want? Have I abused my relationship with Raphaela? Am I going to end my relationship with my apprentice? When I left, I told her to make love to the mall. Am I satisfied with how she has interpreted that request? Or has she failed?

"Both of you ladies must want to know the truth to all these questions. And I want to know the truth about both of you. The deepest truth possible. Instead of spending a lifetime together and ending up disappointed, why not use the CD technology to save ourselves a lot of grief. Let's plunge into each other's minds and find out the naked, unvarnished truth. Let's find out who we really are and what we really believe, what we really value — and who loves who the most, and the best. And do all this in a context that makes it impossible for us to hide from each other. What do you say, ladies?"

Raphaela sat stone still for a span of seconds, her eyes cold as they locked onto Maurice. He gazed back at her, faced her squarely so she could stare unendingly at that beautiful face she loved so much.

She slapped him.

"I see now my role in this drama you have engineered," she told him. "You have abused my goodwill and used me for purposes hidden. You spent a weekend with me in Seattle and never once mentioned that you had an apprentice. You flew me to your home and still said nothing. Then you spring it on me like this. All so you can have a dramatic CD experience, is that right?"

"Let's be clear on what has happened, Raphaela," said Maurice. "First of all, you invited yourself. I let you come because I wanted you to meet Diane. I didn't tell you about her because I wanted to protect your innocence — but also because I knew this weekend was an important test for Diane. I had no idea what would be waiting for me upon my return. But I knew it would be something special. And I knew having your voice, judgment, and opinion beside me would be valuable, both for me, and for Diane. So I ask you now, as one Mall Master to another: please join me as I judge my apprentice Diane. Stand beside me as I confront her with my judgment and challenge her self-esteem. Have I not done the same for you in years past?"

Raphaela slowly turned away from Maurice, her eyes finding me as a subtle smile gently returned to her face. "As I said: unyielding," she said. "Very well. Diane, it is time for us to experience the Conscious Dreaming."

***

So now I knew what was to happen, and why Maurice had brought Raphaela. And just as in the Festival of Arete, all that remained for me was to relax and be myself. Would that be enough? I would have my answer soon.

We left the therapy room and went to a CD chamber. I buzzed an available therapist and explained what was needed. Soon, we were all three locked in the CD chamber, strapped down into comfortable recliners, fitted with the CD helmets, and slowly brought down into the

Conscious Dreaming state.

During normal sleep, the self is submerged into the sea of subconscious and drifts randomly, encountering memories, information, fantasies, fears. Where one goes, and how one gets there, and what one finds when finally arrived, are very much uncertain and open to interpretation.

During conscious dreaming, we would all be completely aware of what we wanted, how to get there, and what to do with the information once we had it.

But there was more: we were three powerful, passionate, self-confident personalities linked in an integrated dream sequence. Where would we all go? Who would lead, who would follow? Would one of us dominate the others and set the agenda, guide the dream? What if we all went in different directions, in search of different information, what then?

And if I wanted to gain entrance into the deepest core of Maurice Sully's mind, would he allow me to enter?

I thought I would have the advantage. I was experienced in the CD state. I knew what to expect, and how to navigate inside. I expected that I would be able to lead, forcing the other two to follow me.

Before crossing the border of consciousness into the CD state of mind, my last thoughts were ruminations on the meaning of what Maurice had said to Raphaela. Maurice wanted to challenge my self-esteem and test me.

Test me how?

***

The boy stood alone in the middle of a field. He raised his head and gazed up at the sky. Diffuse light glowed all around, coming from nowhere — and everywhere. There was no sun. The sky had a metallic glint. The air held the scent of rain, but was warm and close. The grass was knee-high, and very soft. He looked far off to the horizon. He saw a white house at the base of some hills. He turned away, looked behind him, saw a great red barn rising up into the sky behind him. The color of the barn was like a force on his eyes, he experienced the red color with an intensity that caused his head to ache. But he didn't look away. The barn was beautiful. He wanted to go inside. He felt compelled to go inside. He had to see what was in that barn.

"Look what I have built," said Diane.

Maurice was calm. "No, I have built this."

Laughing, he ran through the grass. It didn't hold him back. He ran across a circle of dirt and then into the barn.

Inside, the barn was beautiful. Clean and well-ordered, dimly lit, but clear. Rows and rows of beautiful colored glass bottles lined the shelves inside the barn. No animals were present.

The boy walked to a shelf and took hold of a glass bottle, held it up into a shaft of green light slipping through the open doorway. The bottle illuminated as if a flame burned inside. The boy examined it, rolling it from one hand to the other, watching the light play through the bottle. The light was beautiful and he liked to watch it. All around him the colored bottles glowed like jewels along the clean straight lines of the shelves. He was filled with wonder and didn't find it curious at all that a barn should be built and hold nothing but bottles.

He noticed a ladder leading up into the loft. He climbed up and went immediately to the wide swinging doors of the hay loft that opened out upon the field. He swung the doors out and looked down and away. He was so high and he liked the view. He looked far to the horizon and saw a city in the distance. Beautiful towers gleamed with a promise of the future.

Down below him now, children danced and sang. He called down to them, but they didn't hear him, never looked up to see him, didn't notice him. He yelled again, got no answer, lost interest.

He noticed something on the floor of the hay loft near his left hand. Partly in shadow was a yellow disc of plastic. He picked it up and smiled. It was a frisbee. He looked out at the field. So high up! Look how far I can throw the frisbee! I bet I can sail it to eternity!

He twisted his body, cocked his wrist, gave a quick flick, flipped the frisbee out of the barn, into the air, out over the field —

The frisbee spun out in a sharp tight arc. Then, like a boomerang, it swept around to the right, tracing an ellipse through the air, and came right back towards the hay loft.

The boy sat watching, didn't move a muscle, didn't say a word, didn't breath. He didn't even have to move his right hand. The frisbee floated back and landed in his right hand, the same hand that had thrown it.

How did I manage to do that? he wondered.

And then he screamed down at the children. "Did you see it? Did you see what I did! Did you see the frisbee! I threw it and it came right back to me! Did you see it?"

"What happened?" asked one child. "Why are you screaming at us?"

The boy told them what had happened.

"I don't believe you," said a child.

"Do it again," said another.

That seemed a reasonable request. He tried it again. He tossed the frisbee out, trying to mimic the movements he had made the first time. The frisbee sailed out over the field and landed in the grass. Nothing miraculous about that.

The other children lost interest. Some called him a liar and a spinner of tale tales. They wandered off.

He went out into the field to find the frisbee in the tall grass. But it was lost.

"This is a true event from your childhood," said Diane.

He looked up. The girl with long curly black hair stood before him. She wore a red dress and had a serious face.

"Yes, it really happened," said the boy. He had blond hair and blue eyes.

"The other children thought you were a liar. They didn't believe you."

"No."

"Why have you shown this to me?"

The boy waved at the barn. "My first mall. Do you like it?"

"Yes. But what does this have to do with love?"

The boy smiled. "Look across the field. See the house?"

"Yes."

"I lived there as a child. Come, let's go see."

They stood in the yard of the big white house.

A bicycle was parked underneath a tree. Blue and white, glowing in the strange light, its sleek lines and extreme angles gave it a blurred quality, as if even sitting still it was in motion, and all you could do was catch a glance.

"Where is Raphaela?" asked Diane.

"She's waiting for us," said Maurice.

Anton Layvanwick appeared on the porch of the house. "Maurice, time to get dressed up! We're going girlfriend hunting!"

"Come on Diane, you can help!" said Maurice.

They raced into the house, ran up the stairs, entered a huge bedroom. Anton had laid out fine clothes for young Maurice. Maurice changed clothes, put on a nice tie, then stood in front of a mirror combing his hair. Anton was laughing and jolly, ignored Diane, who kept talking to him. But he didn't seem to know who she was, and she grew silent and sad.

When Maurice was ready they left the house, jumped on bicycles, flew down a long hill south of the house. Anton raced on ahead and disappeared down a side-street. Maurice and Diane kept going straight ahead down the endless hill, the wind whipping her hair and his necktie.

They reached the bottom of the hill. Just as they hit the bottom they heard a bone-jarring crash from the intersection ahead. They pedaled even harder and arrived to find a tremendous car crash. Two cars, twisted and crumpled like giant accordions, were strewn across the intersection. One car had impacted the side of the other.

Maurice jumped off his bike and ran to a girl lying in the street. She had been thrown from one of the cars. Lying on her back, beautiful and bloodless, her green dress unspoiled, her brown hair unmessed, her green eyes vivid and devoid of pain, she gazed up at Maurice, let him take her up into his arms. He kissed her and she smiled. "Will you be my girlfriend?" asked Maurice.

"My hero," said Raphaela. "Of course I will."

"This can't be the way you two met," said Diane.

"Yes, it is," said Maurice and Raphaela, in tandem, using one voice. "This is the abstract meaning of our love. Can you find the theme? Don't you see the abstraction? Use your aesthetic training, Diane. And be quick. Try to keep up with us. Here we go —"

Raphaela took control of the dream. She took us away from Maurice's childhood scene. Now we stood on the rain-drenched patio of a huge stone house facing a stormy ocean. Lightening flashed in the sky. Wind whipped and lashed our bodies with stinging pellets of water. Warm light glowed from the windows of the house, and a doorway beckoned. But neither Maurice nor Raphaela gave any indication of wanting to get out of the rain. They faced the dark ocean, walked to the edge of the stone patio, looked down across a rocky beach to the waves boiling in from the storm-drenched sea. Just when it seemed the storm would sweep us off the patio and into the sea, Raphaela raised one hand and swept it across the sky in a motion of imperial dismissal. In time with the motion of her arm, the stormy scene was swept away, the entire landscape faded into a warm sunny daytime scene of blue sky, golden beach, gentle blue waves lapping at a pristine shore. Darkness vanished, blue sky swirled above, the sun was an orange haze of dull metallic fire. Now our skin was dry, the house was dry, the stone beneath our feet was dry. In the dream, this all seemed perfectly natural.

Raphaela slipped out of her dress and stood naked before Maurice. She stepped off the patio and into the sand. She turned and beckoned to Maurice, holding out one hand and motioning for him to follow. "Come, Maurice, swim with me."

"No, I'd rather not."

"The water is fine. You'll see."

"I don't want to swim."

"I love the water, I want to share it with you."

Maurice took a step back.

Why was he so afraid of the water?

I looked out at the sea. My eyes scanned the shore, watched sunlight reflecting off the rippling waves. The ocean seemed alive. The beauty I saw was forceful and insistent, much more intense than anything I had ever seen in real life, in my waking hours. Raphaela's mind — and mine in turn — had stylized this ocean so that I saw it as a living work of art. It almost hypnotized me. But not enough so that I missed what the ocean held.

I gasped. Did Maurice see what I saw? Was *this* what frightened him so much?

Two bodies floated out on the ocean. Two bodies face down, what looked like a man and a woman. They were drifting out to sea. The waves had not captured them yet, were not bringing them back to shore.

"Maurice, don't go!" I shouted.

Raphaela laughed. "Don't worry, Maurice. I won't let you drown. I am a good swimmer, you'll see. I can teach you how."

"I'd rather go in the house," said Maurice.

"Then I will swim by myself," said Raphaela.

She ran towards the ocean. Maurice made no move to run after her, to stop her. Nor did he turn away and enter the house. He stood on the patio and watched Raphaela run to the water, dive into a wave as it crashed around her. As she swam, she took me with her.

I was naked in the water beside Raphaela. She swam to me and smiled, both of us stopped in the water, the two of us lifted in tandem as a wave rolled past and moved in to shore. "Isn't the water lovely?" asked Raphaela. "Let's see how far we can go!"

"Raphaela, did you see the bodies?" I asked, swimming after her.

"Never mind that. The bodies are always there. Maurice brings them. They are his spiritual baggage, don't you see."

I finally made the connection. Of course. Thanks to Anton, I knew the story. These bodies floating in the sea had to be Alan Benton and Sarah Fletcher.

But something was off. This was wrong. Alan and Sarah had survived and still lived in New Athens — did they not? They had lived happily ever after. Why did Maurice represent them as dead bodies floating in the sea?

But this was Raphaela's dream. She controlled these images, did she not?

I asked her. "Raphaela, is this your image, or Maurice's?"

She did not answer, just kept swimming. She was starting to lose contact with me — and getting closer to the bodies.

I felt the lure. I wanted to see the faces. I wanted to see what Alan Benton and Sarah Fletcher looked like, even dead, even in a dream.

I swam hard and caught Raphaela just as she approached the bodies. Both floated naked face down in the sea. Raphaela swam for the female and reached for the head, pulled it up out of the water to show me —

I was wrenched away by a .powerful force. Maurice had cut my connection to Raphaela's dream. I was back with Maurice, standing dry and clothed in the study of the stone house. We turned away from a window facing the sea and faced a fireplace. A huge fire burned, warming my skin. I looked at Maurice. "Why didn't you want me to see?"

"It is my memory. It should be my choice to show it to you."

Raphaela materialized across the room, dry and clothed, her hair perfect, her classic green gown impeccable as when I first saw her. But her eyes were angry. "If you don't want your apprentice to see your memory, then take it from my mind! I don't want your filthy images corrupting my mind! Take them out, I'm sick of seeing them in my most cherished memory of childhood!"

"You asked me for the story. You wanted that connection between us. Do you now disown it?"

"Yes! Take them away! What do those people mean to you? You saved their lives and never once did they offer a single word of thanks! Never once have they travelled to visit you. For all you know they could have children they named after you! And still not a word!"

"You know the reasons for that."

Raphaela walked across the room and stood furious in front of Maurice. I thought she was going to strike him. Instead, she said, "Show her the memory. Show her what you told me. Show us both so I can know it is true. Show us that moment in time, we both want to see it. Show us the moment you lost Sarah Fletcher. Show it to us and let us share your feelings for that woman."

"No, it is mine."

"Diane, tell him. You have power over his soul, I know he cannot refuse you. Tell him you want to see it." She looked at me, her eyes flaming and imperious. "You do want to see it, don't you? Just as Maurice saw it all those years ago?"

I looked at Maurice. "Share this with me, Maurice. Please. I do want to see it. I want to know Sarah and Alan as you knew them. Please show us."

"I cannot," said Maurice.

Raphaela exploded at him. "You cannot hide this from her, Maurice! You are a coward even to try. You have shared it with me, and I am not even your final choice. You *must* share it with your apprentice, the woman you wish to integrate completely into your life and soul. If not her, then who?"

Raphaela's face suddenly changed, surprised, shocked, as a new thought occurred to her. "Or are you hiding something from us? There is something you have not told even me. You wish to hide the memory because there is something there that you dare not confess to either of us. Is the story even true?"

Maurice exploded. "Of course it is true, it's part of the public record!"

I reached out for Maurice's arm, touched him gently. "Darling, I cannot force you. But this is not the place for hiding. Share the memory if you wish. But if you will not, allow me to take you into my dream. Which shall it be, darling?"

Maurice bowed his head, took a deep breath, then looked at me. "I did not want to protect you, Diane. There is no protection against this. But if you want to see what I saw, and feel what I felt — then I hope you learn something from it. Very well. Here you go—"

He took us.

The scene morphed into the interior of a helicopter. We were flying low past the legs of the Statue of Liberty. The helicopter circled some boats down in the harbor of New Athens, then went down, landed on a large rescue vessel. Raphaela and I were together, seeing out of Maurice's eyes, feeling with his body. We were carried by him, guests in his mind, his memory. I could see his youth reflected in the eyes of those who looked upon him, the young Mall Master, the recent hero of the events at the Show Me Mall in Missouri.

He left the helicopter and ran across the ship to a spot where rescue workers were just finishing up on two wet people dragged from the sea. As Maurice approached, the rescue workers receded, like waves from a beach, and all that was left were two wet people, a man and a woman, both of them young, both strong and healthy and saved from drowning. The man was on his back and very pale. The woman held his head in her lap and looked down at his face, caressed his cheeks and forehead, stroked his flesh to warm his body, combed back the wet hair from his eyes. The man's eyes were open and he looked up at the face of the woman with absolute amazement.

As Maurice approached, neither saw him, both wrapped up in the other. Maurice came so close he could reach out and touch them. But so many people swirled around, and it was so noisy on the deck of the ship, the two victims didn't notice Maurice standing right in front of them.

Then it was like we were all three in a spotlight. Everything else receded and there was no outside sound, not even the wind. Just the voices of the man and the woman speaking words of love to each other, with nothing bothering them, nothing disturbing them, the world was held at bay for these few moments as they rediscovered what it meant to be alive and in love.

A woman came and placed a hand on Maurice's shoulder. "Sir, do you need anything?"

"No."

"Everything is under control now. They'll both be fine."

"I know that."

"You are not needed here."

"I know that."

We stood and watched the two young lovers. Alan had a bomb in his head. I had to keep reminding myself of that fact. But right now, he was the only one who knew.

We stood and stared at them both, and I studied the faces, memorized Sarah Fletcher's face especially. I wanted to make sure I recognized her if I ever happened to see her.

And while we watched, Maurice spoke to us — Raphaela and myself — in the dream.

"I came to save them, but I was too late. When I got there, they had already been saved. They did not need me. And Sarah — she did not need me any longer.

"Listen to my thoughts:

"I should say good-bye, I should let them know that I am gone now and they are free, I should say something, I should tell Alan not to worry about the bomb, and I should tell Sarah not to worry as well, because she will, I know her. But I cannot interrupt this moment. I cannot invade this privacy. So this is the end. Just like this. We had breakfast this morning. We were happy and a family. And now, like this, it all ends, and I walk away without saying anything, leave them both alone, leave them on their own. And they will be fine, won't they? My job is done. Am I good Mall Master today? Am I?"

Maurice took us back to the stone house.

The memory was over.

He looked at me. "Now you know the meaning of the first memory I showed you. Everything that happened at the Show Me Mall, and all the aftermath with Sarah and Alan — it was like throwing the frisbee. I couldn't do it again if I tried, not in a billion years.

"But you, Diane, you are another frisbee. I have thrown you out of the high barn loft. And here you go, sailing off. Are you going to come back to me? Will you land softly in my hand? Will you?"

They both smiled at me — and then relinquished the dream to me.

Now it was my turn.

CHAPTER ELEVEN

DIANE COPERNICUS, MISTRESS OF THE MALL

Having the dream relinquished to my control, feeling Maurice and Raphaela step aside and allow me to take over, I felt a surge of power and energy flow through my mind. I was the experienced individual in this realm. I had let the two Mall Masters play around like children exploring a toy for the first time. And I admit they were good — they both learned with frightening quickness and seemed comfortable in the Conscious Dreaming realm.

But they still did not know the tricks I knew. And now I would show them. I would show them what the CD technology had been designed for, and how powerful it really was.

We were all seekers of an ecstatic state of consciousness. Maurice and Raphaela had merely hinted at what was possible through Conscious Dreaming.

Now I intended to give them the reality, in spades. I would string them out in such a manner that when it was over and we awoke and were disconnected, they would fall limp from their couches and have to be carried away on stretchers. I would have them both speaking in tongues.

I grabbed both minds and wrenched them into my mental elevator and plunged us to the base of my soul. I showed them the structure of my mind, starting at the bottom, with my axiomatic concepts. We moved up slowly through my first-level concepts, pausing to contemplate this base and see how it flowed up into more complex concepts. We observed the hierarchy of my mind as it flowered up into the far reaches of higher-level concepts, to my concepts of consciousness, my definitions, the endless strings of abstractions derived from previous abstractions. We followed the hierarchical structure, studied the logic of it all, looked for flaws, found none. I paused here and there to explore single concepts in detail, letting Maurice and Raphaela study the inductive trails that led to each concept. And I let them flow along the paths leading to each successive integration. I let them try as they could to find flaws in my structure, mistakes in my definitions, chaos in my integrations. They could not. We kept moving along, contemplating the structure with wonder, seeing the whole of all the thinking I had ever done, seeing in one unity the entire sum of a lifetime of induction, abstraction, integration, holding it all in our conscious awareness through the miracle of the Conscious Dreaming technology. They knew me and knew my mind in a manner more intimate than if I had written ten thousand books and they had memorized each line. They knew me in the best possible way. And while we toured, I gently instructed them in the art of this mind tour, so that in the future, they could do the same by themselves. They could explore their own minds, and, if they wished, share their minds with others as I was now doing.

They were both silent and respectful as we moved through the corridors of my mind. There was one concept I had held back. We had moved past related concepts, and they could see the paths to this concept, could see that I had blocked them so we could not pursue it until the time was right. They knew what the concept was and understood perfectly, made no attempts to crash the barriers of my mind.

But finally, the time came. I led them directly through the portals of my concept of love. We entered through the definition and inhabited the interior of the concept, explored its every detail and raced out along to every connection and integration I had ever made. It led to every part of my mind. We started at the beginning and I took them on a tour of everything I had ever loved. We began with the toys of childhood and gradually built up to the more important adult values. We ended up with a series of people, and at the end of that trail, was left with only two. I hinted that Maurice was the end of the chain. But I wanted to concentrate on the next-to-last link in the chain, and I wanted to explore that value and show it to them both in some depth.

That was Anton Layvanwick.

Raphaela warned me to be careful and consider fully what I was doing. I noted her comments, then led them both into my experience of Anton.

I showed them everything I loved about Anton. We explored all the connections leading from Anton to all my other values. And finally, when they knew my thoughts and feelings in precise detail, knew what I loved and why I loved it, I plunged us into a memory so they could experience the reality of what I felt for Anton — and what I experienced with him.

***

"I love the feel of your hands on my body," I said.

We were naked in the shower on the morning after our first night together. Warm water streamed over our bodies in the steamy shower. Anton was soaping me down, taking his time, caressing me as he lathered my skin, pausing now and then to kiss my neck and face. In the mist I watched his large hands slide over my body. I leaned back against his muscular chest and felt his warm wet skin pressing against my back. I felt light, even weightless in his arms. There was no danger of slipping and falling in this shower, even though the porcelain tub was slick with soapy water. I stood secure between his two massive legs, feeling as if I was a little girl hiding between two trees in a forest.

Anton lathered my entire body, then moved me into position under the shower and let a stream of hot water rinse over me. When I was rinsed and clean, I stepped out of the shower and he was waiting for me with a huge soft white fluffy cotton towel. He wrapped me up, rubbed me dry, then set me free.

I returned the favor, taking my time as I toweled his body dry, lingering on his shoulders and back, being brusque with his legs, gentle with his manhood. He was pleased with my effort.

I went away to do my hair, left Anton in his closet. I was only away a moment. I tied my hair back out of my face, then returned to him. I rewarded my freshly showered and deliciously clean Anton by padding naked across the thick carpet of his bedroom and surprising him as he stood naked before a full-length mirror, contemplating which clothes he would wear. There, in the dim haze of morning, feeling the warmth from nearby heating vents radiating on my exposed skin, I lowered myself to my knees in supplication and took his manhood into my mouth and pleasured him with my lips and tongue for a good long languid series of moments. I took my time and let him relish the experience. I did the same.

And inside the memory, I directed points of view thus: Raphaela was with me and knew what I knew as a woman; Maurice felt the experience as if he was Anton. So in a way, he knew what it was to have me love him in this fashion. I sent a quick query to Raphaela, wondering how well she knew Anton and if she had ever had this fantasy about him. But no reply came. She was silent, rendered mute by the depth of the experience I was giving her.

After making love, Anton and I dressed quickly. It was mid-morning and the sun was getting hot. We drove south in Anton's open car, followed a winding two-lane highway through the hills south of the city, crossed a bridge over the Yellowstone river, then continued south into wilder country.

"What kind of adventure are we going to have today?" I asked.

"You'll see," he said. "But first, we'll have breakfast."

The restaurant was hidden behind a stand of trees. Built into the side of a hill, it faced north to the city. Our table was at a window. We gazed out to the buildings and homes spread out in the valley beneath the sandstone cliffs of the Rimrocks. We saw fluffy white clouds sail above in slow-motion procession.

Our breakfast came quickly and we both ate with ravenous appetite, speaking now and then of trivial matters concerning the mall, the grocery, the clothing store. Anton got up once to make a phone call. When he came back, he was smiling.

We finished breakfast, then got back in the car and drove even further south. The road curved and winded even deeper into the hills until we finally came out on to a plain that stretched away across a wide valley. Far off on the other side, to the horizon, were the Pryor Mountains, the small first steps of a range leading up to the Rocky Mountains. And in the middle of the valley, in a series of connected fields just off the road, was a staging area for the launching of hot air balloons.

Anton pulled into a dusty parking lot and we got out and started walking towards the balloons.

"Are we going for a ride?" I asked.

"What do you think?" he said.

The balloons were being inflated as we arrived, most of them in various stages of ripeness. They were all the colors of the rainbow, and each with a distinctive design. Here was one painted to resemble the face of an animal; here was the face of a clown; there a dazzling design of flowing, swirling colors that seemed alive as the nylon fabric of the balloon billowed forth with hot air.

We made our way to the far side of the field, winding a trail through all the other balloons, giving ourselves a mini-tour. Anton knew many of the balloonists and waved and said hello to all, stopped to chat with a few, introduced me to several. We finally reached the far corner of the field and saw the last balloon. One of the first to begin inflating, it was now fully ready for flight. It was tethered to the ground by thick ropes. The ropes were taut, belying the force the big balloon was exerting against them, trying to get away, leave the earth, float up into the blue sky.

This balloon was a stunning cerulean blue and was decorated on two sides with the crystal flame, the symbol of the Festival of Arete. The crystal seemed to sparkle in the sunshine, and the billowing fabric of the balloon created the illusion of a flickering flame. It was truly a beautiful balloon. I was dazzled.

"Diane, this is master balloonist Bill Nemes. We call him Captain Nemo. He's been good enough to prep our balloon for us this morning. He deserves special thanks."

I took the hint and gave Nemes a proper kiss. "Thank you, Mr. Nemes. Is Anton competent to pilot one of these things?"

"Oh, certainly, you're in good hands with Anton. I taught him everything he knows. I trust him completely. You can do the same."

Anton stepped up into the basket first, then helped me in. When we were securely inside, Nemes released the ropes that held us to earth and we floated up and away.

It was a gentle, soundless levitation into the sky. The field and all the other balloons receded slowly at first, but then we were high enough for the wind to catch us good and we started moving steadily north, towards the city.

At first my attention was devoted exclusively to the ride, the sky, the view. We moved over the countryside, getting gradually higher. I saw the mountains far off to the west, looking much closer now that we were high in the air. And to the east, endless rolling hills of green and brown. The road back to the city snaked along beneath us, a gray ribbon twisting through the hills. An occasional car or truck inched along beneath us, the vehicles getting smaller as we rose higher. They were finally reduced to noiseless toys. The only sound was the occasional blast of heat from the burner Anton manned. He was nudging us higher slowly, and as we rose, our speed increased as we got up into faster winds. Behind us, more balloons were floating up into the sky, trailing behind us like so many round steps back down to the green fields of earth. We were all spaced quite a bit apart, though, and at this point, interference from other balloons was impossible. As was communication.

I was torn between watching the balloons rise behind me, and facing north to watch the city flower beneath us.

"Are we going to float over Billings?" I asked.

"You'll see."

"This is wonderful, Anton."

"It is."

"How long have you been a balloonist?"

"Many years. My primary hobby."

"Do you have a balloon of your own?"

He frowned at me. "Who else would own a balloon displaying the symbol of arete?"

I squealed with delight. "We must make a habit of this!"

"I would like that."

"Do you take all of your girlfriends for balloon rides?"

"Yes, I do."

He gave the burner a long blast and I could feel the balloon rise, my feet pressed firmly against the basket as we rose as if in a gentle elevator.

"The thing I like best about ballooning is the relaxed pace. I can run the balloon and still carry on a conversation with a woman."

I was watching his face carefully. "And I can't run away, can I?"

He looked directly at me, his eyes hard. "No, you can't. Not if you're sensible."

"Has a girl ever jumped out?"

"A few wanted to, when I was younger. When I was learning the ways of love, I chose poorly on many occasions. I took women for rides before they were ready. I rushed them. I've made all the classic mistakes with women."

"You've made none with me."

"So far."

"Do you expect to make a mistake?"

"I expect there are judgments and values of yours unknown to me."

I turned away from Anton, faced north, felt the balloon pressing into the cool morning air, my hair fluttering gently against my face. "Here we are, floating above the world, disconnected from the daily concerns of our lives, drifting as if in a dream, locked together in a small space with nowhere to go but where the balloon takes us. We have a context conducive to honesty, don't you think?"

"That was my hope."

"Then you have my pledge. As long as the ride lasts, I will be honest with you. Let us be naked with each other. Let us discover the truth of each other, and share judgments and values. What is it you wish to know, Anton?"

"I wish to make a contingent declaration of love."

I turned and faced him. "You did that last night."

"Did I?"

"That is what I felt."

"I was unaware that I had expressed myself so eloquently."

"It was in your body language, darling. And the sound of your moment, when it happened for you. You did not hide it from me, did not keep it to yourself. You shared it with me, you wanted me to feel it as well, did you not?"

"I did."

"Well — you succeeded. I did feel what you wanted me to feel."

"I cannot claim to read your body as well as you read mine."

"You don't have to; I'll let you know how I feel."

"Diane, why have you come to this mall?"

"For my honor. It was time to earn my own way, to make a prosperous life for myself."

"Why not stay in Denver, or go off to the coast?"

I smiled. "Am I so transparent?"

"No, not at all. I honestly don't know."

"You feel I don't belong here?"

"You seem out of place."

"How so?"

"You have a job beneath your person, beneath your capabilities."

"What do you know of my capabilities?"

"I have tested you."

"Oh? And when did that happen? And how?"

"I have my methods."

"I want to hear about them."

"They are secret."

"Have you invaded my privacy?"

"Of course not."

"Tell me what you did."

"I simply observed you."

"And?"

"And sent girls to the clothing shop to measure your competence."

"That explains all the grocery personnel going on clothes buying binges!"

"It was well worth the investment."

"I like working in the clothing shop."

"I know that, it was obvious."

"What is wrong with working in a clothing store?"

"Nothing."

"Well, what else did you learn?"

"I learned that you were a person I wanted to meet."

"And so we are together now. Good for us, yes?"

"Yes. But I still have some questions."

"Are we sinking?"

He gave the burner a blast. The balloon drifted higher, the city got closer.

"Why did you choose this city? A city with only one mall?"

"I expected I would have an easy time here."

"Why do you want an easy time?"

"Because I love the mall — but I am frightened of it at the same time."

"Do you wish to apprentice?"

"Possibly."

"If you do, why?"

"That is a very large question."

"If you wish to apprentice, you must learn to make it a small question. Go ahead. Give it a try. Don't be afraid. We are disconnected from the world up here, so anything you say is merely contingent."

"Very well. Because the mall is of this earth, completely, totally, in every respect. And it is a beautiful integration of all that is good and valuable in human life."

"That is a good general statement, and I understand what you are saying. But I'd like to hear you get more personal. What do you hope to find in the mall, personally?"

I considered that for a moment, then I said, "Two things. I want myself — and I want my ideal man. I can find myself only in the mall because here is where I find my truest expression of my own distinctive sense of life, the quality of existence that I want each day, and every moment of each day. And here is where I'll find my highest type of man, the man of my dreams, the man of my reality, a man who values the mall as much as I do, and in the same way I do."

"If this is true, why have you never asked me of the Mall Master?"

"I gave it no thought."

"Why not? Weren't you curious about him?"

"No."

"Why not?"

"What do I need a Mall Master for when I have you?"

"Aren't you curious why I have never apprenticed?"

"I did not know this was something you wanted."

"Well, now you do. Do you know how long I have been at this mall?"

"No."

"Ten years."

"And the Mall Master won't have you?"

"He has never accepted an apprentice of any kind."

"Why not?"

"That is complex."

I was silent. Anton gave the burner another blast. We were floating over homes now on the southern outskirts of the city. I looked far ahead and could see the gentle etchings of the cityscape of downtown Billings appearing ghostly on the horizon. The buildings were gray-green in the misty haze.

What Anton had said was truly one of the most frightening statements I had ever heard, and I was shocked — and ashamed — at the power with which it hit me. Despondent emotions flowed through me. I had lied to myself. I had evaded facing this. And now here was my new friend and lover Anton thrusting it in my face with no knowledge of the power it would have on me. It was a crushing blow to my spirit. What kind of monster was this Mall Master that he refused to accept apprentices? And what kind of fool was I to come to this place, lying to myself that I didn't care, that it didn't matter, telling myself that I had given up this dream, that I was an adult now and no longer wished to entertain the little-girl notion of being a Mall Master. But I did. I really did. It was something I wanted, something I had hoped for, and something I had wanted to be easy for me in this place. But it was not to be easy. It was not to be at all. Only one mall in town — and a Mall Master who did not accept apprentices. I had never heard of such a thing.

I was angry. And true to Anton, I did not hide my anger. "Who is this bastard? What kind of son-of-a-bitch builds the only mall in a city and then refuses to accept apprentices? He must be a filthy bastard, and as disagreeable as I had suspected."

Anton looked directly at me, his face calm.

"Is he some old man who flunked out of New Athens? Did they chase him away from Atlantis? Or is he some freak from America who wants to try to be a Californian? I have heard of that type. I hope I never meet one. I wouldn't enter any mall run by some Christian filth, even if he renounced that madness and pledged dedication to total logic and the highest standards of arete, I would never step into his mall, even if it was the last mall on Earth. So who is he? After ten years, you must have met him, you must know him. Why haven't others censured him on this policy? Well, tell me. Talk to me. Are we sinking again? Those balloons are above us now."

Anton gave the burner another blast, nudged us a bit higher. We floated closer to the city. I did not consider the implications of that. My mind was focused on other issues.

Anton regarded me calmly. "Yes, I know the Mall Master of West Park Plaza. He is my best friend."

I stared at him dumbly.

"Well, now I know how much you want it," Anton said.

I closed my eyes, took a deep breath. "And so do I."

"A discovery?"

"Yes. I fear I don't know myself as well as I should."

"I'm sure you know yourself. You merely haven't discovered what you are capable of."

"And what of you, Anton? You say he is your best friend. And yet he won't accept you as an apprentice?"

"I have never asked him."

"Why not?"

"Because I know his answer. And I know the reason for his answer. And I respect it."

"I do not want to meet him now."

"Yes you do."

"Well…"

"Diane, it is your destiny."

"What do you know of my destiny?"

"First law of logic. A is A. It is in your nature."

"We'll see. Very well. So you've shown me how much I love the mall. And what of you? How deeply do you wish to pursue this value? How much integration do you desire? Ten years at the grocery. Part of the mall, but not yet master of the mall. What does the future hold for Layvanwick?"

He gave the burner a good long blast, then came to me, put one arm around my shoulders, raised my left arm in his and pointed far off to the city. The towers were growing larger, the shapes cleaner. Anton pointed and whispered in my ear. "There is my destiny. In the city. In the center of the city. I do not wish to become master of a mall. I wish to become master of the city."

"You are a boxboy."

"I am Layvanwick. I can do this."

"When you do, I will be your apprentice."

He smiled at me.

We stopped talking. There was much to reflect on. And there was much beauty to take in. We were well over the city now and it stretched out below us in a sparkling green sprawl. I saw trees and trees and more trees, and houses and buildings and long boulevards shooting away to every horizon. I was hoping we would float over the mall, but Anton went nowhere near that part of town. He guided us high, then took us floating down into the center of the city, maneuvering the balloon with expert precision. I have no idea how hard it really was for him to steer the balloon in the manner he did. At the time, I didn't consider it, just assumed that this was a commonplace thing done with huge billowing hot air balloons all the time: float them over the center of a city and then land them on top of a building. Sure. Nothing to it. Easy as parking a car — or sitting down in a chair. But that is what he did. He took the balloon over the city of Billings — and landed it on the roof of the Bank of Montana. At noon. With traffic heavy in the streets below. Wasn't this sort of thing against the law? I was impressed. Maybe Layvanwick could master the city. But what exactly did he mean by that? What did it mean to master a city? And even if it was possible, how could it be done by someone who was just a boxboy?

I remembered something my father had told me long ago. "You don't need anyone's permission to live. If you want to do something, do it. The people who get things done are the people who want to do those things. Whatever it is. See something you regard as a great achievement? Wonder how the person who did it managed to do it? Very simple. He did it because he wanted to do it. That is the entire secret of life. Make up your mind what you want to do — then do it."

Anton had made up his mind that he would land his balloon on the roof of a building in downtown Billings.

He had made up his mind that he would become master of the city.

Because his best friend wouldn't share the mall he had built.

And what of me? Was it worth making up my mind to do something that Anton had just told me was impossible? I wanted to apprentice at a mall where there was no apprenticeship, never had been, never would be. So what was I going to do now?

I was going to land in a hot air balloon on the roof of the largest bank in the state of Montana.

As we descended, I thought of the Mall Master of West Park Plaza. I had never met him. I didn't know his name. I didn't ask Anton to tell me his name. I didn't want to know. Because I hated him. In the name of justice, I hated that bastard, whoever he was.

***

Within the conscious dreaming, I watched Maurice Sully, I observed his state of awareness and checked his focus. He was completely into the dream. He was experiencing the dream through Anton. The shadow of Anton's soul was reflected in my memory, and this Maurice gravitated to, becoming his best friend as seen through my eyes, as loved through my eyes. If Maurice had feelings or thoughts about my statements and state of mind during this memory, he kept those mute and I could read nothing in him. And the same for Raphaela. From her all I sensed was a rising awe for my ability to direct the depth of this experience. She was hungry for more, wanted to take it to conclusion.

The dream continued.

***

We left the balloon billowing atop the bank in the mid-day sunshine, and we took an elevator down into the building.

A crew had been waiting to receive the balloon and tether it to the roof, securing it in the wind. Anton didn't say a word to them, and they didn't even glance at us, ignored us as we left the basket and made for the doorway to the elevator.

Ten years at the mall, and still only a boxboy? There was something I was not being told.

As we rode down in the elevator, Anton said to me, "Do you know what I am, Diane?"

"What are you?"

"A city worshipper. Do you know what that is?"

"I am a Californian, Anton. We are all city worshippers, you know that. It is our religion."

"Logic is our religion. The city is the body of logic, the physical form of reason. I am one presumptuous enough to want to possess that body. The city is a woman, and I am a man. I want to have the city. I want to make love to the city. I want to penetrate the city. And I want to do it in front of everyone, hiding nothing, ashamed of nothing. For this is what separates those of us who have a calling to the mall. We are the man worshippers who rise above even those who call themselves this. We are the man worshippers *who are worshiped* by the man worshippers."

The elevator opened and we walked across a narrow corridor, then out some swinging doors and onto a modest patio. We were on the tenth floor of a twenty story building. At the edge of the patio was a metal railing. Built into the railing was a telescope. We were facing west. Anton went to the telescope, took aim on the western horizon, then motioned for me to take a look.

I did. I saw West Park Plaza so close I thought of reaching out to touch it. But it was far away. Even so, I could see clearly some strange structure built into the roof of the mall. I asked Anton what it was.

"His home. That is where the Mall Master lives. He built himself an apartment on the roof of his mall."

I laughed.

"Does that strike you as silly?"

"Oh no."

"That is what I brought you here to show you. And now that you have seen it, it is time to leave this building and take a walk."

"Very well."

We took the elevator down to the lobby and left the building. There was a vacant lot across the street from the bank, an entire city block left barren and undeveloped. The grass was getting tall and scraggly. The whole area had a dreary and depressing aura hanging over it. It depressed me to see it, but I said nothing to Anton, not wanting to sour his mood. But strangely, Anton insisted we walk across the vacant lot. We crossed the street and instead of keeping to the sidewalks, Anton strolled right across the lot.

"Why haven't they fenced this mess off?" I asked.

"Good question."

"And why isn't this developed?"

"Good question."

"This is prime real estate."

"Good location, no doubt about it. Feel like lunch?"

"We just had breakfast."

Anton looked at his watch the same instant I glanced at mine. We laughed at each other. "Too early!" I said.

"Well, let's have a cup of coffee at least," Anton said.

We entered a diner across the street from the vacant lot. Anton insisted on sitting at a window counter facing directly across the street at the ugly vacant lot. I ignored the view and watched Anton while he talked to me.

"Have you ever been loved by someone — and didn't understand why they loved you?" he asked me.

While we were talking, a young girl strolled by. She was holding a balloon by a string. The balloon was red and looked brilliant against the dark stone of the buildings. The little girl came skipping by the window, her fist closed tight around the string attached to her balloon. She glanced back, laughing gayly at the sight of her balloon jerking weightless through the air behind her. I saw her eyes shining and her strong little first closed tight around her string, her knuckles white with the force of her grasp. She was not going to let her balloon get away. She was going to hold on to her balloon no matter what. She loved the simple pleasure it gave her. It was her balloon. That made it a special balloon.

In a flash, the child and her balloon were gone. She had only taken an instant to pass across my line of vision. But before my eyes, framed in the window of the diner like a painting, she had been frozen into slow motion, my mind noting the details, my subconscious jolted by a shock of recognition. The little girl was me. Not literally, but in the abstract. I was like that little girl. I had been that little girl once in my youth. And essentially, I still was, although now my strong little hands were concerned with hanging on to other values — and with how to grasp still others. I was a greedy little child aching to get my hands on something. Or someone.

I looked at Anton. "I am not surprised when someone loves me."

"And what of your own loves? Ever been surprised to discover that you love a certain person?"

"Briefly. But after subjecting my emotions to logical analysis, the reasons for my feelings have always been clear — and always justified."

Anton nodded, took a sip of his coffee. "You know, for most people, love is something they don't know they are looking for — until they see it."

"I'd like to think I am more spiritually formed than that."

"It is not a matter of spiritual development. It's more basic. It is the situation of being confronted by the reality of your ideal — and knowing that action is now the only moral option. When you see your ideal, when you meet it, confront it, listen to it, speak to it, share with it — there is no other option, no other choice. You cannot turn away. You cannot hide. Why would you? The terror comes from knowing that only two choices are possible. Turn away from your ideal — and lose your own soul. Or pursue your ideal — and risk the shock of being fooled by twin truths: is your ideal really what you believe it to be — and are you really what you believe yourself to be? That is the risk in love."

I reached out and touched Anton's arm. "Anton, is this what you feel about me?"

"Not exactly."

"Then what?"

"You noticed the little girl with her balloon?"

"Yes! Wasn't she cute!"

Anton nodded and smiled. "You are missing something, Diane. I don't believe you have yet found your favorite balloon."

I gazed at him severely. "You'll have to let me be the judge of that," I said, grasping his forearm and holding on tight.

"I will," he said.

"Besides," I continued. "I have two hands. A girl can hold more than one ballon, if she wishes."

Anton burst into laughter.

"What is so funny?"

He was suddenly serious, as if an inner switch had been touched. "I don't know," he said, soberly.

I scowled at him. "We are being silly now. Finish your coffee and let's go for a walk. I want to see more of the city."

He finished his coffee. We left the diner and walked the city. The sunshine flowed down between the buildings like golden water through funnels, swirled around us in moist, weightless dapples, then was frozen and encased like ice in the brilliant reflections of polished windows and doors. We walked close to the doorways, basked in the glow of our own reflections, kept away from the streets and the busy rush of afternoon traffic. I felt secure and safe, as if all the buildings were armor pressed against my body, protecting me.

Anton led me west, to a series of skybridges connecting various buildings. We made our way to the highest of these and stood in the middle, facing west, into a breeze, our hair blowing back towards the city behind us. Anton took my hand in his, pulled me close, spoke to me once again as he had in the balloon, in the diner. "Diane, for as long as you'll have me — my logic is yours." He kissed me simply, briefly, then stepped back to let me respond.

"Anton, you're so brave. Even when you don't need to be." I hugged him.

"I need to be," he said, and kept on hugging me.

***

I ended the memory with a slow fade, brought us all gently up out of the conscious dreaming state. The visions dissolved into darkness and we each began sleeping normally. Our units beeped alarm signals to the attending therapists, telling them it was time to bring us back up to normal consciousness. We were given the usual ten minutes of regular sleep to give our minds time to transition back to a standard mental state. While we slept, the CD helmets were removed from our heads.

I woke first, found the attendant waiting with a cup of hot broth. I sat up and took a sip, looked over at the bodies of Maurice and Raphaela, both asleep still with very pleasant looks on their faces.

Maurice was first to rise. He was helped into a sitting position by the therapist and offered his broth. He accepted without question. He looked across at me while sipping. I raised my cup in a toast and saluted him.

He smiled weakly and did the same to me.

A minute later, Raphaela was awake. I went to her myself and helped her sit up, gave her a cup of broth, told her just to relax and let herself wake up gradually. She nodded and smiled up at me, did not try to speak, her eyes gazing up at me, her face stripped of age, looking very young, as if her CD experience had brought out the little girl in her.

After several minutes, we had all recovered enough to leave the CD chamber and retire to a lounge next door. This was a comfortable, sumptuous place designed for people to relax and discuss their CD experience. Maurice and Raphaela followed me silently into the lounge and I wasted no time. I wanted to get to Maurice while he was still recovering from the CD experience. I knew his senses were now heightened, his vision startlingly clear, his mind focused sharply. Now was the time to make the impact on him I wished to make.

"Raphaela, I don't mean to be rude and leave you alone, but it is important for me to speak to Maurice alone right now. May we leave you for a few minutes?"

She nodded. "Please, go ahead. Think nothing of me. I will be fine."

I signaled for a therapist to attend Raphaela so she would not be alone, then I took Maurice by the hand and led him from the lounge, telling him, "I want to show you why I shared that particular memory with you, Maurice. I want to explain what it all means and why it is significant."

"I know what it means and why it is significant."

"Perhaps. But I must share this with you now."

I led the way to my private elevator and we rode it up to my penthouse. When the doors opened, I led Maurice out into my living room. I said nothing, merely showed him what I had done.

He looked around at the sun-drenched octagon of my dwelling, his eyes growing larger by the second. His gaze paused for a long moment on the window showing his own penthouse. Then he continued his visual tour of my apartment. He walked around, touching the stone walls, glancing out the glass windows, stroking the drapes. He kicked his shoes off and walked barefoot through my plush carpet. He admired the art on my walls, stopped to caress several sculptures. He eyed the titles of the books in my shelves and noted the music stocked in my entertainment center. He found his way into my bedroom and I followed him as he stood in front of my bed and studied the feminine details of my most private chamber. Then he returned to the living room and sat down in a chair, looked up at me as I stood in front of him.

"Do you understand why I have done this?" I asked.

"Yes."

"Do you understand what it means?"

"Yes."

"Do you understand what I want now?"

"Yes."

"Have I earned what you brought me here to earn?"

"Yes, you have. Why do you think I brought Raphaela home with me?"

I bowed to him. "Does she understand why she is here?"

"She does now," he said, smiling.

"Very well. I wish to proceed at once. Is this agreeable to you?"

"It is."

I closed my eyes. "Thank you."

He stood up and came to me, held me in his arms in a tight embrace for a long moment. His arms and his strength were still not enough to stop me from trembling.

I felt his lips kissing my cheeks, his fingers gently wiping away the tears that flowed uncontrollably from my eyes. He whispered in my ear, "The frisbee has returned to my hand perfectly. I am as amazed as you are relieved, darling. You know the mall so well, Diane. You know me so well. I want you to be the mistress of my mall."

"Yes."

"I want you to be the mistress of my mall."

"Yes, I will, I will."

"You are the mistress of this mall. You are the mistress of West Park Plaza."

"Yes, I am."

"This mall is yours as much as mine, in body and soul, I swear by my logic, this is true."

"Yes, it is."

I opened my eyes finally when he held my face in his hands, kissed my lips. "Thank you for coming back to me, darling," he said.

"Where else would I go?"

***

That evening at dusk, on the roof of West Park Plaza, in the space between our two penthouses, we were joined in a sacred union by she who had the authority to do so: Raphaela Capuletti, Mall Master of the Emerald City Mall of Seattle. Maurice had brought her home to perform our wedding, and this she did with severe elegance and passionate austerity.

I do not know what it would feel like to marry a man I loved to another woman. But Raphaela managed to do it.

We stood facing the setting sun. Purple and red light flowed out from the edge of the earth and reached up, warming the cold blue of the coming night. All around us, warm fires blazed in white torches bearing the symbol of arete.

Maurice wore his finest purple silk ceremonial gown, with the symbol of his mall on one breast.

I wore white silk.

Raphaela stood before us in flowing green. She began the ceremony.

"The union of a Mall Master with his apprentice is one of the most sacred bondings that exists in our culture. It is my obligation as a Mall Master to remind you both of the solemnity of this occasion. You are both assuming grave responsibilities. If your integration is to remain and hold true over time, you must both face this event honestly and with clear minds.

"First, you, Maurice Sully. You built this mall with your own hands and judged this woman with your own mind. Is it your wish to make the final integration and invite her into your life completely as your wife?"

"Yes, it is."

"And you, Diane Copernicus. Have you entered this mall of your own free will and is it your wish not only to work with this man and support the life of the mall, but to achieve full integration by becoming his wife?"

"Yes, it is true."

"Then I will ask you both to make an oath to each other. Maurice, you may speak to Diane first."

Maurice turned to me and said, "I built this mall so that it would bring me a certain kind of woman. It took a long time, but she finally showed up. This mall is for you, Diane. That is why you feel so at home here, and that is why you wish to live here with me. That is why you built an apartment on the roof. My oath to you is that I will remain true to the highest standards of arete for as long as we are together. My logic is yours. All I do in the mall and for the mall will be done in your name. The essence of the mall universe is the pursuit, achievement, and enjoyment of logical values. Therefore, my most solemn promise to you is that any logical value you wish to have, I will never deny. The mall is no place for the evil of sacrifice. I have banished it from my mall, and as long as you are the mistress of this mall, values is all you will find, all you will know. Oh, and by the way — I really do love you."

Raphaela turned to me, her face implacable, unmoved, untouched by any emotion brought on by Maurice. "Diane, now you must make your oath to Maurice."

I gazed up at Maurice, saw his face framed by twin flames, his skin glowing in the dusk, his face radiant, his hair like a flame in the subtle breeze.

"My earliest memory of childhood is my love for the mall. It is the first place I remember visiting as a child. I knew even before I had the words to describe it that a mall was the distilled essence of life on earth. Life is sacred, and that which supports life is sacred. Production and trade are sacred, and men are at their best, their most logical, when they concern themselves with production and trade. What I love about the mall is that it integrates a huge variety of business activities into an artistic experience, and that it does this in an environment designed to facilitate the experience of our most profound emotion: man worship. As a child I was nurtured in an atmosphere of man worship within the mall, and it helped me to grow into a woman deserving to be loved by a man like Maurice Sully. For this, I thank the mall. Especially this mall in which I now stand.

"The essence of a mall is man. They are built by men, for men, to please men. And this pleases me, a woman who worships men. I have always loved men who understand the mall in the same way I do. For as long as I remember, a Mall Master has been my highest hero, the highest type of man I know, the master idealist who stylizes reality for me so I can love it all the more. Maurice Sully has done this to a degree unequaled by any other Mall Master I have ever heard of or known of. And more: he has understood who I am and what I have needed. He knew why I came to this mall and what I was looking for even more than I. He said it himself: he built this mall so it would bring him a certain kind of woman. Well, here I am. I am real, so the mall is true. And Maurice Sully is a master of total logic. What a delicious integration this has been! Reality is real, A is A, Maurice is what he is, the mall is what it is, I am what I am — and now we can all fit together into a seamless whole, two human lives surrounded by human values, human purpose, human worship. There is nothing more for me to desire, ever. I am home. This is my home. This is where I belong. This is where I will stay, forever — with my husband, Maurice Sully, whom I love dearly above all other men."

I did not look to see what was on Raphaela's face. I was gazing at Maurice. I heard Raphaela's voice. There seemed to be a slight tremble in it, but it may have been the roaring in my ears. Maurice shimmered before me. The sky was very dark and the flames of the torches surrounding us seemed abnormally bright.

Raphaela was saying, "Thank you for your oaths. The mall has heard them and I, as the officiating Mall Master, now use my authority as a priestess of commerce to announce that your final integration is logical and true and now exists as an independent fact in reality: you are man and wife. May you achieve ecstacy and wealth in unlimited measure for as long as you live. Please kiss each other to seal your oaths."

I kissed Maurice. He kissed me back.

When we finally pulled apart, Raphaela bowed to us both, then turned to me and said, "Congratulations, Diane. I hope someday to surpass you in thought and action."

Then she moved quickly to Maurice, who was waiting for her. She took his hand, held it to her cheek, closed her eyes for a split second, then dropped his hand. "I will love you forever, Maurice. I will never hide it." Then she quickly left us alone on the roof. She exited into Maurice's apartment. We saw no lights go on inside.

Maurice took my hand. "My Mistress. Mistress of my mall. Mistress of my life."

We let the torches burn.

Inside my penthouse, our integration was completed.

***

That is the story of how I became the wife of Maurice Sully, the greatest of all the Mall Masters. And that was actually the boring part of my life. There is more to tell of me and Maurice, and Anton Layvanwick, and others. But these parts of the story should be told through other voices, so I will be silent now and let you hear what remains from those who can tell it best.

Good logic to you!

BOOK THREE

THE PRIDE

OF

ANTON

LAYVANWICK

CHAPTER TWELVE

APHRODITE'S FABULOUS MASKED BALL

Here we have Layvanwick, master of his mall. On the morning of the Festival of Aphrodite he rises naked from his bed of purple silks and walks to the edge of his golden skyscraper to meet the dawn. He stands naked in the light of morning and raises his arms to the sun, letting the city see him stand together with his creation.

Layvanwick Tower is a thirty story mall rising in golden tiers into the misty blue sky. The sunlight glows along the edges of the building, the great glass sheets of the facade catching light from the stone and steel frame and reflecting it back out over the city.

Naked in the morning, that glow now returns to Layvanwick, who stands at the top edge of his building, his body serving as a pinnacle to the tower, and his form cocooned in a nimbus of vital warmth matching the stone and steel of his creation, matching even the sun he faces.

Layvanwick Tower is a thrust of transparent glass framed with edges of stone and steel. Inside, each floor of the tower is open to the sky, filled with light and visible from all the city. The great glass walls are composed of transparent light-sensitive glass that darkens like sunglasses in the day, protecting shoppers from the heat and glare of sunshine. At night the walls fade to crystal clarity and leave the interior of the building naked and open to the sight of the city. On a busy day, looking up from the street below, pedestrians see a dark pedestal of glowing luminescent black. At night, the building is transformed into a giant chandelier flowing with champagne, elevators rising and falling like bubbles up and down the sides. Inside, activities blur into a miasma of action, colors flowing into colors as people move from level to level and go about the sacred business of production and trade. From a distance, all this activity makes the tower seem alive and conscious. Beside it, the other buildings seem dull and lifeless.

Now, having greeted the dawn and the city he loves, Layvanwick returns to his chambers and prepares for the day ahead. His mall has been open and doing business for a month, but today is the official birthday, the Grand Opening, scheduled to coincide with the Festival of Aphrodite. Layvanwick planned it thus so that his mall would be officially presented to the community on the day when love is celebrated. "My mall is the mall for lovers," Layvanwick tells the journalists.

***

The day progresses as the sun moves across the sky, light playing across the face of the skyscraper mall in an ever-changing interplay of sun and shadow, sunlight splintering through clouds into multiple focused beams that flash across the building like searchlights. Later, the clouds thicken and shadow the mall. Still later, clouds clear away, the sky darkens as dusk approaches, and finally, the brilliant mall fades briefly as the sun sets — then comes alive again as the walls fade to clarity and the lights go on inside and out, and the gleaming golden tower flows with brilliant power, like a fountain of electric water.

Finally darkness reigns, the city is dim and faded — all but Layvanwick Tower, which stands supreme among the buildings of the city. Light flows upward and out in a golden geyser of brilliance that illuminates the entire town. The skyscraper mall is a lighthouse in the middle of a placid ocean, casting its beam across the waters, guiding the ships safely to shore.

At ground level, spotlights shoot up into the sky, silver swords of light clashing in the night, beaming the message of the mall to the heavens, the white beams celestial escorts for the golden tower as it seems to levitate into the heavens, as if challenging the gods.

But the gods never show up, making way instead for the true masters of reality — men and women.

***

The Festival of Aphrodite is a costumed affair, and the guests who begin arriving at dusk do so in all manner of flamboyant array, faces masked until midnight, identities hidden until the hour strikes when all must reveal themselves to those they have chosen to love. Some masks are simple and cover just the eyes and face, but others are more elaborate and cover the entire head, giving no clue to facial features, and even muffling the voice to disguise identity further and fool those who play the game of wagering on who is who and what is what.

By nine in the evening the festival is in full force and the mall is filling up with guests arriving from all directions, entering the mall from each of the four entrances. At precisely seven minutes after nine, at the western entrance, a white limousine delivers two guests: a tall man costumed as an Eagle; and a woman costumed as a colorful Harlequin. Upon entering the mall, they bow to each other, then — in keeping with custom — separate, going alone into the mall to explore and see what they might find.

At that precise moment, on the opposite side of the building, entering through the eastern entrance, is another couple: a man costumed as a Musketeer of Old France, complete with a sword on his hip; and the lady at his side a masked Sorceress in a gown of sequined purple, a cloak of starry dusk. These two enter the mall, bow to each other, separate — then find each other moments later and stay together as they move through the ground floor level, ignoring conversation and partaking of no food or drink.

At twelve minutes after nine, a dark figure descends in a private elevator from somewhere high in the mall. He is disguised as a Panther, his mask hiding his eyes and most of his face, the lower half of his mask projecting fangs down past his jaw. His costume is composed of soft black fur covering his entire body, hugging his physique closely, accentuating his powerful shoulders and massive legs. Just like the cat he imitates, he moves silently, gracefully through the crowd, speaking to no one, but stopping here and there to sip a drink and nibble a bit of food. Even disguised, his identity is easy to guess, and those who surround him let him pass, do not approach him or speak to him, even though most of them want to, especially the women. But the time for that will come later.

On the other side of the room, the Sorceress and the Musketeer stand together and notice the Panther. The Sorceress nods to the Musketeer and then leaves him, moves across the room towards the Panther, her eyes never leaving his form, her movements careful and precise, her motion taking her slowly, inexorably towards the Panther; but not too fast, and not directly, not yet. She wants to approach him without being noticed.

Meanwhile, the Musketeer has spied the Harlequin. She is alone and unescorted and moving across the room with a slow, confident strut. He steps into her path and bows, stopping her motion, forcing her to look up at his masked face. "Pardon, dear lady, but the dance is about to begin and we both lack partners. Will you do me the honor of escorting you through the dance?"

She bows and accepts. "Thank you, fine sir. I would be honored."

She offers herself to his arms and he holds her gently as the music begins. A stately, elegant, well-mannered waltz, old-fashioned, archaic even, but perfect to begin these festivities. The Festival of Aphrodite always begins in well-mannered elegance.

"Which musketeer are you?" the Harlequin asks.

"Aramis."

"Ah, the spiritual one."

"You admire the spiritual?"

"Of course. That is why I have come tonight."

"You consider yourself a spiritual woman?"

"Most certainly."

"What spirit do you celebrate?"

"Tonight, the spirit of love, of course."

"You are Aphrodite in disguise?"

"If I was, I would not disguise myself. Love should not be hidden. That is what we celebrate tonight. And you?"

"I am hiding. But not from love."

"From what do you hide?"

"From what is outside. From the darkness."

"You have found the right place."

"Your first trip to this mall?"

"No, I've shopped here before."

"What did you buy?"

"Lingerie."

"Oh. Are you wearing it now?"

"No."

"Ah!"

"And you? Have you visited the mall before?"

"My first time."

"How do you like it?"

"It is a great concept and should meet with much success."

Meanwhile, on the other side of the room, the Sorceress has approached the Panther and broken protocol by asking the man to dance. "Forgive my breach of etiquette," she says. "But arete compels me to be bold in your presence, sir. I wish to dance with no other. Will you have me?"

The Panther smiles behind his fangs and glides to her, takes her in his arms as the waltz begins. "You have cast your spell over me, Sorceress. I can do no else but bend to your will."

They spin through a swirl of colorful characters, the room swaying with the rustle of fabric in motion against the dark wide windows of glass walls facing a maze of dim buildings.

"Is it too soon to guess who you are?" she asks him.

"Not at all. But I enjoy the suspense of waiting till midnight, don't you?"

"You don't want to know who I am?"

"I want to be surprised."

"You will be."

"Do I know you?"

"In a manner."

"Then let it be. Midnight will strike soon enough. Before that, let us relax behind our masks and enjoy the mystery."

"I don't like mysteries."

"Some mysteries make life exciting."

"You disappoint me, sir."

"How so?"

"Mysteries are for mystics, don't you think?"

"When it comes to women, all men are mystics."

"Why compliment me by disparaging yourself?"

The Panther lowers his hand from her back to her hip, draws her closer as they spin, then holds her tight and looks deeply into her eyes, trying to fathom her nature.

"You have an exquisite shape, dear lady," he says.

"You change the subject," she says, spinning away and vanishing into the crowd, leaving him stopped in the middle of the dance, surrounded by waltzing couples in outlandish costumes, the entire scene resembling a cartoon, and he, a heroic character graceless and ill at ease. He steps back, waits a moment for a path to appear, then plunges into the crowd in search of the Sorceress.

While the dance flows on like a lost wave captured from the ocean, the Eagle glides alone to an elevator and rises to the next level. He steps out and walks across a lucite floor through which he can look down to the ground level. The dancers spin and twirl below him like toys in a doll house. He smiles and looks up at the windows. Spotlight beams cross into X patterns at each window and then flash away for brief moments, revealing twinkling window lights randomly spaced in the buildings across the street. The effect is delicious. He thinks himself a mote rising upward through a fountain. He feels weightless and at ease. He stops in the middle of the floor and looks down, tries to find a harlequin he knows. He spots her dancing with a musketeer dressed in purple and black. Who can that be? he wonders.

Downstairs, the Musketeer says to the Harlequin, "Do you know the Mall Master?"

"Aren't you the Mall Master?"

"If I am, I must remain silent on that subject."

"Do you wish an introduction?"

"No, just curious."

"We shouldn't speak of such things. Talk to me of love!"

"I love the mall."

"As do I. But which one?"

"This mall has a rival?"

"Indeed."

"West Park Plaza."

"Yes."

"Are you familiar with that mall?"

"Yes."

"I have not visited that mall yet."

"It is worth a look."

"Will I see you there?"

"Perhaps. Shop there long enough, you see everyone in the city."

"This mall makes me sad."

"How can that be?"

"It is so beautiful and full of life. So new and fresh and young."

"Why does that make you sad?"

"Someday it will be old."

"With age comes virtue."

"Then someday it will be dead. It will be an empty skeleton bereft of shoppers. What virtue is there in that?"

Harlequin stops the dance. As she stands and stares in stunned anger at the Musketeer, the room flows with applause and laughter as the dance ends and the dancers bow to each other and move arm in arm to the elevators rising up to the next level. As people flow away, Harlequin's eyes are locked into a cold stare at the Musketeer. "Why speak of such things? It is not to be contemplated."

"I contemplate it."

"Then you must dance with another, sir." Harlequin leaves the Musketeer standing alone and disappears into a crowded elevator.

The party rises.

The Panther has found his Sorceress and rides an escalator with her up to the second level. His hand rests lightly on the small of her back, his fingers caressing her skin. They look up through the lucite roof above, watching the shapes of people grow closer and come into sharper focus.

"Why did you run away?" asks the Panther. "We've only just met."

"I wanted you to chase me."

"I will chase you all the way to the top."

"Then that is where you shall catch me."

"I seem to have caught you here."

"I'll let you think that."

"The celebration rises with us," says the Panther.

"How high will it go?" asks the Sorceress.

"All the way to the roof."

"What happens when we reach the top and can rise no further?"

"Then we must enter the spiritual realm, where there are no limits. And then continue to rise."

"Take me with you to the top!"

"Very well. And the spiritual realm?"

"You may have me there as well."

"Then let us rise."

On the second level, Harlequin finds her Eagle and moves to his side. "There is evil in this mall," she says.

"What do you mean?"

"I have spoken to it."

"Who?"

"The Musketeer."

"What did he say?"

"He spoke of the death of this mall."

"On this night? We celebrate Aphrodite, and he speaks of death?"

"It was obscene."

"To speak of death during a birth truly is. Do you have a clue to his identity?"

"No. I didn't recognize his voice."

"I will try to speak to him. Do you see him near?"

"There. Turn around."

The Eagle spins and faces the Musketeer across the crowded second level. For one instant their eyes meet, but then two sets of couples move past and when the line of sight is clear again the Musketeer is gone.

"Where is he?"

"I don't know, I didn't see what direction—"

"Find him again. Keep track of him. You follow him. I will follow you. I will get close and see if I know his voice or manner."

"Very well."

"If he approaches you again, try to be compliant."

"That may be difficult."

"You can do it."

"And you?"

"Remember what we are celebrating tonight. The form of our celebration may become defensive. But we will still celebrate."

"Yes. We will."

"Now go. Don't lose him."

"He will probably seek me out again."

"Then let him."

They separate once more.

The second level is mostly food and drink and comfortable couches to lounge on before rising up to the third level and the great attraction of the festival: the erotic sculpture garden of Alexios M.

The Panther pauses on the second level only a moment, then he takes his Sorceress on up to the third level. This time they take an elevator. They are locked alone in a crystal cage sliding up against the black sky. He holds her close and they face the night sky. They see their own reflections in that dark mirror. And behind this, violent light and colorful tumult moving through the building behind them. Alone in the intimate glass elevator, they seem to float up into the night sky. But it is only a brief moment in time. Their eyes meet and they look at each other frankly, smiling behind their masks, showing each other the laughter in their eyes. Then the elevator ride is at an end and they turn and exit onto the third level. They are one of the first couples to arrive.

"Have you heard of Alexios M?" asks the Panther.

"I have, but I have never seen his work," says the Sorceress.

"Now is the time. It was created for this festival. Aphrodite lives in his stone figures."

In front of them, in the center of the third level, are two statues, a naked man, and a naked woman. Their arms beckon forward into a labyrinth of cubicles created by strategically placed screens. Panther and the Sorceress enter the maze and commence a tour of a series of statues done in white marble, portraying a man and woman engaged in the type of self-worship proper to those in love.

Here is a woman on her knees, reaching up with one hand to gently touch the erect manhood of her partner, who stands looking down at her with implacable lust.

Next is the same couple, only this time, the woman has the manhood in her mouth and the expression on the man's face, rendered with utter candor by the artist, is one of absolute rapture. Hands outstretched, head raised, hair flowing off to one side, it is the moment of his complete lack of control caught and frozen in stone by the sculptor.

The next statue has their positions slightly changed, and now, the man's penis is withdrawn from the woman's mouth, with only the tip of her tongue still just barely touching the head of his manhood.

"He renders their facial expressions with such perfection, don't you think?" says the Panther.

"Oh yes," whispers the Sorceress.

"I have never seen the spirituality of sex expressed more perfectly in any work of art."

"Nor have I."

They continue. The sculptures grow more explicit. Now the woman is on her hands and knees and the man is entering her from behind. The woman's head is raised, a smile of utter bliss on her face. The man looks down at her lovingly, gently, his hands lightly on her hips, his face delicate and serene.

"He has entered her politely, can you tell?" asks the Panther.

"Look at the arc in her back. The craftsmanship here is flawless."

"It goes beyond craftsmanship. Look at the details."

"The white marble is perfect for these statues. It gives them an excellent combination of the abstract and the concrete. For this kind of subject matter, white marble was the best choice."

The next statue has the couple in the same position, but now full sexual energy has been unleashed and the man is captured frozen in the middle of a furious thrust. The expression on his face has changed. He is now an unbridled animal and he is having this woman in the bluntest way possible. Hair flying, mouth twisted, eyes wide open, tiny beads of sweat appearing on his forehead, his hands grasp her hips tightly and the muscles of his legs flex as he drives his pelvis into her. The woman is now face down, head twisted, hair flying, one hand reaching back for the man, the other thrusting a finger into her mouth, her eyes closed, her face twisted in a combination of pain and pleasure.

"There is no mystery about this," says the Sorceress.

"It leaves nothing unhidden."

"When we reach the top, will we remove more than masks?" asks the Sorceress.

"It is your choice, dear lady."

"I don't wish to remain hidden."

"We'll make no firm commitments until our masks are removed and we know our respective identities."

"That is a wise policy."

"I am getting the impression that you have never attended a ceremony of this kind."

"I have. But in another part of the country. You know, customs vary from community to community."

"So I have heard. What city are you from?"

"No fair! I don't want to give you clues to my identity!"

"You're not from Billings?"

"Let's see what this sensuous couple is up to now."

They move along to the next set of statues. Now the woman is on her back, her legs in the air. The man enters her with her legs draped over his shoulders. She reaches up to him, her fingers just brushing against his chest, her eyes open to him, seeing his raised face, his eyes closed, feeling nothing but his own delight; and the woman's teeth clenched, mouth open, lips searching for something to kiss.

Panther approaches this statue and kneels close, studying the fine detail, contemplating the face of the woman and paying close attention to the angle at which the man enters her and the depth he has achieved. The Sorceress stands beside him, looking closely at the man's face. "He is lost in his love."

"No, not lost. He has found it and knows exactly where it is. He is simply enjoying the moment."

"There is great pleasure in contemplating the act of love, don't you think?"

"Sculpture gives us a concrete abstraction. This makes our contemplation easier — and deeper. Have you studied aesthetics?"

"Yes, in some detail."

"Alexios has managed to express the spiritual by portraying the physical. That is a great achievement for a sculptor."

"Indeed."

"Which aspect do you find most compelling?"

"Why separate the two? They are one and are compelling by virtue of being joined. But we know this because we know the meaning of the act they perform."

"So you have some experience with love."

"Oh yes."

"I am glad to know that."

They move on to the next statue. This one has the man on his back, the woman on top, straddling him, her arms reaching back towards his feet, supporting her as she raises her hips from his manhood, her head thrown off to one side, her face ecstatic, her breasts pointing straight up, her flat stomach frozen in a quiver of ecstacy, her womanhood surrounding the top half of his manhood.

"Is she withdrawing, or thrusting down?" asks the Panther.

The Sorceress is more intrigued by this statue than any of the others.

Now it is she who kneels to study the set in close-up. "She is just getting started. This man is holding tight to a whirlwind."

"Look at the exquisite detail of the penetration."

"This is truly a delicious moment."

"I've had a curious thought."

"Which is?"

"I wonder if these statues will satisfy those who see them — or make them desire sex even more."

"I'd say the latter."

"Speaking for yourself?"

"Is this celebration to end in an orgy?"

"Not officially. But what people do when they leave is their own business."

"The festival ends on the roof, at midnight?"

"Yes."

"I have heard that there are Mall Masters who make their homes on the roofs of their malls."

"Yes, that is true."

"What do you know of this Mall Master?"

"He does have his home at the top of this mall, that is known."

"How exciting. It must be thrilling for him to wake up every morning and see the city spread out around him."

"I suppose it would be."

"I'm curious. Do you know who began that tradition, of having a home in the mall?"

"Yes. It was started here in Billings."

"But not at this mall?"

"No. The other mall."

"Are you afraid to speak the name?"

"No."

"And the Mall Master? Can you speak his name?"

"Yes."

"There is much history in this little town. Why do you think that is?"

"Because certain individuals made it so."

"Why did they come from this place, and not somewhere else?"

"Because they came from here."

"That is a simple answer."

"It is a true answer. You sound like one who wishes to apprentice."

The Sorceress laughs.

"Why is that so funny?" asks the Panther.

She stands up. "This is the last set of statues. Fine gentleman, take me please up to the next level. And talk to me of love. I wish to hear your thoughts."

"Very well."

They exit the sculpture garden and move to an elevator, rise up to the next level.

At the moment they are leaving, the Harlequin is arriving on the third level. The Musketeer is waiting and approaches her. He bows. "Fine lady, forgive my earlier spiritual brutality. I apologize if I offended you. Perhaps these sculptures can remedy my soul. If you will consent to join me in the tour, I promise to remain a dignified gentleman."

"A dignified gentleman does not ask for forgiveness."

"I was illogical."

"You were obscene."

"Aphrodite has challenged us both by making us adversaries. I accept the challenge and intend to overcome it. And your choice, fine lady?"

The Harlequin offers her hand. "Your refusal to give up shows excellent self-esteem. I will accompany you on a tour of the sculpture."

"Let us proceed."

They enter the sculpture garden.

Behind them, the Eagle follows and is intercepted by two women wishing to escort a lone male. They slow him down. Another couple enters the garden ahead of the Eagle, separating him from those he must watch. But the Eagle is relaxed and enjoys the company of the two women. There are levels yet to reach. He will learn what he needs to learn. For now, he keeps moving and enjoys the sculptures.

Harlequin and the Musketeer follow the path. One by one they experience a series of statues glorifying the sex act. They notice the titles. "Anticipation" — "Man Worship" — "Lust Lingers" — "Gentle Conqueror" — "A Wild Ride Down Passion Boulevard" — "Deeper" — and finally, "What a Woman Knows."

Musketeer is silent as he escorts the Harlequin through the maze of silent stone sex. But he watches her face.

She looks to him often, afraid of what he might say, hoping for silence, but anxious at it just the same. They move through the entire series without saying a word to each other. Ahead of them and behind, eager couples gasp and exclaim, comment and critique, laugh and applaud, stand awestruck and worshipful. But these two are dumb mutes limping through the display without showing any passion.

And then they are out. Harlequin turns to the Musketeer and says, "Well, did you enjoy it?"

"I enjoyed your company."

"You didn't say a word."

"I feared I would offend you, so I held my tongue."

"Greatness such as this deserves some comment from a man."

"It was excellent sculpture."

"Is that all?"

"I don't feel competent to analyze art of this type."

"I have been so hard on you, Musketeer. May I call you Aramis?"

"I see no reason why not. That name will do for now."

"Very well. Tell me, do you have a love?"

"Oh yes."

"What is her name?"

"Agnes."

"Haven't you shared such passion with your Agnes?"

"No, I never have."

"Your love has not been consummated?"

"Not like that."

"Is there another form of consummation?"

"Yes."

"I would be interested to hear about that."

"I must not tell you of it. Agnes has forbidden it."

"I admire a man who can be loyal to a woman like that."

"I am loyal to Agnes."

"Is she here tonight?"

"No, she is at the other mall."

"West Park Plaza?"

"Yes."

"Why did you not attend together?"

"I am here with my other love."

"You have two loves?"

"Yes."

"I underestimated you, Aramis. Now I am beginning to respect you. A man who can love two fine women must have great arete."

"They have told me I have fine qualities."

"What is the name of your other love?"

"I have promised not to tell."

"Loyalty to a second woman? You are growing more magnificent with each moment! Let us rise!"

"You will meet her when the evening ends and masks are lowered."

"I look forward to it."

"I think she will want to speak to you."

"I welcome the opportunity."

"Now I have a question for you," says the Musketeer. "Why this mall and not the other?"

"This mall is new and unusual. There has never been anything like it before. This is history. I could not miss this!"

"Are you a special guest of the Mall Master?"

"We are all his special guests, you know that."

"Some are more special than others."

Harlequin laughs. "You have no idea how correct you are!"

"Oh, believe me, I know."

"*You* are a special guest of the Mall Master?"

"Yes, I am."

"Now you have made me curious. I want to get personal. I must pry because I am a woman. You have not shared passion with your Agnes. Is that to happen tonight?"

"I hope so."

"And what of your other love? You have shared passion with her, have you not? These statues we have seen; you have known the kind of love portrayed in these masterpieces?"

"With my other love, I have known all."

"I am relieved to hear that. I hope you will experience the same with your Agnes."

"Your concern is appreciated."

"Then let us rise!"

"Here we go. Make way to the elevators! I am anxious to get to the top."

"Up we go!"

As they move to an elevator, the Eagle swoops in, leaving his escorts behind for a moment. He stands directly in front of the Musketeer and grabs him by the lapel, shakes him and looks through his mask, into his eyes. "Weren't they magnificent! Have you ever seen such beauty and passion? What did you think?"

The Musketeer is paralyzed for a moment as he stares into the Eagle's eyes, saying nothing. Then he regains his senses and spins abruptly away and runs into a crowd exiting elevators just arriving from below.

Harlequin and Eagle stare after him, struck dumb by his bizarre behavior. Eagle looks at Harlequin. "Well, anything?"

"I was doing fine. I had established a connection."

"Allow me." Eagle runs after the Musketeer. "Sir, are you ill?"

Musketeer holds up a hand and motions Eagle away as he escapes into the closing doors of an elevator — and is taken down.

Eagle returns to Harlequin, who says, "He was eager to get to the top, yet when you arrive he races back downstairs."

"Perhaps he does not know what he wants."

"Or perhaps he knows full well and wants it to remain hidden from us."

"Why us?"

"Enough of this. My festival will be spoiled no more. Let us stay together. If he wants anything from us, let him state it in the open. If not, he can stay away and I will be pleased."

"As long as there is no threat to the mall."

"I don't believe there is. He is just a fool. Probably an American."

"Very well. Then let us rise."

"Let us rise!"

On the fourth level they find arcades and games, more food and drink, and relaxing lounges facing the dark windows. Couples sit together facing stars and buildings and the dark earth spread out below and they talk about the art they have seen. They talk of sculpture and sex and love and what the night still holds. The masks hold firm, are not removed, and no one guesses at anyone's identity. It is too soon for that.

Panther takes his Sorceress higher, on up to the fifth level. This time, they are the first to arrive, but other couples soon follow. The evening is becoming a race. Who will reach the top first? And what will they find when they get there? What will be the answers to the mysteries confronted during the evening?

"Did you come here hoping to meet a special person?" asks Panther.

"Yes," says the Sorceress.

"I hope you find him."

"Perhaps I already have."

"What do you seek to gain?"

"My love."

"What do you have to trade?"

"My soul."

"What is your price?"

"What I want is priceless."

"A limitless love?"

"For which I will do anything."

"Then tonight is your night. May Aphrodite bless you and be with you."

"May the mall bless me and be with me."

Panther raises his hand to the Sorceress, a smile hiding behind his mask. "Come, let us rise!"

"Let us rise forever!"

They find an elevator and continue up into the building.

Downstairs, the Musketeer has left his elevator and found a bathroom. There, he hides in a stall, removes his mask, bends down to a toilet, washes his face with cold water from the toilet, then dries his face with wads of toilet paper. He lingers over the toilet, his body shaking, face sweating, cold shivers rippling through his body. He pauses, expecting vomit. When it doesn't happen, he sags to the floor, relief deflating his tense body. He closes his eyes, raises his head, breaths slowly, steadily, until he is relaxed and composed. Then he replaces his mask and leaves the rest room, walks directly to an elevator and thumbs the number 30. He is heading for the roof *now*.

Meanwhile, on the fifth level, Eagle dances with his Harlequin. "Are you glad we came tonight?"

"What kind of silly question is that? There is nowhere else to be!"

"It has been an interesting evening so far."

"I think it will only grow more interesting."

Eagle faces the eastern window. He sees an elevator shooting straight up through the floors, not stopping, disappearing into the upper reaches of the building. Inside the glass elevator, alone — a Musketeer in purple and black.

"You are right, darling, as usual," says the Eagle. "It has just gotten much more interesting. I ask your indulgence: I must leave you for a time. But I'll be back, I promise."

"Where are you off to?" asks the Harlequin.

She gets no answer. She merely watches as the Eagle makes his way to an elevator and shoots for the roof.

The Musketeer reaches the thirtieth floor and his elevator opens and lets him out. This is the Skyview Terrace, the most elegant restaurant in town. Musketeer faces an empty restaurant — except for groups of waiters and restaurant workers preparing the tables for the midnight celebration. One of the waiters notices the Musketeer and approaches. "Sir, you are early. We are not ready to receive guests yet."

"How do I get to the roof?"

"None but the Mall Master has access to the roof."

"Isn't the final ceremony taking place on the roof?"

"No. It is cold and windy up there. The midnight unmasking will happen here, in the restaurant, where it is warm."

"I need to get to the roof."

"That is not possible, sir."

Musketeer draws his sword. "Either I am on the roof, or your guts are on this floor."

"Let me find the manager—"

"No! The responsibility is yours! What kind of Californian are you? If you know the way to the roof, show me now! Do not toy with me, boy! This sword is not a prop, it is a real blade and is capable of finding blood."

Back in the kitchen, looking out on the developing scene and remaining unseen by the Musketeer, the restaurant manager hits a button that sends an emergency page to the Mall Master. In seconds, the page is answered.

"We have an emergency up top, sir. You need to get up here right away. There's a lunatic with a sword who wants access to the roof."

"I'm on my way," says the Mall Master.

The Musketeer now faces ten waiters arrayed against him, and behind them, numerous cooks and kitchen help. He faces them with his sword still held ready. "Well? Who among you is willing to assume responsibility for escorting me to the roof?"

"We don't have access, sir," says the head waiter.

"Make access," says the Musketeer.

"The only way up is a private elevator. Only the Mall Master has the key."

"Nonsense. There must be a stairway up. Elevators break down and there has to be a backup. Now quit stalling."

"Sir, perhaps you should discuss this with the Mall Master."

"I intend to soon. But first, I'm going to discuss it with you." The Musketeer walks forward to the youngest of the waiters, waves the others away with his sword, reaches out and grabs the young waiter, pulls him to his side, presses his sword against the lads neck to give him a taste of what his cold steel feels like, to let him know that this situation is real and serious. But then he lets the boy stand easy and relaxes him with a hand on his shoulder. "What's your name, son?" asks the Musketeer.

"James."

"Well, James, I suppose you consider yourself an intelligent young man, is that right?"

"Yes sir."

"And do you consider yourself responsible?"

"Yes sir."

"You think you understand what is happening here?"

"No, sir."

"Why not?"

"You haven't explained it to me, sir."

"I have said that I wish to reach the roof, have I not?"

"Yes."

"What is so complicated about that?"

"Your request is illogical, sir."

"Ah, logic. Tell me, what good is logic when you have a sword at your neck?" The Musketeer places his blade against the young man's neck. "Well?"

"Logic tells me to remain still and follow your instructions."

"My instructions are for you to take me to the roof."

"Very well. This way, through the kitchen."

"Everyone out of the kitchen!" screams the Musketeer. "We are coming through and want no interference!"

The kitchen empties as white-uniformed chefs and cooks and dishwashers pour out of the kitchen and into the restaurant. When they have all come out, the Musketeer guides his waiter ahead of him into the kitchen. "Show me the way, young man, and I will set you free."

"This way." The lad takes him to the rear of the kitchen. There, a metal ladder leads up to a roof hatch.

"Climb up and open it for me," says the Musketeer.

"Very well." The boy climbs up, disappears into the darkness. There is the sound of a hatch being unlocked, then thrown open. A gust of cool wind comes rushing down into the kitchen. The Musketeer raises his masked face to the breeze and feels it cool his hot sweating face.

The boy comes down, his face white. "There you are, the hatch is open, the roof is yours."

"Thank you very much," says the Musketeer. "You may leave me and go back to your work. Prepare the tables well. There is a party to follow and it will go on as scheduled."

"Thank you, sir."

The boy leaves. The Musketeer is alone in the kitchen. He notices a platter of desserts sitting on a counter. He raises his mask to free his mouth, then plucks a cherry off the top of a cake and eats it. He smiles, smacks his lips, lowers his mask, sheaths his sword, then climbs up the ladder and onto the roof. Once there, he shuts the hatch and locks it so no one may follow him. Then he turns to the dark wind-swept roof and faces across to a glowing glass structure. It is the Mall Master's penthouse apartment. "Let's go see if anyone is home," says the Musketeer. He marches toward the glowing apartment.

Meanwhile, on the lower levels, celebrants have noticed a number of elevators rising straight to the top. Rumors begin to swirl through the party. "Everyone is heading for the top! Let's go see what's happening!" The elevators begin to rise.

Crushed into the rear of one crowded elevator are two women, a Sorceress and a Harlequin. They are pressed against each other and forced to stare closely at each other.

"What is happening?" asks the Harlequin.

"My escort abruptly left me," says the Sorceress.

"Mine as well. Where was yours heading?"

"Straight to the top."

"Something is happening up there."

"Rumors are running wild. I fear much irresponsibility has been loosed."

"Have you seen an Eagle?"

"I didn't notice. Did you see a Panther?"

"Nowhere. I did see a Musketeer."

"Oh?"

"He was acting very strange."

"How?"

"He spoke obscenities of death in the mall. And when my escort approached, he ran away without speaking."

"Your escort was the Eagle?"

"Yes."

The Sorceress is quiet and looks away.

"I fear there will be some unmasking before midnight," says the Harlequin.

"Perhaps that will be for the best," says the Sorceress.

Their elevator flies up into the night.

In the restaurant, the first elevator to arrive unloads the Eagle and a contingent of security guards. They face a group of frightened cooks. "What has happened?" asks the Eagle.

"He is up on the roof. I think he wants the Mall Master."

"Show me which way he went."

The head chef shows him.

"Very well," says the Eagle. "You security guards, take the elevator up to the penthouse. Use caution. Await my instructions. The rest of you — people are coming up. Seat them as you normally would and let the party continue. Say nothing of what has happened. You sir, have you contacted the Mall Master?"

"Yes."

"Is he on his way up?"

"Yes."

"Very well. Did he say how he was coming?"

"No."

"We'll assume his elevator. Very well. You all have your instructions. Proceed."

Having spoken, the Eagle flies for the ladder to the roof hatch.

Up on the roof, the Musketeer's purple and black costume blends with the night sky, makes him seem a slice of cloud come to walk atop the buildings. He marches up to the warmly lit penthouse and rings the front doorbell. He hears the chimes sound inside. Then, in a moment, the door is answered — by a Panther.

"Good evening," says the Panther. "What can I do for you, sir?"

***

The Eagle is having trouble with the roof hatch. Unable to get it open, he retreats back into the kitchen. Now it is full of chefs. Once more they go about their business of preparing the feast. They ignore him as he exits the kitchen and makes for the private elevator to the top. On his way, the first of a series of elevators arrives and a loud mass of costumed Aphrodites tumbles out, screaming for wine. They are met by waiters who seat them immediately, as far from the kitchen and the private elevator as they can.

The only two to make it past the phalanx of waiters are the Harlequin and the Sorceress.

Harlequin spots the Eagle and follows him to the elevator. "What news?" she asks.

Eagle turns. "He is on the roof. We don't know what has happened. We're going up now."

Sorceress hangs back, standing at an angle so the Eagle cannot see her masked face. She says nothing.

"Shall I join you, or remain down here?" asks the Harlequin.

"Remain here, darling. Speak of this to no one."

Eagle disappears with two security guards into the private elevator.

Harlequin turns to her Sorceress friend. "Shall we find a table?"

Sorceress nods.

***

Musketeer faces the Panther. "Ah, here you are at last."

"Do I know you, sir?"

"If you don't, I will be disappointed."

"I don't recognize your voice."

"Then allow me to introduce myself."

Musketeer removes his mask and smiles at Panther.

Behind his own mask, Panther's reaction is unseen. But his voice is steady. "I have failed your test. I do not recognize you, sir."

"Does my face shock you?"

"Your face is your face."

"Do you think it beautiful — or ugly?"

"I don't believe you wish an honest answer to that question, sir."

"Perhaps you are right. Then I will hide behind my mask some more." Musketeer replaces his mask over his face. "Well, are you going to invite me in?"

"That depends on what you want to discuss."

"I want to hire you for a job."

"What job is that?"

"I need someone of your skill to retrieve something I have lost."

"You wish me to recover property for you?"

"Yes."

"What makes you think I am competent to perform such work?"

"You are a Mall Master. You can do anything."

"What makes you think I am a Mall Master?"

"I know who you are and what you have done. I have not come to this task unprepared, you see."

"Very well. Step inside and let us talk further."

Musketeer enters the penthouse.

"Shall we sit or stand?" asks the Panther.

"I prefer to stand."

"Very well. Now tell me, what property it is you have lost?"

"Something has been taken from me."

"Who took it?"

"Another Mall Master."

"I see. Anyone I know?"

"Yes."

"Why not approach this man yourself?"

"I wish you to intercede on my behalf."

"What is it that was taken from you?"

"Something that I did not value at the time I lost it. But since losing it, I have come to love a woman named Agnes. She has taught me that it was my highest value, my greatest achievement, and that I should not have given it up so cheaply."

"What was it that you lost?"

"I will get to that. But first, I want to explain why it is important for you to act on my behalf. And to explain to you how I intend to reward you when you retrieve what was taken."

"I'm listening."

Outside, four security guards approach the penthouse, take up strategic positions outside, peer in and see the two men facing each other and talking. The security guards radio positions and report activity, then remain still, awaiting instructions.

Inside, the Musketeer keeps talking.

Outside, the Eagle finally arrives. He notes the reports of the security guards, then approaches the penthouse. He walks up to the front door and rings the doorbell.

The door is answered by the Panther. The Musketeer sits behind him, relaxing on the sofa.

"Is everything all right?" asks the Eagle. "We were worried about you downstairs. We feared your party had lost control."

"Everything is fine," says the Panther. "I was just discussing some business with my friend, the Musketeer."

"Ah, he is a friend of yours?"

"He is now, yes."

"His manner of introduction is overly dramatic, don't you think?"

"Have the guests assembled in the dining room?"

"They have."

"Then let the celebration continue. Aphrodite beckons. We must not keep her waiting." Panther turns to the Musketeer. "Will you join us below for a toast?"

"I think now is the time."

Musketeer jumps up from the couch and strides past both Panther and Eagle, leading the way to the elevator and the restaurant.

When the door opens below and the three walk out into the dining room, they are faced with a party in full force. Every table is full, wine is flowing, food is being served, toasts are offered at every table, and eager celebrants watch the clock on the wall as the minutes edge closer to midnight. Many grow eager to unmask and stand revealed to those they have chosen. Others tensely bear the stress of curiosity drawn taut in waiting to see who waits behind the masks they have smiled at all evening.

CHAPTER THIRTEEN

MIDNIGHT IN THE TEMPLE OF MAN

Having silently escorted the Musketeer down from the penthouse, Panther and Eagle lead the way to a table near the elevator. Musketeer follows. Seeing the three men approach, Sorceress and Harlequin rise as the men arrive and join them at the table.

"It has grown late and you have been too long from our presence," says Harlequin to the Eagle.

"Excuse my absence, dear. It seems our mysterious friend had business up top."

Harlequin turns to the Musketeer. "So you are a man of some substance after all?"

Musketeer bows to the Harlequin.

Panther raises a glass of wine. "Let us toast."

The others raise glasses and wait for Panther's toast.

"To the drama of love," says Panther.

"To the drama of love," say all, in unison, each sipping their drinks through slender straws.

"I would like to hear from the Sorceress," says Eagle.

The Sorceress is silent.

Into this silence leaps the Musketeer. "The Panther has her tongue."

"Or could it be the Eagle?" asks Harlequin.

"Who is it that has your tongue, Sorceress?" asks Eagle. "Panther or Eagle?"

"Neither," says Sorceress, softly.

They all sit down. Eagle stares across the table at the Sorceress. She refuses to look in his direction. Her eyes are on the Musketeer. The Musketeer ignores everyone, is eating and drinking with gluttonous intensity.

Harlequin smiles through her mask at the Panther. "You have strange friends, Mr. Panther."

"My friend is merely in character. He is dressed as a Musketeer, so he acts like one. You can't say the same. You dress as a Harlequin, yet you complain sullenly all evening and show not a shred of gayety. Where is your benevolence, dear lady?"

"It was used up in tolerating this rogue."

Eagle says, "I'm curious about what business a Panther has with a Musketeer."

"Our business will be transacted when our masks are removed," says Panther.

Sorceress continues to stare at the Musketeer, who ignores all. Finally, Sorceress reaches across the table and lightly touches the Musketeer's arm. This the Musketeer notices. He responds by gently patting her hand — then shoving it away.

This action does not go unnoticed by the others at the table.

A brightly costumed woman passes the table and stops. "I see two women and three men. May I join your table?"

"Away with you, wench!" bellows the Musketeer. "We have no use for you at this table!"

The woman giggles behind her mask. "Such an actor you are!"

"It is not an act! Now be gone, wench, before I slap your silly mask off!"

The woman runs away to another table.

The Musketeer has drawn attention to the table and now all eyes in the restaurant are on him and his guests. "There is drama at that table," say some celebrants. "Let us observe."

"I think that is the Mall Master's table!"

"Are you sure?"

"Yes! Layvanwick cannot hide himself behind a mere mask. Watch and listen."

The restaurant is quiet.

All eyes move from Panther to Eagle, and back again, waiting for reaction.

Musketeer interrupts the silence with a massive belch.

Harlequin stands in anger. "Sir, you mock our values!"

"Sit down, dear," says Eagle. "This isn't necessary."

"It is! I refuse to have this beast at my table!"

"This is my table," says Panther. "I want him to stay."

"Then you are as foul as he is!"

"You have lost your logic, dear lady."

"Me? What about him?"

"His logic is yet to be discovered."

"Why don't you people talk like normal human beings?" asks the Musketeer.

"He mocks the customs of our festival!" says Harlequin. "He degrades our exaltation. Sir, I demand you unmask and reveal your identity!"

"It is not midnight. What about your customs?" asks the Musketeer.

Sorceress stands and moves quickly to the Musketeer, grabs his arm, pulls him up and away from the table. "Dance with me, Musketeer."

"I'm eating! The dance is over!"

"Our dance has just begun. I insist."

She pulls him away. There is no music. The two dance alone between the crowded tables, while silent celebrants watch in fascination for the bizarre. Sorceress and Musketeer move towards the glass wall and dance free along the edge of the night, looking as if they will fall away out into the dark vast night that hoods the city.

At the table, Panther motions to a small group of musicians just setting up. They have arrived late, having chased the eager celebrants up to the top. Now, at Panther's command, they hurry into a dance. The dining room fills with a small but lively tune. Still, Sorceress and Musketeer dance alone. No other celebrants rise to join them.

Sorceress has spun the Musketeer into a corner of the dining room where they have relative privacy. There she stops the dance and spins the Musketeer with his back to the glass wall. Behind him is a dark landscape of twinkling lights. Sorceress says, "What are you trying to do? Have you forgotten why we have come here?"

"I know exactly why I am here."

"Are we no longer a team?"

"We are still a team. You just don't know what game we are playing."

"You spoke to him alone?"

"Yes."

"You went up without me and spoke to him alone?"

"Yes, I did."

"How much did you tell him?"

"Only what I needed him to know."

"Now I need to know it."

"Darling, let us not quarrel in this. I know why you brought me here and who you wish me to meet. I even know what you hope to gain from such a meeting. But you must know that I am beyond all that now. Whatever your plan was, it has been superseded by my own."

"And what is your plan?"

"You honestly don't know?"

"Does it involve Agnes?"

"Of course it does. Everything involves Agnes now."

"Have you brought that woman to this city?"

"I have."

"Is she here within this mall tonight?"

"No."

"That is all I need to know."

Sorceress starts to turn away, but Musketeer grabs her shoulder and pulls her back to him.

"No, you must know more. I hid my truth from you once before and hurt you greatly. I do not wish to do that this time. I want you to know my truth. I want you to know what it is I have come here for, and what I hope to get."

"You have spoken her name and that is all I need to know."

"You have not lost me, darling."

"Haven't I?"

"No matter what you think, there is much more to be gained than you can conceive."

"I am returning to the table now. Follow if you wish."

Meanwhile, back at the table, Eagle says to Panther, "Let us speak plainly while they are away. Do you know who the Musketeer is?"

"He unmasked for me above. So yes, I know who he is. And the Sorceress as well."

"I recognized her voice, finally. This is a most exciting evening!"

"Is it?" asks Panther, soberly.

"Who are they?" asks Harlequin. "Don't hide this from me! Tell, tell!"

Eagle's excitement is muted by Panther's serious tone. "You don't share my excitement. Can you tell me why?"

"I have been asked to broker a trade."

"What kind of trade?"

"Musketeer wishes to make an exchange."

"With who?"

"With you."

"Why does he not approach me directly?"

"He wishes to honor you by waiting till midnight when all masks fall. Then he will reveal himself and make his offer."

"What does he wish to exchange?"

"A life — for a soul."

"Whose life?"

"The Sorceress."

"Whose soul?"

"His."

"I see."

"Do you?"

Harlequin watches silently, her mouth set like marble, her tongue frozen inside her. Curiosity still makes her tremble with expectation. She looks at the large clock on the wall and notes how much time till midnight. But now her palms sweat and her knees tremble, and behind her mask, within her privacy, her eyes widen and her mouth dries as she listens to the voices of the two men she knows so well. They are calm behind their own masks, but speak now in tones too gentle for a normal party. From this, Harlequin's feminine senses pick up the subtle vibrations of danger. She remains silent, watching, listening, hoping she can learn something quickly so she can help them master this situation, whatever it is. She straightens her back and squares her shoulders in anger at not being told the secret.

Panther nods across the room to Sorceress and Musketeer, the two locked in embrace against the far window. "Look at them. Sorceress is trying to reason with him, trying to bring him to his senses."

"They work at cross purposes?"

"It appears so."

"He will listen to her."

"I fear it is another woman that has his ear."

"How do you know this?"

"Look, they're coming back. We'll find out if she succeeded."

Sorceress and Musketeer return to the table and sit down. "Forgive our absence," says Sorceress. "My friend the Musketeer is not himself. We needed a moment apart."

"But everything is fine now," says the Musketeer. "Our party can continue. Ho! Look at the time! Midnight draws near. Is it not delicious?" He stares across the table at the Eagle. "Can you stand the suspense, Eagle? Or has my loud voice spoiled it for you?"

"One suspense has merely been replaced with another."

"The customer must always be satisfied, right?" says the Musketeer. "Tonight I think we will all get more than we bargained for."

"Who will get the most?" asks Eagle.

"Whoever has the most to trade," says Musketeer.

"Or whoever asks the highest price."

"If you ask a high price, you must have much to bargain with."

"Just so you know — there are certain currencies the mall does not accept."

Musketeer nods across the table to Eagle. "We'll see."

Panther raises his arm and waves over a security officer, who comes to the table. "Bring the waiter over," says Panther. Then he looks at

Musketeer. "We have serious business to attend, sir. A complaint has been lodged against you."

"Can't it wait?"

"No, it can't."

The security officer returns with the young waiter Musketeer met earlier. Panther says, "This young man claims you threatened his life."

"There was no threat. I merely borrowed his life for a few moments. I held it securely in my strong, competent hands, and when I got what I needed, his life was returned to him, undamaged."

"Has it occurred to you that his life was not yours to borrow?" asks Panther.

"Yes. But has it occurred to you that borrowing a life is sometimes the greatest way in which to honor those who oppose us?"

"Your morality is illogical, sir," says Panther. "You cannot gain value by threatening the only thing that makes value possible."

"You wish to debate philosophy with a Musketeer?" asks the Musketeer.

"And a drunken Musketeer, at that," says Harlequin.

Panther raises his hand. "This is a serious legal inquiry. Please, hold all comments. I will make this as brief as I can."

Panther removes his mask.

"Protocol demands that I reveal myself and face the accused truthfully. Sir, I am Anton Layvanwick, Master of this Mall. You stand accused of threatening the life of this waiter. What do you have to say for yourself?"

The Musketeer turns and faces the young waiter. "James, is it?"

"Yes sir."

"Do you wish to press charges against me, James?"

"Yes sir, I think I am right to do so."

"I am sorry you feel that way. My wife Agnes will be sad to hear of what has happened to me."

"You are married to a woman named Agnes?"

"Agnes is my wife, yes. Do you know Agnes?"

"I do know Agnes."

"Agnes has borrowed my life, you know."

"Agnes is a good woman."

"I trust her completely. I have no fear to allow my life to be held in her hands. I know that if I perish with her, it will be a graceful death."

"Agnes will not let you die, Musketeer. I think you should be happy to give your life to her caretaking."

"Perhaps after me, some day you can do the same for yourself."

"I would be honored."

Musketeer faces Layvanwick. "Very well, Mr. Mall Master. What is next?"

"It is as I thought," says Layvanwick. "James, do you still wish to press charges against this man?"

"Forgive my illogic, Mall Master, but I feel it would be wrong for me to do so at this time."

"And why is that?"

"Does the law compel me to offer an explanation?"

"It does not."

"Then I have none to offer."

"Very well. James, I do not tolerate illogic in my employees, nor do I forgive. You are not of the Mall. If you do not wish to press charges against this man, consider yourself fired."

James raises his head, straightens up for a moment, as if shocked. Then he relaxes and looks at the Musketeer, to the eyes behind the mask. "My logic remains untouched by your standards, Mall Master. I will leave the mall."

"Do so at once." Layvanwick motions to security to escort the young man away.

Musketeer rises, goes to the young waiter James, and shakes his hand. "Agnes would be interested in meeting a young man without a job. You should seek her out and speak with her."

"I will do so at once. Thank you for your concern, Musketeer."

Musketeer bows to the waiter as he is escorted to an elevator by security officers. When he is gone, the party continues.

Layvanwick relaxes in his seat, gazing severely across the table at the Musketeer. "So, Musketeer, you got away with that much. Look at the clock. The hour approaches."

"Who is this Agnes of whom you speak?" asks Harlequin.

"You will meet her someday," says Musketeer. "She will kiss you and you will love the taste."

"I doubt that," says Layvanwick. "Would it surprise you to know that I am familiar with your Agnes?"

"No, it would not surprise me. It would shock me if you were to tell me you have wed her."

"I have not wed her, nor do I intend to."

"I am sad for you."

"Don't be."

"Are you Agnes?" asks Harlequin of the Sorceress.

"No, dear. I am her rival."

Eagle looks at the clock. Sorceress watches him and sees the longing in his eyes. He wants the moment to come.

"Eagle, never mind the clock," says Sorceress. "Look at me. You know who I am, don't you?"

"Yes, I do."

"Then there is no mystery, and no suspense. Relax. When the moment comes, our masks will fall, and then we can speak honestly."

"I speak honestly now," says the Musketeer. "Why let a clock rule your actions? Why not let our masks fall now, as the Mall Master has done? Look around you. All of the other tables watch us. We are the entertainment. Let us shock them and give them a good show. Come on, what do you say?"

Layvanwick picks up his mask and replaces it. Masked once more, he stands and raises a toast to the entire room, to the total gathered assemblage of masked celebrants waiting for midnight. "To the drama of love!" he says.

The room responds with hands raised in toasts. "To the drama of love!"

"Bravo Layvanwick!"

"May Aphrodite bless the mall!"

"Love has never been more dramatic than tonight," says the Musketeer.

They all rise and face the clock hanging over the entrance to the kitchen. It is now 11:59 and thirty seconds. Everyone watches the second hand sweep along inexorably towards midnight.

"Time is such a curious thing, don't you think?" says the Musketeer. "Eternity has come down to these final moments."

"Another eternity will follow," says the Sorceress.

The second hand sweeps towards midnight — hits midnight — passes midnight.

The room erupts into applause. The celebrants cheer each other. Every table is an explosion of joy released after great anticipation.

Every table, except one.

At Layvanwick's table, there is no applause, no cheering. At Layvanwick's table, they all simply stand and stare at each other, none of them moving to remove masks.

Around them, at all the other tables, the masks fall and reveal smiling, happy, thrilled faces finally facing those they wish to share love with in celebration of Aphrodite.

At Layvanwick's table, Harlequin tears off her mask first and faces the Musketeer with her eyes blazing.

"There, are you satisfied? I went first. Now honor demands that you follow suit."

"I have no honor. And I don't know who you are, so your unmasking means nothing to me."

Eagle removes his mask and stares across the table. "You recognize *me*, don't you, Musketeer?"

"Oh yes. You I know."

Next, Layvanwick removes his mask and looks across the table at Musketeer. "We three who are of the mall stand revealed to you, Musketeer. Now you must show yourself to my two friends so that they may finally know the truth of this situation."

Musketeer looks at Sorceress. The two pause a moment — then remove their masks.

Layvanwick's eyes move to his two friends, Eagle and Harlequin, watching intensely so that he might know their feelings.

Eagle's face floods with the recognition of what he has already known and is paralyzed with emotions too great to allow him to speak.

Harlequin recognizes both and wails at Eagle. *"In the name of logic, this can't be! Not here, not like this, not tonight!"*

"What other night would fit as well?" asks Musketeer, staring across the table at Panther — who is Anton Layvanwick — and Eagle — who is Maurice Sully — and Harlequin — who is Diane Copernicus.

The three Mall Masters stare across the table at a woman with tired eyes and worn face, her bearing proud, yet her face twisted by pain, regret, embarrassment, apology. She looks across at Maurice Sully, her eyes sad. "I tried to save him. I have failed," she says, lowering her eyes.

And the unmasked Musketeer faces the three Mall Masters with a face painted in bizarre lines of primitive color, like a savage from the jungle, his eyes bright with a glint of madness, hysteria, insanity. "No, dear, you have not failed," he says to the unmasked Sorceress. "You have succeeded. We both have. Now I can reclaim what was taken from me."

Diane Copernicus touches Maurice Sully and says, "Tell me I have not gone mad. Are these two really who I think they are?"

"Yes," says Maurice. "She is Sarah Fletcher. And he is Alan Benton."

***

Using mental techniques taught to her by her husband, Diane Copernicus freezes the moment into her consciousness, so that it can later be recalled in vivid detail. She looks hard to the essence of the two faces she sees and files away the fundamental characteristics to her eidetic memory.

"I recognize you both from conscious dreaming," says Diane. "But you are different."

"It has been ten years," says Alan Benton, smiling at Maurice.

"You have changed," says Maurice.

"Have I?"

"Oh yes."

"I think it is an improvement."

"That remains to be seen." Maurice Sully looks at Sarah Fletcher. "It is good to see you, Sarah."

"It is good to see you, Maurice. And this is your bride?"

"She is Diane Copernicus, the Mistress of my Mall."

"She is beautiful. I am happy for you."

"I wish I could say the same for you. But your face tells me that would be illogical. So let us get to it. Why have you come to us tonight and conducted yourself in this manner?"

Sarah Fletcher bows her head in resignation. "I sought your help in saving my husband from madness."

"I will help you if I can," says Maurice. "But do I have Alan's consent in this matter?"

"You do not," says Alan Benton. "I do not want your help. I am not mad. I have come seeking justice."

Alan draws his sword and jumps up on the table. He turns to the room of celebrants and raises his sword.

"Hear me, all you pagan Aphrodites! I am Alan Benton of New Athens. I have come to make a claim against Mall Master Maurice Sully. Anton Layvanwick, Mall Master of Layvanwick Tower, has agreed to judge the justice of my claim. I have traveled far and crashed your party to reclaim a value taken from me long ago by Maurice Sully. I come to ask for its return."

Alan turns around and looks down at Maurice Sully. "Mall Master, do you know what it was you took from me all those years ago?"

"I saved your life."

"That is how you remember it."

"I have no memory of taking anything from you."

"You are morally blind, sir."

"Tell me what it was I took."

Alan turns and faces the room.

"I am Alan Benton of New Athens. This is my wife, Sarah Fletcher.

Perhaps some of you know our story. Ten years ago, I lived in America. I fell in love with Sarah. She was the daughter of the Governor of Kentucky. He could not accept our relationship and tried to have me murdered to keep his daughter from me. We tried to escape together, but only Sarah made it out. I remained behind and was captured. Sarah made it to the Show Me Mall and was granted sanctuary by an apprentice Mall Master named Maurice Sully. He wedded her and took her to New Athens. While all this was going on, my captors implanted a bomb in my head and ordered me to bring Sarah back, or they would let the bomb explode. I was sent to New Athens to kidnap Sarah and bring her back to America. But I did no such thing. It was never my intention to do any such thing.

"You celebrate love, tonight? You celebrate Aphrodite? You know nothing of love. I know about love. I loved Sarah. I went to New Athens with that bomb in my head. I knew the exact hour it was to explode. I was working on a time table, a schedule. I had to get her back to America before the bomb went off and killed me. But I loved Sarah and knew she could not live happily in America. So I went to her, to see her one last time, to make my peace, to pronounce my love for her in the only manner left me: by giving my life in saving hers. When the bomb went off and I was killed, Sarah would be safe forever. Those who sought her would have no chance to get her back.

"But my plan did not work out. Because Sarah was with Maurice Sully, a Mall Master. I had heard that Mall Masters were special people, with special talents. But I had no appreciation for how extraordinary they could be. I could not have conceived of what Maurice Sully would do to me.

"Look at me, you Aphrodites! What do you see? You think you see a man. But I am not a man. I am a ghost. I am a zombie. I have been dead for ten years, but have still walked among you living.

"For ten years I have awakened each morning and looked at the face of my beloved Sarah. For ten years I have looked at her and thought, 'Is this the last time? The last morning, the last day, the last night? The last time I will hold Sarah in my arms, the last time I will kiss her, the last time I will make love to her?'

"Because the bomb is still in my head. It has remained in my head for all these years and it has never gone off. It has never exploded. It has never killed me. Now how can this be?

"It can be because Maurice Sully made it so. Maurice Sully activated a spiritual alchemy within me that rendered the bomb mute.

"But what he never knew, what my Sarah never knew, was that it was too late. When he rendered the bomb mute, I was already dead. I had made my peace with death, I had said good-bye to Sarah, good-bye to the world, good-bye to all my values. I was ready to go. I was already gone. I was a dead man already. I was waiting for the bomb to finish the job.

"But the job was never finished. Twice I tried to die, and twice I was saved. Once by Maurice Sully, when he stopped the bomb inside me. The second time was when Sarah pulled me out of the Pacific Ocean at the feet of the Statue of Liberty. Once I was saved from murder; once I was saved from suicide.

"I should have died twice, but was saved both times. I am twice a zombie. Like a cat, I have been granted more than one life.

"But I do not want more than one life. I had one life, and it ended, and I was happy to have it end.

"I have made my peace with my wife. Now I have come to make peace with Maurice Sully. I have come to ask him to return to me what he took so long ago: my death.

"Maurice Sully stole my death. I want it back."

Now Alan Benton turns and throws his sword down on the table in front of Maurice Sully. Then Alan kneels down and bows his head, raises his arms, bares his chest to Maurice.

"Pick up the sword, Mall Master."

"I will not," says Maurice.

"Pick it up and put the blade in me, damn you!"

"I will not."

"I want to die by your hand, in this mall, tonight, to celebrate love! This is how I celebrate Aphrodite! With sacrifice! I sacrifice for Aphrodite!"

Alan picks up the sword and moves to thrust the blade into his own chest.

Layvanwick pounces like a cat, is on Alan in an instant, has him in a choke hold, gets Alan's arm pointed upwards, the sword in the air, Alan's hand and arm twisted by the irresistible force and strength of Layvanwick. Alan's fingers release and the sword clatters harmlessly to the table. Security guards rush forward and help Layvanwick wrestle Alan to the floor. He is handcuffed and sedated, then dragged from the room to an elevator while Layvanwick whispers instructions to his head of security.

Maurice Sully moves past Diane Copernicus and goes to Sarah Fletcher, holds her and speaks to her as they take Alan from the room.

When Alan Benton is removed, Layvanwick goes to a microphone in front of the band and addresses the room.

"My apologies for letting your celebration be spoiled. I invited you to my mall to celebrate love and allowed a madman to enter our sacred festival. But it is over now and will be dealt with by those responsible. Those of you who wish to stay and spend the night in the mall and continue the celebration till dawn are welcome to do so. But my recommendation is to leave this place tonight and take your celebrations outside the mall. Again, I apologize for spoiling your evening and hope to make it up to each of you in the future. Good night."

Layvanwick follows Maurice, Sarah, and Diane into his private elevator and rises to his penthouse.

The Festival of Aphrodite ends, Layvanwick Tower empties, the celebrants disperse throughout the city, most of them looking back at the skyscraper mall with longing in their eyes, saying, "This is a night which will live in memory for many years."

Meanwhile, up in Layvanwick's penthouse, the Festival of Aphrodite continues, as it must, because the mall can never sleep.

***

Diane Copernicus is furious. "He has brought the filth of death worship into your mall, Anton! You must deal with this in the harshest way possible. He spoke of sacrifice at the Festival of Aphrodite! It is the worst obscenity I have ever witnessed in my life!"

"It is," says Anton.

"Then why do you bring him to your private chambers?"

Alan Benton is asleep on the bed in Anton's bedroom. Two security guards stand watch over him. Anton has called a nurse, who has yet to arrive.

"I have assumed responsibility for this matter. I intend to resolve it completely."

Maurice Sully says, "Anton, it is my responsibility. Alan feels I have done him an injustice."

"He has contracted with me to help him in this matter."

"He is insane and you should not honor the contract," says Diane. She bows to Sarah. "I appreciate your tragedy, Miss Fletcher. But what your Alan has done in this mall tonight cannot and shall not be forgiven. Mall Masters do not forgive."

"You are presumptuous, Diane," says Anton. "It is not your decision to make. It is mine. It happened in my Mall, it happened with my knowledge. I know more than you think. I knew who Alan was as soon as he came to me, and I know who controls him. Alan Benton has sanctuary within this mall. If you do not like it, return to your own."

Diane raises an eyebrow. "Sanctuary? From what? From whom?"

"From his death."

Diane approaches Anton closely, looks at him face to face, eye to eye. "You wish to be my rival in this issue?"

"You have no say, Diane."

"I am curious. You say you have contracted with him. What payment did he offer?"

Anton smiles, glances quickly at Maurice, holds his eyes for a moment in silent understanding, then looks back at Diane. "You, darling. He offered me you. Diane Copernicus was to be my payment."

Diane's face goes cold. She looks at Maurice. "Do you hear this, Maurice? Your wife is the object of a trade between a madman and a fool."

"Diane, Anton knows you are harsh because you love him so much," says Maurice.

Diane ignores Maurice, maintains her gaze on Anton. "Tell us more, Mall Master. Tell us what is happening."

"In Alan's mind, Sarah Fletcher is still the one true love for Maurice Sully. Alan came to me and asked me to help him regain his death. Since it was Maurice who took it, Maurice is the one who must give it back. But Alan can't ask Maurice because he knows the answer will be no. So he comes to me and promises me reunion with the woman I love — Diane Copernicus."

"I am married to Maurice," says Diane.

"Yes. But if Alan is dead and Sarah is near, Maurice will go to her. And you will come to me. Don't you see?"

"This is absurd," says Diane.

"Of course it is."

"Then why do you deal with this man?"

"First principle of how to defeat evil. What evil wants is irrational and cannot be made to exist. So the easiest way to defeat evil is to pretend to give it what it wants and watch it destroy itself in attempting to achieve unreality."

"I see," says Diane.

"Alan is not evil," says Sarah.

"I am not so sure about that," says Anton.

"He is not evil, I tell you!"

"We will determine that, Sarah. But you know the Agnes of whom he speaks. She is evil. Completely evil."

"In this, you are correct, I think."

"You know it, Sarah. If you do not comprehend how completely evil, then I will teach you."

"I would like to hear more about this Agnes," says Maurice. "Sarah, tell us everything. From the beginning. I want to hear it all. How long has Alan been like this? When did this all start, and how has it come to pass? Why does he want to die? Why does he characterize my saving his life as 'stealing his death'?"

Sarah Fletcher gazes up into the face of Maurice Sully. Her face is old and tired, worn out, but still proud. She looks up into the glowing young face of a man still untouched by tragedy. "You have not aged at all, Maurice. And you are still so innocent."

"I am not innocent, Sarah," says Anton.

Maurice looks at Sarah. "Tell us what happened."

Diane brings a cup of hot coffee for Sarah. Sarah sips the coffee and relaxes into her chair. She gazes up at the faces of the three Mall Masters. Her gaze stops on Maurice and her focus intensifies, the years fall from her face, her lines tighten and her features grow sharper, as if she has become young again. She smiles at him, remembering.

"We were happy for a few years. Alan suffered occasionally, but not very seriously, so I thought nothing of it. We were survivors. We had gone through hell, but come through finally and found ourselves in what we thought was heaven. When you went home and we left the mall, Alan started writing again. He got a job on a magazine, doing feature stories on all aspects of California society. He became a cultural explorer. Most of what he found was good. But there was some madness as well, even in California, the land of reason and logic.

"What of me? I found a new life designing clothes. I started a clothing store and lost myself in the business. You know Californians love their clothes, and go through them with wild abandon. Business was good. Alan and I were doing well.

"But then three years ago he got an assignment to do a story on one of those weird cults that spring up from time to time. Most of them come from America and go nowhere here. But this one seemed to be home grown. A California cult, can you imagine such a thing? This one was headed by a woman named Agnes. That is all I know about her. I have never met her, never seen her. I asked to be introduced any number of times, but it never happened. I think Alan was hiding her from me. Now we know why. He claims to be married to her. I do not know in what sense this is true. But she has made some kind of powerful spiritual connection to Alan. He is devoted to her and her ideas."

"In what does she believe?" asks Maurice.

"What does she preach?" asks Diane.

"It is true, what you said earlier, Diane," says Sarah. "It is death worship. But a special kind of death worship, designed for certain people, designed to appeal to those who have been injured or malformed in some way. Her followers all seem to be sick in some way, either physically, or mentally — sometimes, both."

"Those who are not sick, she makes ill herself," says Anton.

Diane looks at him. "You know of this cult?"

"I have studied it."

"I had no idea you had an interest in such arcane matters."

"My interest is in protecting my mall from evil. To do this, I have come to know the face of evil."

Diane looks at Maurice. "And you? I have received no instruction in these matters. Have you held back on me, Maurice?"

"No. I am not an authority in these matters. I have a different strategy in facing evil."

"Which is?"

"To maintain a ruthless innocence."

"Which means?"

"I do not study evil. It does not interest me. When I recognize it, I render it irrelevant."

"Is that a euphemism for killing it?"

"I do whatever is necessary, prudent, and legal to remain untouched by evil. If it is a self-defense issue, I am prepared to deal in death."

"Have you ever had to do so?"

Maurice looks at Sarah Fletcher, his eyes remembering so many years ago. "I have come close," he says.

Diane looks at Anton. "How does your strategy differ from Maurice?"

"In essence, our strategy is the same. I merely wish to have complete knowledge of my enemies."

"Well, if this Agnes shows up at my mall —" Diane stops, covers her mouth with her hands, her eyes wide in sudden terror.

"Diane, what is it?" asks Anton.

"When I danced with Alan earlier, he spoke of his Agnes. He told me that she was at the other mall this evening. She was celebrating the Festival of Aphrodite at West Park Plaza. She has been to our mall, Maurice! She may be there now!"

Maurice reaches quickly into a pocket and brings out a cellular phone. He pushes a speed dial button and gets the security desk at West

Park Plaza. "This is Sully. Tell me, how did the evening go? Oh? Everything's okay? Peaceful? No disturbances? Nothing out of the ordinary? Okay. Yes, we had a wild night over here, you've heard about it? Well, it's a free country. Listen, we've had news over here that there may be a threat to the mall. No details right now, it's kind of arcane, but you should go on alert. There is a woman named Agnes, leader of a weird cult, she may have something planned. No, we don't know what. Just stay alert. That's all I know right now, but we'll be finding out more soon. We'll be home as soon as we can make it, but I'm not sure when that will be—"

"I going over right away, tell them to watch for me!" says Diane, yelling into the phone.

"Yeah, she's a bit worked up right now," says Maurice, smiling into the phone and twisting away from Diane. "Listen, I'd like you to concentrate your attention on any Aphrodites spending the night in the mall. She may be among them—"

Anton shakes his head no.

Maurice grimaces into the phone, frustration creasing his features. "Anyway, I'll be in touch, keep you as informed as I can. Stay on top of things, I'm counting on you." He turns off the phone, slips it back in his pocket while walking towards Anton. "Well, what do you think?"

"She would not be an Aphrodite."

"If she is in the mall, what will she be doing?"

"Waiting for you."

"Why?"

"To ask for Sanctuary."

"I will not give it to her."

"You might not have a choice."

"It is my mall, I always have a choice. Where is Diane going?"

"Outside!" says Diane, leaving through a side door, which she leaves open, allowing a gust of cold wind to blast in.

"Why is she going outside?" asks Maurice.

"Probably to use one of my telescopes," says Anton.

"I think I will join her," says Maurice.

Anton looks at Sarah Fletcher, the two of them left alone. "Well, shall we join them?"

"I could use a breath of fresh air," says Sarah.

Outside, Diane reaches a telescope first and zeros in on West Park Plaza. The mall is lit up huge and bright for the Festival of Aphrodite. There is a carnival in the parking lot and she can see a Ferris Wheel spin against the night sky. She studies the mall closely, looking for anything strange or out of the ordinary. "It looks fine to me," she finally says to Maurice. "Here, you have a look."

Maurice takes a look. He sees nothing strange. He concentrates his sight on the twin apartments built onto the roof. The lights are on inside both, but he sees no evidence of movement inside or out.

"This is no good," says Maurice. "We have to go home and make sure all is well. Come Diane, let's be on our way."

Anton stops Maurice with a hand to his shoulder. "Maurice, pause to consider my thoughts."

"Very well."

"If you rush off to the mall now, and she is there, you will be playing into her hands. You do not know who she is, what she looks like, or what she is capable of. I do. Your place is here right now, with Sarah and Alan. You should deal with that right now. Talk to Sarah, spend some time with her, and make sure that when Alan wakes up he is cared for properly. I will go to your mall. I leave you in charge of mine. We will switch, for one evening, for this one task. I will go find Agnes and learn what she seeks. Depending on what I learn, I will either deal with it myself immediately, or return to you and report on what I have learned."

Maurice looks at Diane. "Can you stand to relinquish control of this issue to Anton? Can you stand to be apart from the mall when you believe it is in crisis?"

"I ask the same of you," says Diane.

"I can. Anton has saved my life in the past. I trust him completely. He has offered to take care of our mall. I say let him. We will take care of his."

Diane turns away from Maurice, goes to Layvanwick, faces him squarely. "Do you swear an oath that you will defend our mall, that no harm will come to the mall, nor to anyone who is of the mall, while you walk the mall and defend it?"

"I swear."

"Swear it on my lips."

Layvanwick takes her face in his hands and kisses her deeply, seriously. When the kiss ends, he releases her face and speaks to her gently. "I swear by Aphrodite that I will protect your mall, and all those who are of the mall."

Diane steps back and bows to Layvanwick. "Very well. Do it."

Anton disappears across the roof, into the night, a Panther without a mask.

Maurice Sully goes to Sarah Fletcher and says, "Give us one moment, please."

"One moment," says Sarah, her smile twisted by pain. "What is one moment to me now?"

Maurice takes Diane aside. "Here is my plan, darling. I must remain with Sarah and talk to her, try to heal her soul. I want you with Alan when he wakes up. The nurse will help you. She will medicate him so he is under control. I want you to talk to him. Explore his mind. Find out how damaged he really is, and whether he can be redeemed. This is a difficult assignment for you, darling. Not like selling a suit to man who already knows its value, or teaching a child how to think about values by guiding him through the selection of a toy. Your job here is to find the man Alan once was and show that self to him again. Let him see himself as he was, as he should be, as he could be. And you must see him the same way. You must forget the crude, drunken Musketeer who spoiled your evening. Now you are a Mall Master and you must fill this man's soul with the mall. Will you do this?"

"I will. But Maurice…"

"Yes?"

"What if the bomb goes off?"

Maurice smiles. "The bomb will not go off."

***

Watch now as Layvanwick races to West Park Plaza.

In the elevator on the way down, Layvanwick is on the phone to his head of security. "I'm leaving the mall. In my absence, Maurice Sully and Diane Copernicus have complete authority over all mall operations and all mall personnel. Please pass this message along to all employees. I don't know how long I'll be gone. I hope to return by dawn, but I can't guarantee that. I want security on full alert. I'm transmitting a file to you, code-named 'Agnes.' Look it over, it will have all the information you need to protect the mall. Any questions, see Maurice Sully. I will talk to you when I get back."

On the ground floor a car waits for him. The door is held open by an attendant and Layvanwick jumps into the already-running car, shifts into drive, accelerates down the street.

His skyscraper mall lights the night sky behind him. Around him, downtown is a dazzle of light and color, the restaurants all open late and filled with Aphrodites celebrating love. Some recognize his car and cheer as he drives by. They toss flowers into the air after his car, the petals falling lightly onto the hard asphalt street. He drives slowly through the city. Soon he leaves it behind and heads west, accelerating down Grand Avenue, the street wide, dark, empty, his car alone in the middle of the street, sprawling suburban homes on either side. As he nears West Park Plaza, he sees the sky glowing with the colors of the carnival. He smiles.

At the intersection of Grand Avenue and Plaza Way, the carnival is in full sway against the night sky. The sounds assault his ears through the glass and steel of his car. Traffic thins briefly and he accelerates through the intersection as the light turns yellow. In his rear view mirror he catches a glimpse of a car behind him clip his rear fender while attempting to change lanes. The force sends Layvanwick's car swerving out of control into the opposite lane and he collides head-on with a car heading east.

His seatbelt holds and his airbag deploys. The sound and impact deafens him. His next awareness is of gazing fuzzily through his cracked windshield at the crumpled mass of a car in front of him while blood drips down into his eyes. His vision blurs and he wonders why he can't hear. In trying the wipe the blood out of his eyes, he smears it across his face, obscuring his features. Gradually the sound fades back in, he hears people shouting and screaming. He turns to his left, feels sharp pain in his neck and shoulders, stops moving, listens, watches, tries to think of what he should do next. But the sound is fading again. And with it, his vision goes. He feels himself falling sideways out of the car. It seems to take forever. He waits for the ground to hit him, but it never does. He is still falling, somehow in slow motion, when all goes black and silent.

***

He never makes it into the mall. He wakes up in a carnival tent and looks up at a group of people standing above him.

Here is a man with a patch over one eye; a woman with one arm missing; another man with a wooden leg; another woman with half her face missing, eaten away by some horrible disease. They all stare down at him, none make a sound, they just watch.

And there is one more person. A woman in a gray shroud. She is near him and looking at him intently. She studies his face with intense fascination. Her shroud covers all of her body and part of her face. He sees only a tiny bit of hair. Her age is hard to judge; she might be old, she may be young, she is some strange intermediate between the two. She is homely in a crude way, as if nature has chosen to insult her by making her neither plain nor ugly, but a strange mix of both, a mongrel of homeliness with neither the redeeming excuse of plainness, nor the complete finality of total ugliness, but a quirky integration of both that manages to achieve a freakish kind of invisibility, as if light bounces off her and anyone who tries to look at her ends up seeing nothing but a blur.

Or perhaps it is just that his head hurts.

"You have been injured," says the woman.

"Where is the doctor?" he asks.

"I am your doctor," says the woman.

"What is your name?"

"Agnes. What is your name?"

He starts to speak, but stops.

"I can't remember."

CHAPTER FOURTEEN

DAWN WAITS FOR ETERNITY

"You are my baby," says the woman in the shroud.

"Who are you?" asks the injured man.

"I am your mother."

"I don't remember you."

"We will make you a new memory. Here, relax, close your eyes, don't think, don't struggle. Let me take care of you."

"I hurt."

"I know you do. Let me take care of you. I'll take your pain so you don't have to feel it."

"I can't see. What's in my eyes?"

"Your face is covered in blood."

"Please wash it away."

"I will clean you. Close your eyes and relax and let your mother clean you."

"Very well."

"Don't speak, just be silent."

The injured man relaxes, closes his eyes.

The woman in the shroud bends over his head and silently begins to lick the blood from his face, her tongue lapping at him like a dog's.

"What are you doing?" he asks, alarmed.

"I am cleaning you."

"You are licking me."

"Your blood is sweet. I like the taste."

"What kind of ghoul are you?"

"I am your mother and I will wash away your pain. Now lie still and let me do my job. Can't you feel it? Each drop of blood I remove from your face means that much less pain for you."

"I still hurt."

"You hurt because you speak. Now lie still and be silent and the pain will vanish."

"Who are those people behind you?"

"Your brothers and sisters."

"Why do they stand and stare?"

"They are taking your pain unto themselves. They will suffer so that you do not."

"Who am I?" asks the injured man.

"You are my child and I will care for you. Now lie still and let me clean your face."

He lies still. He is silent. He feels her breath on his face and feels her wet tongue sliding across his skin. She licks up his blood. She smacks her lips, relishing the taste. He is frozen in horror — because he knows this is wrong — but he cannot answer her nor defend himself, nor get away. He lies still. The pain washes over him and he sinks again into a black hole. His last memory is of her long tongue slithering across his cheek like a snake, a small wet snake looking for an entrance into his body, his mind, his soul.

But he has none of these things; his body is smashed, his mind is a disjointed jumble; and his soul — this is lost, because he cannot remember who he is, where he came from, what he was doing before he awoke to see this strange woman leaning over him. So he lets sleep take him again.

And while he sleeps, the strange woman in the shroud licks the blood off his face.

***

Approaching one o'clock in the morning of the day after the Festival of Aphrodite, high above the city on the wind-swept roof of Layvanwick Tower, Maurice Sully guides Sarah Fletcher back down into the calm and serene interior of the building. The lights are all still on and the colors are brilliant, spot lights shining onto beautiful walls, paintings, sculptures, flower arrangements, furniture. But the spacious halls are deserted now, empty of all human contact. No parties, no dancing, no lovers embracing, no tables full of laughter and conversation.

Maurice guides Sarah along, holding her hand, guiding her down the empty corridors as if they are explorers moving through unknown territory. He seems to know where he is going, so Sarah says nothing, follows along, trying to keep up with him. Maurice moves quickly, almost running. And he holds her hand with a subtle extra pressure, as if afraid she will get away.

She watches his face, remembering so long ago when he acted under stressful circumstances to save her life. He is older and wiser now, more experienced. How many lives has he saved since the Show Me Mall?

How many desperately rational people has he helped since then? How many others owe him their lives and happiness? She merely wonders, doesn't bother to ask.

And Maurice: not once does he glance back at her to check her face, to see if she follows merely as a body in motion — or as a mind and spirit eager to travel with him back into a realm of values and happiness. But he does not let go of her hand.

They travel several floors down from the roof, to the floor just below the restaurant. Here Maurice leads her into a private lounge located within the Alexios M Art Gallery. They sit back together on a comfortable couch that faces a glowing painting hanging on the opposite wall. The scene is from early California history, an idealized portrait of the author of the Constitution of the Individual's Republic of California, Mykonos Kiriakos, standing in his first mall and presenting his Constitution to fellow merchants.

Maurice and Sarah ignore the painting, sit staring at each other for a long moment, neither speaking, neither wanting to speak. They sit alone together, enjoying the silence, the peace, the serenity, the intimacy of being alone in the skyscraper mall, in the museum, in the dim museum light, with the painting looking out at them both, as if they are the work of art and not it, as if they have been put on display for Mykonos Kiriakos, and he looks out at them from his painting, across time and space, into the room, seeing the reality of these two lost lovers who have suddenly found each other again, and saying to them, "I wrote my constitution for you, so that you could both live as you have lived and reach this moment and know the meaning. This is what a free country is for: so people like you can find love and happiness and know the meaning."

"None of this has happened as I planned," says Sarah.

"I know."

"I feel I have not mastered this situation as I should have."

"You have mastered it more than you think."

"What is going to happen to Alan?"

"He is being cared for by Diane. Alan is in good hands, I assure you."

"I fear Alan is finally lost to me completely, Maurice. I think he has gone away to a place of madness and that he will not return."

"Diane will bring him back."

"I would feel better if it was you."

"Diane is my female self. Whatever confidence you feel for me, you can expect the same of her, I give you my word."

"And you are here to bring me back, is that right?"

"Do you feel you need to be brought back?"

"I feel I am capable of chasing Alan all the way into madness. Wherever he goes, I must follow, spiritually as well as physically. He has gone to a dark place and I have rushed in after him. Now I've lost sight of Alan, and I've lost sight of the way back."

"But I am here with you."

"You have no idea where I am right now, Maurice. You see my body. You see me sitting here with you in this museum, in this great mall, in front of this beauty and this memory of greatness on the wall before us — but you cannot see where my mind has gone, where my soul has been. Love has been brutal to me."

"I am not going to tell you to let go. I'll merely mention that you must consider the possibility, because it may be necessary. But only you can know how much you are willing to take, and how far you are willing to go. If you wish to go mad and die with Alan, that is your choice. I will not judge you immoral for that choice. I just want to remind you of how strong you are and how good you are."

"Ten years have passed, Maurice. Can you be sure I am still the woman you remember?"

"Yes, I can."

"How?"

"You knew where to come when you needed help."

"I should not have needed help in the first place."

"Don't be ashamed of that."

"But I am. You saw it on my face when I removed my mask. It was obvious you were shocked to see what a mere ten years had done to me. Don't pretend you weren't, there is no sense evading this fact."

"I was shocked. I won't deny it. But give yourself credit, Sarah. You have endured what would have crushed a lesser person long ago. And you have the strength left to face even more. I want to help you survive till the end, see this thing through, and beat this evil and achieve happiness again with Alan. You are both still young and have many good years ahead of you."

"So what can be done? What is your plan?"

"Alan has lost his intellectual sovereignty. He no longer believes that his own mind is competent or capable of perceiving and judging reality. Losing this has left him vulnerable to a cult that presumes to be a substitute for his mind and judgment. What we must do is give Alan back his mind and his judgment. We must return his intellectual sovereignty. When he has this back, the cult will be powerless against him."

"How do we return such a thing to Alan? Isn't this something he must do for himself?"

"Yes, the primary choice must be Alan's. But we can help him. We must show him what his true values are and urge him to make the choice. He has been captured by death worship because he feels powerless with the bomb in his head. We must help him to see how powerful he still is, how much life still has to offer, and how easy it is to live properly if he simply makes the choice."

"I thought I understood all this and that I could bring Alan back. But so far I have failed. What have I been doing wrong?"

"Perhaps nothing. In a situation like this, it is possible to do everything right and still lose. You are dealing with Alan's volition. He has to want a rational life and rational values. If he does not, there is no power on earth that can sway him."

"What do you wish to try?"

"Alan is still in love with you, or else he would not have come here with you. Perhaps he has a different agenda than yours, but he does still love you. We must use that love to get Alan back. Has Alan asked you to join him in the cult?"

"Yes."

"And so far you have refused."

"Yes."

"Then what you should do is join him in the cult. We must test how far he is willing to see you go. If he wishes to make you a sacrifice, we must learn exactly what kind of sacrifice."

"I fear I will be put in danger."

"What makes you think that?"

"What little I have been able to learn about this group leads me to believe that they are capable of murder."

"Do you know that they have actually killed people?"

"No. I have no direct evidence. It is just a feeling. My subconscious screams warnings to me. I have never met the leader, Agnes. But I have had some contact with others in the group, and they have all been extraordinarily unhealthy individuals. They give me the creeps. They are worse even than people I knew in America."

"Then it will be your decision as to how far you go, and how much contact you have with these people. We will make sure we exercise extreme caution. But I do believe that if we can create the illusion that you are in jeopardy, and confront Alan with the possibility of actually losing you, we may be able to shock him out of his current state of mind.

Remember how all this started? Alan came to us with the bomb in his head, did not tell us, made his peace and said good-bye, then went off alone to die. He wanted to spare you the pain of witnessing his death."

"But now he wishes to share his pain. He wants me to become a part of it."

"He thinks he does. What he really wants is for you to save him."

"But I have been trying!"

"But not in the way that counts. In New Athens, he did not want to be saved, he ran away to die alone. But now he does want to be saved, but it has to be in a specific way. The first time, he understood his situation to mean that he really was completely powerless, physically and spiritually, against the bomb in his head. But this time, the demon he fights has been created by his own mind, his own will. He has made a choice. What he wants is for you to save him from that choice. He wants you to rescue him from his own irrationality. You have been treating Alan as an adult and urging him to re-think his actions and values. But he is actually a child. Lectures and explanations are useless against him in this state. What you have to do is march in, take control, grab him by the neck, yank him out of his world and back into yours. You have to be brutal and blunt about it. What Alan needs is a kind of spiritual shock therapy. And you are the person to deliver it, because you are who he loves. Because he loves you, he cannot ask you for this help in a straight-forward and simple way. At least not just yet. Eventually, if he sees that he really is going to lose you, he will ask. That is the point to which we need to bring him."

"What if the cult won't have me?"

"Alan is the only one who counts. If he believes you have become a death worshipper and are prepared to sacrifice or be sacrificed, then he will be on the cusp and faced with his ultimate choice. And then you will finally know."

"So he still might choose death."

"Yes."

"Whose death?"

"Yours. His. Maybe both."

"What about you?"

"We'll have to ask Alan about that. Judging from his actions at dinner tonight, he may wish to see me dead. If he does, that can be arranged."

"What do you mean?"

"Ceremony is a big part of a Mall Master's job, as you know. I have some knowledge of the theatrical arts, including the art of illusion. If

Alan wants to kill me, I can easily fake my death for him, see how it affects him."

"Please don't do that. I think it would just encourage him."

"Perhaps. We'll see what happens. Now then. I think we should start getting ready right away. We'll need to act quickly when the time comes. Our chance may come as soon as tomorrow. So I have a mission for you. I want you to go to West Park Plaza immediately. Find any cult members and try to gain entry into their circle. If you can get access to this woman called Agnes, do so at all costs. I think she is the key. You have listened to Alan speak of her and her group. Mimic his language. As of now, you are part of the group. Agnes is your wife, your sister, your mother, however it is that women speak of her. Conduct yourself as a member of the group."

"They know me too well, Maurice. I fear they will not fall for a lie."

"A lie is the first thing they will fall for. Lies are what they want more than anything. I know the psychology of a cult like this. The social dynamic is predicated on lying. Those who rise to highest rank in a cult like this are those who lie the best. By which I mean: whoever tells the biggest whoppers the most consistently. So don't be afraid of lying. If you tell them what they want to hear, they will welcome you with open arms. Now correct me if I am wrong: in the past, you have approached this group as an outsider wishing only to remove Alan from their group, is that right?"

"Yes."

"Now will be different. Alan has converted you completely, so you are a true believer. Dress as they dress, talk as they talk, and you will gain entrance. Do not ask about Alan, express no concern for Alan at all, and they will welcome you."

"You wish me to leave right away?"

"Yes. I want you to leave Alan in my care and put all worries about him out of your mind. Your focus should be to make contact with the cult. If you are hungry and tired right now, use that to your advantage. Those who worship Agnes will love you for being tired and hungry."

"How do you understand so much about this group? You've never met any of them and you've not studied them at all. Yet you speak authoritatively on exactly what they want and how to deal with them."

"I understand the principle of what such a group is, how it functions, and what it functions for. Knowing that principle, the implications follow as a matter of simple deductive logic. Do you think I am wrong about anything so far?"

"No, I think you are right."

"Very well. I'll let Layvanwick know you are coming and what you are up to. If you have contact with him, stay in character. You serve Agnes and you are not of the Mall."

"Very well. Will you call a car to take me?"

"No. You should walk."

"Are you serious?"

"Absolutely. Change your clothes, wear appropriate garb to be presented to Agnes, then start walking."

"Are you doing this to be deliberately cruel, Maurice?"

"Not at all. You need a long walk. You need to think about what you are doing and why you are doing it. And if there are any cult members between here and West Park Plaza, I want them to see you and wonder what you are doing."

"You want a woman to walk alone across a dark city in the middle of the night?"

"Yes. Are you afraid?"

"Should I be?"

"No. Billings is as safe as New Athens. Especially on the evening of the Festival of Aphrodite. You will be in no danger. Most likely anyone who approaches you will be a member of Agnes' cult."

"Very well. If this is what it takes to get Alan back, then I will do it."

"This is also what it takes to get Sarah Fletcher back. And that is my primary concern."

"Then I am on my way."

"Good logic to you, Sarah."

"Good logic to you, Maurice."

They rise together and leave the gallery lounge. In the hallway, Maurice goes one way, Sarah the other. Maurice rises in an elevator back up to the penthouse. Sarah disappears down to the street. Behind them, hanging on the wall of the art gallery, the painted eyes of Mykonos Kiriakos stare after them, implacable, watchful, wise.

***

In the penthouse, Maurice retires to Layvanwick's study and gets on the phone to the head of security, listens to an update on the status of the building. All is well, all is peaceful. Maurice instructs the security chief to send a tail to follow Sarah Fletcher to West Park Plaza, make sure she gets there safely and to observe her actions once she does get there.

Next, he calls West Park Plaza and asks to be connected with Layvanwick. Told that Layvanwick has not arrived yet, he leaves a message about what Sarah is up to and what her mission is. This done, Maurice turns to Layvanwick's computer and accesses the file code-named "Agnes" and begins reading. It is a big file and he reads for a long time, his focus intense, his mind relaxed and receptive to all he reads. He pays no attention to the clocks in the room and time moves past him, carrying him along in a dark flow towards dawn.

***

In another room, Diane Copernicus sits with a slumbering Alan Benton. The nurse has come and gone, Alan has been medicated, but not so much with sleeping drugs. He is supposed to wake soon and Diane composes herself for the task ahead.

Alan has been stripped of his musketeer costume and lies naked under a clean white sheet. He sleeps calmly, pleasantly. Diane watches his eyes, observing subtle movements beneath his eyelids. Before, there was much movement. After the nurse delivered her medication to his system, there has been less. Now, it has stopped completely. Alan's chest rises and falls in a peaceful rhythm. Diane watches and thinks about her memories of the conscious dreaming, what she learned of Alan from that, what she learned of Maurice's perceptions of Alan. She also thinks about the public record of events Maurice and Anton have told her about.

Here is a man who insists on death worship and my job is to speak to him of the Mall. Now how should I approach this? What is the principle involved here? Should I treat this man as sane — or crazy? Healthy — or sick? What does he *need* to hear? What does he *want* to hear?

She tries to call Maurice, but he doesn't pick up. She could leave the room and talk to Maurice, but Alan could wake at any time, so she stays and solves the problem on her own. If she was still an apprentice, she would consider this a test. But she is a Mall Master, so it is more than a test — it is life. The life of the Mall, and her happiness within the Mall, depends on her judgment and actions. I am responsible, she tells herself. So is Alan Benton. My responsibility is to make him understand his own. And to show him what he owes — and to whom. I act selfishly to serve my love — Maurice. Alan must be shown the way to act selfishly and serve his love — Sarah.

Alan's eyes flutter open and the first thing he sees is the smiling face of Diane Copernicus.

"How do you feel?" she asks him.

"Calm. Rested."

"Just relax. You don't have to get up if you don't want to."

"Did I injure Sully?"

"No. Maurice is safe."

"Where is Sarah?"

"She is with Maurice."

"Am I your prisoner here?"

"You are a guest in my care."

"What are you going to do to me?"

"What do you need me to do to you?"

"Kill me."

"You have a bomb in your head. Do it yourself."

"You are cruel."

"And you are kind?"

"I enjoyed our evening together."

"Then you are still mostly human. Congratulations."

"You mock me."

"If you are sensitive to being mocked, that is two points for my side. See, you are not so bad after all."

"So this is the way it is going to be. Playing mind games with me."

"No. I'll hide nothing from you, Alan. Tell me about Agnes. I want to hear about her."

"No you don't."

"Don't you enjoy talking about her?"

"You wouldn't understand."

"Your own understanding is all that should matter. Do you love Agnes?"

"Oh yes."

"Why?"

"She takes away my pain."

"Where do you hurt?"

"Everywhere."

"Physically?"

"Spiritually."

"And Agnes takes that pain from you?"

"Yes."

"How does she do that?"

"She lets me share it with her. She understands what has happened to me. When I talk to her, she listens. And when she touches me..."

"Yes?"

"She shows me what the pain means. Why the pain is important. She allows me to love my pain."

"Why do you love your pain?"

"Because it is unavoidable, final, complete. It is the end of my road, my final resting place, the essence of my being. To suffer is the essence of life. It is what life does to us. We must learn to love our suffering. That is what it means to be human. Man is He Who Suffers. That is her great wisdom. That is what she shows us. I mean Agnes. She is our mother who nurtures us with suffering, who cleanses us with pain."

"Agnes knows you have a bomb in your head?"

"Yes."

"She knows the entire story?"

"Oh yes."

"She is not afraid of the bomb going off?"

"No. She would welcome it. She has prayed for it to detonate. I have prayed with her. All of us have, all of us together, all my brothers and sisters, all of Agnes' children, we have all prayed. I am to deliver my family to heaven. They want to be taken up with me. All of us together, in a conflagration of mind. Agnes especially loves the symbolism: the mind of man annihilated. The mind of man blown to kingdom come."

"Who do you all pray to?"

"Jesus Christ."

"So you are all Christians?"

"Of course we are. We are the true and honest Christians."

"What does Sarah think of all this?"

"She does not understand."

"Do you want her to understand?"

Alan is silent.

"When you set the bomb off, do you want Sarah to be at your side?"

"Only if she understands."

"What does she need to understand?"

"How powerless she is, how impotent is her own mind, and how sublime is the essence of suffering. You see, for we who worship Christ, the highest form of worship is found in those who suffer. Christ died for us on the cross and took all the sins of humanity upon himself. To worship this, we seek out those who suffer the most. When we touch one who is sick, we are touching the body of Christ. When we touch one who is in pain, we experience the pain Christ felt on the cross. When we suffer with those who are dying, we become Christ-like for a short time, we take on all the pain of the sick and dying, we suffer for them so that they might find peace in the final moments of their lives, and enter heaven in a state of grace, and be blessed and be greeted by Christ himself as they enter the kingdom of eternal happiness."

"Have you ever explained all that to Sarah?"

"Of course I have."

"Do you remember when you first met Sarah?"

"Yes."

"What did she look like?"

"The first time I saw her? Radiant. She had such a powerful energy emanating from her skin and eyes. Her face was like glowing stone, like a sculpture burning with heat and light. Her bookstore was dim, but when I saw her, it was as if the entire room was ablaze. I thought she had the most perfect face I had ever seen. Such a spiritual face. I thought she was the essence of..."

"Yes? The essence of what?"

"Of the spiritual."

"What aspect of the spiritual?"

"I was young, what did I know?"

"Go ahead, you can say it. Was it something false?"

"Yes."

"What was it?"

"Reason. I thought her face held the essence of rationality. I thought her eyes were the beauty of logic."

"And you found that beautiful?"

"At that time, yes."

"We're you raised a Christian in America?"

"Yes."

"Yet you had a passion for reason to such an extent that you actually identified a woman's face as containing the essence of reason and fell in love with that face? Didn't you take your Christian lessons seriously?"

"I ignored them. It meant nothing to me when young. I knew nothing of life."

"Do you still love Sarah today?"

"Yes."

"What do you see in her face now?"

"Just memories."

"Sarah is only a memory to you now?"

"No. But our best years have passed. I have grown spiritually, while she has remained a pagan."

"Do you love Agnes more than Sarah?"

"That is a nasty question."

"Three points for my side. If you think that is a nasty question, there must be some conflict in your mind between Agnes and Sarah. Do you feel a conflict?"

"You seek to put words in my mouth, pagan bitch."

"Ah, you are waking up and becoming insulting again. Very well. Never mind that question. Tell me more about Sarah when she was young, when you first met. Tell me what kind of fun you had."

"No."

"Tell me about your first date."

"No."

"Tell me about the first time you kissed her."

Alan closes his eyes. "No."

"Remember the first time you held her hand?"

"No."

"Remember the way her hair smelled and what her skin tasted like?"

"No."

"Remember the sound of her laughter?"

"No."

"Remember the first time you made love to her?"

"You are obscene."

"It was not obscene, it was beautiful, remember? Remember how good it was?"

"It is none of your business."

"You don't have to tell me about it. Just remember. Think about how wonderful she was. Think about how she felt, and how she made you feel. Remember how it was to look at her face, to hold her face in your hands, to look into that face that was the essence of reason, the beauty of logic, and to hold that face in your mind, that body in your arms, and experience the exquisite ecstacy of her love while seeing that face and knowing what it meant to you, and understanding all of the values implicit in that face, and all of the meaning of life in the moment you two shared together while making love? You can't forget something like that. You can't forget the meaning of something like that. You have the memory still, I know you do. Relish it. Take it out and hold it in your mind and go deep into the memory and re-live it. You are that young man again. You love Sarah because she is reason to you, and reason is what you need more than anything else, what you want more than anything else, reason is the oxygen of your soul, reason is what raises you out of the darkness of a Christian childhood in America, reason is the force that compels you into this woman's arms, even when you know she is the daughter of the Governor of Kentucky and that loving her might cost you your life. Reason is the force that compels you to follow this woman to California, to New Athens, to the world of the Mall Masters and a land of reason and logic and science and Man Worship. If

Sarah is reason and you still love her, then you still love reason — and all that follows from reason."

Alan Benton exhales a deep breath, raises his hands up over his face, shudders briefly, then breaths deep, catching the scent of Diane's perfume. He drops his hands back to his sides, turns his head slightly, opens his eyes, looks at her.

"You are a witch."

"No. I am a Mall Master."

"You have never had your reason taken from you."

"Who took yours?"

"The evil bastards who put this bomb in my head."

"How did they take your reason?"

"Don't you understand? It was not my choice. And once it was done, nothing I do or say matters anymore. My judgment is useless. My mind is useless. Any choice I make is useless. Because my mind is not under my control."

"You contradict yourself, Alan."

"I have heard this before, from Sarah."

"Now you will hear it from me. They gave you orders to come to California and bring Sarah back, correct?"

"Yes."

"Did you follow those orders?"

"No."

"So who is in control?"

"You don't understand."

"And when you thought you were going to die, whose choice was it not to tell Sarah? Whose choice was it to leave her out of that situation? Who picked the place to die? Who chose to be in the presence of the Statue of Liberty when the bomb in your head went off? And what did that mean? Who chose to plunge himself into the sea and suicide by drowning himself? Who chose to struggle against even the arms of the woman he loved, the woman he sought to protect, when she came to drag you from your watery grave? Who chose that? And what did that mean?"

"You understand nothing."

"What don't I understand?"

"That was not the bad part. All of that was the easy part. Don't you see? Dying was easy. Preparing to die was easy. Saying good-bye to Sarah was easy and resigning myself to death was easy. Diving into the harbor and plunging into the cold icy deep was easy, trying to suicide was easy, all of that stupid dramatic crap was easy, don't you understand!

"When the bomb didn't go off and I knew I was going to live — *that* was the difficult part. That was the beginning of the end for me. That was when I lost my mind. That was when I remembered all I had been taught as a boy about Jesus and Christianity and religion and God. And that was when it all made sense and all came together and came crashing into my soul and obliterated my reason, my arrogant man worship, my love for California and the Malls and your science and technology and your sybaritic culture, all of it was washed away, blown away by a spiritual epiphany in which Christ finally entered my soul and I understood how small I really was and how great God is, how good Christ is, and how and why I had to give my life and mind over to him and let him be my savior.

"But you cannot know any of that, and I cannot explain any of it to you. That is something you have to experience for yourself, it has to come from being directly in the presence of the Holy Spirit. If you have not felt something like that, then there is nothing I can say to you."

"So you were a Christian from that first moment on the boat, when Sarah held your head in her lap and kissed your wet face?"

"Yes, I knew it even then."

"Yet it was several years before you discovered Agnes."

"Yes."

"Tell me of your love for Agnes."

"It is different."

"Different how?"

"It is spiritual."

"You said Agnes is your wife. What does that mean?"

"Exactly that. We have been wed."

"So you are really man and wife?"

"On the spiritual level. It is a union of souls."

"So you don't have a physical relationship?"

"Don't be disgusting."

"Do you want a physical relationship with her?"

"I do not need that from her."

"Do you want it?"

"No."

"Would you accept it if she offered herself?"

"She would do no such thing. Your questions have grown offensive, I will answer no more. To speak of sex in relation to Agnes is grotesque."

"You are right."

"She is beyond such desires."

"Are you?"

Alan lies silent, his eyes shut, his jaw tense, the tendons in his neck flexing.

"Do you feel passion for Sarah?" asks Diane.

Alan says nothing.

"When is the last time you made love to Sarah?"

Alan hears this question — and is stopped by it. He sits frozen on the bed, his eyes glassy, staring past Diane to the wall behind her. There is nothing there but white paint, white wall, like a blank slate, an empty palette. He stares, as if mesmerized by nothing.

"Don't you remember the last time?" asks Diane.

"No."

"Has it been that long?"

"Yes."

"I don't believe you."

Alan laughs. "Do you really expect to heal me by getting me sexually aroused and sending me chasing after Sarah?"

"That would be a step forward."

"If you believe that, why don't you try me yourself?"

"Do you want me?"

"No."

"Is rejecting your sexuality part of your religion?"

"I have not rejected it. It is simply of no importance."

"What about Agnes? Has she rejected her sexuality?"

"Of what significance is that?"

"I want to see where your values have taken you. And what your values really are."

"Agnes is my value. The holy quality of suffering she shows us is my value."

"Why do you hate Maurice?"

"I don't hate Maurice."

"Why did you want him to kill you?"

"I thought a Mall Master would be capable of rising to the occasion. I thought he would understand what I wanted, and why it was right for me to want it."

"But to ask a Mall Master to take the life of a man he previously saved — and to do this in a Mall, in the middle of a celebration of the Festival of Aphrodite — do you see what an obscenity this was? Do you comprehend why we who are of the Mall were so horrified by your actions? Why we see it as a vicious, nihilistic attack on our values and beliefs? What did you hope to accomplish by all that?"

"I wanted to make myself a sacrifice to Agnes. She believes that this culture of the mall you people have is evil and should be destroyed."

"Did she put you up to it?"

"No. She knew nothing about any of this. She knew I was coming. But what I did was my own idea. I wanted to die at the hands of Maurice Sully because he was the man who took my death from me."

"I do not understand how you can value something such as death."

"Christ suffered and died. To become like Christ, we must suffer and die. The ultimate spiritual moment comes in the experience of suffering and death, when you have suffered your most and in the last moments of your earthly consciousness, you become one with Christ as you die. That is the state of grace we seek. That is how we get to heaven. That is the key that unlocks the gates into the eternal kingdom. Our earthly existence is low and vile. It is not to be enjoyed, it is to be endured, and the more suffering you can endure on earth, the greater will be your happiness in heaven. What you call 'death worship,' is not that at all. It is simply acknowledging the fact that existence as such is evil and that to transcend this evil, one must suffer a sickness unto death. So it is not 'death worship.' It is the worship of suffering, the glorification of suffering. Suffering as an end in itself. Because that is all reality deserves from us."

"Do you want Sarah to suffer with you?"

"Yes."

"Hasn't she suffered enough?"

"There is no such thing as suffering too much."

"Alan, do you have any photographs of Sarah from ten years ago, when you first met, when you first got married?"

"Yes, we still have our photos."

"Can you remember what she looked like? Is there a favorite photo you recall? Can you think of it, remember how Sarah looked? Or remember her face when you first saw her?"

"I remember."

"Now match that face with what Sarah looks like now. Look at what all this suffering has done to Sarah. Is this what you want? This is what you want to see happen to your wife's beautiful face? You want to see that radiant face of proud reason turned into a twisted mask of tortured pain? Is that what you want to look at all day — knowing that it was your worship of suffering that turned her ugly?"

"That is why I married Agnes. Hers is a face of true spiritual grandeur. Suffering has molded her features into a mask that insults reality by matching its wretchedness. True beauty lies on the spiritual realm. When Agnes becomes an angel in heaven, she will be a vision of glowing beauty. But on earth, in this reality, all the world deserves is gray wrinkles."

"Tell me, since suffering is your value — would you suffer if Sarah was no longer with you? How do you feel about losing Sarah?"

"I want to lose her. I want to lose her to Agnes."

"What if you lost her to the Mall?"

"Then I damn her and forget about her."

"But would you suffer?"

"I suppose I would."

"Wouldn't you want to suffer intensely?"

"Perhaps."

"And if you lost Agnes? Would you relish that suffering?"

"When Agnes dies, I will be there to share her suffering."

"Why don't you just kill Sarah?"

"That ignorant question shows how little you understand."

"Death only has value if it includes suffering?"

"Suffering is the only value. Death is simply stepping through a doorway, from one room into another."

Diane is suddenly quiet for a long time. She ignores Alan and sits thinking. For a while, she sits with her eyes closed, as if meditating. She does not move a muscle, except to breath slowly, her body relaxed.

Alan watches her, wondering if he has reached an impasse with her. Is she thinking of more questions to ask? Is she stumped? Is she trying to figure out a new plan of attack? Alan smiles at her. He is happy to see her struggle. He feels pleased to have confused a Mall Master.

Look at this woman, he thinks. See how proud she is? I have defeated her pride. She cannot touch me with her reason and logic. Her glorious mall has no sway over my soul. I am not of the Mall. I am of Agnes. I am of Christ. I know the true nature of reality. She thinks she is going to heal me, save me, bring back to the Mall. But she is wrong.

Diane finally opens her eyes and stands up, looks severely at Alan, her posture and tone of voice indicating that their little session together is at an end. "Very well, Alan. I've made a decision. I'm going to help you."

"Help me what?"

"Help you suffer."

"How are you going to accomplish that?"

"I'm going to let you go."

"Really?"

"Yes."

"Go where?"

"Wherever you need to go, to do whatever you need to do."

"Well, that's very *logical* of you," says Alan, laughing darkly.

"Wait here. I'll bring some clothes, then you are a free man."

"Isn't there some legal action to be brought against me?"

"Maurice does not intend to press any charges against you."

"Oh."

Diane leaves the room. A few minutes later, she comes back with some clothes. She leaves the door open and steps outside to wait for Alan to dress himself.

When Alan is dressed, he steps outside to find both Diane Copernicus and Maurice Sully waiting for him. Both look at him seriously with faces austere in implacable judgment. Before Alan can say a thing, Maurice addresses him.

"Alan Benton, you are banned from this mall for life. You are no longer of the mall and your presence here is a blemish on our happiness. If suffering and death is what you want, then suffering and death is what you will get. You are irrational, illogical, and immoral, and I want nothing more to do with you. Whatever moral debt or obligation you felt you owed me is dismissed. You owe me nothing and are obligated in no way. You are free to pursue whatever madness you wish. But you will find no sanctuary or solace in this mall, or any other. You are banned from West Park Plaza as well. I'm sorry that after ten years our reunion has to end this way. But you are beyond redemption. There is nothing we can do for you, nothing we want to do for you."

"You have defeated us Mall Masters," says Diane. "I hope you are pleased with yourself."

"Where is Sarah?" asks Alan.

"She left an hour ago," says Maurice.

"Left? To where?"

"I don't know," says Maurice.

"You just let her walk away?" asks Alan.

"Just as we are letting you walk away," says Maurice.

"Didn't she want to stay here?"

"No."

"Didn't she want to wait for me?"

"No."

"Are you going to find her?" asks Diane.

Alan's tense face relaxes. He looks at the two Mall Masters and sees right through them. "No," he says. "That is what you want me to do, isn't it? You want me to go chasing after Sarah, find her, rescue her, regain my lost soul by finding my highest value, my one true love. That is what this has all been about. Well, you have failed. I will not find her. I will not look for her. I renounce Sarah Fletcher from my soul forever. Agnes is my wife. It is to Agnes that I will return. Sarah Fletcher is no longer my concern. We came to this place together, each hoping to find common ground, each hoping to convert the other to our values. But there will be no conversion for either of us. We are now on different paths. Hers leads to the Mall. Mine leads somewhere else. So if you see her, tell her I said good-bye."

"Good-bye," says Maurice.

"Farewell," says Diane.

Alan steps into an elevator with two security guards his escort. The elevator plunges to the lobby and lets him out. He walks across the spacious lobby with security guards at each elbow. They let him out into the cold, dark street and then lock the glass doors behind him, turn away, walk back into the skyscraper mall.

Alan glances back at the mall briefly, just once. Then he turns and walks into the darkest alley he can find, disappears into the city, leaves the mall behind.

***

Upstairs in the penthouse, Diane says to Maurice, "Do you really think this will work?"

"It is the only chance he has. If he wants it to work, and lets it work, he will be saved. But if he truly does wish to die, then there is nothing else to be done. Don't worry about it, darling. We have done what we can. Now it is all up to Alan. So let us turn our attention to other matters. Anton should have arrived at our mall by now. Let's see if we can get him on the phone."

***

"Mother Agnes, we have news."

"Yes?"

"This man we saved from the car accident, we know who he is."

"I know who he is."

"Truly?"

"He is Anton Layvanwick, Mall Master."

"Yes, Mother Agnes. What are we going to do?"

"We will do what we came here to do. Now is the time. We have what we need. Pass the word along to the others. We will move against the mall immediately so that it is ours before dawn. When the sun rises, West Park Plaza must be in our control."

"What is to happen to this Mall Master?"

"He will be crucified."

"Yes, Mother Agnes."

CHAPTER FIFTEEN

GARGOYLE CARNIVAL

Yes, Sarah Fletcher could walk down Grand Avenue, but instead, she chooses a side street deserted of traffic and dark with a lack of street lights. She walks past stately old homes, broad lawns, huge trees. A breeze picks up as she strolls along, the branches and leaves above her rustle gently in the night. The windows of the homes are all dark here. It is late. Or early. However one wishes to think of it.

It is late, thinks Sarah. It is getting later all the time. Late for me, very late for Alan, late for the Mall Masters. And what of Agnes? Late for her — or early? Perhaps I can have a say in that. If I succeed, it can be late for Agnes as well.

I have never met this woman, yet it is she who has controlled my life for the last several years. My husband has a mistress. If only it was sex he wanted from her. That I could deal with. But instead, they have an affair of the spirit. A mingling of souls. And to what end?

And now I am to join with her — this Agnes — this cult that worships suffering. So get used to it. Are you tired yet? No? You will be. Keep walking. Is that a hill up ahead? Good. I hope it is a large hill. I want to feel my lungs burn. I want to taste some sweat in my mouth. I want to feel my legs ache. These shoes don't fit right. Fine. I'll have a blister. When I find Agnes, I'll say, "Look, I have a blister on my foot! Can I joined your cult? Is a blister enough?" Maybe my feet will chaff and start to bleed. That would be good. If I show up with bloody feet, they're bound to let me in. "I am Sarah, she of the bloody foot, and I come to suffer with Agnes!" That would be good.

She hears a dog bark. More dogs join in, a chorus of howling commences, some of it close by. The dogs sound vicious, the menace of their howls magnified by the darkness and wind. The wind moves through the trees like a ravishing lover and makes the trees moan. On her left, the sky glows with lights from Grand Avenue. To her right, the sky is dark, the Rimrocks invisible. She doesn't see a single star anywhere. Where are the stars? she wonders. Hidden behind clouds? Or sucked from the sky by Agnes? No, she doesn't have that kind of power. She has no power at all. Then why am I going to meet her? Why am I going to join her? Whose power is it that I am fighting?

She doesn't answer herself, letting the answer hang in the back of her mind unacknowledged. She gazes ahead. The street is dark and endless. What if she gets lost? This is a strange city. Don't worry. The route is simple. I walk due west, I end up at West Park Plaza. Keep Grand Avenue on your left, you will find it. Can't miss it. It is a mall, after all. See that glow up ahead? Faint, just a touch of light. That is the Mall. The Festival of Aphrodite was held yesterday, just this past night, at all the Malls in all the cities of this country. An entire nation has just celebrated the glory of love, the joy of love, the sacred ecstacy of sex. They are all screwing their brains out now. Most of them. And what of me? I trudge along in the night in a strange city in ill fitting shoes, looking for an ugly old woman who has kidnapped my husband's soul. Now that is a hell of a way to celebrate the Festival of Aphrodite, is it not?

Ah, this is good! I am feeling sorry for myself. Agnes will love this! Yes, I am getting into the right frame of mind now. I won't have any trouble fitting in with these people. I will have bloody feet and a sad tale of woe.

Shut up and walk. Think about what you have to do. What do I have to do? Show up, join the cult, then wait for — what? Alan to rescue me? Layvanwick to reveal me? Agnes to reject me? Maurice Sully to —

Never mind. Wheels have been set in motion. I am just a cog in a great integration of events set in motion by that wise benevolent Mall Master. I will let the events play out. I know what I want. I want to save Alan. I want to help Alan save himself. I want to bring Alan to his senses by throwing myself on the flames and seeing if he wakes up and drags me out before I burn to death.

She catches a scent of burning wood in the air. Someone's fireplace. Ah, they are making love in front of their fireplace. They are naked on a great bearskin rug and can feel the heat of the flames on their skin. They pleasure each other on the soft and sweet-smelling carcass of a dead animal that if alive would tear them both to pieces and eat them. How is that for a symbol emblematic of Man's mastery of nature?

She closes her eyes, walks a few steps blind up the sidewalk, letting the soft breeze caress her face. The air is warm and smells sweet. The breeze carries away the scent of burning wood and replaces it with the aroma of trees and grass and flowers. What time of year is it? Spring. The Festival of Aphrodite is held in the spring. But what day is it? She does not remember. Now isn't that strange. This is the day I have lost Alan forever, I should remember the day, you'd think I could remember a little thing like that. What is it, May or June? Never mind.

She stops. Out of nowhere, an overwhelming emotion hits her and she stops. Tears flow, her throat constricts, she cannot speak, she moans, sobs, tears flowing down her cheeks. She turns and faces down the hill. Through her tears, she can see the skyscraper mall glowing through the trees, standing tall and still bright above the city.

"Maurice...why are you not with me? Why have you sent me away to be alone in the night, to walk across the city? Why are you not here with me? Maurice. I want you here with me. I want Maurice. I want Maurice."

She sits down in the soft grass under a tree. There. Have a good cry. My goodness. Where did that come from? Just relax, go ahead, you're alone, it's the middle of the night, go ahead and cry, who's to know, who's to care?

That bastard Maurice. This is all his fault. All of it. Right from the start. He started the whole thing ten years ago. If Alan would have died then, then Maurice and I —

There. That is what you were looking for, isn't it? That forbidden thought. Go ahead, don't be afraid. Let it out. Bring it out, take a look at it, get used to the idea. Say it out loud.

"If Alan would have died ten years ago, I would be with Maurice and we would be happy."

There, that wasn't so tough. Now how do you feel?

I am a horrible person for thinking such a thing!

Are you really?

I don't know.

Well, let's just let it sink in and see how we feel about it, shall we?

She says it again. "If Alan would have died ten years ago, I would be with Maurice and we would be happy."

Is that what I want now? Do I want Alan to die so that I can go back to Maurice? But Alan does not even have to die. Just let him run off to the cult with Agnes. Never have to see him again. Yes. It would be that simple. Can it be that I am that close to being free of his suffering? Do I really want to save him — or just walk away and be done with it all? He has put me through hell. He has dragged me down into his pit and ravaged me even as he has ravaged himself. He has destroyed my life and made me miserable in his quest to indulge his pain and anger at those who annihilated his mind. Do I really want to save him? Do I really want to try?

She pauses a moment, is very still, her mind empty. For a second, she is aware of nothing except the wind and the sound of the leaves above her. Her soul is empty and motionless.

I have been through this before, she thinks. When Alan is gone and I cannot see his face and body, nor hear the sound of his voice, I am angry at him and I hate him for what he has done to us. But when he returns and I see him again, hear his voice, I know that I am powerless not to love him. So I will continue to fight for him. Whatever tiny speck of human soul is left within him, I will fight for that small piece of virtue and whatever happiness will come from it. And if Alan perishes, I will perish fighting for him. Because I know that while I fight for him, I fight for myself. I fight for she who was saved by Maurice Sully. And whatever I end up saving of myself will be something that Maurice Sully can love. And for Maurice and I, that will be all we can have.

She rises and begins walking once more. She is getting closer to the mall. The lights are getting brighter. She is almost there. The darkness and the wind does not bother her now. She has a mission. She is on a mission from Man. A mission to reclaim the soul of one particular man. And the woman who loves him.

***

When police officer Rod Black pulls his motorcycle to a stop at the scene of the car accident at Grand Avenue and Plaza Way, he sees two crumpled cars ruined by a head-on collision. He radios in the accident location, calls for an ambulance and backup, then approaches the scene. A crowd has gathered and he has to fight his way through. He orders people to disperse and they do so. When he finally gets close he looks into both cars and cannot see any bodies. He does a double-take, then checks again, this time looking slowly, methodically, checking front seats and back. There is nothing. He sees blood inside both cars, he finds blood drops in the street around both cars. But no bodies.

He looks up from the accident and surveys the crowd. "Did anybody witness this crash? Did anybody see what happened?"

Nobody answers him. Some stare at him with blank faces. Others turn and walk away.

"I saw it," says a woman.

Officer Rod Black looks at her. She is skinny and pale and her face lacks arete. "What happened to the passengers?" Officer Black asks. "Were they thrown clear?"

"They walked away," says the woman.

"What?"

"They walked away."

"Walked where? What direction?"

"To the carnival."

"They walked away from *this* — and went to the *carnival?*"

"Yes."

Officer Black doesn't trust the woman. He is suspicious of one with so little arete in her face. So he looks back to the cars. Never mind what people say — or don't say — look at the evidence. Look at these cars, look at the blood. Follow the trail of blood. Here, see where the drops lead? They lead — towards the carnival. But they stop just before the sidewalk. Officer Black looks up from the street, from the last tiny drops of drying blood — and he stares at the wild scene of screaming lights before him. The carnival is still going. People still swirl about, moving from ride to ride, from attraction to attraction, the densely packed and noisy center of the carnival so loud and boisterous that these people probably didn't notice the crash, couldn't even hear it.

They *walked* away from this crash?

Officer Black looks back to the crumpled cars. There is something oddly familiar about the big black sedan. He runs a check on the license plate and his suspicions are confirmed when he learns the identity of the owner.

He takes a deep breath and considers his next actions carefully.

When his backup arrives, he gives them instructions. "We've got a serious car crash and no bodies. I suspect foul play. I want this carnival closed down and searched. Make it slow and methodical and don't miss a thing."

"Yes sir."

From his motorcycle radio, Officer Black calls the security desk at West Park Plaza. While waiting to be connected, he stands in front of the crash in the middle of the street, looking past the carnival at the brightly lit mall. A chill runs down his spine.

"Mall Security."

"This is Officer Rod Black of the Billings Police Department. We have a serious car crash here on Grand Avenue in front of your mall, but no bodies. I've done a check and one of the vehicles belongs to Anton Layvanwick. We have a missing Mall Master. We're checking the carnival out here, but I'm wondering if he made it into the mall."

"We've heard nothing here, but I'll have my men do a check and question the aphrodites."

"Is Maurice Sully home tonight?"

"He's at Layvanwick Tower."

"You should let him know what has happened."

"I will."

"I'd also like your permission to enter the mall with some officers and do a search and ask some questions."

"That permission will have to come from Mall Master Sully."

"I understand. Let me know the answer as soon as you get it. Meanwhile, I'll be searching the carnival."

"Very well."

The connection ends. Officer Rod Black heads for the carnival.

***

In the old car he and Sarah drove all the way from New Athens, Alan Benton is detoured by the accident to the rear of West Park Plaza. He parks the car and walks around to the carnival side. He sees police cars with lights flashing all along Grand Avenue. The carnival is shut down and silent, lights are dimming, and people are drifting away. So, it has begun, he thinks. Good. Let it begin — then let it end, quickly.

He makes his way to a dark tent on the eastern side of the carnival. Inside, he is met by one-eyed Manny Kantor. "I'd like to see Agnes, please," says Alan.

"Soon. Did you see that it has begun?"

"Yes."

"Soon the mall will suffer with us."

"Let us pray that it is so."

Alan is surprised when Agnes comes out to meet him. He had expected to be escorted in to her. Agnes greets him by coming to him, placing her hands on his cheeks, staring into his eyes seriously through her veil. "Did you lose what you wanted to lose?" she asks him.

"I have lost Sarah."

"Have you renounced her?"

"I have."

"Your eyes hold much suffering now."

"I love my suffering."

"I believe you. That is good. It is good that you suffer. Very well. So you have seen outside?"

"Yes."

"We have begun. I intend to have the mall by dawn. Are you with me?"

"Of course I am. I want to see this mall suffer."

"Good. Come, I have a surprise for you. We have claimed a great sacrifice."

Agnes escorts him to the darkened rear of the tent. There, behind a barrier, hidden from view, she shows him a bloody and delirious Anton Layvanwick sprawled on a blanket.

"He was injured in an accident and providence has guided him into our hands."

Alan looks down at the helpless Layvanwick. Layvanwick does not see him. Alan bends down and looks closer at Layvanwick's face. Alan's eyes widen, his lips part, his breathing grows quicker, he feels a tension in his chest, whether terror or excitement, he does not know. It is a curious kind of pleasure he has never felt before, but mixed with a pain he ignores, pushes aside.

"He was so powerful just a short time ago, when he presumed to pass judgment on me. Now look at him. Reduced to this."

"Yes," says Agnes. "Look at him. What do you see?"

"Pride humbled."

"Yes. But there is more."

Alan looks at Agnes. "He is to be a sacrifice?"

"Yes. And I want you to be responsible. I want you to be the agent of Heaven and do God's work. If the mall is to be sacrificed, it is fitting that a Mall Master be sacrificed as well. I want you to take care of this detail for me. Are you willing? Can you do it?"

"What do you wish?"

"Once we have the mall, this Mall Master will be crucified. We will put him on a cross and he will burn when this mall burns."

"Those who refuse to suffer, must experience God's justice."

"Yes."

Alan turns again to Layvanwick. "Does he not hear us?"

"He hears, but he does not understand. The crash has taken his mind, wiped out his memory. He does not know who he is, nor what he is."

Alan reaches out a hand and touches Layvanwick's cheek, turns his face towards him, watches to see if his eyes focus on him. Layvanwick looks up at him, but there is no recognition in his eyes.

"Hello," says Alan. "Do you recognize me?"

"Are you one of my brothers?" asks Layvanwick, his voice soft and ragged, weak, with no force of mind or arete behind it.

"Yes," says Alan. "I am one of your brothers."

"Are you here to take away my pain?"

"Yes. That is what I am here for."

Alan turns Layvanwick's face away, back towards the colorless material of the tent, and the Mall Master returns to his reverie.

Alan stands and joins Agnes, both of them facing away from

Layvanwick, their voices low, as if hiding their words from the Mall Master, even though there is no danger of being understood.

"What is the point of sacrificing someone who does not know who he is?" asks Alan.

Agnes looks at him soberly. "There are others who know who he is."

Alan understands her.

"Very well. I accept. I will do this thing."

"You are not afraid?"

"Of what? If there is suffering to relish, I want to be there."

"Then let us begin. First, we must take the mall. My plan is simple. Listen —"

***

Agnes and her entourage enter the mall through the back door. Anton Layvanwick is their key.

At three AM the carnival is dark and silent. Police have wrapped a yellow barrier all the way around the carnival and are slowly working their way through the people inside, questioning everyone and searching every structure inside the yellow barrier.

Agnes sends someone out to count how many police officers are present. When she has the number, she gives orders to have twice that many of her followers go out and approach the officers, talk to them, distract them. While this is happening, Agnes and her core followers gather Layvanwick and pack him into a box, load the box onto the back of a truck, then drive the truck to the nearest exit. While her followers harass and berate the police as they try to question her and search the truck, Agnes is meek and compliant. The box is opened and looked at, but nothing is found because Layvanwick is hidden in a false bottom. He makes no sound because he has been told not to, and in his mindless state, he follows the orders he is given. He can conceive of no reason not to. He is going with his brothers and sisters to a place where all his pain will be taken away. That is all he understands.

Once through the police barrier, the truck is driven around to the back side of the mall and Layvanwick is unpacked, dressed in a coat to cover up blood stains on his shirt, then walked to the rear entrance of the mall. It is a painful and slow walk for him, and he has to be held up between two men, but they manage to cover the small distance in a reasonable amount of time, and Layvanwick, although he weeps some, does not cry out loudly, nor does he lose consciousness.

"What is this place?" he asks.

"It is to be our church," says the one-eyed Manny Kantor, who holds up his left side.

"It is to be your home," says Alan Benton, who holds up his right side.

Agnes approaches the door. It is locked. Inside, a security officer approaches warily, stares at them through the glass. Agnes steps aside and motions to Layvanwick. The security officer speaks into his radio, then steps forward and opens the door.

"We found this poor man wandering the street. He has been injured and needs help."

"Please, come in, I recognize Mall Master Layvanwick, you have rescued a Mall Master! How badly is he hurt?"

"He will be fine," says Agnes. "It is you I am worried about."

"Excuse me?"

"You have been injured."

"I am fine."

"No, you are in pain. Here. Let me help you."

Agnes reaches out and takes the security guard's hand. "Here, sit down on this bench. You need to rest."

"No, I have to radio in, I have to tell them I've found Layvanwick."

"Don't worry about that, I'll take care of it for you. You don't have to be responsible. There. Now you're sitting down. Don't you feel better?"

"I feel dizzy. What has happened to me?"

"I told you, you are ill. Can you feel the pain?"

"I have no pain — wait — oh, what is happening, what have you done to me? Who are you?"

"I am Agnes. Tell me where it hurts."

"The pain — moving up my chest — can't breath — why –"

Agnes rubs her hands across the guard's chest. "This is where it hurts, right here?"

"Yes, there, my chest, my heart, my lungs burning—"

Agnes sticks her fingers inside the guard's shirt, her hands making contact with his naked skin. The guard slumps down on the bench, his eyes closing, his last sight of the group of freakish people moving away into the mall, Layvanwick in the center, surrounded.

Leaving the guard unconscious on the bench, Agnes picks up his radio and carries it with her as she catches up with the group. "Guards first, everyone. Confiscate their uniforms. Ignore the aphrodites. Control all entrances and exits. Once the security force is rendered mute, we will deal with the aphrodites. Now let us begin."

The followers of Agnes swarm out into the mall, heading into the center court, then spreading out down each arm of the mall, and onto every level, like a toxin entering the bloodstream of a body.

The limping, wooden-legged man, Augustus Stein, clatters into the center court and is met by two security guards. Stein falls to the floor of the mall in front of them and begins weeping and wailing. "Please, my leg, my wooden leg, I am in pain, touch my leg, there is something wrong with my leg." Stein holds his wooden leg up to a kneeling security guard, who touches the leg, takes it into his hands and examines it while his partner shines a flashlight onto the scene. The guard holding the leg touches the wood. Unknown to him, the wood of Augustus Stein's leg has been coated with a special chemical. The chemical is absorbed into the guard's skin, into his bloodstream. Within seconds, the fast-acting compound is putting him to sleep. His partner bends down to see what has happened and Stein kicks him in the face with his wooden leg, scrapes the leg across the guard's face, making sure to scrape some good wounds across his skin so that the chemical sleeping compound gets into his skin. Soon, the second guard falls to his knees beside his slumbering partner, and then seconds later, while mumbling incoherently and trying to activate his radio, he collapses unconscious on top of his partner. Stein strips both men of their uniforms and leaves them naked on the floor of center court, looking like two lost aphrodites in a lust-induced slumber.

Upstairs, on the second floor, the one-armed woman, Carla Marks, is approached by a guard. When she sees him, she falls to the floor and begins weeping. "Pity me sir, I have lost my arm! What am I to do?"

"Are you a lost aphrodite?" asks the guard.

"I have lost my arm. Look at me!" She rips her clothing away, revealing the hideous scar where her arm once was. A red mass of shriveled skin stares the guard in the face. He sees it, looks away in disgust. "You are not an aphrodite! You need a doctor, you shouldn't be here, how did this happen—"

"Touch my wound, please, I am in pain, you must help me, just touch my wound, caress it, please, I beg you!"

"What is wrong with you?"

"I need your assistance, please, my shoulder is on fire, please, I need your healing touch!"

The guard looks at the shriveled skin, the red wound, the garish scars, is repelled and attracted at the same time. "What must I do to relieve your suffering?" he asks.

"Put your hand on my shoulder. Here. Right here. Touch this, press your warm healthy strong hand against my scar and take my pain away."

"Here?" asks the guard, pointing.

"Yes. Right there. Press your hand against my scar."

The guard grimaces, but does as asked. He presses his hand against the dead skin of a long-healed wound, against the cold, sensationless scar tissue of a wound coated with the sleep-inducing chemical. The guard presses his hand against her and Carla Marks grabs him, holds him tight, presses his hand hard and tight against her and twists his palm against her, making sure that the compound is rubbed into his skin. Then she lets him go and thanks him, smiles at him, caresses his face as he collapses onto the floor beside her, searching dumbly for the radio she has lifted from his waist. She puts him to sleep with soft words, finally kissing his lips and then spitting on his face as his eyelids flutter into sleep. Then she strips him naked, takes his uniform, drags his body off into an exit corridor and leaves him to dream dark dreams while she changes into his uniform and rushes downstairs to meet with her brothers and sisters.

Meanwhile, down on the first floor, on the far eastern wing of the mall, directly in front of and below the statue of Athena, Josephina Lennon, the leper woman with half her face missing, smiles through green teeth and rancid lips at two naked aphrodites with perfect bodies. They have been making love in the presence of Athena, but the leper woman has interrupted them. They rise from the shadow of Athena and step out to greet the strange woman, but are frozen in horror when they see her face.

"I want to be an aphrodite too!" says the leper.

"You poor woman, you shouldn't be here!" says the girl.

"Kiss me!" says the leper.

"You are not healthy!" says the boy.

"Don't I have the right to be loved?" asks the leper.

"You must see a doctor," says the boy.

The leper falls to her knees and bows down to the boy. "Won't you be my doctor?"

"I can do nothing for you!"

"You can heal my wounds, I know you can."

"You are mad!"

"No, touch my face and I will be healed, I know I will. I will look like your lover!"

"She is mad," says the girl. "We must call security!"

"No, all I ask of you is that you touch me, hold me, give one moment of your love, please, I am an ugly old woman and Aphrodite still has called out to me. Do you think Aphrodite mad? Can it be that she sends lust to one such as me? Why would a god do such a thing? Why would a god torment one like me, who's body is diseased, who's body lacks arete, I, whom nature has seen fit to torment with a face that falls off? You who are perfect, you have so much while I have so little. Isn't there some small part of the love you have for each other that you can give to me? Spiritual crumbs is all I ask. You who are perfect owe it to me, who is not perfect. You smile, while I cannot. You share kisses, while I share only outrage and horror. You make love while I lie in a bed of filthy rags. You find ecstacy in each others' arms, while I find only cold eyes and colder bodies. I am twice your age and have never once known what you have both enjoyed in this, your golden youth. I have never celebrated the festival of love. I have never been loved. I am a leper and have known only hatred. But why? Is it my fault I am a leper? Who made me thus? Did I make myself a leper? Did I stare into God's face before I was born and say, 'Make me a leper, oh wise one, send me to Earth ugly and malformed, send me to Earth in a shape that will strike horror into the hearts of my brothers and sisters, send me to Earth a creature to inspire hatred and fear in those who see me.' Yes, this is how I wish to spend my days on Earth, this is how I wish to exist, this is the form my sacred life will take, that of a leper with a face eaten away by disease, with a mouth spewing bile and venom, with green teeth and lips that dissolve before they can be kissed by beauty. Did I ask for this? What madness would possess a gentle soul such as I to ask for such a curse? Of course I did not ask for it, nor is it my fault. Chance has dealt me an evil roll of the dice. The tarot deck of life was cut and the cards turned face up and I was dealt the leper card. And you two who are so beautiful, so perfect, so fine and loving, and so happy to share your bounty with each other — what did you do to earn your beauty? You were born. That is all you did. And you did not even do it. Birth simply happened to you. You came into the world and opened your eyes and this is what you saw, this is what chance has given to you: blue eyes, blond curls, perfect skin, healthy teeth, sweet breath from sweet mouths easily kissed, and young spirits innocent of the true nature of Mother Nature, the true hideous nature of this evil bitch you worship so blindly. This is what she does to your brothers and sisters. She makes monsters. She makes me a leper, then sends me as a jester to the Festival of Aphrodite so the young lovers can look at me and laugh. So why don't you laugh? Or am I to be pitied? So then why don't you cry? Why don't you weep for me? Why don't you weep for all those less fortunate than yourselves? Why don't you weep for those who will never know Aphrodite's touch? Why don't you weep for those who will never know a love you take for granted? Again, all I ask is for a touch, a hug. Here, touch my hand. Just reach out and touch me, show me that I am a human being and I deserve love too."

The innocent naked boy stares down at her, his mind frozen by her words, his soul confused.

His girlfriend steps to his side and takes his hand. "Let us help her up and show her the way out. She asks only for kindness, and we can be kind, can we not?"

The boy nods. The two step forward. The boy takes her right hand. The girl takes her left. They help the leper stand.

As the leper stands, the two youths fall. The leper's hands are coated with the sleep-inducing chemical. It dissolves through the skin and into the bloodstream of the two innocent youths with stunning swiftness. They crumble at the feet of the leper, who stands over them, leering triumphantly through her hideous face. Once they are completely asleep, she drags them both away from Athena, to a dark corner of the mall, hidden away from view, the boy on his back, the girl draped over his body, unconscious lovers sharing a final embrace on the morning of the Festival of Aphrodite.

And Josephina Lennon, the leper in the service of Agnes, stands before the statue of Athena, brings out a match, lights a torch, then sets fire to the wall behind the statue, stands watching it burn for just a moment, just long enough to make sure the fire will be big enough and do damage enough. Then she turns and runs away.

***

Downstairs, in the basement, the electricity is turned off and the water pipes closed down. The mall goes dark, and when the flames surround Athena's statue and the fire detectors in the roof are activated, there is just a little water in the pipes flowing through the roof and walls of the mall, and little pressure to push that water out, so the mall sends just a spurt, just a dribble of water out into the fire engulfing Athena. It is not enough to extinguish the fire. It is slowed, but continues burning, spreads, slowly begins to work its way through the eastern end of the mall.

***

Within half an hour, every security guard inside the mall is unconscious. Agnes and her followers have taken the mall.

Locked away inside various stores, slumbering aphrodites remain unaware of what has happened to the mall.

And outside the mall, the police are just finishing up their search of the carnival. Layvanwick has not been found. Nor have any other bodies. And no security officer inside the mall has been able to call outside to alert the police to what is happening inside the mall — and who is being held inside the mall — so the police begin to wrap up the investigation.

Satisfied that the carnival has been searched well, and that carnival attendees and employees have been questioned thoroughly, Officer Rod Black turns his eyes to the mall. He hasn't heard from security since his first communication. Nor has he heard from Maurice Sully. Did Layvanwick make it to the mall? Was he taken there by witnesses? If so, why has no word of this reached anyone in authority?

The mall is the next most logical place to look. So let's start looking, festival or no festival, and even without Maurice Sully's permission, the mall needs to be checked out. He calls the security desk at the mall. The number rings seven times before anyone picks up. It is a man's voice that answers, but Officer Black recognizes instantly that it is a different voice from last time.

"This is Officer Rod Black of the Billings Police Department. I spoke to you earlier about this accident with no bodies. Any news to report?"

"None, Officer. The mall is quiet."

"No sign of Layvanwick?"

"No sign, Officer."

"Any other injured people show up?"

"No one here but aphrodites, sir."

"Very well. I'll check back later."

"Yes sir."

Officer Black clicks off. He climbs on his motorcycle and sits staring at the mall, thinking, going nowhere. Finally, he makes up his mind, starts his cycle, takes a slow ride around the perimeter of the mall. At certain points, he rides up on the sidewalks, close to the glass windows, so he can see inside. At the entrances, he rides right up to the glass doors and presses the front tire of his bike right against the glass and he stares into the mall, watching, waiting, listening. He sees nothing, hears nothing.

Finally, he is satisfied that there is nothing to know, nothing to see, nothing to hear. But still Layvanwick is missing, so what must he do?

He turns away from the mall, looks across Grand Avenue to the dark neighborhoods south of the mall. Did Layvanwick somehow end up out there somewhere? If so, how? Why? Did he go himself? Or was he taken by someone else? And why not to the hospitals? They have been checked, double checked, triple checked. No hospitals in the area have seen anyone fitting Layvanwick's description.

So it remains a crash with no bodies. But the victims of this accident have to exist and they have to be somewhere. They have to be inside the mall. Why do I believe this? Because Layvanwick is a Mall Master. It is where he would go of his own volition, if it was within his power. And if he was injured and had no volition, it is where he would be taken by those wishing to save him. Isn't it?

I must solve this mystery. The answer lies within the mall. So I am going in. With or without permission, I am going in. Even if it means my badge, I am going in. I will violate the sanctity of the mall during the Festival of Aphrodite and I will find the Mall Master, I will find Layvanwick, I will solve this mystery. Because it is my responsibility.

Officer Rod Black parks his cycle, turns it off, then walks to the front doors of the mall.

***

On the roof of the mall, Alan Benton and Manny Kantor have Anton Layvanwick sprawled on the roof while they try to make a cross for him.

In the chilly morning air, there is no sign of dawn anywhere. Layvanwick lies on his back, staring up at the night sky with eyes that see but do not understand. He hears voices and senses movement around him, but it means only that his two brothers are working to take away his pain. That is what they told him. That is what they said was to happen. How it is to happen, he does not understand. Why they have brought him to the roof, he does not understand. He does not think there is anything strange about this. But he feels that *all* of this is strange, all of this is some kind of weird dream, that he is not really this person and not really in this place, and this is not really happening to him. But that conviction fades with all the rest.

At first, the pain was overwhelming. But it has drifted away. Each time he wakes, the pain has lessened. But the confusion grows. He looks around and sees so much he does not understand. He looks at a face and thinks he recognizes it, but when he searches for a name, there is nothing to be found, and when he pursues a memory of how he knows this face, there is no memory to be found. Then by some strange instinct, unable to find answers outside, he looks inward, at himself. But here, the darkness is even greater. He looks for a name but finds nothing. He tries to remember his face, but no image appears. Horror fills him with a psychic pain that rivals that of his body, a pain in his soul that spreads out and engulfs his body, swamps his entire biologic system so that he trembles with a paralysis of *not knowing*, of being *unable to know*. His palms sweat, his chest aches, his breathing grows rapid and ragged, his voice tries to howl itself out of his body, he screams up at the night for some glimmer of light, but nothing comes to him. One of his brothers bends down close. It is the brother with one eye. His brother looks angry and distressed, frustrated with some problem of his own. "My God, why do you howl so?" screams the one-eyed man.

"Show me my face. I want to see my face. I can't remember what I look like. I can't remember who I am. I can't remember what I am."

"You are ugly."

"I don't care, I still want to see."

"I don't have a mirror. Shut up and be still, you are going to Heaven soon."

"What is heaven?"

"It is up in the sky, up above you."

"How am I going to get there?"

"You are going to fly."

"Fly? Did you say I am going to fly? Or did you say something else?"

"Don't talk, I am busy."

The one-eyed man moves away.

So now he stares up at the sky, trying to see what is up there, trying to find something called heaven, this place where he is to go. But he sees nothing but sky. What is a sky? And those tiny points of light, what are they?

They are stars, says a voice in his head.

Suddenly, he is calmer.

There. I remember that.

I know something.

He closes his eyes and calms himself. His breathing slows down. He even smiles just a little. A glowing warmth of confidence spreads through his body. He knows the satisfaction of actually knowing something. All is not a mystery. He knows something.

I know what stars are. I know why they are in the sky and what they are. I know what the sky is. I know that this dark sky is called night, and in the morning, the sun will rise — I know what the sun is, too! I remember the sun! — and it will be day, and the stars will disappear, the sky will be blue, and I will be—

Pain hits him in a flash and he screams. It is not physical, it just feels like it. The frustration hits him like a physical pain. And he is humbled. He knows so little. There is still so much to know. What is my name? Who am I? Why am I here? What are these men really trying to do to me?

They are dragging huge poles of wood around. He hears the sound of a hammer banging against nails and wood. They are building something for him.

His brother named Alan kneels beside him and looks down at his face.

"Am I beautiful?" he asks his brother Alan.

"Yes, you are."

"My one-eyed brother told me I am ugly."

"He sees less with his good eye than he does with his blind. He lied to you. You are beautiful."

"Why does my brother lie to me?"

"Because he hates you."

"Why does he hate me?"

"Never mind."

"Do you know my name?"

"Yes, I know your name."

"Tell it to me."

"Anton Layvanwick."

He considers the sounds, repeats the name to himself silently, in the privacy of his own mind. The sounds are meaningless. He says it out loud, hoping it will help. "Anton Layvanwick," he says, but the music of his own voice saying this sound does not produce even the glimmer of a memory of the face this sound names. "Why can't I remember who I am?" he asks his brother Alan.

"You have lost your mind."

"Help me find it."

"I cannot. I have a job to do."

"What are you building?"

"Don't talk to me, just keep still, be quiet, rest. If you be still and rest, your mind will return, your memory will come back."

"Very well."

He calms himself. He stares up at the sky and considers the stars. Focus on what you know, he says. This knowledge will lead to other knowledge. These small facts you possess will lead to further facts, more facts, more knowledge. If you relax, let it all come to you, let your mind slowly come back to life, you will remember.

He hears his brothers yelling at each other.

"Alan, get over here!" says one-eyed Manny. "We've got work to do!"

"I'm here."

"Hold this while I pound with the hammer."

"Yes."

"Damn you, hold it tighter!"

"I'm sorry."

"Hold it straight, damn you! What's this, trembling hands? You're not going coward on me, are you, Alan? You're not getting cold feet, you're not going to chicken out on me, are you?"

"No, I can do this job."

"Then do it! Hold still while I hammer."

"Yes."

"What's this! Tears on the wood? You're blubbering like a baby! Shedding tears for our enemy! You don't have the guts for this! You can't take it! You're not going to do it!"

"I am, I tell you! Just finish the thing, damn it, before he remembers who he is and wakes up! If he does, we'll both be dead in the blink of an eye!"

"Making fun of my eye, are you! To hell with you!"

He hears a sharp thump and then listens to Alan fall to the ground. He sits up and looks across the roof to the two men working in the chill darkness. Alan is slumped over in a heap. Manny drags some kind of wooden construction across the roof, yelling to himself that, "I'll do the job myself, cowardly bastard, to hell with you!" Manny drags the wood only so far, then stops, gets on his radio, calls for help to be sent up right away. Then Manny stops and looks across the roof at him, notices that he is sitting up. "What the hell are you staring at? Lay down and shut up or I'll bang you on the noggin with the hammer like I did your weepy friend."

"You are not my brother."

"Hell no, I'm not your brother! Starting to figure that out, are you?"

"Tell me who I am. Tell me why you have really brought me here."

One-eyed Manny bends down close and gazes into his face. "You are a Mall Master."

"What is a Mall Master?"

"You are going to be crucified."

"What is crucified?"

"You'll know soon enough."

Manny walks away, back to his wooden construction.

Two other men have come up to the roof. They help one-eyed Manny with the wooden construction. It is dragged to an exact position on the roof. Then they all three come to him, pick him up from the roof, half carry and drag him over to the wooden construction. They throw him down on his back against the wooden construction. The wood is round and hurts his back. His legs are tied to the middle of the long wooden pole. His arms are pulled out like wings to long round sections of wood on either side of the main pole. They tie his hands to the ends of these poles with rope. When he is securely tied to the wood, they hoist the entire construction up in the air and stick the end of the main pole into the round end of a small chimney sticking up out of the roof. There is a small puff of smoke coming up out of the chimney, but it stops as soon as the pole is inserted. The pole of the cross — it is a cross, he understands what that is now — fits snugly into the chimney and it makes a good stand.

He hangs tied to the cross and looks down into the dark faces of the men below him. They look up at him. There is still fear in their eyes.

Why are they afraid of me? he wonders.

"There you are," says one-eyed Manny. "You just hang there for a while, okay?"

"Why has this been done to me?" he asks.

They walk away.

"This is some kind of punishment, some kind of torture. Why is this being done to me? What have I done to deserve this? What kind of justice is this? Why am I to be hung from a pole like an animal and left in the cold night air? *Tell me why you have done this!*"

One of the other men turns to one-eyed Manny and says, "We'd better shut him up, huh?"

"I'll do it," says Manny.

Manny returns to the cross. While he walks to it, the Mall Master watches him approach and begins screaming, howling into the night, at the top of his lungs,

"I am Anton Layvanwick! Anton Layvanwick! Layvanwick! Layvanwick! Layvanwick!"

He still does not understand what this name means. He still does not remember what a Mall Master is. But he knows he is hanging from a cross and he knows that this is wrong. So he screams, hoping someone somewhere will hear the name and know what it means, know who he is, and come and rescue him from this cross.

Below him, as he screams into the night, one-eyed Manny reaches into his pockets, brings out fingers coated in the special chemical Agnes has taught him to use, and he rubs the chemical into the naked feet of Anton Layvanwick, who soon falls asleep tied to a cross on the roof of the West Park Plaza shopping mall.

***

Sara Fletcher is one block away from the mall when she hears the voice screaming in the night:

"A ton of hay is slick!"

What? Such an odd thing to be yelling in the night. What kind of festival are they having here tonight?

As she gets closer, she listens more intently. The voice keeps screaming. Not understanding the words clearly, she focuses on the emotional intensity of the sound. This is some desperate soul yelling for help. This is someone in distress. This scream is for help. Someone needs help. Where is the sound coming from? Still too far away. She breaks into a run and covers the last half block quickly.

Here I am, finally. Here's the mall, just across the street. My God, look how dark it is. As if it is dead. They have killed the mall already. No lights, no life. Even the carnival shut down. And what of the aphrodites, where are they? They will be locked away within selected stores. So perhaps they have no part in this festival yet.

Finally she is at the mall. She hears the last scream and clearly identifies the word being yelled: Layvanwick.

Somebody is screaming for the Mall Master. And it's coming from the roof. Someone up on the roof screaming for the Mall Master.

What is happening? What have I gotten myself into? What has Alan led me to? What has my quest for love led me to?

She finds her way to a mall entrance. There are no lights anywhere, inside or outside the mall. The entrance has been barricaded. Piles of benches and chairs have been stacked in front of the doors to stop anyone — or anything — from entering easily.

They have taken the mall. Agnes has actually done it. She has taken a mall. She has taken West Park Plaza from Maurice Sully.

The unreality of it makes her laugh. She lies on the cold cement steps in front of the north entrance to the mall, in the dark, in the cold early morning, and she laughs.

And she thinks:

Somehow, I feel that I am to blame.

She is quiet.

The roof is quiet also. No more screaming from the roof.

Am I too late? she wonders. Are we all too late?

She rises to her knees and bows down before the mall, her hands grasped together in prayer, and she screams out to the dark and quiet mall,

"Mother Agnes, I am your child and I wish you to take away my pain! Save me, Mother Agnes, please save me! I pray for you to save me!"

Then she collapses against the glass of the entrance doors and sobs for the memory of Maurice Sully's mall.

CHAPTER SIXTEEN

BROTHERS AND SISTERS

In Layvanwick Tower, Maurice Sully calls West Park Plaza. "Has Anton arrived yet?" he asks.

"No sir. But there is some kind of traffic accident in front of the Mall. Looks pretty bad. The police are on the scene and we're checking with them. They've got some streets blocked off and traffic on Grand Avenue is moving slowly. Plus the main entrance to the Mall is blocked off right now."

"Let me know as soon as Anton arrives. If he's involved in the accident in any way — let me know immediately."

"Yes sir."

Maurice hangs up, looks at Diane. "More complications."

"What now?"

"Still no Anton. Plus some kind of accident."

"What do you want to do?"

Maurice pauses just a moment, carefully watching Diane's face for any sign of a subconscious event. Her face holds its shape and color, her mouth remains relaxed, her nostrils do not flare, and her eyes are calm, so — no, she feels nothing, senses nothing, has thought nothing. He maintains his own control so as not to reveal what has happened inside him. He looks her straight in the eyes, but does not smile. "We're both tense, stressed, high strung. Neither of us will sleep tonight. Not in this strange Mall, no matter how much we love it. We both need reassurance about what the status of our mall is. So one of us should take a trip home and see how Anton is doing."

"You'll go, of course."

"That was my plan."

"Very well. I'll stay here. I can't leave Anton's mall unattended. Not after making him swear on oath on my lips."

"No, that would be a breach of Mall Master etiquette."

"How long will you be gone?"

"Just long enough to see that both the mall and Anton are all right."

"Which one of you will be coming back?"

"I'll discuss that with Anton."

"I will wait for you both, then."

"It won't take long."

Maurice leaves her on top of the tower, rides an elevator down. Waiting to be delivered to the ground floor, he grasps the hand rail, closes his eyes, surrenders to the sensations of vertical transport, and thinks about what he has been reading in the file code-named "Agnes."

Once in his car, he drives north through the city, towards the Rimrocks, takes a left on Poly Drive and heads west, planning to approach the mall from the back side. There is no traffic anywhere. He flies along the streets, building speed as he gets further west, flying down wide Poly Avenue. Halfway to the mall, his phone rings. It is the security tail he sent to follow Sarah. "Talk to me!" commands Maurice.

"She has arrived at the mall, sir."

"Is she inside yet?"

"No, she's still outside."

"What's going on?"

"Hard to say. The mall is dark, all the power has been shut off. The carnival is shut down, the police are gone. The place is deserted. Mall is like a ghost town, sir."

"I'm only minutes away. Keep Sarah in sight. If she makes it inside, let me know. If she has contact with cult members, or anybody who looks like a cult member, let me know. Which entrance is she at?"

"Northeast entrance to Sears."

"I'll arrive at the north entrance of the mall in just a few minutes."

Maurice turns left off Poly Drive and flies south to the Mall. He slows down as he enters the mall parking lot, pulls up to the north entrance, stops in the NO PARKING zone, gets out, looks to the glass doors of the entrance. Inside the mall, there are no lights, the place is dark. But even in the dim light, Maurice can make out the form of a solitary security guard standing motionless, watching him. The guard seems to be missing an arm. And his uniform does not fit very well. As Maurice moves away, the guard slowly raises a radio to his mouth, as if speaking into it.

Maurice walks away, having noted that much.

Halfway to the northeast entrance to Sears, he is forced off the sidewalk and into the side of the building by a pack of screaming shadows that come running past. It is a pack of four men dragging an unconscious man behind them. Maurice recognizes the man as the security guard he sent to tail Sarah. Before he can react or say anything, one of the shadow-men detaches from the pack and runs up to him, screams, "Filthy aphrodite! To hell with you!" and spews a mouthful of bile onto his chest. Then the shadow-man races away to catch up with his mates.

Maurice dials 911 on his phone as he races to the Sears entrance, hoping to find Sarah.

Where the building slants in to the Sears entrance, he races around the corner and the first thing he sees is a column of smoke rising above his mall.

He knows that type of smoke. He can't see the flames, but he knows his mall is on fire.

The 911 operator answers his call as he looks down and sees Sarah Fletcher sprawled motionless on the cement in front of the entrance.

"Emergency 911, how may I help you?"

"West Park Plaza is being attacked by cult terrorists. I've got an unconscious security guard at the north entrance, and what looks like an unconscious woman at the northeast entrance to Sears. We need a police presence here as soon as possible, including hostage negotiators. Also, the fire department. They've set fire to the mall. I am Maurice Sully, Mall Master. I'm going to leave my phone on so you can monitor me while I attempt to deal with some of this."

"Sir, if you are in danger, you should get out of there!"

"Too late for that."

Maurice pockets his phone and bends down to check on Sarah.

At his first touch, her eyes pop open and she sits up, conscious, alert, uninjured — and screaming angry.

And also, completely in character.

"Bastard aphrodite!" she screams, slapping his face.

She spins away from Maurice, into the on-rushing arms of the suddenly returning shadow-men. They surround her on four sides, with Maurice off near the entrance.

"I am Sarah, daughter of Agnes!" she says.

"You are no daughter we have ever met!" say the shadow-men.

"I wish to suffer with Agnes," says Sarah.

"Suffer with us instead!" says one of the shadow-men, bouncing closer to her.

"I wish to make a sacrifice."

"We will sacrifice you!" say the shadow-men, the four now jumping like apes close in around her, all of them hunched over, none of them facing her directly, all of them glancing from her to Maurice and back again, as if they are nervous about Maurice and don't want him any closer.

"If you are to sacrifice me, do it in the mall," Sarah tells the shadow-men. "Take me before Agnes and let her eyes see my sacrifice, let her eyes know my suffering, let her see what has become of the former wife of Alan Benton."

"Alan Benton is dead," says one of the shadow-men.

"Then it was I who killed him," says Sarah. "Let Agnes see the blood on my hands — and the blood on my soul. I must find redemption through Agnes. I am on my knees and at your mercy."

Sarah falls to her knees and bows her head, raises her hands in prayer.

Maurice freezes the shadow-men by diverting their attention to him. "Sarah, don't do this! It's too late, the charade is off! The Mall has been taken and entering it now means certain death. Come with me away from this place!"

"I must enter the mall and face Agnes."

"No, Sarah, you can't face Agnes. Agnes is not what you think she is."

"She is the Angel of Mercy."

"She is the Angel of Death!" say the shadow-men.

"Do not interfere with me, or I will tell them who you are," says Sarah to Maurice.

"If you tell them who I am, they will kill me for certain."

The shadow-men stop and stare at Maurice. "Who is he?" they ask. "Tell us who he is, and we will take you to Agnes!"

Sarah raises her head, opens her eyes, stares at Maurice through the spaces between the shadow-men. Maurice stands frozen, watching her, ready for anything.

The shadow-men bounce on their feet as they try to decide which way to move, which person to grab. Should they break up into two groups of two and take man and woman at once? Or should they return to the mall and forget about these outsiders?

When a moment of silence hangs between all six people, and while the loose folds of Sarah's dress flutters in the night breeze, the tiny voice of the 911 operator can be heard coming from Maurice Sully's pocket.

"He is possessed by a demon!" says a shadow-man.

"He's got a phone in his pocket, you idiot!" says another shadow-man, this one finally letting a tenor of serious thought enter his voice.

"The police are coming. We must enter the mall and prepare," says a third.

"Agnes will handle the police," says the fourth.

Sarah stands up. "I will enter the mall, either by myself, or with you men as my escorts. Either way is fine with me."

She starts to walk away, heading for the north entrance.

Maurice yells out to her, "Sarah, don't go! Can't you see the mall is on fire! They're all going to burn!"

When they all whirl to face him, Maurice points to the roof. Against the dark sky, the shadow-men and Sarah see the darker smoke billowing up from the roof.

The shadow-men are suddenly hysterical. "Fire! The mall on fire? It's too early for fire! Who set the mall on fire? Are they trying to burn out the aphrodites?"

"We must put out the fire!" says the leader of the shadow-men. "This is not a part of Agnes' plan! We must quench these flames, else all is lost!"

The shadow-men race off in four different directions, each forgetting Maurice and Sarah.

Maurice walks forward and takes Sarah's face in his hands. "Forget the mall, Sarah. It's too dangerous. We must let the police handle this."

"No. You gave me a mission, I want to finish it."

"I'm calling it off."

"I am not. I must save Alan."

"Not by sacrificing yourself."

"Yes, that is exactly what I must do. It is the only way now."

"Sarah, this is for real. They intend to burn the mall down — and anyone who's inside when it burns, goes up in flames with it."

"You are a fool for standing here talking to me while your mall burns. You should follow those shadow-men and try to put it out." Sarah turns away from Maurice and heads for the north entrance.

The first wail of sirens can be heard in the distance now.

"Save your mall, Maurice," says Sarah, calling back to him as she breaks into a run. "And I will save Alan."

"He will not come for you!" screams Maurice.

Sarah stops and turns to him. "Do you still hold him in Layvanwick Tower?"

"No. We released him. But he renounced his love for you. I have no idea where he is or what he is doing."

"He will go to Agnes. If she is in the mall, Alan will be in the mall."

"You are taking a terrible chance, Sarah. Please don't do this."

"Everyone else has taken terrible chances. Now it is my turn. Even if I don't find Alan, I will find Agnes. And I will deal with her."

"You don't want to find Agnes, Sarah, believe me."

"Unless you have facts and reasons to offer about why that is, I have nothing more to say to you."

"Have you seen Layvanwick?" asks Maurice.

"No, I have not."

"Have you seen any aphrodites?"

"No. I think they are all locked away inside."

The wail of sirens is closer now. The first police cars are entering the mall parking lot. Fire trucks are close behind.

"You find Layvanwick," says Sarah. "I will let Alan find me."

She turns away for a final time, sprinting for the north entrance.

Maurice starts out after her — but then stops, watches her go. He reaches into his pocket, turns off his phone. The 911 operator is still yelling at him. He clicks her off in mid-sentence. He turns away just as a firetruck pulls up. He directs the firemen to the flames. When the firemen are putting water on the roof and have smashed through the barricaded entrance, Maurice joins them in entering the mall and beginning the search for aphrodites.

***

In the management offices at the center of the mall, far from the fire and far from the tumult, Agnes sits in a chair recently occupied by Maurice Sully. She surveys his desk, his office, she an island of serenity amongst her followers.

"What is our status?" she asks.

"Layvanwick is tied to a cross on the roof."

"Very well."

"Alan Benton has failed and Manny had to knock him out."

"Good. Put Alan on a cross as well."

"Yes, Mother Agnes."

"What of the aphrodites?"

"We haven't encountered any yet."

"No?"

"We think they are somewhere up in the arcade level."

"Locate them."

"Yes, Mother Agnes."

"They need our help. They are suffering terribly and we must relieve them."

"Yes, Mother Agnes."

Two shadow-men enter the office with the leper woman Carla Marks held between them.

"Mother Agnes," says a shadow-man. "We have news. The mall is on fire. Carla set fire to the statue of Athena in front of Sears."

Agnes rises and goes to Carla Marks. "Is this true? You set fire?"

The leper woman smiles at Agnes, her eyes gleaming. "I could not help myself, Mother Agnes. I saw the naked aphrodites and the statue of Athena and my urge was simply to burn."

"You did not follow my instructions, Carla."

"No, Mother Agnes."

"You have failed, Carla."

"Yes, Mother Agnes."

Agnes walks forward, holds the leper woman's face in her hands, bends down to her, kisses her leprous face, strokes her sores. "I love your failure, Carla. To fail is to achieve a holy state. Our Lord was a failure on Earth. He suffered on the cross for his failure, and that is how he achieved his holiness. You do the same. I bless your incompetence. Your soul matches your face. You are the holiest of my holies. Now go forth into the mall again. Go to the arcade level and find the aphrodites. When you locate them, help them to find the beauty in suffering."

"Yes, Mother Agnes."

The shadow-men release Carla Marks and she disappears back out into the dark mall.

"How serious is the fire?" asks Agnes of a shadow-man.

"It will be contained. But firetrucks and police are surrounding the mall right now. They will be entering soon. They are already inside Sears, putting out the fire."

"Then let them enter. Spread the word, quickly! The police and firemen must suffer with the mall. Let all who enter the mall know the exquisite ecstacy of suffering. They will be the children of our church before this day is born, so let them slumber like children until the sun rises. Now do it!"

"Yes, Mother Agnes."

Agnes sits back in Maurice Sully's chair. She pulls his rolodex forward and starts looking through names and phone numbers. Quickly, she finds what she wants and picks up the phone, makes a call.

On the other end, a phone rings twice, is picked up on the third ring. A woman's voice answers. "Yes?"

"Let me talk to Maurice Sully."

"He is not here. Who is calling, please?"

"Where is Sully?"

"You must identify yourself, please. How did you get this number?"

"Tell Maurice Sully that he needs to go to West Park Plaza immediately."

"Why?"

"Because I am here. I have taken his mall."

"Who are you? What are you talking about?"

"I am Mother Agnes. I have taken his mall and I intend to convert it into a church. Sully might wish to discuss this with me."

There is only a slight pause at the other end, then the woman's voice says, "Very well. I will inform Mall Master Sully."

"You do that. And one last thing…"

"Yes?"

"When I am done here — you're next."

Agnes clicks off before the woman can respond. Then she just sits staring at the wall, not happy, not pleased — just staring, her face empty. There is no one else in the office with her right now. Because the power is off, the only light in the room comes from a lantern sitting on a shelf high up on one wall. The yellow light slants down across her features and sends a ragged shadow onto the wall on the other side of the office. The flame in the lantern flickers for a moment and the shadow dances and twists. But Agnes does not notice. She is watching the black empty doorway, wondering who will come to her next, waiting for the next pair of eyes and the next consciousness to give her existence by virtue of seeing her and speaking to her. Until then, she is simply an empty vessel waiting to be filled.

Soon she hears a tell-tale clicking on the tiled floor. She knows who approaches. She waits for him. Then Augustus Stein appears in the doorway, his features like ancient parchment in the yellow light.

"She is back," he says.

"Who?"

"That woman."

"What woman?"

"The one you have always refused to see. She who claims to be Alan Benton's wife."

"Oh." Agnes' eyes drift away, her features meditative.

"She claims now that she is your daughter. She has renounced Alan and wishes to make him a sacrifice."

"Does she?"

"That is what she says."

"Do you believe her?"

"She has the mark of suffering upon her."

"Has she been injured?"

"Only in her soul. Her eyes and face bare the mark of much inner torment."

"Well, that is an improvement for her."

"What shall I do? Throw her out? Put her to sleep?"

Agnes raises her veil back over her face and stands up. "No. The time has passed for that. Now is the time for me to see this woman. And for her to speak to me. Stein, do you know who she *really* is?"

"No."

"She does not know who she is, either. But now is the time for revelation. Do you believe in miracles, Stein?"

"Yes, Mother Agnes, you know I do."

"You are a liar, Stein. But that is why you are here. Now I am going to show you what a liar you are and always have been. I am going to show you a *real* miracle."

"I am eager to see it, Mother Agnes."

"Show me this woman. Take me to her. But mark my words: do not let her look upon my face until a time of my choosing, or I will burn you on a cross. Do you understand me?"

"Yes, Mother Agnes."

"If you wish to burn on a cross, then fail in this. I will honor your failure with the reward of suffering. But if you wish to see a miracle, do not let this woman look upon my face."

"As you wish, Mother Agnes."

"Now let us go."

They leave the office and journey out into the dark mall. Augustus Stein carries a lantern and limps along, his wooden leg clattering through the hallways, sending pathetic little echoes rattling out into the black empty spaces of the mall. The yellow light of the lantern flows out around them, enveloping them in a thick yellow circle of murky light, as if they are bugs glowing in the night, or translucent earthworms oozing across the soil of some dank basement. They travel slowly towards the north entrance. Halfway towards the doors, four firemen with axes come smashing through a wall and plunge out into the dark mall. Black shadow-men pounce on them instantly, smearing sleep dust into their faces. The firemen fall to the floor of the mall and shudder into silence and blackness as Agnes and Stein move slowly past, ignoring them, unconcerned, carrying their yellow light away, leaving the firemen in silent darkness, forgotten.

Stein takes Agnes to an alcove just off the north wing of the mall. Here, they find Sarah Fletcher kneeling underneath dim emergency lights, the pathetic beams of the weakened lights glowing down on her as if a transparent angel has blessed her with a vision. Sarah's head is bowed, her hands raised, her lips moving in a silent, unheard prayer. She is intent. Shadow-men watch her, motionless in the darkness. Two leper women stand nearby, obviously aching for the chance to put this radiant beauty to sleep. But they move away as Agnes approaches. Stein holds his lantern high above Sarah, illuminates her so that Agnes can see it is she. Agnes stands well back in shadow, her outlines visible, but her features hidden behind two veils; one of darkness, the other of silk.

"For what do you pray, woman?" asks Stein.

Sarah stops, is silent, her lips motionless. Her eyes snap open, she takes in the features of the wall in front of her, illuminated by the yellow light of the lantern. But she does not turn her head to see clearly who is with her. She merely senses the presence of her visitors. Far away, deep within the mall, there is the sound of screaming.

"I pray for Agnes to bless her daughter's suffering," says Sarah.

"How do you suffer for Agnes?"

"I have renounced my love for Alan Benton and I offer him as a sacrifice. I have renounced my former love for the universe of the mall. This is the last mall I shall ever enter. When it becomes a church in the service of suffering, I wish to worship my pain here, within these walls that Agnes has destroyed."

Agnes finally speaks. From the shadows, her voice is thin and cracked, with a slight rasp, as if the sound is being warped by a ragged file. She says, "What is your name, child?"

"Sarah."

"Sarah what?"

"Sarah Fletcher."

"Tell me about your family."

"They are gone."

"And before they were gone?"

"My father was the governor of Kentucky, once, a long time ago. But he is dead now. My mother was a good woman. My father killed her for political gain. He made a sacrifice of my mother. He sacrificed her for the good of the people of Kentucky."

"Did you have siblings?"

"I had a brother."

"What was his name?"

"Stephen."

"Did you love him?"

"I sacrificed my love. I ran away to America and left him behind."

"Did you love him?"

"No."

"Not ever?"

"When we were small. When we were children, I loved him."

"Why?"

"He had a sweet, innocent soul."

"What happened to your love?"

"As we got older, he changed. The world changed him. He was not strong enough to deal with our world. His innocence was changed to corruption; his sweetness eroded into cruelty."

"What happened to your brother?"

"I don't know. I haven't seen him, nor heard from him, in ten years."

"Do you remember the last time you saw him?"

"Yes."

"Tell me about it."

"The Show Me Mall. Ten years ago. He came to my sanctuary ceremony to plead for my return to America."

"And that was the last time you saw him?"

"Yes."

The two pause. Sarah jumps into the pause with a question. "Mother Agnes, is my brother one of your children? Is he here within this mall?"

There is a long hesitation from Agnes. She stands motionless in the shadows. But finally, she responds, her voice weary. "Stephen Fletcher was sacrificed long ago."

"Then you knew him?" asks Sarah.

"Do not speak that name again. You have said you wish to make a sacrifice. If you are serious, I will take you to the sight of your greatest."

"What do you ask of me?"

"Sacrificing Alan Benton will not be enough. If you wish to be my daughter, you must sacrifice your love for Alan Benton. And more: sacrifice the memory of your love for Alan Benton. There must be nothing left. I want you to give it all up. Your soul must be empty. There must be nothing of value left inside you. Do you wish to attempt this?"

"Yes."

"Do you comprehend the pain you are welcoming?"

"I do not wish to comprehend it. To experience it will be enough."

"Very well. Then let us begin. Shadow-men! Escort this woman. Follow Stein. Do not allow her to look upon my face, or I will burn you all on crosses, is that understood!"

"Yes, Mother Agnes."

"Why do you not wish me to see you, Mother Agnes?" asks Sarah.

"Be silent and follow."

"Your voice somehow sounds familiar. Have we met before?"

"No, we have never met," says Agnes, turning away into shadow and letting Augustus Stein lead the procession away. When all are past, Agnes follows, staying well back, hidden completely in darkness.

They travel to the roof.

When they come up through the roof access hatch, they are met by one-eyed Manny. Augustus Stein goes first, followed by Sarah, several shadow-men, then Agnes, far behind, the last to arrive, she actually waiting several minutes while Stein and Manny each grab an arm of Sarah Fletcher and guide her forward to what awaits her.

They have come up onto the western roof of the mall. To their right is empty roof followed by a drop to the parking lot. To the left is an octagonal structure of stone and glass. The windows are dark, there are no lights inside. Past this is another structure of metal and glass, rectangular, a soft glow of some dim light coming from within.

Sarah opens her eyes as Stein and Manny guide her forward. She looks up and sees the huge lights of the colored mall signs on Grand Avenue lighting up the sky. And against these colored lights, she sees the silhouettes of what looks like two men hanging on crosses.

The man on the right is larger, more powerful, and his cross is large. He faces west, to the darkness. He is silent and motionless, either dead or unconscious, impossible to tell which.

The man on the left is smaller and his cross faces straight out to Grand Avenue and the lights. He is motionless as well.

Stein and Manny lead her between the two crosses, then stop her, turn her around so that she faces the smaller man.

She looks up and sees the face of Alan Benton looking down at her.

His eyes are open, but motionless, unblinking. For a moment, she thinks he is dead.

"In the name of logic, no! This can't be!"

The scream escapes her without warning, before she can think or stop it. And with her scream, she sees movement in Alan's eyes. Slow movement as he tries to focus and turn his head toward her sound, so he can see who it is come to feel anguish at his fate. She stares up at him and sees his eyes focus, watches the recognition slowly spread across his face, sees the tortured combination of happiness and sickness her presence causes him to feel.

"Sarah..."

"Alan, what have they done to you?"

"I have done it to myself."

"No, this can't be your final choice."

"I am facing the ocean, Sarah."

"No."

"It is far away — but I can see it. I can smell it and taste it, really I can. I remember it. Are you here to save me again?"

"Do not speak."

"What's this? Agnes is with you?"

Agnes has moved around behind Sarah, some distance away, but still close enough to hear and be heard. She calls out in a firm voice, "So, Sarah, your true convictions are revealed."

"I was shocked by this sight. You did not prepare me."

"What you saw down below was not enough? What kind of preparation do you want?"

"Who is this other man?"

"Do not concern yourself with that."

"It is Lay—" starts Alan, but one-eyed Manny lashes out with a stick and smashes him in the mouth. "Silence!"

"Gag him!" orders Agnes.

One-eyed Manny follows her order, climbing up the cross to wrap a gag around Alan's mouth.

"Hold the woman," orders Agnes. She walks up behind Sarah, ties a blindfold around her eyes, then steps back, still behind her, even with the blindfold. "You offered a sacrifice," she says to the blindfolded Sarah. "Does your offer still stand, or have you changed your mind?"

"I still wish to make a sacrifice."

"What do you offer?"

"You!"

"Ah. So you have not given up your love for Alan?"

"No. I will never give it up."

"Do you know why he is up here?"

"Because you are a murderer."

"And so is he. It was he who helped put this other man on the cross."

"And this is his reward?"

"Yes. Alan is weak, you see. He does not have the stomach for sacrifice. But I do. I had a father once, did you know that? My father had a stomach for sacrifice. He could do what was necessary. Did you know I had a father, Sarah?"

"No."

"He was murdered. Do you know who murdered him?"

"You did."

"No. Don't be surprised by the answer. It was Alan Benton who murdered my father, did you know that?"

"You are a liar."

"I saw it happen. I was there. Alan shot him dead, a bullet to the stomach."

"Oh my God," says Sarah.

"What? Now it's God you appeal to? What happened to logic? Logic isn't good enough for you now?"

"Logic will destroy you!"

"No. It is I who will destroy logic."

"Do you intend to put me on a cross?"

"I am waiting for you to recognize me."

"What do you want from me?"

"I want you to love me."

"What kind of sick person are you?"

"Listen to my voice, Sarah. Listen to my voice. You asked me earlier if we had met before."

"You sound strange. Familiar...yet, alien."

"Yes, alien. That is the word. I am an alien here in the land of the Mall Masters, am I not? Sarah, did you know I had a sister once?"

"I don't care."

"I know you don't care."

"You probably murdered her."

"No. Actually, she sacrificed me."

"So you blame your sickness on her."

"No. I do not blame. I forgive. That is my entire secret. Do you know what forgiveness is, Sarah?"

"No."

"It is tolerance for that which is intolerable. You see these people around me? Have you seen that they are all malformed, sick, insane, retarded, warped, destroyed, helpless, worthless? That is intolerable. But I tolerate it. These are the unwanted. But I want them. These are the unneeded. But I need them. These are the unloved. But I love them. These are the incompetent. But I trust them with missions of life and death. Why? Because I forgive them. What we have done to this mall today is intolerable and unforgivable. But we will all be forgiven for this sin. And it is a sin. I know that. Some of my followers do not understand, but we gathered here do.

"To answer your question: yes, I am going to hang you on a cross. I will hang you beside your lover Alan, so you die together. But I want you to know who I am and why I have done this thing."

"An explanation? You contradict yourself, Mother Agnes. An explanation is an appeal to reason. And there can be no reason for putting people on crosses."

"It takes a genius to find the reason, that is all."

"You seek to justify yourself to me. Why me? What makes me and what I think so important to you?"

"That is what I want to explain to you. Your sacrifice means nothing unless you understand who it is that receives it. So be still and listen to me.

"I will start with these questions: have you ever wondered what has to happen inside a man's soul to turn him into a cold-blooded killer? Have you ever pondered upon the contents of a murderer's soul? Have you ever ruminated on what it would feel like to live inside the skin of a man who has soaked his hands in innocent blood? Can you conceive of such a thing? Do you want to? Probably not. But we have time before this mall burns, so I am going to explain it to you. Because you are why I am here, and why I am doing these things. You — and your lover Alan — and one more man, whom I have yet to face, and for whom this other man on this other cross is substituting as a proxy victim until I get my hands on the other. You know of whom I speak. Is he near? Is he coming to save his mall? Is he coming to save you a second time, as he did at the Show Me Mall? Yes, of course he is. He is a Mall Master. This is what he does. But I will defeat him. Because forgiveness trumps logic. You don't believe that, but I know it.

"Now listen to me: I will tell you the secret of murder. You want to know what it takes. I will tell you. Look at these men around us: they are all murderers. They have taken lives on my orders. And I have taken lives myself. Innocent lives, healthy lives, lives that looked us straight in the eyes and pleaded in horror as we murdered them, and we ignored them, went right ahead and took the life out of them. What made us do it? What made us able? What made us willing? One word, one thing: sacrifice.

"Before a man can take a life, he must first have given up his own. No, not in the obvious way, but in an invisible way. In the privacy of his own mind, in the secrecy of his own soul, in the deepest part of his mind, in the center of his ego, at the heart of what is referred to as 'the self,' it begins with that one word, that one act: sacrifice. And it starts with a thought. A thought is the first thing to be sacrificed.

"Do you want to know how to create a murderer? Program him with sacrifice. And do it in this way:

"First, start at where people live: with values. Do you know what a human being really is? A value seeker. The essence of a human life is the long-range systematic pursuit of values. Divorce a human life from values, and it is utterly meaningless. So to create our murderer, start there: take away his values. But that is not enough. What we want is deeper. You have to tell a man to give up his values. And then to give up his *desire* for values. And then to give up his desire *for desires*.

"Let's follow the pattern and see how far we can get. We have an innocent man and we want to turn him into a cold-blooded murderer. Here is what we tell him: if you have something you want, let go of it. If you have something you love, give it away. If you have a desire, give up that desire. If you have a code of values upon which your desire is based — give up that code of values. If you have a principle on which your code is based — give up that principle. If your principle was the result of your own thoughts — give up those thoughts. If you think your own thoughts are important — give up that idea; they aren't. If you think your thoughts are important because you value your life — give up that notion, your life means nothing. But if you value your life because you have self-esteem — sacrifice that self-esteem to your brothers and sisters who don't have it! You can't think yourself better than other people. To do so is an act of oppression. And if you want to keep all these thoughts, and still pursue values because you love reality — give up your love of reality, sacrifice it. Give it all up.

"Do you see how it works? Do you see where we started, and how far into the human soul we were able to penetrate? Right to the core. Right to the center. Burning down a mall is nothing, compared to torching a soul. And that is what I am, at root: a spiritual terrorist. I explode souls and bomb minds the way some do airplanes and buildings. That is who I am and what I do. And that is how I create murderers. Kill off the mind, quench the soul, destroy a man's capacity to value, to even think about values, and he is left an empty husk with nothing inside. And what happens next? He has no thoughts of his own, no mind of his own, no values of his own. So what becomes important to him? Other people. But something very specific about those other people: their values, their minds, their very consciousness. When you empty a man by killing his soul, he attempts to fill himself through other people. But it can't be done. Others can't give him an identity; he has to supply that himself. If he can't, he remains empty, no matter what. And a soulless man is a dangerous thing. He has no values, no self, no love, no passion, no goals; nothing. So for him, taking another life becomes an easy thing.

"And here is what he will tell you when you chide him for being a murderer: Regret? About what? No right to do it? Well, I just did it, so why tell me I can't? The meaning of a human life? It has no meaning, so why worry about it? Did I feel anything? Feelings come from thoughts, and I have none, so no, I didn't feel anything. Empathy? Not a chance. Someone closed down to his own inner world loses all capacity to sense the soul of another.

"So that is how it happens. That is where men like these you see before you come from. In order to be willing to sacrifice another person, a man must first have been willing to sacrifice his own self. Whenever you hear of a murder, you can know that two killings have taken place: the murderer had to kill his own soul before he could kill another's body.

"But remember what I said earlier? Murder is intolerable and unforgivable? I tolerate it, and I forgive it. And those who have reached the stage of being capable of it — I am the type who knows how to use them.

"And am I the same? Have I traveled down that road of sacrifice myself? Of course I have. But I am different from most in this one respect: I have done so consciously, with no illusions, and no regrets. I wanted this dark world you see before you. I wanted all these botched monstrosities you see before us. Because that is my world. This is where I belong, the only place where I have any metaphysical power at all.

"So, have you guessed yet who I am?"

"I do not care to guess," says Sarah, her voice weary. "I do not want to know."

"Stein! Manny! Put her on a cross!"

"Yes, Mother Agnes."

The two men go to work while two shadow-men hold Sarah. She does not struggle. She does not call out. She holds her head up to Alan's cross. "Alan, are you there? Can you hear me?"

Alan grunts through his gag.

Sarah seems satisfied.

Two more long wooden poles are brought up from down below and strapped together with twine. Sarah is grabbed by four shadow-men and stripped down to bra and panties, then held down against the cross, tied to it securely, then carried to another round chimney sticking up out of the roof. The cross is stuck into the chimney. Sarah faces west, looking at Alan, and past him, the other man. Who is the other man? She can't think about him. She can only think about Alan.

When Sarah is up on the cross, Agnes stands in front of her, looking up at her for a long time. All around the mall they can hear the sounds of sirens as police cars and firetrucks continue to arrive. Lights flash and blink in a kaleidoscope array all around the mall. Agnes stands in front of Sarah. "Look down at me, child. Now that you know what sacrifice is, it is time for you to know my identity."

Through the darkness of her blindfold, Sarah pictures the image of Alan. In her mind's eye, she sees him in his ideal form, as he was in their beginning, when she fell in love with him, and when he loved her in the truest and most selfish form. And while holding this image in her mind, she says to Mother Agnes, "I do not care who you are. I do not want to know."

"Yes you do. When the time comes, you will not be able to resist. You must know who it is has brought this evil into your life. So look. See. Stein! Remove her blindfold!"

Stein does as instructed.

Sarah looks down at Mother Agnes.

Mother Agnes looks up at her and smiles with a freakish kind of ecstacy. "See here. I lift my veil. And now watch the lights play across my features. Do you recognize me? How does this make you feel?"

Sarah shuts her eyes and refuses to look. "You have no power over my soul."

"I think I do. This is to be your greatest torture. I wish the fact of your seeing my face and knowing my identity to be an act of sacrifice. Perhaps it can be. Only you can tell me. Only you can look upon my features and say what it does to your soul. Pain? Regret? Sadness? You tell me, sister Sarah. Tell me what it does to you, my sister."

Finally, the voice reaches her. From out of her past, it crawls up through the dim recesses of her memory, and from locked vaults in her soul, and it comes out. A voice she had forgotten. A voice she had tried to erase from her memory. A voice she had heard for the last time on the stage of the Show Me Mall in St. Louis, a voice that had pleaded against sanctuary, against freedom, against joy, against fulfillment. A voice that had pleaded for sacrifice. A voice that *always* had, even before that moment. A voice from her youth, a chastising voice, a reprimanding voice. An envious voice.

Her eyes open and she finally looks down, to see if what she is hearing is true, to test the reality. Perhaps this is fake. Perhaps this is a delusion. How can it be?

Agnes stands below her in the flickering light. Her veil is gone, and now she removes her shroud as well, revealing a bald head. Agnes is a woman who has sacrificed her hair.

Sarah stares down, watches the colored lights flicker and flash across the garish features of the bald woman who speaks with the strange voice from her past. "Are you woman — or man?" Sarah asks.

"Perhaps neither."

Sarah looks at the flat chest of the person standing before her. Not even a hint of breasts. Have those been sacrificed as well? "If you are a woman, then you cannot be the person you wish me to believe you are."

"Say it."

"You are not my brother, Stephen Fletcher."

"Don't I resemble him?"

"There is a vague resemblance."

Agnes pulls her shroud back up over her head. Her veil she folds and places in a pocket. "The rationalists have taught you skepticism. You do not believe the existence of what is right in front of your eyes."

"My brother Stephen could not have fallen so far."

"Perhaps he did not fall."

"He would not put his sister on a cross."

"If he learned the art of sacrifice from a father who murdered his mother, perhaps he is capable of things you cannot imagine."

"Then I will not imagine them."

Agnes comes forward and stands close below Sarah, reaching up and touching her feet, stroking her toes, caressing her ankles. "I feel your pain, Sarah. But do you feel mine?"

"You are not on a cross."

"I was on a cross from the day I was born! You put me on that cross. You drove in the nails. You made it impossible for me to get down!"

"No. I had nothing to do with it. Any cross you bear, you picked up yourself."

"Listen to me. Don't you want to know what happened to me after my failure at the Show Me Mall? Yes, it was a failure, I admit it. I was sent by powerful people to bring you home. I was a hostage to a sister who hated me. I knew you did. I knew you didn't care. And I didn't want to go, because I knew it would be useless. But I was to be a sacrifice on top of a sacrifice. I was a brother who hated his sister — under the control of men who cared for neither, but felt obligated to sacrifice both — out of a duty to a collective that hated them in turn — as you and I hated each other. It was a great, grand, glorious circle of sacrifice, a link of people joined together with only one thing in common: that they hated each other and did not want to be joined, but held hands nonetheless because they feared to stand alone and walk away. They all believed that sacrifice was moral, practical, necessary — and inevitable. And so they all joined hands in a great collective orgy of sacrifice. Except you. You stood alone and walked away, right into the waiting arms of a Mall Master. And I? I pleaded for you in my ineffectual way, then went back and faced the contemptuous stares of men who would have done no better in my place, but felt free to judge me as incompetent because I was the patsy who actually had to take the position of attempting what all knew to be impossible.

"So I went back. I watched my sick father die of the gunshot wound delivered by Alan Benton. And I faced an inquisition of government officials who treated me like a retarded child. They put it all on my head. Because I was family. Before all this, I had hated you. Now, I really loathed you, because I was linked to you, responsible for you, even though you were now in another country and leading another life, even though you were beyond the reach of all. Or so I thought. They didn't think so. They fixed Alan good and sent him after you. I thought that was funny.

"When that failed, more people fell into disfavor. I was forgotten and allowed to go back to my life. Such as it was. And what was my life? Do you remember it? Probably not. You never paid any attention to me, so how could you have known?

"For a few years I lived in obscurity. Our family was destroyed, all the power our father had accumulated was gone, we were all in disrepute, stricken from the records, that sort of thing. I was actually the only one left. And no one remembered me, no one remembered our family, no one remembered what a powerful and feared man our father had once been. I thought I was home free.

"But two years after you disappeared into California, Filbert Duckworth got control of the government. He began setting himself up as a dictator. He began systematically erasing everyone with any links to his past, anyone who knew who he had been, what he had done, what deaths he had ordered. All of that. And he remembered me. He put my name on a list. I was to be erased. He didn't want me showing up and spoiling the party. He didn't want me telling any stories, naming any names, pointing to any graves. So he sent the shadow-men after me. His shadow-men were a little different from mine. But only in style. The essence was the same.

"I found out. In the circles in which I traveled, there were many people in just my position, and word traveled fast amongst us. When I found out that Duckworth wanted me dead, I had to vanish even more completely than I had the first time. This time, I would have to change my identity in a, shall we say, slightly more comprehensive way?

"Duckworth was simply playing into my hands. He was an amateur in the game of power — remind me to tell you how I killed him, some day, but not now, no time right now.

"Yes, sister Sarah, I became a woman. I undertook a sex change. I emasculated myself. How is that for sacrifice? No, I had no desire to be a woman. Nor did I really hate being a man. Either sex was, and is, completely irrelevant to me. No, I was not motivated by a quest for sexual identity, or a desire to seek a form of sexual pleasure that was more in tune with my nature. It had nothing to do with that. I surrendered my manhood because by that time I understood the sublime power of sacrifice, the metaphysical power of sacrifice, the power of sacrifice to alter the consciousness of other people, to bend their minds to my will, to shape their formless souls into what I wanted and needed to achieve my ends.

"I was a failure as a man. I would have been as much a failure as a woman. But as neither man nor woman, I have been a complete success. Mother Agnes does not love men. She does not love women. But she is worshiped by both, and controls both, because those who wish to be selfless see the void within me, and I teach them to love it to such a degree that it envelopes them, they vanish, become the creatures you see all around you here in this mall.

"Look at this mall. It is a symbol for the soul of man. Once proud and clean, with a firm purpose and identity, and filled with values, now it lies in ruins, a sacked and looted hulk ready to be burned, to go up in flames and take all with it.

"Do not ask me why. That is the most ignorant question of all. This is sublime religion, don't you see? What did I do in all those years between losing you to California and losing myself to Duckworth? I worshiped mystery. That is the essence of this religion. The unknown is sacred and holy and to be feared. The greatest unknown is the unknown self, and we who practice the art of sacrifice do so because our selves, our values, our identities, are unknown to us. Who am I? I do not know. What do I believe? I do not know. Why do I do the things I do? I do not know, it is a mystery. And now all around you, look upon the consequences and results of that mystery. Here is your answer. The mall took my sister from me. Now I have taken the mall from my sister. The Mall Masters built these palaces of selfishness. Now I have taken this mall away from that one particular Mall Master, the one who stood young and arrogant in the Show Me Mall and achieved more value in one afternoon than others find in a lifetime. I have taken you away, and his mall away, and soon, I will take him as well. Think of it, Sarah. Would you like to see Maurice Sully on a cross? Him I will not tie to a cross. Him, I will nail to a cross. I will drive the spikes in myself, and his blood I will lick up into my mouth and make his flesh part of mine. And his cries for mercy I will not hear.

"So I have had my revenge on all those who mocked my incompetence. My mother lectured me for being a little monster. Now I am a large monster. My father told me I was weak and would never have the stomach for sacrifice. Now I have surpassed him in the art of sacrifice. He murdered our mother? That is nothing next to killing you, your lover, two Mall Masters, and an entire city. And you: you held me in contempt, told me I was not a man and would never amount to anything? Well, I am not a man, I am not even a woman, but have I amounted to anything? I am the leader of a new race of men. I am the creator of a new religion. And I am the living God on an altar of death. And your Mall Master lover, Maurice Sully? I had a chance to take you from him once, on his terms. But now he has to take you from me, on my terms. And who will win this battle, dear sister? Who has the upper hand now? Who has the power? Who is consistent with reality now? If reality gave a damn, I would be stopped. But reality does not care. Nature is blind. So I and my shadow-men go marching on."

Sarah reflects on the life of her brother, contemplates his actions and beliefs. The awesome logic of it all leaves her calm. "The Mall Masters see. And you will be stopped."

Agnes looks up to her sister's face, her eyes searching, her face longing for something that is not there. "What, no tears? Why do you not weep for me, sister?"

"If I weep, it will be for this mall. And for Alan."

Nearby, Alan has heard all, including Sarah's latest statements. Behind his gag, he grunts and moans, strains at his bonds, thrashes about on his cross, trying to knock it down. But he has been secured well, and there is no chance of his getting free.

The shadow-men stand by silently, mesmerized by Agnes' words.

Augustus Stein and one-eyed Manny stand near also, gazing with ignorant mystery worship at the woman they have chosen to follow. They have seen her deeper than any others now — but they still do not understand who or what she is.

"Where is your Mall Master, Sarah?" asks Agnes. "Where is he? Why does he not come to save you? Where is Maurice Sully?"

Sarah does not answer. She hangs on her cross, stares over the roof to Alan, her beloved.

Before she can start screaming, they gag her, then replace her blindfold.

Mother Agnes is done talking. She disappears from the roof, takes her shadow-men with her. Soon, the three crosses stand alone and silent in the early morning darkness.

CHAPTER SEVENTEEN

A CHILD REMEMBERS HIS FIRST LESSON

In Layvanwick Tower, Diane Copernicus is still trying to get through to Maurice Sully on his cell phone. The line has been busy for the past half hour and she has left message after message. She has called the mall security office at West Park Plaza, but has gotten no answer. She has spoken with the police and fire departments and been told they are on the scene. She has raced out to the roof of the tower to look through the telescope and see West Park Plaza burning and surrounded by the blinking spinning lights of firetrucks and police cars.

Still, she is not satisfied. She cannot know peace until she hears from Maurice.

For most of this crisis, she has reacted like a frightened wife. But now, her mind is asserting itself, and she remembers she is a Mall Master, and she commands herself to think like a Mall Master.

What must I do? How must I help Maurice? What can I do to save the Mall? How can I fulfill my obligation to Layvanwick Tower and act in defense of West Park Plaza at the same time?

I can't get Maurice on the phone. I must assume the worst. Layvanwick has vanished. I must assume the worst. I have seen the mall dark and surrounded by the authorities. I must assume the worst.

When a Mall Master is faced with a worst case scenario, what does a Mall Master do? When reason has ended and brute force enters the mall, what does a Mall Master do?

Finally, at four o'clock in the morning, after much pacing, she picks up a phone and dials an operator.

"Get me the number for the Office of the First Citizen."

***

Inside Sears, surrounded by police and firemen, Maurice Sully rushes through smoke and darkness only far enough to make sure no aphrodites are in Sears. There are not supposed to be any, but he wants to make sure. All aphrodites wishing to spend the evening inside the mall are supposed to be on the arcade level. But Maurice knows that young people are liable to wander anywhere in the mall, including Sears.

His brief push into the store shows him that a large fire is burning right at the boundary between Sears and the mall. He cannot get into the mall this way; nobody can until the fire is put out, so he quickly retreats and lets the firemen do their job.

When he is back outside, he has a brief coughing fit. After fresh air and some water, he is fine and notices that in his pocket, his cell phone is ringing. He answers and listens to Diane's voice on the other end.

"Maurice, I have called the office of the First Citizen."

Maurice kisses the phone. "You are a brave woman."

"I could think of no other logical next step."

"It was the right thing to do. Who did you talk to?"

"An assistant. I told all I have seen through the telescope here — I can see the fire!"

"It is under control, don't worry about it."

"Has the mall been lost?"

"It is in the hands of Agnes right now. But the police are moving in. Any commitment from the First Citizen?"

"They are going to monitor the situation and call me back. They are in touch with the police here and if the police ask for military assistance, the First Citizen will most likely authorize it."

"To my knowledge, no mall has ever been assaulted in this manner. This is an unprecedented situation. I'm sure the First Citizen will give it his full personal attention."

"I hope he does. Now how are you? What is happening there?"

"The fire department is moving into Sears, putting water on the fire. Police are moving into the mall — but none are coming out."

"Any sign of Anton?"

"No, nothing."

"What about Sarah and Alan?"

"Sarah is here. She has gone inside, even after I pleaded with her not to. Alan hasn't been seen. Sarah feels certain she will find him here. I hope she is right. She has taken a great risk."

"Are you staying?"

"Yes. I'll see this through to the finish. If you hear anything from the First Citizen, let me know, okay?"

"I will. Maurice, one last thing—"

"Yes?"

"She called me. I spoke to her."

"Who?"

"This Agnes person. She called me and told me I am next. Maurice, be careful. I think she is out to get you. Not just your mall, but you personally."

"I know she is. I read Anton's file. I know who Agnes is."

"What do you mean?"

"Read the file while you wait to hear from the First Citizen. You'll understand."

"Just be careful. She wants you there. If she knows you are there, she will act against you."

"I am safe for now."

"In the name of logic, make sure you stay that way!"

"Yes dear, I will do as you say."

***

Officer Rod Black uses a billy club to smash his way into the mall through the glass doors at the front entrance. Once inside, he is immediately set upon by shadow-men who rush at him from all sides. He has a second to wonder — in a bemused fashion, as he smashes heads, knocks hands away, kicks people off their feet —, where have all these destructive maniacs come from? And he knows the answer even as he asks the question, because he has already interviewed most of them: they have come from the carnival. The entire crew of the carnival has descended upon the mall and is savaging it. Why this is, he has no idea. While he swings and punches and kicks, he listens to his radio squawk. New back-ups are arriving all the time — and then back-ups for the back-ups. It must be the entire active duty force of the Billings Police Department descending on the mall right now. Will it be enough? He is not sure. Even as he fights his way into the mall, he realizes he has made a serious mistake. There are too many of them. And they come from every angle. His only chance is to get away and lose them in a store.

He feels a man grab his face briefly. Something on the man's hand rubs off. Some kind of sticky powdery substance with a medicine smell. He feels his cheek begin to go numb as he staggers off the mall and through an access door into a service hallway. He runs down the narrow hallway with no one in front of him, but many dark feet behind him. He drops his flashlight and runs headlong into darkness. Behind him, the flashlight glows briefly, then is extinguished. All he senses is running feet catching up with him. A wave of nausea hits him and he skids to a halt, slams into a wall on his left, rebounds into a door on his right that flies open and catapults him into the dark back room of a shop. He staggers past stacks of light cardboard boxes, pulling them down behind him as he feels his mind start to go. He knows he has been drugged and must think and act fast. He only has seconds and must make his final act definite and of some impact. So what can he do?

What kind of shop am I in? What is in these boxes? I can see nothing. My radio is gone, my flashlight is gone, my billy club is gone. Here, pull down more boxes, slow them down. Hear them all? How many of these dark shadow-men are chasing me? Sounds like a hundred. Listen to them scream. Are they animals? What can I do? What can I use? I can't see anything, I have no light, I am helpless, they have me, I am going fast. I must protect the mall. How can I protect the mall? What can I do to protect the mall?

He makes it out of the back room and into the store. This store has a south-facing window that lets in some light. He can see that he is in a party supply store. He races forward towards the window and slams into a heavy metal rack in front of the window, pushing it forward. The tall upper shelves fall down and smash against the window, cracking it. Through the cracks in the window, the last thing he sees is three police cars pulling up outside and fellow officers charging forward, billy clubs ready. He sags to the floor as the shadow-men swirl all around him. He hears shouts, screams, the sound of smashing glass. He wonders if he has made a difference. Then he falls to the floor unconscious and is buried in a drift of tissue paper pushed from a table by a shadow-man racing forward to smash out more of the front window.

Around the slumbering body of Officer Rod Black, shadow-men taunt the police officers, sucker them deep into the mall — then vanquish them all with sleeping dust.

And when all is finally silent in the party store, Officer Rod Black lies slumbering beneath tufts of tissue paper, unaware that the front windows of the store have been completely smashed out and a breeze from outside has entered, swirled around inside, then moved back outside, pulling with it a number of brightly-colored helium filled balloons that have lined the ceiling of the store. These balloons drift out of the store, then rise into the dark morning sky, like drops of blood from the mall.

***

On the arcade level, the aphrodites slumber in sweet innocence, unaware that a dark force moves towards them.

All throughout the arcade level, in every individual chamber, regular lighting has been turned off. Illumination comes from only a single love lamp inside each chamber. Soft yellow light glows warm across the naked bodies of each couple. They sleep now, limbs entwined, hair meshed, breath mingling with radiance from dreams stemming from a deep well of shared values, and from memories of the Festival of Aphrodite just held on this dark night.

The festival begins at midnight. While the mall empties of conventional celebrants, those chosen to stay behind and share love within the mall gather in front of the statue of Athena and swear an oath to love rationally, logically, and with full arete. This done, two guards are left behind to honor Athena. The rest of the aphrodites pair off into couples and travel to pre-selected shops chosen to reflect some value affinity expressed by the merchandise within. Merchants place gifts for the young lovers wrapped in red paper and hidden in easy-to-find places. The couples find the gifts, unwrap them, and swear a value oath to each product.

"In the name of my sacred ego, and the beautifully selfish life it supports, I pledge to value this object with full arete and make it a part of my soul for as long as I own it. My value choices create my soul; in turn, my soul creates my value choices. Therefore, let this value add to the beauty of my soul, and let my soul always recognize value of this type. I make this pledge with full commitment to logical values. In the name of reason, let my satisfaction be complete."

Most often the gifts are works of art, small paintings and sculptures, or items of clothing in which the aphrodites can dress each other for the trip upstairs.

Within an hour, all the aphrodites make it up to the arcade level and find their way into small private chambers designed especially for couples. Here, they spend the night making love. In the morning, the ceremony ends with the aphrodites rising at dawn and returning the gifts back into the shops and stores. These items are then marked as having superior value because they have been used selfishly and blessed with superior arete during a Festival of Aphrodite. Items used in this manner are then sold to newlyweds or people celebrating anniversaries. But they are also highly prized by single people trying to find true love, and hoping to help themselves along psychologically by drawing focus from objects known to have been loved in the presence of the most honest, clean, and true form of selfishness known to exist.

But on this early morning, at five AM, one hour from dawn, these aphrodites gathered in West Park Plaza are going to miss this last rite of the Festival of Aphrodite.

Walking silently to the first chamber, Mother Agnes looks in and
sees a young couple sleeping with such radiant serenity that she is
mesmerized for a few moments just watching, gazing upon this scene of
domestic bliss. They are a young couple. He has curly brown hair and
finely muscled shoulders. She has long black hair spread out against her
silk pillow. Her skin is olive and glows with even more beauty in the
dull yellow light of a dying love lamp. They breathe lightly, chests rising
and falling gently, faces clean and pure, unaware of what a rogue array
stands just outside their chambers.

Such a picture of innocence, thinks Agnes. They have shared a
sacred privacy tonight. They have enjoyed the glory of moral innocence.
They know nothing of me and my world. They think they are safe inside
this mall, that the mall has blessed them and will protect them. But there
is no protection from me. Shall I disturb them? Shall I wake them and let
them stare into my face and know who it is shall corrupt their love? Or
shall I leave them as they are? The aphrodites sleep until dawn. Give
them another hour? Or use that hour to let my shadow-men hold sway
over this garden paradise?

Mother Agnes kneels down over the two beautiful aphrodites. She
touches the shoulder of the girl. The girl's eyes blink open and she looks
up into the haggard face of Mother Agnes.

Agnes smiles down at her. "Child, you are injured. Here. Let me
help you. Let me feel your pain."

***

Outside, in the sky above the mall, two helicopters roar and flash
and flutter in a mechanized dance, like two giant insects on a mating
flight. One helicopter is from the police, sent by a hysterical department
on the verge of panic, sent to assess the situation from the air and remain
untouched by the forces below that have defeated an entire city's police
force. Information is kept tight, but those at City Hall know they are in
trouble. They have sent in everything they have and the mall has sucked
it all up like so many pieces of dirt into a vacuum cleaner. The fire
department has arrived and put out a fire — but the price has been the
disappearance of every single fireman who has entered the mall. So the
police chopper circles the mall, lower and lower, a searchlight flashing
across the sides of the building and down onto the roof. What they see
near the western end of the roof strikes absolute horror into their hearts
and minds. They radio back for instructions. Do we land? Do we attempt
a rescue? The answer comes back: negative.

The second helicopter is from a local television station. It has a searchlight and a camera. Its beam flashes across the roof, jousting with the police beam. They see the same things as the police. Only these images are captured by a camera and beamed by satellite to television stations all over the country. Soon, everyone everywhere will know what is happening at West Park Plaza.

***

In Denver, at the residence of the First Citizen, the old man has been roused out of bed by a call from an assistant. He has the TV on to the cable news channel, hoping for a satellite feed from the affiliate in Billings. It comes in sooner than expected and he watches it while tying his shoes. He sees what has happened to West Park Plaza — and what is on the roof. He picks up his phone and gets an assistant on the line. "Have my plane prepared immediately. I am going to Billings." Then he clicks off, dials another extension. "Get me on the phone to Layvanwick Tower, Billings Montana, office of the Mall Master."

***

Maurice Sully is about to do something stupid when he gets the call from Diane Copernicus.

"The First Citizen is in the air," she informs him. "He'll be here in two hours. He wants you to meet him at the airport."

Maurice laughs into the phone.

Diane hears his laugh. "Maurice, where are you?"

"Home."

"What?"

Maurice raises his eyes to the Rimrocks. He can see lights blinking up there. The airport. He is so close, yet so far away.

"Maurice, do you hear me?"

"Yes, darling."

"Where are you?"

"I am on the roof. I am hiding against the north wall of my penthouse."

Above Maurice, the helicopters whirl and tilt and thunder against the air, sending voluptuous waves of sound beating against his head. Twin search beams play across the night sky, but neither finds him. And lucky for him, neither do they find any shadow-men racing to meet him. He is alone on the roof, as far as he knows. But he does not like this. Where are all the police? Vanished. Where are all the firemen? Vanished. But I am home, at least. I have them on my home turf. So I have the advantage. Don't I?

Diane is screaming at him from the phone, but the helicopters are so loud he can't hear her. He presses the phone hard to his ear, but he still can't hear her. Now the helicopters move away for an instant and he has a second in which he can actually hear Diane, but all she says is, "Come back—"

At Layvanwick Tower, Diane stands in front of a television, tears streaming down her face, she screaming into the phone at Maurice. "Get off the roof! You are in danger on the roof! Get off the roof! Do not go into the mall! Get off the roof!"

And she thinks, Do not tell him what you see. If he knows this, he will not leave, and he will end up on a cross as well. What if he sees it? He must not see it. He must listen to me and get off the roof and come back. He must meet the First Citizen. This is a job for the First Citizen. Maurice is a merchant. The First Citizen is a soldier. Let a soldier deal with this hell. Let my Maurice come back to me safe.

And while she talks with one part of her brain, thinks with another, there is a third part asking itself: "Who are these three people hanging from crosses on the roof of my mall? Who has put them there? And what have they done to deserve this torture?"

On the roof, Maurice presses his back flat against the steel wall of his penthouse and his arms press out and back against the wall, his body forming a cross against the wall. He stares across the city, up to the Rims, knowing now that the First Citizen is on the way and wants to meet him up there. Does he have time? For what? His wife is screaming at him from the phone. He leaves it on and lets her scream, but he does not listen, does not respond. This is his mall. He is the only defense left. Where is Anton? Where is Sarah? What choice has Alan made? When will he face Agnes — and what will he do when the moment comes? There is so much here that is unknown. How much time do I have? The aphrodites are scheduled to awake in an hour. What is to become of them? Or has it happened already? How much time do I have? If I wait for the First Citizen, will it be too late? If I leave the mall now, will I be able to make it back? I know Agnes wants me. Shall I face her now? Can I defeat her now, on my own? Where is Anton? Why isn't Anton here to fight by my side?

He turns around and presses his face to the metal of his penthouse.

This is my home. I built this place with my own hands. I am this close. I go in through my penthouse, I enter the mall through the secret passageways that only I know about, and I find Agnes and her dark army and I stop them. And how do I stop them? The police couldn't stop them. The firemen couldn't stop them. What makes me think I can stop them? Anton couldn't stop them. Did they stop Anton? What have they done to Anton? What has Sarah done to herself? I told her not to—

Make a decision. Going or staying? Leaving or fighting?

The helicopter beams are at the other end of the mall. He has just a moment. He runs and slips into his penthouse.

There. Finally. Some silence, some peace. He slides to the floor of his penthouse living room and holds his phone to his ear. Now he can hear Diane clearly. So let her hear me clearly.

"Diane, listen to me. I am inside now. I am in my penthouse. I am staying. I am here to fight for my mall. You must meet with the First Citizen and you must follow his instructions and advice. Is that understood?"

On the other end of the phone, Diane Copernicus cries into his ear. "Maurice, look out your western windows."

"What is there?"

"Something you must see."

Maurice crawls to his western windows and then carefully looks outside, taking care to make sure he does not make himself visible to the helicopter beams still passing over the roof.

He sees what Diane has wanted him to see.

He sinks to the floor of his penthouse.

"Can you recognize who they are?" Diane asks him.

"No."

"Are they alive?"

"I can't tell."

"Are they moving?"

"Doesn't look like it."

"What are you going to do?"

"I am going to get them down."

***

Fifteen minutes later, Maurice is ready for his assault on the crosses. He has changed clothes, now wears black slacks and sweater, black gloves to cover his hands, and a knit cap pulled over his face. In his bedroom, in the dark, he still sees a faint image reflected in his bedroom mirror. Funny, he thinks. I look like a criminal. A mugger, a burglar.

How ironic.

In his kitchen, he arms himself with several sharp knives. Two small steak knives he inserts into each of his socks. A medium-size knife he slips into his belt at the small of his back. A large butcher knife he carries in his right hand.

He pauses at his kitchen window and looks west, across the dark roof of the mall, to where the three crosses stand. He scans the area all around the crosses for guards or lurking shadow-men. He doesn't see any, but he decides to assume they are there anyway. By now he knows it is important not to let any shadow-men touch him. All the evidence points to some kind of sleep-inducing agent being used on mall personnel. It isn't gas, so it has to be something delivered individually, person-to-person, one victim at a time.

Between him and the crosses is one obstacle that worries him: Diane's apartment. It is dark, he watches it carefully, taking time to thoroughly study every inch he can see. His eyes linger on the windows, hoping to catch a glimmer of movement within. There has to be someone else up on this roof watching the crosses and waiting for him — or anybody — to try a rescue.

Those shadow-men earlier didn't seem to recognize me. But I'm still assuming Agnes will know I am here — and that she will come for me. Or send others for me. So where are they?

He walks to the door of his private stairway leading down into the management offices. As far as he can tell, no one has been up into his apartment. He finds that odd. They should have set some kind of trap for me here, some kind of ambush. Perhaps they are not as clever as I think.

He slowly opens the door just an inch and waits, listening, his knife ready. After a moment of tense anticipation, he closes the door again and steps away.

Back to the window, back to the crosses. Now is decision time, action time. No more time to waste and wait. Whoever these people are on the crosses, they are coming down now.

He exits his apartment. Back out into the cool morning. The air feels good on his hot face. He runs across the roof and stops at the wall of Diane's apartment, crouches down below the window line to hide himself, and he waits, listening, watching, taking just a moment to suck in deep breaths and relax himself. Now another test to find out if harm waits within his wife's apartment: he picks up a pebble from the roof and tosses it up at a window. Then another, larger pebble, throws this one harder, hears it hit the glass squarely and make a definite *tick* . He waits some more, still hears no sign of movement within.

He looks right, looks left — then something catches his eye across the roof.

Shadow-men.

Inside his apartment.

Through the glass of a window, he sees a flash, then a flicker, then a soft glow that flares into a brilliant flame.

They are setting fire to his apartment.

In just a matter of seconds, his penthouse is burning beyond the point of being rescued. It happens so quickly, he doesn't even have time to feel anything. Mesmerized by the flames, he ignores the shadow-men as they leave his apartment and lope across the roof to Diane's apartment.

Four of them now, coming across the roof at him.

Do they see me?

He sits motionless, hidden in the shadow of Diane's apartment. Two shadow-men go left, two right. He hears windows being smashed, then a door kicked down as they enter Diane's chambers and begin starting fires. None of them have seen him. So now is his chance. The only chance he has left. If the serious and final burning is to begin now, then he must move.

He jumps up and runs out of darkness, into light, heading for the first cross. When he reaches the cross, he cuts without even checking to see who it is. First the feet, then the hands. He notices it is a woman, gagged and blind-folded. He cuts her waist free and she falls on top of him. He tries to catch her and drops his knife. The woman pulls off her blindfold as he looks past her to Diane's burning apartment and sees two shadow-men come dancing out of the flames, celebrating with each other and not seeing that one cross is now empty. Maurice reaches for his knife and then looks down into the face of Sarah Fletcher. She pulls her gag off and stares up at him with awe in her eyes. "I knew you would come."

"Have a knife," he says, giving her the knife from his back belt. "Cut down the others. Don't let these shadow-men touch you."

"I know." She takes the knife and runs for the second cross.

Maurice stands and faces the shadow-men. Now all four are out of Diane's apartment and they see him. They leap and scream and charge across the roof to him.

Sarah cuts down Alan. They stand together and move towards Layvanwick's cross.

Just past this cross, at the edge of the roof, is the access hatch leading down into the grocery store. It flies open and shadow-men come crawling out, scurrying across the roof like cockroaches. Behind them, smoke and flames soon flicker from out of the open hatch.

It is a race to Layvanwick. The shadow-men win because they are closer.

"I am lost unless I save Layvanwick," says Alan.

He turns with Sarah to see Maurice pull down Sarah's cross and use it as a battering ram, charging forward at the shadow-men and knocking them down. Alan and Sarah follow his example and rush to the second cross, pull it down, then turn and face the shadow-men who come at them from Layvanwick.

Behind them, Maurice yells, "Get off the roof! Save yourselves!"

"I must redeem myself!" cries Alan.

He and Sarah rush forward to the shadow-men standing in front Layvanwick. Some are hit and fall down, but others grab on to the cross and hold tight. A tug of war ensues, Alan and Sarah against three shadow-men.

The shadow-men are stronger. They have not been hanging on crosses for several hours.

The shadow-men get the upper hand, control the cross, drive Alan and Sarah back across the roof, to the edge of the roof.

Maurice is in the same trap. Two shadow-men have grabbed his cross and they drive him back. He lets go suddenly and dances away as the two shadow-men fall forward onto the cross. Maurice runs for Alan and Sarah.

But he is too late.

He skids to a halt and watches the shadow-men drive Alan and Sarah off the edge of the roof.

First Alan goes tumbling into darkness.

Then Sarah falls from sight.

He hears nothing but the screams of the shadow-men. He screams for Alan and Sarah, but even his voice is lost in the howling of the shadow-men. Now they turn and see him. They howl louder and charge.

He turns around. Two more shadow-men now up on the roof and running at him.

The mall is burning all around him. His apartment is gone. Diane's is in flames. Where to go? What to do? Jump off the roof after Alan and Sarah?

His foot hits something.

Another access hatch down into the mall.

He bends down, pulls it open, dives down, pulling the hatch shut after him. He locks it from the inside.

Above him, he hears the shadow-men pounding on the hatch and yelling at each other. He ignores them and descends the ladder down into the store.

He is in Pacific Orchid, the clothing store. No flames here yet. He races out, finds his way to the front of the store and out into the mall.

Unconscious police and firemen litter the floor everywhere he steps. In the middle of center court, a great bonfire is blazing. Soon, the entire mall will go up.

He makes his way to a service hallway nearby and begins his journey to the basement. His mission is to turn the water back on so the fire sprinklers can activate.

On the way down, his mind is haunted by the image of one lone man hanging on a cross, alone, unsaved, unrescued. Who was that man? Do I want to know? Do I want to think about it? But I don't have to think about it. I know who it is. It can only be one person. And I if I am to save him, I must stop these flames. So do this, then get back on the roof. And hope he can last till I make it back to save him.

He glances at the glowing face of his watch. It is five-thirty in the morning. A little more than half an hour until dawn. And then this evil night will finally end.

***

At seven minutes past six in the morning, the first rays of sunlight shoot over the eastern sky and light up the burning mall. Sunlight flows into flamelight and the two radiances join in a deep red glow. Above the light, smoke gathers in a black cloud above the mall. A light breeze pushes the smoke west. Sun-beams and flame-glows flow up into the smoke and are stirred into a deep red pigment, as if the smoke is blood transformed from liquid into gas, and the mall is bleeding up into the sky — instead of down into the earth.

Near the western edge of the roof of the mall, within a small triangle of safe, unburned roof, Layvanwick hangs alone on his cross. He is awake now. The scent of smoke and the heat of the flames on his naked skin have roused him. As awareness floods his mind and his senses grow alert, he looks around, through the smoke, past the flames, at the world renewed with sunlight. Up past the smoke, he sees patches of blue sky. He raises his face to the sky and tries to gulp down some clean fresh cool morning air, but he gets too much smoke and he coughs and chokes. His mouth is dry. He needs water. He remembers water. He knows what a drink is. Picture a drink, he thinks. See a tall glass of clean pure water, the glass sitting in the sunlight, the glass covered in beads of condensation. Pick the glass up, feel the slick wet glass in your hand, taste the clean water as it flows down your dry throat. This is a drink of water. You can't have one because you are tied to a cross.

He has been hanging for so long, his body is starting to come apart. His wrists are sore, the rope around his waist is starting to loosen and slide up. He can feel his back scratching against the main pole of the cross.

This is the only existence I have ever known, he thinks. I have been on this cross my entire life. And what has been my life? Only the memories of the last several hours, the evening past. I was born into a dark world of ugly people and constant pain. I have no name, no identity, no purpose that I know. My job is to hang on this cross. What is a job? Something that needs to be done. Why? I don't know. My job is to hang on this cross? Why? Who decided this? Why is *this* my job? Why is *this* my purpose? Isn't there some other possibility?

He looks out away from the mall. He sees houses and trees and cars, and far away, more buildings. He sees traffic lights blinking over an intersection. He sees a sign with big letters. GRAND AVENUE. That seems to mean something, but he's not sure what.

Where is everybody? Why have they left me here to burn? Where is my mother, Agnes? Where are my brothers? The man with one eye? And the blond man with the sad eyes? Where have they all gone?

The flames are getting closer. The smoke is getting thicker.

A gust of wind hits the side of his face and he looks to his left. The smoke clears for a moment and he sees a curious thing.

A balloon.

A single balloon drifts past his line of vision, carried up and away by the wind from the east.

He smiles. A balloon. Some poor child has lost his balloon.

An image crashes into his brain. He slams shut his eyes and the image flashes briefly, burning itself into his brain.

An afternoon cityscape, the background for a smiling, laughing little girl who chases a balloon trying to get away from her.

It is a memory.

Now why is it that a balloon is what I choose to remember in the hour of my death?

Another image flashes into his brain. This one hurts his head. His eyes shut and his teeth clench, his hands ball into fists and his arms surge against his bonds.

A cerulean-blue hot air balloon drifts against the sky. In the basket, a smiling dark-haired woman looks at him with love in her eyes. She laughs with him and kisses him. It is his balloon and she is riding in it with him.

Who is *him*?

His eyes open and he sees more balloons following the solitary one. They are all different colors. Here is a red one, there a green, now a yellow, next some orange, blue, gold. They flow up into the sky, pushed along by another gust of wind, and lit up by sunlight from the east. They don't seem to mind the smoke and flames, they are in the air, they are safe, they are flying away from this burning mall.

And he must do the same.

I must follow these balloons, he thinks. They will tell me who I am. They have the answers. Balloons.

He begins rocking and shaking his cross. He throws his weight from side to side, then back and forth, using his weight to move the cross, just get it moving a little—

Another image flashes inside him.

A full moon sits in the night sky in front of him, looking just like a big yellow balloon. It hangs in the sky and it smiles at him, and he smiles back. A young man in a crisp white shirt and black slacks. He sits on the roof of the mall and smiles at the moon. And hears music.

He opens his eyes, screams against the smoke and flames, then looks inward again, to another image.

A beautiful woman with long black hair. She wears a red sweater and a black skirt that hugs her hips tight. She laughs and smiles and dances with a mannequin.

The same woman was with him in the balloon. Who is she? What does she mean to me? Why can't I remember her name? If I remember her name, I will remember my own name, because we are linked somehow.

He gazes at the balloons. Still more of them drift up into the sky. Now the sky is filled with them. Are the balloons all that can escape this burning mall? That cannot be. Look at how soft and delicate they are! They race the smoke to find the heights. But the smoke is blind and disappears, while the balloons have eyes and find the sunlight. Look at them rise. Let them rise!

Another memory-flash sears his brain:

A man and a woman in brilliant costume ride an elevator up the side of a beautiful transparent skyscraper. They smile at each other behind colorful masks and say, "Let us rise!"

Layvanwick shakes the cross furiously now. He knows what is

behind him. He knows what rises on the eastern horizon. If he can just turn around and look through the smoke, he will be able to see it, that skyscraper is real, it exists. It is right behind me, I can look at it, I can stare at it, I can get down on my knees and bow before it and worship it, because I know what it is, I know what it means! They have put me on this cross and faced me in this direction to keep me from seeing this structure, to keep me from remembering who I am and what I have done—

Who am I? What have I done?

He rages against the smoke and flame, thrashing furiously on the cross, trying to tear his hands out from the bonds, trying to generate enough force with his movement to snap the cross at its base and free his legs.

Even if I do not get free of the flames, at least let me see that golden skyscraper before I perish. I want to see my dream real. I want to know that my memory is not false, that it really does exist, that somebody really did build it—

Who built it?

Who do you *think* built it?

Another memory-flash overtakes his mind.

On the roof during a hail storm. Stepping carefully across a crystal skylight. A beautiful blond man in white smiles back at him. The skylight collapses and he grabs and holds the man before he can fall. As he pulls up, he sees the blond man's lips moving in slow motion. He is calling out a name. It is the name of the man who holds him. It is the name of the man who's first act of friendship is to save his life. What is the name? What is he saying?

And then he remembers.

You have heard it before, you silly fool. Your brother told you your name, but the sound meant nothing.

Say it again. Say it out loud, and now understand what it means.

"ANTON LAYVANWICK!"

Finally, it all comes rushing back. He knows who he is. He remembers what he is and what he has done.

"I am Layvanwick!" he screams to the smoke and flame. "I am the boxboy! I am Layvanwick the Mall Master and those who put me on this cross will pay for it with their lives!"

As if hearing his voice and fearing his power, the cross snaps, as if the wood itself is cowardly and wishes to fight him no more. The cross falls to the right, hits hard, but with his weight going forward, so he falls to the roof face-first, the cross on his back, his legs free. He staggers to his feet and spins around, scanning the roof for a safe path. The fire is serious, he can feel the heat all around him. The roof is burning his bare feet. The best way to go is north, towards the Rimrocks. He staggers across to the edge the roof and collapses. To his right, he can see Maurice Sully's penthouse apartment completely engulfed in flames. Behind him, Diane Copernicus' apartment is suffering the same fate. "I will avenge this," he says to the cross, as if it is a person.

With his feet and waist free and the cross loose across his back, he can move his arms against the ropes at his wrists. Twisting and turning and pulling has loosened them enough so that finally he gets a hand free. With this he unties the other side and is finally completely free of the cross. It collapses beside him like giant chopsticks and he kneels for a long moment, head bowed, taking deep breaths. His thirst is powerful and he allows his pain and exhaustion to reach his full conscious attention for just a moment. But then he raises his head and stands up straight. *I will rest after I have slain at least one of those who have defiled this mall.*

He picks up the main mast of the cross. The end which snapped off is a spear of jagged wood, with a sharp tip. He picks it up and carries it lightly in his right hand, like a javelin. He steps to the edge of the roof and looks down.

Deserted firetrucks and empty police cars sit silent in the cool morning. He searches the area for signs of people, but sees none. The best way off the roof from here is further east, towards the dome over center court.

He carries his wooden spear and jogs across the burning roof, twisting through a path of flames, his feet burning, his skin scorched, his eyes filled with smoke. Finally he makes it close to center court, to an access hatch that he knows leads down into the arcade level. He pauses a moment and faces east as the smoke clears away for him and gives him an unobstructed view of the eastern horizon. He sees his beautiful golden skyscraper mall sparkling in the morning sunshine. No flames there, no smoke. Is his mall safe?

I swore an oath on the lips of the woman I love that I would protect her mall. Once it was my mall. It has always been my mall. It always will be my mall, by virtue of my loving it, and by virtue of my loving the people who do own it in fact. Maurice and Diane. Do they know what has happened? They must know. Then let them know that I am here. I will take the mall back.

The access hatch flies open and a shadow-man sticks his head up. Layvanwick thumps him hard with the blunt end of his spear and the man falls away.

Layvanwick follows, down into the mall.

***

Mother Agnes is about to bless the dark-haired aphrodite girl with the gift of suffering when she hears screams of alarm behind her. She pushes the aphrodite away and turns around to see several shadow-men race to a stop in front of her. "Layvanwick awakes! He is down from his cross and in the mall!"

"Slay him!"

"He slays us instead!"

Past the shadow-men, coming out of a service hallway, Agnes sees two shadow-men fly out away from the walls and land limp on the floor of the mall, blood draining from chest wounds.

Behind them comes Layvanwick. What was once a wooden cross he carries as a spear. He twirls and thrusts and spins the spear in his hands like a baton, pounding and stabbing his way through the shadow-men who get close. He has them all in retreat before him. Those behind him are dead. He stops a short distance from Agnes and gazes through the yellow murk at her.

"You are responsible," he says.

"I am," says Agnes.

In one swift motion, Layvanwick raises his spear to his shoulder, steps forward quickly, puts the weight of his body into his throw, and javelins the broken cross on a line to Agnes' chest.

Agnes does not move.

The spear flies through the air.

To one side of Agnes, Augustus Stein stands still just long enough to know the throw is true — then he throws himself in front of Mother Agnes and catches the spear straight through his chest.

Spear and man fall together to the floor of the mall. Augustus Stein looks up at his Mother Agnes, blood in his mouth, worship in his eyes.

Agnes looks down at her faithful follower, her face blank, no words on her tongue.

Stein's last words gurgle out of his mouth. "Tell me this was not a lie."

And then he is gone, another sacrifice complete.

Agnes stares up at Layvanwick.

Layvanwick marches resolutely towards her.

Both are dumbfounded when it starts to rain.

The ceilings suddenly sputter as fire sprinklers cough to life, spitting out brief squirts of water, then flowing freely and powerfully as water finds its way back into the mall. In seconds, Agnes and her shadow-men are drenched, soaked, and Layvanwick also. They stop and stare at each other through the rain. Layvanwick opens his mouth and relishes the sensation of cool water entering his body for the first time in — forever. But his eyes remain open, alert, watching Agnes. Stopped for a moment, he continues forward.

"You are not alone in the mall," says Mother Agnes.

"I am here to help you consummate your worship of death," says Layvanwick.

"You will not kill me," says Agnes.

"I will."

"Logic says otherwise. I have a bomb in my head just like Alan. Only mine is programmed to detonate at the moment my life ends."

Layvanwick only smiles through the rain and still marches forward.

The left side of Agnes' face starts twitching. She realizes Layvanwick is serious. He means to do her in and does not care what it costs.

"Shadow-men, take me away from this place!"

Layvanwick breaks into a run and charges for Agnes.

But the shadow-men swirl in and rush Agnes away. When Layvanwick reaches the spot where Agnes just stood, he is alone with Augustus Stein. He pulls his spear out of Stein's chest — and collapses.

Naked aphrodites awakened by the water pick him up and carry him to the nearest exit.

When he wakes up, he is lying in grass on the north side of the mall, and Maurice Sully is kissing him.

***

On the south side of the mall, Alan Benton has a broken arm and leg. He landed first. Sarah landed on top of him. He broke her fall; she broke his body. Now they lie together in the grass under a tree. They missed the tree. It could have caught them, but there was no time to aim.

With dawn, the city is coming back to life. From homes in neighborhoods all around the mall, people come out and soon cross the streets to the mall to do what they can. The mall is sacred and holy, and even though seeing such a place desecrated in this fashion stuns many people into silence, they are not paralyzed into fearful immobility. So they come.

Alan and Sarah crawl through the grass to the edge of the parking lot and are met by a man and woman who help them and comfort them. Soon, they are in the back seat of a car and on the way to a nearby hospital.

Sedated and calm, Alan stares up into Sarah's eyes, he seeing her truly for the first time in many years.

Sarah smiles, because she sees her husband's soul returned to his face.

But Alan does not smile. He is grim as he looks at the woman he has put through hell. "Do not forgive me," he tells her. "Do not ever forgive me."

"I do not forgive you," she says, smiling, kissing him on the forehead.

***

Agnes and her shadow-men steal police cars and firetrucks and race off down Grand Avenue on a wild caravan to the city. There are no police to meet them and stop them; those all lie asleep in the soggy mess that is West Park Plaza. Citizens up early along the route see but do not yet understand what is happening. By the time information flows and a citizen resistance is organized, it is too late. Agnes and her shadows have crashed firetrucks through the glass doors and windows of Layvanwick Tower and begin their assault on the second mall.

***

At shortly before eight o'clock in the morning, a golden jet glides down out of the blue sky and lands at the airport. On the side of the jet is the gold seal of the Office of the First Citizen. As the jet maneuvers into position at the gate, three figures watch it from the wide glass windows looking out onto the runway.

Maurice Sully stands in a clean ceremonial robe brought from Layvanwick Tower. Beside him, holding his right hand with her left, is Diane Copernicus, also wearing a ceremonial robe brought from Anton's mall. And beside her, sitting quietly in a wheelchair, his legs covered with a blanket, is Anton Layvanwick. His eyes are bright, intense, clear, two vivid circles of consciousness in a face ravaged with fresh wounds and scars. His left hand is held in the right hand of Diane Copernicus, who glances down at him often, as if checking to make sure he is still there, still whole, still alive. Anton does the same to her. She barely made it out of Layvanwick Tower in time, escaping just before Agnes and her shadow-men arrived.

The three Mall Masters hold themselves erect as they wait for the arrival of the First Citizen. When it is time, they move away from the window and go to the gate. Diane pushes Anton's wheelchair. Maurice's eyes are intent on the arrival gate.

Finally, the First Citizen arrives. There is no entourage. There is no media. There is no announcement. He just shows up.

An old man, eighty years old, but still radiating powerful arete, he walks with certainty and purpose down the ramp of the arrival gate and out onto the airport carpet to meet the waiting Mall Masters.

With no preamble, he addresses Maurice. "Let it be known that I am the warrior of reason and the defender of arete."

"It is known, First Citizen," say all three Mall Masters together, at the same time, their voices integrating into a chorus of resolute purpose.

The First Citizen smiles — but with his eyes only. His face remains hard. He bows down on one knee in front of Layvanwick and looks up into Anton's clear eyes. "You remain unsacrificed, Mall Master."

"Yes, First Citizen."

"I hope someday to surpass you in thought and action."

Layvanwick does not smile. "I hope you do so very soon, First Citizen."

"Before this day is done. I swear an oath on your wounds, Mall Master Layvanwick, that it will be so."

Then the First Citizen stands up straight. "Let us retire to a conference room and discuss what you know and what our status is. Afterwards, I will tell you how I intend to kill the terrorists."

CHAPTER EIGHTEEN

MASTERS OF INTEGRATION

First Citizen Peter Sharnok listens to the facts presented by the three Mall Masters. Maurice does most of the talking. Anton does the least. There isn't much for Anton to say. What he has been through is written on every inch of his body and speaks for itself. However, he does have one piece of information which is of immediate interest. "Agnes claims to have a bomb in her head. It is programmed to detonate at the moment of her death."

This doesn't seem to surprise Sharnok. He reacts to the news passively, as if he knows it already — or as if it is of no consequence.

"I have a request, First Citizen," says Maurice.

"Which is?"

"I wish to be deputized. I want to take the oath."

The First Citizen stares hard at Maurice. "You called me to do a job, young man. I suggest you let me do it."

"I would not be so presumptuous as to tell you how to do your job, First Citizen. The logic of my case is simple. I do not want merely to kill Agnes. I want to kill the idea she represents. I want to kill the belief in this idea. I want to eradicate all its claims to virtue. I want to kill the moral power of this woman, and the moral power of the ideas she holds. I want to annihilate the philosophy she represents."

"And how do you intend to do this?" asks the First Citizen.

Maurice proceeds to tell him.

Maurice speaks for a short time, uses simple words, logically presents a brief outline of his case, explains a definite plan. Diane and Anton listen without comment. They are hearing it for the first time as well. But neither has anything to add. Anton looks grim and says nothing, only the light in his eyes indicating that he is pleased with his friend. Diane is calm.

When Maurice is done talking, First Citizen Sharnok is even more serious than when he arrived. He looks at Diane and Anton. "This plan cannot work without your participation. Do you consent? Do you wish to take the oath? Are you ready to assume the responsibility of becoming soldiers for the Individual's Republic of California?"

"I am," says Diane.

"If Agnes is to die, it will be I who slays her," says Anton.

"Very well." The First Citizen hits a button on his wristcom, speaks briefly to a soldier waiting on the plane. "Bring me the reliquary."

While they are waiting, Sharnok stares hard at the three young people, watching their faces for signs that they understand what is about to happen.

Here is Sully, standing proud and tall, his face austere, his eyes filled with a soul-flooding vision of the possibilities he has conceived. Yes, he knows what he is doing. He wants to contain these events to his own mall and this city. It must not spread and he does not intend to let it. Very well. Sully I can count on.

And his wife, Diane. The woman. See the fire in her eyes and the steel in her face. This is a hard woman. But does she understand the risks being taken here? Does she understand that if she fails, then what has happened to Anton will befall both her and her husband? And that what has happened to her mall will befall other malls all across the country? Look at her hands. Steady, no trembling. She stands relaxed but alert. Her body is integrated with her mind. She is ready for what will happen, whatever it is. She can adapt. A Mall Master yesterday; today a soldier. Does she understand the connection between the two? Does she see them as opposite sides of the same coin? Is she repelled by evil? Or willing to deal with it? Look at her mouth. Lips held firm, eyes in focus and filled with thought, the planes of her cheeks smooth, composed. Nervous ticks? No. Trembling? No. She is placid. She faces reality and sees it for what it is, integrates herself into the flow seamlessly, pursues her values with total logic. Did you expect anything less? No. You know this woman's history. But I was eager to see her in the flesh and to experience her in a self-known moment, see the logic inherent in her soul. So here she is. I am getting an erection. Final proof of the ineluctable flow of logic.

And Layvanwick. Look at him. Beaten to a pulp and almost murdered and still his pagan life force thrusts itself into the world. Look at the passion in his eyes. He is already a soldier, probably has been for years. Listen to his voice when he takes the oath. What a poetic sound it will be. I long to hear him speak the words. Even in a wheelchair he has more power than most men.

Within moments, two soldiers enter the conference room. Between them, they carry a square box of bronze metal, polished and well-cared for, but still ancient. First Citizen Sharnok ignores the reliquary and the men who carry it into the conference room. He watches the faces of the three Mall Masters to see if they recognize and understand — and what this means to them.

The reliquary is carried by two powerful soldiers in dress uniform. They set the metal box down on a table between Sharnok and the Mall Masters, then step back, awaiting orders.

"Officers of the Box, you must witness this event," says Sharnok. "These Mall Masters are to be sworn in as soldiers for the Individual's Republic of California. First Officer of the Box, please insert your key."

One soldier steps forward, brings out a long key, inserts it into the side of the box, then stops, waiting for his mate to do likewise on the opposite side.

"Second Officer of the Box, please insert your key," commands Sharnok.

The second soldier steps forward and inserts his key.

"Open the reliquary," orders Sharnok.

Both keys turn in unison, the box clicks open, the top pops up. The two soldiers remove their keys and step back.

Sharnok steps forward and opens the top of the box, reaches inside, pulls out a wooden storage tube, opens one end, reaches inside, pulls out a papyrus manuscript. This he lays down on the conference table and unrolls to its full length: fifteen feet.

Sharnok watches the eyes of the Mall Masters. They all recognize what this papyrus roll is. They say nothing. Their eyes feast on the manuscript and wait for the orders of their commanding officer, First Citizen Sharnok.

"You are all about to undertake the solemn responsibility of becoming soldiers sworn to the defense of the Individual's Republic of California. You are to swear an oath on this, the original copy of the Constitution of the Individual's Republic of California, as authored and signed by Mykonos Kiriakos. Maurice Sully, step forward and witness the signature of Mykonos Kiriakos on this sacred document."

Maurice Steps forward, looks down at the ancient manuscript, sees the signature. "I have seen the signature, First Citizen."

"Now all of you, bow down before the memory of Kiriakos and prepare to swear your oath. Listen to my words and answer truthfully when I put questions to you."

Maurice Sully is the first to kneel. Diane helps Anton out of his wheelchair and steadies him as he kneels with her, the movement and position of his body obviously painful, but no self-pity in his eyes. And there is no solicitous consideration for him on the faces of those facing him and witnessing his oath. Anton's eyes widen as he looks to the sacred document, seeing it as a love letter to his arete, and something addressed to him individually. He looks on it with his best friend and former lover and integrates the meaning with total logic and full arete.

Sharnok looks down severely on the three Mall Masters. "Government exists to protect individuals from the evil of force," he says. "This document defines and delimits the manner in which the government of the Individual's Republic of California endeavors to protect individual rights by securing property rights, enforcing contracts, and leaving men free to pursue life, liberty, and the quest for perfect arete.

"You three Mall Masters are to become members of the military of the IRC. All those who serve in the government of the IRC are in the military and are subject to the uniform code of military justice. The military is divided into two distinct classes. The First class are those soldiers charged with the physical defense of the nation. They are the army, navy, and air force. The second class are those charged with the philosophical and moral defense of the Constitution — of the laws — and of the ideas upon which these documents are based.

"As Mall Masters, you are to serve as fully integrated soldiers charged with both the physical and moral defense of the nation. In this task, you are are acting as agents of the First Citizen, who is the sole member of the government who is daily responsible for both defenses. If any of you object to this responsibility, please say so now."

The three Mall Masters are all silent.

Sharnok continues. "Very well. Then all three of you hold these words in your minds and secure a self-known understanding. Then prepare to achieve full logical integration into your own individual arete. 'I swear an oath on the Constitution of the Individual's Republic of California, that I am personally committed to defending the individual rights of each citizen of this nation; that I am committed to defending the physical security of all citizens against enemies foreign and domestic; that I am committed to defending the physical property, be it large or small, of all citizens of this nation; that I am committed to enforcing all legally binding contracts between sovereign citizens of this nation. I swear this oath on my own sacred arete, and if I speak falsely, let the truth crush me. Do you three swear this oath?"

"I do," say all three Mall Masters, together, in one voice.

The First Citizen continues. "The logic of identity says that government is government by virtue of having a legal monopoly over the use of physical force. This awesome and frightening power is made moral by virtue of a government's commitment to using force in a moral manner. Moral force is used in retaliation against those who initiate physical violence against individuals, or who attempt the destruction of the mind through fraud and fakery. Therefore, as soldiers for the Individual's Republic of California, you must swear an oath that you will always use force morally and never knowingly initiate violence against innocent citizens. Do you swear this oath?"

"I do," say the Mall Masters.

"More important even than the physical defense of citizens is the intellectual defense of the ideas that make our government moral. As soldiers in the defense of this republic, you are warriors for reason and defenders of arete. You must swear an oath of allegiance to reason, logic, and perfect arete. Do you swear?"

"I do," say the Mall Masters.

"You must acknowledge that each individual citizen you protect is an end in himself, and that the perfection of his own arete is the only reason for his existence. You must acknowledge that no individual exists to serve the needs or desires of any other individual, or group of individuals, and that no citizen exists to serve the state. Do you acknowledge this and swear an oath?"

"I swear," say the Mall Masters.

"Finally, you must swear an oath to banish the evil of sacrifice from all social interactions among men. Do you swear?"

"I swear."

"I say: death to sacrifice. What say you?"

"Death to sacrifice!"

"Very well. You have sworn your oath, and I have witnessed it, along with the Officers of the Box. You are now soldiers in the armed forces of the Individual's Republic of California. I salute you."

The First Citizen snaps to attention and crisply salutes the three Mall Masters. The two Officers of the Box do the same. And the three Mall Masters return the salutes, hold them frozen like statues for a short span of seconds, then stand at ease.

"Your last act to make this ceremony sacred is to bow down and kiss the signature of Mykonos Kiriakos, and while you feel the touch of this sacred document pressed against your lips, make his logic yours, and know the freedom he created in your own soul, your own mind, see it clearly with totally ruthless logic, know its value, pledge eternal love for this thing for as long as blood flows through your veins. This is your own sacred, private moment. The only valid motivation for pursuing any value is personal, private, not to be shared. So whether it be a person, a thing, an idea, or any combination of these, introspect now and know the truth of your soul and the logic of your values. Whatever it is you wish to defend, swear an oath to defend it to the death."

One by one, each mall Master bows down to kiss the parchment. Maurice Sully is first, Diane second, Anton third. When Anton has kissed the Constitution, he steps back, pushes the wheelchair away and stands up straight by his own power.

Diane says, "Anton, you should let yourself recover. You are still weak."

"A soldier does not go to war in a wheelchair," says Anton.

The First Citizen surveys his newest soldiers and nods approval. "Very well. This ceremony is complete. Now then — let us engage the enemy."

***

Preliminary matters are handled by the First Citizen. His first order of business is to consult with the local justice of the peace with jurisdiction over the city, present the facts of the situation, and ask for a legal sanction for military action. This is granted within half an hour, the judge having seen the wreckage of West Park Plaza. With the legal writ of sanction in hand, First Citizen Sharnok declares martial law throughout the city and calls in his troops. The green rookies are dispatched to West Park Plaza to help with the clean-up. His experienced front-line troops, those who have seen action before, he calls to surround Layvanwick Tower, initiate surveillance, estimate the enemy's numbers and strength, determine if any surrounding buildings have been taken by Agnes and her shadows.

Layvanwick Plaza is all she has. Apparently, it is all she wants.

While all this is going on, the Mall Masters work out the details of their own plan. Maurice explains in detail exactly what they will do, how they will do it, when, and for how long.

It is a sunny day. Layvanwick Tower stands opaque before the city. There is no communication from inside, no demands, no announcement of hostages, nothing like that.

"Agnes knows we are coming," says Anton. "She is waiting for us."

"Let her wait," says Maurice. "She will have us soon enough."

First Citizen Sharnok commands his soldiers. "I want an assault before sundown," he says. "What is to happen should remain hidden from the city."

The main unit primed to lead the initial assault is the 7th Air Cavalry commando squad, jetted in from Malmstrom Air Force base in Great

Falls. As sunset approaches, they move into position all around Layvanwick Tower and prepare for action.

At one hour before sunset, an army glider flies silently over the skyscraper. From inside the belly of the glider, six commandos jump from the glider, parachute soundlessly to the roof of the building, and begin the assault.

The warriors of reason and defenders of arete are mostly young men from aristocratic families, some even the sons of Mall Masters. They are intelligent, well-trained, highly-motivated, fully in focus, and charged with moral fire by knowing that they are defending a sacred place from the evil of death worship. They enter the fight with clear eyes and clean souls. They are dressed in form-fitting uniforms designed with utter practicality in mind. They enter the dark building and become invisible even to the shadows. They carry weapons designed to deliver a soundless death instantly. Their orders are clear and unequivocal. There is no confusion or hesitancy in any of the men, nor in any aspect of the mission. It is all ruthlessly efficient, implacably logical, and as absolute as the reality to which it is directed.

The shadow-men don't have a chance.

Within half an hour, every last one of the shadow-men, the minions of Agnes, has been exterminated by the commandos. When this is done and the building is secure, the bodies are removed as quietly as the commandos entered.

Agnes is found in a small room in the basement of the Tower. She is asleep. The commandos do not wake her. Instead, they inject her with a drug that puts her into an even deeper sleep. Then they put her on a gurney, wheel her to an elevator, and take her up to the penthouse, where she is undressed and placed between the clean silk sheets of Anton Layvanwick's bed. She is left to sleep peacefully, blissfully, her face serene, even innocent. Except for an occasional tremor in her left cheek.

Agnes is left alone within the building. The commandos all disappear, their mission complete.

Now it is time for the Mall Masters to swing into action.

***

When she wakes up it is night and she can see the stars through the glass ceiling of the penthouse. The night sky is clear and the stars twinkle down at her, tiny silver points of clean white light, each star like an individual thought integrated into a beautiful concept, a galaxy of abstractions representing a concrete universe understood by virtue of having an identity. She thinks back to her youth, to a love she once had, a love for the night sky and the objects she saw there, the planets and stars. I wanted to be an astronomer once, she thinks. I thought I would travel to those stars and planets some day. Why didn't I? Are they unreachable? Or was it I who refused to reach far enough?

What is this? Something on my head. Here, touch it. Oh. Some kind of helmet.

She takes it off, pulls it down to her chest so she can see it clearly in the dim light. As she pulls the helmet away, she feels connections to the skin of her head pull loose. And she smiles.

Ah, so this is what they have done. They want to trick me. Make me think this is a dream. Or that what has all just passed has been a dream. But the trick will not work. I am not susceptible to the conscious dreaming. I will not take part. My mind is too strong, my will too great. They will not overcome me. They do not understand me. They underestimate me, as they always have. So much for the conscious dreaming.

She pushes the CD helmet away and rises out of bed. How did I get up here? No matter. Where are my shadows? The time has come to burn this mall. Set it on fire and watch the Mall Masters rush in to save it. Where are my shadows?

They are dead, says a voice inside her.

She stops. A cold wave of chilly emotion washes over her. Am I hearing a voice from outside — with my ears? Or a voice from inside — with my mind? The fact that she cannot tell bothers her. So she asks the question of herself, silently, inside her own mind, without using her voice:

"Who said that?"

No answer comes.

It was me, she thinks. I told myself. I know my shadows are dead. The Mall Masters have come while I slept and killed all my shadow-men, all my children, my babies. My slaves. There are no shadows. There is only myself. It is to be me and my soul against the mind of the Mall Masters. It is to be my emotions against their logic. Who is going to win?

She walks to a mirror and turns on a table lamp, looks at herself in the mirror.

She is beautiful.

Oh my.

Flowing blonde hair, long and lustrous. Face sculpted to feminine perfection. Large blue eyes. Full lips. Ample breasts. Wide hips. Long legs. She is perfect. She is a woman. She is truly a mother.

She turns to the bed and looks back at the CD helmet.

It is disconnected, but still I dream?

She does not have time to think about it.

There is a knock at the door.

She moves to answer the door, but before she can get there, it swings open and a woman walks in.

"Hello Agnes," says the dark-haired woman.

"Diane Copernicus. What are you doing here?"

"I have brought you your clothes."

"That is an evening gown."

"Yes. Isn't it beautiful?"

"I do not want to play this game."

"What game?"

"You are toying with me. This is all a conscious dream."

"No, this is reality."

"I have a bomb in my head."

"I know that."

"Who told you?"

"Anton."

"I will blow you all out of my mind."

"No, you won't."

"Why not?"

"Maurice turned your bomb off."

"How did he do that?"

"By waking you up."

"I am not awake. This is still sleeping, and you are just a dream."

"You are about to have a dream date. Get ready, your lover will be here soon to pick you up."

"And who is my lover?"

"Anton Layvanwick."

"That is laughable."

"Look at yourself in the mirror."

"I have."

"Then you know that it is true. Agnes, come here, look at me."

She walks to Diane and stands close. Diane holds her face in her hands, looks into her eyes searchingly. "I can see your soul through the windows of your eyes. You are a beautiful person. You are a good person. Anton deserves you, and you deserve Anton."

Agnes opens her mouth to protest. "I—" is all she can say. Something stops her. She cannot tell what it is. She begins to panic. She starts to tremble and inhales deeply, gathering enough air into her lungs to power a scream that even heaven will hear.

But Diane Copernicus stops her with a kiss.

A woman's lips pressed to hers: powerful, strong, passionately assertive, then suddenly gentle; the lips grow soft and part her own, find her tongue, kiss her sweetly, with a shocking intimacy that she is powerless to resist.

You will kiss Agnes, and you will love the taste.

Her mind is lost in the kiss. She has never experienced anything like this before. She has never felt a love expressed this intimately. She feels Diane's love for her. She understands that *she is loved by Diane*, that it is real and true, this is no fake, this is no lie. Diane Copernicus loves her enough to kiss her like a man.

While she enjoys the kiss, the shadow of some force passes over her, through her, like a moonlight ripple in a midnight lake, something gentle and imperceptible, lost and unnoticed behind the power and fury and passion of the kiss.

She pulls back when the kiss ends, opens her eyes, looks into the beautiful smiling face of Anton Layvanwick.

"I love you, darling," he says to her.

"I love you, Anton," she says.

"Hurry and get dressed, dearest. We don't want to be late. And do me one favor—"

"Yes?"

"Don't wear any panties."

She giggles and blushes — but complies with his request.

Her evening gown is on the bed. She walks naked across the room. Deep red sunlight slants down through the skylight of the penthouse and flows into the room like airborne wine, an intoxicating burgundy she can smell in the air, as if a flower has taken liquid form and induced drunkenness with its aroma. It all makes her tremble with giddy happiness.

While Anton waits in the next room, she dresses herself in the delicate silk finery chosen for this evening. She slips the dress over her naked body, relishing the softness. The air is warm up here and it feels good to be naked — but even better to be dressed in a delicate fabric that accentuates and highlights her naked form. The ethereal texture of her silk gown sends ripples of pleasure through her body, as if she is being tickled gently by a lover. And what is that? Yes. Soft music playing in the background. Soft strings and a harp intertwining in a rhythmic dance melody, a slow dance, the dance of lovers, an evening dance, a twilight dance for sultry summer evenings in late August when the air is heavy with moisture and the sky an ocean of gray clouds swirling into purple dusk.

Listen to the music. It is your gown singing to you. See how it makes your nipples hard. Walk across the room and step into your heels. Now sway as you walk. Look at yourself in the mirror. What a pleasure it is to contemplate my beauty. And to anticipate how I will give myself to my Anton later this evening. Ah! But now, let the evening proceed slowly. There is much pleasure to be relished in this night. Make it last.

Before she leaves the bedroom, she glances one last time up through the corner of the skylight. She sees only blue sky fading into deep purple. She is on the tallest building in the city and can see the tops of no other buildings. But she knows they are there. She watches the sky for an instant, just a brief moment of expectation, hoping for something from the sky, something she has not named or identified. It does not come. She pushes the longing from her mind and goes out to the living room to greet Anton.

They leave the penthouse together and take an elevator down into the mall.

This is my mall, she thinks. Look at how beautiful it is. A masterpiece of aesthetic integration. All of it designed to showcase the productive capacity of Man's mind, to frame Man's mastery of reality, to focus Man's conquest of nature. See all the shops and the vast array of products and services. All of it exists so that I can enjoy an evening such as this. A healthy clean body in fabulous clothes, out to share an evening of love with my magnificent Anton.

She smiles at him and he smiles back. He can see the pride in her face. "Your mall becomes you," he says.

"You become my mall."

Together, they walk across the intimate lobby, the only sound their heels clicking against the marble floor, she feeling that each step is a kiss on the body of her mall, each glance from her eyes a caress on the soft skin of a living being. The mall is not really alive. But she is. And that makes all the difference. The mall does not care — so she has to. Nature does not care — so she has to. The world does not care — so she has to. And she does. And she knows what it means, takes pleasure from this fact, and is proud to know the meaning of what she knows.

On the way out the doors, she notices how the fading sunset flows between the other buildings of the city and surrounds their skyscraper mall, floats through the clean windows in delicate pink tufts, as if the light moves in slow motion just for her, the physical laws of the universe trained and directed to serve her purposes.

Outside, a breeze gusts gently through the trees above Anton's car. The attendant smiles and holds the door open for her. Anton drives. They pull away from the sidewalk and the car surges powerfully down the street.

"Do you mind?" she asks, punching up her passenger-side computer screen. "I want to check my portfolio."

"Not at all," says Anton, his eyes on traffic.

She accesses the web and brings up her portfolio via her investment firm's website. She smiles while watching the computer screen change colors and the information flow beautifully up into her eyes. Such delicious art to present the hot lust of numbers! And then she purrs to herself like a big cat, looking at the numbers, row after row, column after column, doing the math in her head, adding up the numbers, subtracting other numbers, multiplying, dividing, using complex equations of her own design to judge, forecast, predict, understand. She finds mathematics downright erotic and calculations such as these are for her usually a prelude to sex. Math turns her on.

"Are you still rich?" asks Anton.

"Oh yes."

The car glides to a halt at a stoplight and Anton uses the pause in driving to stroke her exposed thigh with his right hand. His strong hand caresses the soft skin of her thigh and she trembles with satisfaction.

"Will you still love me when I am poor?" she asks.

"You can never be poor. Even if you hadn't a cent to your name, you would still be the richest woman in California, because you are rich in logic, and rich in values. That potent combination cannot be resisted."

The light turns green and the car surges through the intersection.

They drive to the base of the Rimrocks, to the home of their best friends, Maurice Sully and Diane Copernicus. Maurice has built a new home into the side of the cliffs and wishes to celebrate with a proper dedication. In his home, his cathedral of privacy, he has invited his best friends to share an evening with him and his wife.

Sully's house looks like a spaceship stuck into the side of the cliff. Anton and Agnes take an elevator up to the first level, then a spiral staircase to the next. They are greeted at the entrance by Diane, who kisses them both, then leads them outside to the jutting thrust of the main patio, which shoots out towards the twinkling lights of the city of Billings, like a launching pad for rockets, showing them all of the city as it flows it a swirl of colored lights out along the Yellowstone Valley. They see the last faint hints of the sunset on the western horizon and smile at the glowing city as it comes to life for the evening.

After a few moments, Maurice greets them wearing an elegant leisure tuxedo. The subtle colors laced through the design are perfect compliments to Anton's own evening wear. Maurice comes to Agnes first and takes her into his arms, holds her and kisses her for a long moment, then pulls back. "I'm so proud of what you've done with your mall, Agnes. I saw the reports today. Your profits are truly gorgeous."

"And the reviews are in on the aesthetics of the mall, as well," says Anton.

"Well, you shouldn't have worried too much—" says Maurice.

"I didn't," says Agnes.

"After all," continues Maurice, "It was Diane who wrote the major review for the Billings Gazette."

"She is my rival, so it was logical for them to choose her," says Agnes, smiling and taking Diane in her arms.

Another long kiss. Remember this? Yes, she does remember. Diane Copernicus is her lover. That is something worth remembering.

"No city in California can boast two Mall Masters as beautiful and competent as we have here in Billings," says Anton.

"New Athens will come calling and try to woo them both away," says Maurice.

Diane looks at Agnes and pouts. "If they ask you to New Athens, will you leave us all alone?" she asks.

"Never, darling. You and Maurice are my inspirations. The only thought and action worth surpassing is yours."

Maurice bows to Agnes. "To be valued so selfishly by one such as you, Agnes, is an honor I relish."

"Do we get a tour of the house?" asks Agnes. "And what kind of feast have you prepared for tonight? We'll we eat before — or after?"

"You are the guest, darling," says Maurice. "You get to decide. But a tour is in order. I hope you will appreciate my house in the manner I intended."

"You will know — soon enough," says Agnes, walking to Anton and taking his hand, letting Maurice and Diane lead them further into the house.

She tours the space Maurice has designed. Agnes opens her mind to the logic of the space. The house surrounds her, then sets her free. The spaces are intimate, yet hint always at unexplored horizons just around the corner. The house hides and protects her, but lets her see the world and the city outside. The house makes her feel as if it is natural for human beings to live on the side of a cliff, as if a voice spoke to the stone and said, "You should be a house," and the cliff responded and transformed itself.

The tour ends on the top floor, in the master bedroom, a circular room with a glass dome for a ceiling. The dome reveals cliff on one side, sky in the center, and sprawling city lights on the right. In the center of the room is a large circular bed. Above the bed is a hanging love lamp, lit now, glowing with an intimate luxurious radiance that draws her forward, smiling, to touch the silk bed sheets of Maurice and Diane's most intimate chamber.

Maurice and Diane, to honor their best friends, let Anton and Agnes use their master bedroom.

Anton and Agnes are left alone in the bedroom. Maurice and Diane disappear into another part of the house, to pursue their own sacred privacy.

Agnes gazes at her beautiful Anton. "I wish to share a sacred privacy with you tonight, my dearest," she says, unhooking the straps of her gown from her shoulders and letting it slip to the floor, revealing her own nakedness.

Anton smiles. "My soul is yours, and my body as well," he says, letting his own clothes fall to the floor.

Then he comes to her and smiles at her beauty, speaks his oath to her.

"By the logic of existence, the sum of all values are to be found in human form. I find my values in your form. Your arete is mine, your logic is mine, your values are mine. Tonight, I will share the ecstacy of sexual union with you, so that we both might experience the integration of body and soul."

"You will know me completely, my husband," says Agnes.

They move to the bed and she takes him there, he submitting first to her, she tasting every inch of his clean masculine form.

She is making love to Anton Layvanwick. She knows who he is and what he has done, and she knows what it means to be this intimate with this man. Her pride in his person takes physical form via his body. Anton is the physical incarnation of her own self-esteem. His body is exquisite.

But look at his face. He trembles with ecstacy at my touch. He is within my power, submitting to my control. I own him in this moment. His life is in my hands. But I hold this life only to derive pleasure from it. See his eyes. See him watch me. Look at the beauty that comes from me. His vision is filled with my form, but his understanding of my form comes from his understanding of my soul. He knows who I am. I am his equal. I am the female form of Anton Layvanwick. I am the Queen of

Mall Masters. And the creation of my mall has brought me to this moment when I meet him naked in this dramatic setting, and we compete with each other in love. Who can give the most pleasure? Who can take the most?

Anton has taken plenty, and now wishes to give. He gently takes control, maneuvers Agnes onto her back, spreads her legs wide, and enters her slowly, gently, to his full length.

She listens as her own voice cries out her need of Anton. Dimly, in the background, as if she is watching herself through Anton's eyes, and hearing herself through his ears, she can hear herself cry out with ecstacy. She calls to Anton in her moment of rapture. Her voice is like music. The sound fills her ears with pleasure, and this feeling is transmitted throughout her body, flowing to her thighs and her womanhood, her warm moist essence filled now with her Anton, and the sound of her voice takes form in his face, she looks up at him, sees him looking down at her, sees her own beauty in his eyes, his face a ruthless mask of passion driving on with implacable greed towards the bright happiness he wants from her, and she wishes to give — and then she does give it to him, he takes it, answers back, and their two voices join in a chorus of love and ravishment.

But Anton does not stop. He continues. His greed knows no bounds. His loving recognizes no limits. She thinks she has experienced the ultimate, but there is more. She thinks there is no more to feel, but there is, and she feels it, experiences Anton in his boundless lust for her.

She feels his rhythm as a musical chord that vibrates up through the bed and into her body, spreading gradually like a delicious singing flame that surrounds her in a warm envelope of sound that drives her body into the rhythm, the two integrated, soon inseparable, her music harmonizing with Anton in a symphony of physical spirituality — and then spiritual physicality — and then something made of both, something named and witnessed only in a brief moment when her body tells her through direct physical perception what the meaning and purpose of her soul is — and her mind tells her body what the meaning of its existence is — and she holds both in her arms, integrated via Anton's naked form, that form driven by that soul, sending both into her, filling her with body and soul, she in that moment neither female nor male, but a union of both.

The drive to exaltation is her drive to life. This is a wild ride down Passion Avenue, but she knows the street. It is a beautiful boulevard filled with all the memories of her life. She sees the straight logical line of her life leading to this moment, this place, this man, by virtue of all the values she has ever held. The irreplaceable moments of their lives is what she has been driving towards. This is the road, and those who know her values have always been her goal. Once she was a little girl and had her first glimpse of the city. And within the city, a mall. And inside the mall, a man. And with the man, a woman. And orbiting around both, a universe of values integrated via the activity of business. It touches even this moment. Why are we here? Why am I here? Why do I come to this place to share love with this man?

Anton answers her with his love, by holding her face in his hands and gazing into her eyes and taking from her soul the matching ecstacy that renders his body the instrument of her joy. She is the meaning of his ecstacy. And she is the meaning of his. And because they know who they are, they know what it means, and the physical pleasure they experience becomes magnified via the arete flowing from each to the other.

I love this man because he is the best possible to me. To want the best, to recognize it and want it, is the highest moral act. Then let me see it. Let me see it and feel it and know it while I share my body with this man. If we are sovereigns who own our lives, then it is more than right for us to share our love in this way. To ignore each other would be to renounce life and values and happiness. So let us take it, yes. Let him take me. And let me take him. And let us be proud that our logic has led us to this kind of ecstacy, this kind of pleasure.

The house, as beautiful as it is, does not care, does not notice. The walls, floors, ceilings, windows of the house are seen by me, but they do not see back. I am aware because I am alive. The house has meaning only because I am here to give it meaning. Without me, the house would be like the cliff. A part of blind nature, unseeing and unfeeling, passive and at the mercy of the blind forces of the earth.

Outside the windows of the house, there is a blank stone wall. I can see it. But it cannot see me. It does not know my manner of existence. It cannot know this feeling I have. It is not conscious. But I am. Therefore, let me know. The stone cliff does not care — so I must.

And here is the blue sky, fading now. The sky looks down and does not see, but I look up and understand. I know what the sky is, but the sky does not know what I am. Does the sky love the sun as I love Anton? No. It cannot. But I can. The sky does not care. Therefore, I must.

And the city. Does the city care? See the twinkling lights and the wide boulevards and all the beauty created and ordered by Man. Does it see, does it understand? No. Like the house, it does not know. It does not care. It is not conscious. I am conscious. Because I am conscious, I must value. And the logic of my values has brought me here, to love Anton

Layvanwick. The universe does not know how good he is, and the universe does not care. But I know, and I care. So let us be conscious together, and let us understand together what the sum of our lives is. If we are values to each other, then let us show it, know it, feel it, share it. Let us trade arete.

Anton has loved her to his limit. He wants to stop. But she will not let him. Now it is her turn to show him the miracle of their love. She will bring him back. She will fill him with lust once more. Because she is that which has no limits, and via her, his love will have no limits. With her, he drinks to become thirsty, and feasts to starve himself.

My Anton. The master of my mall. The final stop on Passion Avenue, the final address on the road of my life. Here he is. Look at how fine he is. Oh how I relish the love he gives me. Oh how I relish his masculine form, and the mind which animates it. What a master of arete he is. Look at what I have the power to make him feel. He has just shared sex with one of the most powerful women on earth, a luscious creature of sensuous arete who has taken all he has, challenged his manhood to rise, received all his masculine power and energy. He should have nothing left. But he returns to me and I have the power to make him rise yet again, with even more potent life force. Between my thighs he finds his final spiritual home. Within my arms he finds his truest mirror. He looks to me and finds the reality of his own self-esteem. In my mind he finds the reality of his own purpose. In my arete he finds the reality of his own reason, and the truest power of his own logic.

And now I am conscious of his body inside me. He fills me with his manhood and connects to a deep memory lost within my soul. I look into his eyes and see myself as a man. I hold his body in my arms and feel his strength — and for an instant, I know what it is to be a man and have a woman such as myself. I feel what he feels, experience what he experiences. I am Anton Layvanwick making love to Agnes — who is me — and I know the greatness of this woman by the greatness of the man.

Everything he has done in his life is so he can be worthy of a woman like me. Every thought has been clean, rational, true, his mind a metallic structure of logical chains caging a wild reality so he can control and direct it. All of the beauty he has ever touched has been a quest to be held within the vision of a soul such as mine. Each creative thought he has ever had he has put into the service of this love he knows with me. The skyscraper mall is the symbol of his love. It is his advertisement calling across the world to me. It is a manifestation of his arete facing all horizons and pulling at me like a force of gravity. Even before it was born, the wind moaning through the naked steel beams of the growing edifice was his voice calling out to me. And this is what it said, what I understood it to say: Come to me, woman, for I am the master of reality. I am the lord of this earthly realm, and with me, you can enjoy your womanly existence completely. I am the man who demonstrates the metaphysical competence needed to tame your power. Yes, you can do as I do, think as I think, build as I build. Your logic is as true as mine, and your values as clean as mine. But you long to worship. And I — to be worthy of your worship.

And how does he know the final answer? By looking down into my eyes during this naked moment, when his soul is intermingled with mine, when he sees in my face what he has longed to see, when he glimpses in my eyes what he has longed to glimpse, that vision of his youth, when he saw the road ahead, and knew that if he traveled far enough, I would be waiting. At the end of the road, there would be a mall filled with many beautiful values. I am one of them. I am the greatest. I am the woman of this Mall Master. And he is the master of this woman. What does it mean to him?

Hold him tight as he drives his body to that highest moment when he gets the sum of all his values. Feel his desperate passion as he reaches even beyond what you have to give, and takes something more, something you have because he has given it to you, something you both own together and which empowers you both.

He loves the mall as you love the mall, but in loving the mall, it does not see him and love him back.

He loves the sky as you love the sky, but in loving it, the sky does not see him and love him back.

He loves the city as you love the city, but in loving it, the city is blind and cannot love him back.

And in this house, he is alone unless you are here with him.

And in that most electric moment of union, when male and female become irrelevant for a brief few seconds, both know the joy of loving another consciousness, of seeing another mind and being known by that mind, being understood and loved and valued, and knowing what it means, and knowing that the time they share is finite, and being greedy for as much of that time as they can get, and wanting it to be quality time, and making it so via their bodies, the vessels of their souls, the engines of their logic, the motors of their values.

And when it is over, the sweet memory fills both with a supremely confident peace. They lie motionless, smiling, feeling weightless, wanting their bodies to rise off the bed and float in the air, held by the house, as if the house is holding them up to the earth and saying, "This is Man, who knows what existence means, and he is the pinnacle of the universe. And you, blind nature, that has existed always, you take meaning because these eyes see you and love the joy existence gives to them."

A house on the side of a cliff: the messenger of Man to nature.

"Thank you, darling," says Anton.

"Thank you, my dearest," says Agnes.

Later, they get dressed and return to the living room. Maurice and Diane wait, both glowing with the inner radiance of a love just shared. The four smile at each other, all knowing what each as experienced, all happy for each one individually. They do not discuss what they have achieved tonight. They simply look at it. Each face contains the reality of the evening, and the lifetime behind the evening. That is enough.

Diane has prepared a feast. This too, will be a spiritual event. The food she presents has been prepared with the same competence she brings to all her actions. That it is food to please the people she cares for most in the world, is a fact which gives deep meaning to the entire process of preparation, presentation, and eating.

Agnes watches Maurice's face as he looks to his wife in the kitchen. He has just had her naked body in his arms, and satisfied his most spiritual physical need with her. Yet watching her move gracefully through her kitchen, preparing the food which will nourish his body, keep him alive to love her another day, his face seems to glow with a lust even beyond that of the bedroom. Can it be that a kitchen lust rivals that of the bedroom? Agnes smiles. This is a secret no man has ever revealed to her, but now that she knows, she will use this knowledge to please her Anton. He will watch me in this manner while I cook for him. He will see me in the kitchen and be transfixed with this special love. And I will surprise him. I will transform that kitchen lust into a bedroom lust and I will have him in the kitchen. Just wait, my Anton. Your wife has plans for you!

Outside it grows dark, but they sit in the light, gathered around an intimate dining room table, and they eat and talk and drink and share stories and memories. Maurice's eyes make love to Agnes, and Diane's eyes do the same to Anton, and they smile back and forth, knowing the pleasure of spiritual comrades.

Dessert is so sweet, it seems her very essence becomes sugar. She is dazzled with brilliant delicacies that leave her drunk with a hyper-awareness of her surroundings, as if, instead of being cut-off from reality and seeing the world as a blur, she is in super-focus and sees all in total clarity, and more: she sees the connections of all to all, the relationship of all to all, and understands why the world has to be what it is, and why the nature of that world dictates her nature as well.

She is sitting alone at the table now, smiling, her eyes closed, her ears filled with the soft music of a stereo system that seems to put a symphony orchestra right beside her, the music perceived as coming from the space surrounding her.

The music fades, and she hears a voice call out to her.

"Agnes?"

"Yes?"

It is Diane speaking to her. "Have you enjoyed yourself this evening?"

"Of course I have, my friend."

"I am pleased."

Agnes gets up from the table and walks out onto the balcony. She leans out over the city as if she is standing at the edge of a knife that is cutting the sky. The city is a strand of twinkling stars that has bled down out of the sky, giving life to the earth. She smiles at the city. She remembers the evening. She thinks of her friends. The breeze is soft and warm. The music disappears behind her. Only the sound of nature hums around her now. She is alone on the balcony. She stands there for a long time. She loses track of time. She does not know how long she has been standing there. She suddenly realizes that she has been alone too long. Why does no one come to join her on the balcony? Why do they leave her alone for so long? Where is her Anton? She wants to hug her Anton and share this view with him.

Look at my glorious mall, shining in the night! What a scene of beauty! I built that. I designed it. I thought of it. I created it. I brought it into existence. Look at it and let the feeling sink in. Relish it with a glorious selfishness. This is what it means to be selfish. This is what it means to love existence. Now I know. Now I understand. Because I have shared this evening with these people. And I have been worthy of them all.

She wants to speak to them. She turns around and looks into the house.

The house is cold and dark. There is nobody home.

In shock, she turns to the city.

The lights go out, vanish before her eyes.

She screams.

"No!"

"Yes," says an implacable voice behind her.

She turns once more and faces the house. Still cold, still dark, still empty. But three people stand with her now on the balcony: Anton Layvanwick, Maurice Sully, and Diane Copernicus. Their faces are cold, their eyes empty. They do not see Agnes, Mall Master. They see someone else.

"We wanted you to know what manner of existence we share," says Diane.

"We wanted you to experience what it is you could have been — and should have been," says Maurice.

"And we wanted you to know the judgment of a Mall Master," says Anton. "Because this is what you have earned."

She screams, but has no control.

The balcony morphs into a living cross that grabs her, holds her tight, her limbs nailed to the burning wood that singes her skin. She screams in agony, the vision of what she has known with these people burned into her brain, vivid, eternally vivid, something she will never forget. And she sees the equation. She sees the logic, and knows how easy it could have been, and always is, for those who live in the world honestly. But for her, now, the reality is this cross. And she hangs upon the cross, and she looks out at the beautiful city and sees it flow with flames, reduced to ashes in an instant, the streets black smears of death stretching out across the hellish landscape of a dark horror show. And here, where once before, moments ago, she saw the proud bright skyscraper mall alive with color and life, there stands an exploded stump of melted metal and glass fused together into a twisted sculpture of chaos and death. It is the skyscraper mall, Layvanwick Tower, destroyed, burned to the ground, as she wished to see it burned, as she wished to present it to the earth as a symbol of man's evil and metaphysical insignificance. The entire city, and she on the cross, presented to her non-existent god as a sacrifice for the sin of having been born.

She screams out at the dead city. She sees shadows swirl up out of the dust of ashes. The shadows come for her. Her screams cannot stop them.

And the Mall Masters have left her. She is to hang on this cross for all eternity, having been given what she wanted, and what she came to this place for.

She hangs on the cross, and sees her world, and even in hell, even knowing a manner of existence beyond what she has chosen, she feels a certain dim satisfaction with what she has ended with. Because deep down — as the Mall Master's logic shows her to be true — she knows that she has been given what she wanted. And what she wanted was this:

to be taken care of. To have responsibility wrested from her hands and to be dictated to. And to be given a reality that is entirely constructed of consciousness. For this is not real. She knows it is not real — but that does not bother her. This is a conscious dream, one the Mall Masters have locked her into, a mental prison from which there is no escape. But it is a prison she has wanted. And the suffering she feels here satisfies her as much as any she had out in the real world. The difference is this: now she knows what she could have been. And this is her torture: to have the moment of her death suspended into an eternity, and to have to contemplate forever the evil of her desires, and the glorious reality which she will never have.

She hangs on her cross. She watches the city burn. And she screams. *Forever.*

***

In the basement of Layvanwick Tower, a shrine is established and dedicated by Maurice Sully.

"Monsters should be kept under glass and studied, so that men may learn how to defend themselves. And so that men may learn how to recognize monsters when they see them. Mother Agnes was a monster. And here she will remain, locked within a conscious dream for all to contemplate who doubt the nature of evil. This shrine will remain here in the Mall she sought to kill. Let those who are unfamiliar with the face of evil connect to this dream and see the reality of Agnes — and the reality of her ideas, her values — her results. Let them stay for as long as they care. And let all who gaze upon this spectacle come away with a clear understanding of what it is they have seen. For make no mistake: this is evil. And when you encounter it in reality, there is only one proper response: kill it."

The first person to connect to the dream is police officer Rod Black. He stays connected for only thirty seconds. That is enough. When he disconnects, he staggers away to an elevator and rides up into the clean bright mall. And he cleanses himself — by shopping for his wife.

EPILOGUE

Sarah Fletcher and Alan Benton say good-bye to Maurice Sully and Diane Copernicus at the train station. Anton Layvanwick does not come to say good-bye. Alan does not speak of it with Maurice and Diane. None of them has to. He understands, and he does not blame Anton.

"We want to go back to America and build a mall," says Sarah. "A real mall. I think our old country needs a taste of California. I want to try to show those people another way, another manner of existence."

"Perhaps we will fail," says Alan. "It's possible the Americans simply will not be open to these values. But we have to try. Mostly for ourselves. I know you'll both protest when I say this, but the truth is: right now, I don't feel I deserve to stay in California. Not after what I have done, not after the manner in which I allowed myself to be used. So I will return to my roots, start at the beginning, and re-grow my arete. And hopefully, save some young people who are on the same path Sarah and I were when we met."

"You have chosen a worthy challenge. I think you will both be equal to it," says Maurice.

In a proper farewell, Maurice kisses Sarah good-bye.

Diane bows to Alan.

As the train moves away to the eastern horizon, Diane looks back and asks Maurice, "Do you think they will succeed?"

"They already have," says Maurice.

***

For Man, there are no endings, only beginnings. Like the universe which gave him birth, Man is eternal. All of his stories have beginnings; none of them have endings.

The beginning of this story is this: on the bright morning of Anton's very next birthday, Maurice Sully and Diane Copernicus arrive to present gifts to honor their best friend. Anton meets them in the lobby of Layvanwick Tower and says he has a surprise.

"What could you possibly do to surprise us?" asks Maurice.

Anton leads them across the wide lobby, to the center lounge, where they sit down on a couch in front of an escalator. They sit with Anton and talk for a few minutes. Anton does not seem to be himself. He seems nervous, excited, even boyishly young. The scars on his face have healed long ago and his eyes retain the innocence they have always loved. But he does not seem himself, and Maurice and Diane exchange glances, both curious as to what is up.

And then Anton smiles, looks across the spacious lobby, to a wide set of swinging doors. They open inward and they catch a glimpse of sunny street, green leaves hanging down from a tree.

Sweeping in off the street, entering the mall as if she owns it, is a long-legged blonde woman. She waves across the lobby at Anton and strides quickly to meet and greet him.

She is a statuesque blonde with huge blue eyes, perfectly sculpted face, exquisitely feminine body. She carries in her baring a wealth of arete which leaps off her person and announces her nature even before she arrives and shows the light in her eyes.

"Allow me to present Electra D'Ambrosio," says Anton. "She is to be my apprentice."

"Bravo, Anton!" says Diane, clapping her hands together and jumping up and down like an excited little girl.

Maurice takes the hand of Electra and kisses her arete ring. "Electra. One of the daughters of Atlas."

Electra bows to him. "Mall Master Sully. I hope someday to surpass you in thought and action."

"Considering your teacher, dear girl, I think you will!"

Diane hugs Electra, then waves at the beckoning escalator. "It is a beautiful day to go shopping, don't you agree?"

"Yes!" says Electra. She turns to Anton. "What do you say, Anton? Shall we?"

Anton steps onto the escalator and waves his friends to follow.

"Let us rise!"

And they do rise.

Forever.

THE END